BUT WE DIDN'T
GET THE FOX

BY RICHARD LLEWELLYN

BUT WE DIDN'T GET THE FOX
THE END OF THE RUG
DOWN WHERE THE MOON IS SMALL
SWEET MORN OF JUDAS' DAY
A MAN IN A MIRROR
UP, INTO THE SINGING MOUNTAIN
CHEZ PAVAN
MR. HAMISH GLEAVE
A FLAME FOR DOUBTING THOMAS
A FEW FLOWERS FOR SHINER
NONE BUT THE LONELY HEART
HOW GREEN WAS MY VALLEY

Juveniles

WARDEN OF THE SMOKE AND BELLS
THE FLAME OF HERCULES
THE WITCH OF MERTHYN

Richard Llewellyn

BUT WE DIDN'T
GET THE FOX

DOUBLEDAY & COMPANY, INC.,
GARDEN CITY, NEW YORK
1969

50003710

Library of Congress Catalog Card Number 69–13644
Copyright © 1969 by Richard Llewellyn
All Rights Reserved
Printed in the United States of America
First Edition

2-26-69 Northday 3.81

For LeBaron Barker
My friend and editor, and virtual
founder-in-chief of the Trothe series.
FLOREAT!

BUT WE DIDN'T
GET THE FOX

1

Rome welcomed me with lit fountains, a melon-slice of moon, the Company's Rolls-Royce, and the comfort of a suite at our Head Office, just above the Piazza di Spagna.

I needed all the cossetting there was. I was tired to the bone after six weeks of flying between Cairo, Bahrein, Teheran, Istanbul, and Beirut, discussing the detail of pipeline construction —which I'd had to learn—with our engineers, and having to endure the talk, the would-be serious, piffling talk, hour after hour, with diplomatists in each country, from Foreign Secretaries down, and the dozens of lads representing "interests," the fingers-in-the-pie, the pressure groups and lobbies, or, if everything had its proper name, the blackmailers.

"Mr. Trothe, you have my word," Garagesh had told me, the night before. "Point-five of one percent is what I ask. It's so much? You have no trouble' fifty years. If I am refuse', you don't bring a co'pling in theez countr', pipes and pomps, 's a jok'l'"

I knew that Garagesh, and more than forty others like him, among the various countries were merely front men for Ministers and the groups behind them. Ministers, of course, never accepted "presents," and bribes were out of the question. They were honest men. I'd come to Rome to find out what was to be done about them. Fortunately, Paul Chamby, my Director General, was in

Athens and wouldn't be back till the following afternoon, which gave me a chance to get a little sleep and shuffle my notes in some sort of order. They were too hot to be typed, and only I could read what was fondly called my shorthand. Consuelo was in the Cairo office, and I couldn't think of any good excuse to fly her up. We'd agreed, in any event, almost six months before, that an office "romance" was not for us. We'd simply get on with the job, and when enough time had decently lapsed, we'd get married, she'd leave the Company, and I'd have a new wife and a home. As a widower I had to be careful of our future name. Gossips are the devil.

I went through a heap of mail a courier had just brought in, luxuriating in the comfort of a dressing gown and a generous whisky and soda in a fistful of frozen crystal, spreading Consuelo's ten-page endearing tattle over my knee, and skimming to the hand-written footnote.

A REALLY VERY BEAUTIFUL—(AND WHEN THEY ARE, THEY REALLY ARE, AREN'T THEY?)—AMERICAN WOMAN CALLED IN JUST AS I WAS FINISHING THIS. SHE'D BEEN TO SEE THE MUSEUM—WHEN ARE YOU GOING TO TAKE ME?—AND HEARD FROM A MUTUAL FRIEND YOU WERE HERE. SHE DIDN'T SIGN IN DOWNSTAIRS OR LEAVE A CARD, BUT I THINK I HEARD MRS. WHEATRIDGE—EDRIDGE?—AND NO CHRISTIAN NAME. ANYTHING FROM THIRTY. LESS PERHAPS, BUT ANY MORE'D BE LIBEL. THE BLUEST EYES I EVER SAW. THEY WENT STRAIGHT THROUGH ME, HEAD-ON. NO LIPSTICK AND EASILY THE NICEST SMILE, BUT SOME-THING I CAN'T EXPLAIN COLD AND QUIET ABOUT HER. I TOLD HER YOU WERE BROILING IN DESERT SUNS AND HADN'T AN IDEA WHERE YOU WERE OR WHEN YOU'D BE BACK. SHE WAS REALLY VERY SORRY, AND SAID SHE'D WRITE, REFUSED TEA, AND WENT, ALL INSIDE TWO MIN-UTES. IT'S NOT LIKE ME TO LET SOMEBODY GO WITHOUT TAKING A NAME. AS YOU MAY IMAGINE, WE HAD A MAD TIME TRYING TO TRACE HER THROUGH THE UNITED STATES EMBASSY, CONSULATE, TRAVEL AGENCIES, HOTELS, ALL FOR NOTHING. NOBODY COULD PLACE HER. HOW ANYBODY COULD LOOK AT HER AND FORGET HER IS INCONCIE —ISN'T IT I BEFORE E—I NEVER COULD SPELL AND THE DIC'S DOWN-STAIRS. ANYWAY, ADORING YOU AS I DO, I WOULDN'T BLAME YOU IF

YOU'D SHARED A BABA AU RHUM OR TWO WITH HER. OFTEN WISH I WERE A MAN. THEY'D HAVE TO SHACKLE ME. AS IT IS, PLEASE READ THE FINAL PARAGRAPH AGAIN WHICH I REPEAT & EMPHASISE, AND BE SURE THERE'S A BABA WAITING FOR YOU. THAT IS, AT THE RIGHT TIME. LOTS OF RHUM. I ALMOST FORGOT. I FEEL ASHAMED TO TELL YOU SHE LEFT BEHIND TWO BUNCHES OF WHITE VIOLETS WHICH WE TRIED TO DELIVER TO HER. YOUR CALM & STABLE, PASSIONATELY IMPATIENT,

CONSUELO

I almost spilled the drink.

Two bunches of white violets?

No room for error.

In other times, the less ordered days of war, two white any-things were a prime warning to get out, drop it, don't dally.

And, obviously, my disappointed visitor must have been Druxi. Nobody else came within a mile of fitting the bill. But what was I being warned for? I was no longer part of the Service, or engaged in anything but the most exacting type of commerce, and I suppose building a pipeline is that, and not about to jink into anything more exciting than a breakdown of mileage and pressure-statistics, with a thought here and there for the palms held ready for greasing.

Druxi, a queen-pin of the CIA wasn't the sort to waste her time. Was the office itself a target? Any thought of Consuelo in danger made me feel lightheaded. Her letter had come by the morning courier. Could anything have happened since?

I put through a call to Cairo, and went out on the balcony to look at night under Roman stars, listening to a mandolin below the steps, and a tenor voice like a fiery vein, in and out of traffic moans, singing a love song I knew and whistled in breath, till Vox flashed yellows for an interior call.

"No reply from the Cairo office, or from Miss Furnival's apartment, sir. Night service is engaged. Keep the calls in, sir?"

"Please. And put a call out for Mr. Chamby. When did you last hear from Miss Furnival?"

3

"Daily report, noon, Cairo time, sir. Mr. Osterley's expected in from Aden tonight, that was all. Shall you be using the box at the Opera, sir?"

"Might as well."

"I'll send up the program. It's Box C. Nine o'clock. You could take up to six guests, sir."

"God forbid!"

I had a most unusual bath—a fitting supplied a froth of small bubbles which floated me up on the surface—that beat the tiredness out of me, and in a glow, and a splash of Knize, I got into a dinner jacket, gave the bow an extra fillip, and went to the vase for a maroon carnation. There must have been three or four dozen, of all tints.

But there were only two whites, in the middle.

I had to lift the vase into the light to make sure. Reds, pinks, apricots, tints in between, maroon.

Only two whites.

Coincidence?

I rang for Marlq' Ben Ab. I don't think even he knew his real name. But that's what his papers had called him for the past thirty years, and in that time both Paul and I had known him to be incomparably the best houseman-valet there ever was— except one—(and I was already in touch with him)—and as close-mouthed as a mute. He's saved my life once, and Paul's twice, all three times by shooting an eye out of the would-be, and once, while he was serving coffee, I saw him flick out the old-and-rare Smith & Wesson, and drop a shadow in the garden, a nobody we were never able to trace, with three primed grenades in his rags, a Luger strapped to his thigh, and a yard of razor-blade steel with a homemade wooden handle, possibly the most vicious weapon I ever saw, wrapped around his waist. He'd meant business, though on whose behalf we never managed to find out. At that time we'd both been after Mao Tse-tung's boys playing games in Kenya and the Congo, and we'd tried to pin the attempt on one or other of them, but we couldn't, and it was pigeonholed as a mystery.

4

His tap on the door was his own, a ripple of knuckles, and he came in, a little taller than the handle, almost as wide as the oak, hands slightly behind, feet together, milky tea complexion, a broken hawk's nose, and the pale-grey eyes and reddish hair of the Berber.

"Who arranges these flowers?" I asked him.

"Housekeeper, sometimes, Miss Masters, sometimes, sir," he said, chin jowled in a starched collar. "Housekeeper buy every three days. Seller come back door. You don't like, I tell!"

"I wondered why there were only a couple of white carnations, that's all."

"White carnations all in Mr. Chamby's office, sir. Two pots. Roses only, the desk, one pot."

"Have we had any American visitors recently?"

"I bring the book, sir!"

Two bunches of white violets, two white carnations, two pots of whites in Paul's office. Was this, perhaps, coincidence going slightly cracked? I poured a small drink, flitted my mind over the staff we had in Rome, Angela Masters, secretary to Paul, Estelle Greig, her secretary, George Coburn, engineering stores specialist, Enzo Mariotti, international jurist-economist, Wayne Miles, pump engineer, and Emma Toverell, the accountant, all first-class, vetted by our own Intelligence Unit, with office staff, cooks, servants, all cleared by the Police. Not a blot anywhere.

Knuckles rippled, and Marlq' Ben Ab came in with the blue visitors' book, and opened it to Monday of the week before.

I ran down the signatures, turning the pages, a little surprised at the eclectic bru-ha-ha there must have been in our plate-glass lobby, day after day. Most of the names were unknown to me, though I was rather touched by a Luke Mander, whoever he might be, writing in the Reason for Visit column: *None. Just wanted to hear English again, that's all.*

But I wasn't shocked, or relieved, so much as amused to see a signature which I knew had been written to pull my leg, a large sharply angular extent of blotted calligraphy which dominated the page, written two days before by Mrs. Mitchell Rowan Crane of Ann Arbor, Michigan.

Alias, of course, Druxi.

Two white carnations, then, and two pots in Paul's office, were no coincidence.

Should I clear out, then and there, or stay? Nothing had happened so far. After all, we had a police department. These weren't the old days of touch and run. Further than that, I had a duty to the Company, as well as to every member of my staff. I had no choice except to stay.

I'm sure Marlq' Ben Ab had seen nothing to suggest any change in me, and I gave him the book.

"I'd like a cab at the side door in five minutes, and if I'm wanted, I'm at the Opera House. If I'm wanted after that, I shall be at Pasetto's. Call at five forty five in the morning with orange and lemon juice, China tea, and honey, and the usual papers. I shall use the East Room to work."

He bent his head sideways and went. I looked at the two white carnations. Why was Druxi warning Paul and me? Obviously somebody on the staff was working for CIA. Druxi couldn't have gone through the place, planting white warnings without a little help, and since we had a strong staff of *carabinièri* pensioners, "wandering" could be a dangerous business.

Who'd helped her? Or who'd taken her instructions?

But, far more importantly, what did she want to tell us?

Paul and I were the only two who'd recognise the two-whites warning.

I felt a distinct relief. Having once been part of the Service, that feeling of Things Happening seems to stick. It's like having an extra sense. When they did, and undoubtedly they were about to, I was perfectly happy to know that Druxi, possibly the most remarkable woman of her time, was on our side. We'd worked together in the good old days of what she always called the Great Woh-wuh, when we all remembered her as a beautiful slip of electrified wire, still at the Sorbonne, studying the Mathematics of Probability, Archaeology, the Left Bank and the younger

6

staff officers of the Wehrmacht. I suppose she got more information over a tablecloth than a generation of courtesans from a mountain of bedlinen. She even became engaged to a colonel of the Luftwaffe to find out more about the V.1 and 2—I believe the first inkling we had of them—what they were, where they were being built, transported, mounted. All she had to do was follow him to the little rendezvous he planned, ask her own sort of playful question, fly to the arms of her chaperone when things got too schmaltzily-smeltery, and when she had the facts, parachute back to southern England. That was her type of blossom, as the head of her Service had once called her, a magnolia forged out of brand-new Bethlehem Steel tramlines. Which reminded me, that Mike Bowles, our supplies director, was still in Cairo, hoping to buy a disused rail-line along the Suez, and I should have heard from him. The Company's aircraft was out, I supposed with Paul, and I taped the travel desk to get me a flight to Cairo next afternoon, and put in a call for Mike, but there was still no reply from the Cairo office. I rang the Swiss Consulate, and a girl said ah, but yes, there had been an explosion, but only the glass doors and a few windows had been broken. The staff had been sent to Lausanne by Mr. Chamby. Yes, he was there, but he left this evening. The Police had put on a guard, the glass had been replaced, and everything now, so far as she knew, was normal. I thanked her, got an appointment with the Swiss Consul for the following evening, and made another drink.

Those glass doors opened into Consuelo's office, and I've seen glass shatter before. Any notion that she might have been there made me feel, not so much ill, or sick, as murderous. I had Paul to thank for getting her out of it. But long before that, Druxi knew, and warned us.

But where did the threat arise? I couldn't believe it had anything to do with a competitor. Skullduggery in commerce on certain levels had to be accepted, but planting bombs, menacing a staff of innocents must have taken a little time to plan. And if so much was already done, what was to be expected in the near future? I suddenly felt a little chilled. We, in fact, were not only

7

in the dark, but defenceless. I had to do something drastic without knowing where to turn.

I called for the monthly reports and staff lists. I tooth-combed the reports, but there wasn't a detail out of place. I looked through the staff lists. Most of our men were already in the desert, the majority Americans, then British, a number of Arabs, all vouched for by our Arabian members of the Board, a few French, Finns, Italians, Poles, and Germans, all of solid experience, those at the top with a degree, all heads of departments well-known in their own field. I couldn't see a weak link, or find in the reports any hint of trouble to come, either from political parties, governments, or from other companies in the industry. I looked through our Intelligence Unit reports, and drew another blank. Yet we were well-served. Our contacts were thoroughly trustworthy, and very little escaped them.

What were we to look for? Where?

Who was after us?

It didn't seem the sort of question to ask on a fine, quiet night, but I made sure of my little friend in the shoulder holster, got my muffler, overcoat, blew in the white gloves, pressed dimples in the felt, and went down the side stair to find Marlq' Ben Ab waiting with a cab door open.

"Don't wait up," I said. "I don't know what time I'll be back!"

He pressed his jowls sideways in the starch.

"China tea, honey, and Al Achram, ironed, five forty five," he said, with a motion to suggest the iron used on the pressing pad. "Blue barathea, lightweight, white voile shirt, black town brogue, blue Locke. Good night, sir!"

I took the cab to the Grand Hotel, sauntered through the lobby, and went out to the right, downhill, caught another cab, and told him to go to Arturo's, off the Via Veneto. I'd had a fifty percent interest in it for the past umpteen years, ever since he'd said he wanted to set up on his own. Some men are born to open a first-class cafe, and Arturo was one. He'd married an English girl, a beauty with a head on her shoulders, a minor in the Service, and since then, they'd made a real business of a cafe with a certain atmosphere, because Lucy didn't permit what she called Rough Stuff, and since she sat in the cash desk, what she said went.

I stopped the cab downstreet, sent the cabman in, and Arturo came out in shirtsleeves and a rush, rolling his apron to help his knees.

"Ah, sir!" he trumpeted. "But what a pleasure! Lucy is just home. I have another son, I call him Edmund, certainly!"

"With my blessing," I said, shaking a damp hand. "Put a couple of men on the building. Watch callers and correspondence. Particularly, watch household buying. Verify and report twice a day, zero eight zero nine and two zero zero nine. I'll stroll in for a cup of coffee tomorrow and drop a *Corriere*. No sign. I'll leave flowers for Lucy, and the christening party's mine, whether I'm here or not!"

A *Corriere* meant I'd be leaving money, we'd give no sign of recognition, and his signals would be waited for at zero eight zero nine every morning, and two zero zero nine each night.

He nodded, bowed, and shut the cab door, and I knew I'd have the last scrap of information on the hour each twelve hours, and I also felt we'd been a little careless in not employing him before. We were, of course, a commercial enterprise, but the nature of our business, the construction of a gas pipeline across southern Arabia, through sheikhdoms and "zones of interest" lent itself to vagary on many levels, and all of them had to be watched for, both eyes well open, and hence a twenty-four-hour-pensioner police guard, and our own Intelligence Unit.

I was worried. Druxi had taken the trouble to leave warnings in Cairo, and here. It shouted, of course, that somebody on our staff was working for CIA. I didn't mind that. It had always been tacit that a good part of our capital was American. But then, if CIA had been clever enough to plant somebody, others far more dangerous might have been just as smart. Which of the staff could be suspect? All of them, without exception, and it was my responsibility to uncover whoever and how many, and I oughtn't to be going anywhere except back to my desk.

But it was a single night off in weeks, and I was obstinate.

It wasn't an opera but ballet, and a favorite of mine—*The Enchanted Toyshop*—and I went into Box C just as the lights went down and applause for the conductor went away in a whisper.

The orchestra plucked those magic opening chords, and instantly I was back in London's Theatre Royal those years ago, with Mel beside me, and the children, rapt. The scenery wasn't what I remembered, choreography had changed, I thought, but the costumes were beautiful, the dancing seemed of angels, and the door creaked behind my chair, and I swung angrily, jolted from a dream.

Paul stood in darkness. I got up and went down the stair.

"Damn nuisance, Edmund!" he whispered. "Been some trouble in the Cairo office. The staff's in Lausanne for a few days—"

"Consuelo?"

"She's fine. She's in charge. Let's get out to the airport. Your plane's fifteen minutes after mine—"

I followed him just as the Cards began their dance, perhaps my favorite vignette. The cloakroom attendant was helping me on with my coat, and I saw the door to Box C fly out against the far wall in a flash of orange flame, and a blast almost knocked us off our feet.

Paul gave me The Long Swords, that palish-blue, half-smiling glance that asked and answered a question in one.

"Any complaints?" he asked gently.

"My favorite ballet, dammit!" I said, and followed him, more than a little mystified, downstairs, stepping aside for the crowd running up. I'd turned to my right to slip between two policemen, and happened to look at the balcony. Not more than twenty feet away, a girl was staring at me—Javanese?—Malayan?—I couldn't tell for the moment, and while I thought how extraordinarily an orange light glittered in dark eyes, she'd gone behind a column.

"Come on!" Paul said. "We don't want any questions!"

2

That airport journey brought us both up-to-date with the Company's business, point to point, reigning Prince to blackmailing jester. Paul agreed we'd have to haggle bazaar-fashion and try to pay the least for most, playing one against the next, relying on our Arabian directors to apply their weight.

"Shouldn't hit us higher than about sixteen percent the lot," he said. "Twenty, top. That's cheap. I'll be happy. Once they've taken that first payment, then we can start grinding. We can make a lot more on the side. Supplies, import licenses, there's a rich field, there. But, look, Edmund. What the bloody hell's happened to Angela? She didn't go home last night!"

"First I've heard of it," I said, startled at his tone. "I got in late. Didn't expect to see her."

"I went across where she's staying. Near the Borghese. An old Englishwoman. She wasn't in, either. I talked to a maid. Wasn't anybody else. Said she hadn't been in. I'm a bit worried. Not like her, is it?"

"What made you come to the Opera House?"

"They told me that's where you were, of course!"

"What's the air trip for? I'm dog-tired!"

"So's everybody. All you've got to do's go to Madrid and pick up a packet at the Air India desk, and take it over to SAS for

Stockholm. I'll be at the Grand Hotel. I want it there soonest. I'm seeing Georg Tamm at the University. He's just back from Teheran. Left messages all over but I missed him. He knows a lot about the Russians we don't, and he's got a couple of good men there we can use. The packet's from Bilat Khan. He's been in Kabul for the past year. Most likely be some interesting stuff, there. I'd have sent Angela—where *is* she?—find out soon's you get back. Hell's she playing at, worrying people?"

"She may have had to meet somebody—"

"How about leaving a note, then? That's a loophole we can block right away. When senior staff leave the office, I want place, telephone number and probable time of return!"

I didn't say anything. It was a backhand at my system of running the offices. I didn't bother to tell him that the rule was everywhere in force. He should have known it.

"How did you get on to the Cairo business?" I asked gently. "Right in the nick, wasn't it?"

"I had the good luck to fly in with Rizkallah Chohfi," he said, bad temper gone. "He was met by that fat Inspector of Nasr Khefi's, the Special Branch wallah. He told me they'd picked up a couple of Yemenis at our place. I mean, just an hour or so before, and they'd ordered everybody in the building outside, just in case. I went one better and sent the entire staff—except the locals—to Lausanne. I'd just signed the travel order in the Swiss Consulate and we heard the thing go off. Took a couple of doors and all the windows out. Anyway, the Consul's in charge of things. Nasr Khefi took a pile of money off the two Yemenis to put the doors and the glass in again, and pay a lot of out-of-pocket "expenses," including plenty for his own. Only thing is, he wouldn't let me talk to them. I'll bet they were no more Yemenis than I am. Any of the Trucial States, Adenis, yes. But not the Yemen. Too many good friends!"

Paul spoke very much under the weather. The verve one had always appreciated wasn't there. For the first time since I'd known him, he seemed not so much sad as tinged with a sort of speculative hopelessness as if, having thought things over, he'd decided we were more or less finished. Nothing gets my rag quite so much as any notion of bending the neck, far less under threat.

"Any idea where all this might be coming from?" I asked, looking out, at the airport's flashing green light. "Any counteraction we might take?"

"Haven't got a drift, Edmund," he said, in the same almost-monotone. "There's nothing in any of the reports. Extra guards on all the offices aren't much use. I'm *very* worried about the girls. I've got an idea they'll all have to go back to London. I'm responsible. Sad start!"

"Won't stop construction. We can deal with the paper from a central office. A staff of travelling couriers for the more important stuff. Might save some money!"

"We lose face, Edmund. You know Arabs. They're like us. They like things right. They won't have half measures. Besides, you don't put a few million into a company to be told you can't have an office wherever you damn' well want it!"

"Beyond the usual supervision, what do you suggest for Cairo and here?"

"Cairo, see Khefi. He's got more feelers than a pussy-moth. Everywhere. He knows who's behind us. I'll see Nabib in Teheran and Othman in Damascus. I'll guarantee we'll know where to look by today week. You get out first. Marlq' Ben Ab's waiting for you in the foyer by the tobacco counter. He's got your passport and suitcase and a return to Madrid. You could stay there tomorrow. Let things simmer down. I'll go to Helsinki, and get back here the day after. I'll wait for the zero-eight-zero-four call. I'm a bit worn, Edmund, I don't mind telling you. There's nothing about any of this I can like!"

I sat back, folded my arms, and looked at him square, lit by passing lights.

"You know a few facts I don't," I said. "What are they?"

"And our dear Druxi almost painting the place white for our benefit?" he said, in a headshake of quasi-regret. "Didn't you hear poor old fair-play died? In good company, of course. The gentleman's agreement, and the word of honor, lovely old landmarks in the verdant sward of chivalry, eh? Where d'you find them, these days? Not even in a game of football. If you look at our potential profits, it might strike you that others'd like to come in, or put us out of it and take control. Perhaps some of the people on our Board. These few months've proved we're right. The bellyachers were wrong. Perhaps they'd like a bigger piece, or all of it. Want to go home?"

"I like a run for my money," I said, and got out, walking to the main entrance. The hall was fairly crowded, but Marlq' Ben Ab had obviously been looking for me, and led over to the desk, taking out an envelope with my passport, ticket, and a sheaf of documents, my shorthand notes, I was relieved to see, among them. I wasn't thinking much about anything because the major part of my mind was on problems ahead. But I suddenly became aware of Marlq's attitude. Ordinarily, he was the sort who'd merge, as it were, into the wallpaper, unheard, unseen. He was looking past me, at nothing, and his widened mouth had pushed his cheeks up into his eye-sockets, an expression I hadn't seen before, and if only for that, alarming.

"Something wrong?" I asked.

"I speak to you, sir," he said, with difficulty, in nods and pauses. "To nobody else. I like to go to Cairo. Rome, to me, it's no good. I please can return, sir? Now, tonight, sir, I am ready!"

"What is it, exactly?"

He looked up at the line of lights.

"Sir, I serve you many years," he said. "I hear bad news in Cairo. My wife and children there. In Cairo, I am home. If things are wrong, I have many friends. Here, none. Rome, for me, it's no good. You please enquire about Miss Masters. Twice she try to enter your apartment. She wants to go in the East Room. I say no, and she is angry. But I say no. I think she has something not correct. I do not permit a woman to speak with me. You forgive, and allow to go, please?"

"Very well. I shall be in Cairo tomorrow. I shall expect to find you on duty!"

He bowed, and I watched him walk away, wondering what

Angela, tall, silvery-blonde, Paul's love—and next wife, most of us thought—and a most efficient secretary, might have to do in my apartment and office. But the top man's right hand would have plenty to do everywhere, in or out of the office.

Out of the office?

Where was she?

Red warning blazed.

Paul had been away more than a month, and so had I. There and then I made up my mind to fly back that night. Marlq' Ben Ab wasn't the type to walk off without good reason. I had plenty to think about on the way to Madrid. It didn't take long to sign for the packet from a smart Air India hostess and hand it in to the freight counter of SAS. My friend the airport manager got me a seat on the Rome flight without passport and Customs fuss, and I went aboard an almost empty plane to drink a scotch and soda while I thought things over and then dozed till we got to Rome. I tried to get Lausanne, but the line was busy—at that hour in the morning?—and I asked for the call to be put through to my apartment number, which didn't have to go through the Company board. I took a cab from the airport and asked him to pass by Arturo's cafe, but as I'd thought, it was shut. Our building was quiet enough. The two night guards opened the gates, and by the time I'd walked to the main door, Dorandi waited to take me up in the Otis. I switched on the electronic lock to my apartment with a distinct feeling of relief.

I went through the small pile of mail brought in by the night courier, picked out a letter from Consuelo, kissed it and put it beside the armchair, and opened a note from the Swiss Consulate in Cairo, asking me to call Mr. Bowles at any time of the day or night. I put the call in, had a hot bath, got into pajamas and a gown, and poured a night cap. I'd just opened Consuelo's letter, got as far as Darlingest, faithless swain, and Vox flashed blues.

Bowles was on the line, holloing.

"Yes, Mr. Bowles!"

"Mr. Trothe? Gee, the time I had!"

"Did we get it?"

"I had it all set. Wasn't so easy. Them Israeli gunners can look through the barrels at us. Hit a matchbox at a mile. The fellahin don't go for it. So I had to get a work force from the interior. Then I had to get trucks, not so simple. From El Kantara to Alexandria, that's a ways. Had to be working day and night, and that's extra money. Well, I got down there day before yesterday, six in the morning, dark. The road turns in and follows the tracks. Remember, the big sign?"

"I do, yes?"

"Wasn't one. I thought I got lost. But just a few yards on, the track's gone, sleepers, signal boxes, barriers, the entire goddam works, start to finish. When I got down there, the last of the guys're getting up in the trucks going back to Port Said. Look, Mr. Trothe, I couldn't recruit one single man there only ten days ago for double pay, triple overtime anything over the eight hours. 'Part from this, in the past week, the freighters got loaded, and they sailed this morning, five of them. I could only charter two, out of Alexandria, and for that I had a lot of official help. As I thought. Somebody has a lot more pull. But worse than that, I had the generator deal signed and paid for. All I had to do was collect. I sent three trucks, they cost the earth to hire, ready on time. They got stalled all day yesterday. Last night my draft came back. There was a figure altered. But it wasn't me altered it. Just an excuse to return it. I got hold of Maluf at the Club, he's the general manager, and he said he was sorry, nothing he could do. But the generators'd been picked up and paid for. I can't find out who by. Anyway, they've gone. I'm sore's hell, but that's the situation!"

"Spend some money. Find out all you can in both cases. Could be even more important than the deals. A pointer's what we want!"

"O.K., Mr. Trothe. I believe I know how. I'd just admire to claw my hooks into 'em!"

I went back to Consuelo's lovenote. New worry throbbed in the forefront of my mind. Whoever had bought that line and the generators must have spent at least three times what we'd earmarked, which was about five times what we'd normally have offered. But they were ready for use, and a mere couple of days' sail from our Mediterranean terminal, which, in terms of manufacture and transport, meant a saving of perhaps a year in time alone.

The spending of so much money, and the efficiency of the move pointed to a large organisation, together with—what I'd imagined we'd enjoyed more than any—cooperation absolute at not less than Cabinet level, and from more than one Ministry. I wondered what the Arabian members of our Board might have to say, and I put in a call for the Prince Azil, a friend of mine for many years, our Vice-Chairman, and a most capable businessman-cum-banker, even though in view of his father's and his own billions, whether in oil, real estate, or the stock market, going to work, as he'd once said, was like adding cupfuls of water to the ocean.

While I waited, I read Consuelo's eight pages, almost drinking the vital strength of her love warm from near schoolgirlish lines, wondering when I could sit down to write with as much freedom and gaiety, and yet imply an utter sadness, a pulsing wound of absence. I didn't feel like trying at that moment, and I put in another call, at eight o'clock, for Lausanne. The voice means more than anything on paper.

I was just getting into bed when the operator said that Prince Azil was in Paris. Knowing something of his night-life, I asked for a person-to-person call at his convenience, folded Consuelo's letter under the pillow, and woke up under my own steam, at a quarter to eight, clear-eyed and fresh as a sunbeam. I hate being jolted out of sleep. It makes me rabid for the day. But I'd forgotten there was no Marlq' Ben Ab, and I had to blow down the kitchen squeaker for breakfast and the papers, making a note for the electrician to adjust for Inter-Vox. Remnants of the nineteenth century, in my opinion, retain all their charm in the museum. Here and now, they merely clutter.

All the newspapers headlined the Opera House bomb. The dancers and orchestra had taken no notice, nobody had been hurt, and Combined Industrial Enterprises S.A. were not once mentioned as ticket holders of Box C, I wasn't, and the remains of a homemade bomb seemed, it was said, to be the work of a madman. I could have told them it wasn't homemade, and whoever planted it was expert. It would have taken me out neatly as a slice of cut cake, with little more damage than cracked plaster and a broken door. I had Paul—and Lady Luck—to thank.

How many among the staff had known I was going to the Opera House? One, Emilia Tagliaferro on the travel desk, certainly. But what advantage would it be to anybody to get rid of me? The Company certainly wouldn't withdraw from the contract—and lose untold millions—if Paul and I and a dozen more were got rid of. There were plenty of people ready to take our places. Why start with me? Druxi had warned in Cairo and in Rome. First correct move, it seemed to me, was to find her and ask. Easier thought than done.

I read the rest of the news with a crackling roll, farm butter— a different taste!—and honey, had a leisurely bath, and I was shaving when Lausanne came through, and Consuelo spoke as if she were in the room, making me not just hungry, but savage to see her again, and I knew that in the next day or so I was going to find the requisite excuse to walk in and kiss the back of her neck just to feel her jump, and then enjoy the fragrant warmth of her arms, and other things I didn't want to think about.

"Edmund, my wonderful, look, I must tell you. Have you seen Mr. Chamby? We're alone and scrambled, aren't we?"

"We're both, and I saw him yesterday—"

"We saw him in Cairo. He looked *deathly* ill. I called Doctor Bittencourt. Naturally, he didn't say anything. Is he sickening for something, d'you think?"

"Business worries, possibly. There's quite a lot that isn't going as we'd like. I shall be in Cairo this afternoon—"

"Darling! Please take care—"

"I shall, indeed, because I intend to be in Lausanne the day after. Reserve a room for me, and our usual table. I'm starving for you—"

"Not long till the day after tomorrow, my sweet. Look, I can't get Angela—"

"She's out, somewhere. I've got to go. If there's anything, call me here. It'll go on the relay. Think of me!"

"Every moment. Tenderly, dearly, darling mine. 'Bye!"

I tried to get Paul and couldn't. Arturo came on with NOY O, Nothing Yet, Out. I got the London signal clear, which meant that I should have got Paul's signal if he'd come on. But he was probably breakfasting with Tamm at the University, as he usually did.

I called down for Angela Masters. She wasn't in. Miss Greig wasn't. Miss Toverell wasn't. I called Miss Corvo in the time-keeper's office. None of them were in, and hadn't been in yesterday. Hadn't? Where was the nurse? At the hospital. All the clerical, stores and messenger staff were in. Three key members were not? What was happening to correspondence? It all went to Lausanne. Had perhaps Angela made her own work schedule? She and the other two often worked on weekends to catch up with the engineers' reports. But she should have consulted me.

I got the board to call her lodging. Somebody—a maid—said she wasn't in. I thought she might be on her way, in which case I'd have a Little Word. I called all eleven of our bases, and got a Normal report except from Eliof, at our Mediterranean terminal, north of Beirut.

"We're getting a little low on tube, Mr. Trothe. We don't have more'n about twenty-two mile in stock. Then there's spares, tires—"

"Tube's being loaded now. The *Shane McFall's* carrying spares of all types. She ought to reach you first, in about ten days. I'll be there before that. How's everything else?"

"Everything swell, Mr. Trothe, sir. Glad to see y'—"

I called Angela Masters' desk again, but the operator said she hadn't been in and couldn't be found at her lodging, the nurse had reported Miss Toverell was unwell at her *pensione* and the Company's doctor was going to see her, and a messenger had gone to Miss Greig's because there wasn't a telephone.

"I believe Miss Masters went to Naples yesterday afternoon, sir," she said. "Captain Tustini called from the airport, something about a couple of engineers going there with her—"

"Ask the travel desk where the order came from, will you?"

"I already asked, sir. Mr. Locatelli said it's an Athens order, sir. Miss Masters was putting the engineers on Alitalia for Damascus—"

"Did she go there with them?"

"Nobody knows, sir!"

I sent queries to Athens and Damascus, and by the time I'd run through the mail, read the reports, made up the daily diary, dressed—missing Marlq' Ben Ab!—noon had struck, and I went on an unofficial tour of inspection. Everything glistened in apple-pie order. In the main office, the staff were going to lunch. The blue light still shone in Angela Masters' office on a raised level at the end. That meant nobody was in, since the opening of the door automatically shut off the light and made the pane one-way from the inside.

I didn't go in because I'd have had to go up to the police office to get the key, and since everything seemed normal, I walked out, through the garden, passing the garage gate, and downhill toward my favorite barber's shop for the usual snip at neck and ears.

The morning was golden Roman, and if I hadn't had quite such a deskful, I might have gone to the beach for a swim and a shell-fish luncheon. I could almost taste a glory of color from a corner flower-stall, and then, for no good reason, except perhaps that I was looking at a mass of yellow daisies, I thought of the Asian girl's face, her eyes, staring at me, black eyes, in that light, basilisk seemed a fair term, the stare of a large cat. But why think of her, on a golden Roman morning, crossing a garden with all the oleanders pink and white in joyous bloom?

Because, trying to remember, there'd been a touch of orange light in that stare, perhaps from the lamps overhead. But why should I be looked at by some unknown Asian girl? And why wasn't she in her chair watching the ballet? Even if she'd been in a box, she hadn't had time to be out there, looking at me. If she wasn't in a box, then what was she doing there? It deserved an enquiry.

I strolled through noon bustle, relishing dry air and morning sun, and the smells of cheese, salt fish and salami from corner grocery shops, wondering again at the resilient spirit of the Italian people, that so little time after war's destruction had put them again in civilisation's front rank. The smiles were there, music and children's voices sounded everywhere, fruit-peddlers shouted and punched bags, waiters put out cafe tables, and the women divided neatly in two, the smartly dressed *en maquillage* going toward the city, or those in pincurls and a headwrap doing the shopping. I was looking at a girl in a cotton dress cheekily puffed by a light breeze to show she wore nothing underneath, and I heard, spacily between the high buildings, a crack! that by reflex side-skipped me into a doorway.

I saw the puff of brickdust just above my eyeline, and stood there, in the lobby of a women's hairdressing salon, sniffing perfume. Nobody looked at me, a man hooded in a sack took a side of veal into the butcher's next door, and across the road, a Coca-Cola wagon stopped at the curb, and the driver climbed up to lift crates. I turned to look down the slight hill, but the crowd walked, other vans unloaded, yelling children roller-skated, and a group of little girls hopped in chalked squares. I judged the bullet to have been a .303, from the crack and *snap!* near my head. I didn't bother trying to look for the sniper's vantage point. While a couple of women shoppers came toward me downhill, I nipped in front of them to the back of the truck, and walked up, in its cover, to the corner, and turned down the lane leading back to the garage.

Bavesi took me up in the lift to the main floor. Morelli got off his knees in front of the Otis, moving his cleaning kit out of the canary cage of brass scrolls smoothed by the brawn of his own and other polishing arms over a generation, that went up silently, not by a button, but a pull on the cable.

"If Lieutenant Truffo's in, I want to see him," I said. "I shall be in the East Room."

21

3

I walked along the parquet to the highest, widest, handsomest office I'd ever had. We'd bought the ruin of a house from a noble-man, and our architect had put in bathrooms, more wardrobe space and a "modern" kitchen, built a wider terrace with more window area, a top floor made into four private apartments, and the dining room, staff club, and a basement garage. Everything else, except for a general scraping and repainting, had been left as it was. The result pleased the eye and rested the spirit, and I sat in the armchair, glad I was still in one piece.

Lieutenant Truffo tapped and came in, a small man, walking stiff-legged as a wary cat, at my nod, sitting on the edge of the chair, one fist on the desk, the other hand clutching a blue folder, looking at me, eyes wide, mouth in a wrinkled cone.

I told him what had happened, in detail, from the time of my arrival the night before, leaving out the visit to Arturo, and he listened without a move until I'd finished.

Even then he didn't move.

"We know who put the bomb there," he said, in English, learned as an interpreter with the U. S. Army years before. "He was found dead in his hotel this morning. No marks. Am waiting for the autopsy report of the Company's physician. There was nothing in his room, not even to shave, change the shirt. Interpol will send a report. For the shot this morning, I shall wait for the report of the man behind you!"

"You had a man behind me?"

He went on nodding slightly as though his neck were on a spring.

"Mr. Chamby's order, sir. Everybody now has an accompanist. It is necessary!"

"Indeed. What about Miss Masters?"

He clasped his hands and looked down at his feet.

"To the best of our knowledge, she is in a house at Anacapri with friends," he said. "My colleagues on the island have the house under observation. Marlq' Ben Ab told you of her conduct, sir?"

"He's gone to Cairo. Tell me about Miss Masters!"

"I am glad Marlq' Ben Ab told you, sir," he said, in a small voice, holding up the folder. "It is a delicate matter. Exceptionally delicate. If you tell Mr. Chamby, it will be better. Miss Masters, sir, you permit me, goes to small clubs. She meets certain men and women. Of bad character. She is with them now. They are wealthy people. Or they spend money. Should I have the report translated, or is it good enough in Italian?"

"Italian!"

"I will enquire about the Asian woman, and I shall hope to present a report about it, as well as the rifle shot, later this afternoon, sir. I have leave, please?"

He put the folder on the desk, and I watched the door close from the corner of my eye, wondering how I was to tell Paul, but really knocked over to think that Angela Masters, that paragon of good breeding and singular accomplishment, could possibly make one little mistake, far less blunder into a complaint of five pages.

The report was a shocker. Angela had been brought back, drunk after luncheon and had to be taken home. There followed a list of names, her companions or fellow-guests, men and women. I knew none of them.

I had a one-way reservation made open, in her name, for London, with a month's salary cashier's docket, and sent a telex to warn Gilbert to meet her.

Athens came through on top of Damascus. Neither knew anything about engineers or Miss Masters. The aircraft hadn't been seen, and neither was it expected. I ordered an all-station enquiry for Captain Tustini, and put in a call for Stockholm. I was certain Paul knew nothing about it.

But he was Director-General, and Angela was his private secretary, and all things being most unequal—because I'd known his wife, Moira, beautiful and very plain-spoken Australian, now in Sydney waiting for a divorce—she'd be the next Mrs. Paul Chamby. She had all the gifts of a first-rate right hand, untiring, of almost intuitive perception, and she'd earned a far higher-than-average Bachelor—though, again, how a girl graduated with a Bachelor's instead of a Spinster's degree had always struck me as being another wordy mess—(which nobody else seemed to think ridiculous or patronising)—and her father was Under-Secretary for Air, which, of course, did her—did us—no harm.

Paul might have given her permission to fly off somewhere without telling a soul in the office. I couldn't believe it. The accountants would want to know every detail of the flight. It was an item in the balance sheet. She knew that. Then how could she go off for a couple of days or so to Naples, or anywhere else, and expect to come back, scathless, a very Daddy's little girl? Our accountants weren't the sort to cover for anybody, and our shareholders were mostly Arabian princes. Their place for women was behind the lattice.

Obviously I had to make a personal—and most discreet—enquiry, if only to protect Paul. He could be damaged personally, as well as officially.

The travel desk said the aircraft still couldn't be located, and I asked for a return ticket to Naples, and took the car to the airport. I don't think there's a more dramatically beautiful flight than from Rome anywhere south, and I got off the plane at peace with the world. Airport control told me that our aircraft had flown the previous day, they understood, to Brindisi. I couldn't think what the pilot might have in mind, and gave up, sending Rome a message to order his return. I didn't spot anyone behind me on the car ride to the harbor, and the little white ship seemed to wait only till I went aboard. There may be pleasanter voyages than from Naples to Capri, but I don't know of one. Sail past the city's piled-up hillside terraces, and the coastline might never have changed since Nero's day. I was thinking of the miles-long bridge of ships he'd ordered built, with the feasting chamber in the middle, and his command to sever the line, so that hundreds of his guests had to swim for it or drown, and a ship's officer saluted and held out a note.

"How did you know this was for me?" I asked him.

"The police officer pointed you out, sir," he said, and nodded behind. "When we reach port, you will please stand nearer the stern. You will be first off!"

The note was a little surprising.

An officer is waiting to take you to the villa where Miss M is staying. You will be under close supervision at all times.

The signature "T" I took to be Truffo's. He was a lot smarter than I'd thought, but then, Italian police work has always been top level.

I didn't worry about the scenery after that. The world's bluest water smoothed by—it was a dream of an afternoon—while I tried to think what Angela could be doing, knowing perfectly well she'd lose the job of a lifetime, and, perhaps, a wealthy husband. Paul, I was certain, would never tolerate a smallest departure from the norms of commerce, especially where it touched the Company's business. He was a martinet of the old school, and by that, I mean he allowed none of the so-called "modern" nonsense of let's-sit-down-and-chat-about-this to affect a decision. He gave none a second chance. They went.

Tilsley, Banham, Muir and Seagram had gone in their first month. Reeves and George had been sent off last week. I'd had the most unhappy job of getting rid of Shanklin, a friend of ours for many a year, good brain, solid experience, but the type of Arab he was dealing with wouldn't tolerate drunkenness, and he'd had to go. It was worrying, because we were losing excellent men, and getting the right sort to fill their places was becoming a task. Each applicant had to be interviewed, scholastic and business details verified, personal record checked by our Intelligence

Unit, but then, on acceptance, and allocation to an area, too many of them seemed to disintegrate. They were drunkards, or taken ill, or comported themselves in such a manner that they were escorted under guard to the nearest airstrip and flown out. Or else, as in Banham and George's case, they sent in a letter of resignation and defied us to sue, as we could have done under Clause 10 of the contract. We didn't, because a contract signed in Athens has no teeth in Cairo, and none of them wanted a contract rising in London because of Income Tax.

I was thinking about all that while we backed into the Mole and a couple of seamen pushed a lane in jostling passengers to allow me an almost lady-like skitter over the cleats of the gangway, and down to a black car, with a policeman holding the door open, and another at the wheel. I didn't ask how they knew I was the one they waited for. I got in, and we turned for the steep hill leading up to the older Capri.

Except for a few new houses and shop fronts, I don't think much had changed since I'd been there years before, and the islanders, of course, have far too much personality to change at all. They've seen more than one civilisation come and go, and it seems their smilingly unspoken purpose to watch a few more crumble, though women over twenty will always wear the Roman black, men will go patched in sun-faded tatter but instantly told apart from tourists, children will still play ancient games and scream cradle-grimed obscenities, Pan will pipe, and Poppeia will ever be empress of vice, all in the braying South Wind breath of the Ass-god, Set, whose hoofmark is on them all. We passed Axel Munthe's lovely old house—but what *is* the use of making a man's house, his intimate shelter of years, into a museum-cum-memorial? Why not let a scholar emeritus live there, and after him, others?—and a couple of miles or so farther on we turned right, down a lane, and stopped at a blue door new-painted in a high stone wall. We were over the sea. The sun was warm, and I could hear flies, the tick of a cooling engine, and the rank of weeds overrode the smells of settling dust and the rubbery heat of tires. The policeman didn't bother to knock. He took out a bunch of keys and poked, gouged, and the door creaked open.

He stood aside, and I went along a flagged path in a garden of fountains, benches and bits of statuary in clumps of flowers, toward an old house still in scaffolding, with canvas over a gap in the tiles. Around the left-hand corner, the ground sloped toward the cliff, with small lawns, roses, lilies, a swimming pool, and under a laburnum, a girl in a white swimsuit lay on an orange towel, reading.

I thought she was Angela Masters. The same drawn-back silvery-fair hair, and when she looked up, startled, the same enormous blue-grey eyes.

But not Angela.

She frowned, got up gracefully without hurry, and stood, looking at me, tall, slender, lovely in her way, but close to, not even remotely like Angela.

"I beg your pardon," I said soothingly, and thinking fast. "I was told I'd find Mrs. Octavius Porilloni here? Isn't she renting the house?"

"I'm sorry, but it's been rented, sir," she said, in fair Italian with a German accent. "Only the housekeeper and I are here. I don't know Mrs. Porilloni. Perhaps it's a house further on?"

My mind was in a gallop. Italian Police were rarely wrong, especially when they'd force a door. This girl was very much like Angela. Only those knowing her would see the difference. Could she—an absurd tangential thought!—have impersonated Angela? Where? For what reason? Where *was* Angela? How could the Police have made a mistake? Should I apologise, and leave? Or persist?

"I regret this inconvenience," I said, and looked at the house. "I'd no idea it'd been taken. Just what I was looking for. Perhaps you'd be kind enough to let me see inside? I know it's a nuisance—"

"But please do," she said, and threw up the poncho of orange towelling to settle round her neck, and walked in front, tying the straps. She wore an emerald on the right-hand little finger, her nails were long, pink, perfect, but she held an air of the "cheap," though I'm not sure why, except for that half-smile in the corner of her eyes.

I felt I was being played for stupid, but I had no intention of rousing the smallest suspicion. Lieutenant Truffo would have some explaining to do. I didn't dream of going to any other house. This one, for some reason that had to be explained, had been pin-pointed by the island Police. Had somebody been bribed?

"The downstairs rooms are still being painted," she said, opening the door. "Upstairs is ready. This is the main room. Beyond is the dining room. Then the kitchen and maids' rooms. When the furniture is in place, it will be a good house for the summer, no?"

She stood in the shadows, back to me, and I might have sworn I saw, I listened, to Angela, except that she didn't speak Angela's Italian. Her voice in that vault was much the same. She walked, gestured, as Angela did.

Eerie, I thought.

But it appears to be a law of merest nature that for one reason or another, the criminal must, by malvirtue, make one more—damning—mistake than the rest of us, their innocent brethren. Paul and I had asked a famous Swiss designer to make a New Year gift especially for Angela, Consuelo, Marguerite and Tara, the four principal secretaries in our now-extinct Department. He'd brought in four draw-string crocodile handbags, quite small, with their initials, replica of their own handwriting, in gold, on the right-hand side, and since each Department worked with a different colored copy-paper, that color was beaded in semi-precious stones on the handles.

Angela's bag, with the turquoise-studded handles, smiled at me on the small table against the far wall under the window. I couldn't see the initials.

I looked about the room, at painters' ladders, pots, pastel colors dabbed on sheets of brown paper, furniture pushed together under linen shrouds humping in the middle, certain I was being watched, as certain that without the two men outside I'd have been put away.

The girl never faced me, never looked me in the eye.

"Thank you for your courtesy," I said. "I wish the house were mine. I apologise for the intrusion. Permit me to wish you good day!"

She smiled, half-inclined her head—so like Angela's!—and I walked out, down the path, feeling the target in the middle of my back, waiting to be shot, pacing down toward the blue door held open by the policeman, with sun splashing white on his bald head.

I got in the car, and we bumped over stones in a turn to the left.

"You didn't find anybody, sir?" the policeman asked, a little anxiously, while we jolted back to the road. "You didn't call, so I didn't—"

"Nothing to call for," I said shortly. "The woman there isn't the one I'm looking for. There's been a serious mistake. Who's in charge here?"

"Inspector Vassilio, sir, but he's gone to Naples—"

Instinct—or experience—I didn't analyse—warned me not to mention the handbag. That could be an ace at the right time, and now obviously wasn't. Stronger than the chauffeur's hair oil, I could smell the familiar odor of chicanery. I knew that the less said, the better.

"Could you get me a motor launch back to Naples? And look, share this with the driver. You've been most helpful!"

I got the best launch on the Marina and two enormous smiles, and away we went across the Bay, beating a couple of schools of dolphins, passing one of our destroyers—I don't know why the White Ensign always gives me a small boy feeling of absolute pride—painted in most delicate shades of green and grey, and an enormous American aircraft carrier in plain-jane grey, a magnificent sight, not a soul to be seen anywhere, and not a sound.

But whether or not I enjoyed the day's sunshine, green water, blue mountains, and Vesuvius' mauve cone beneath a smoky cap, my mind was on the Angela Masters' mystery. The girl I'd talked to was Austrian or German, about the same age, and a fair twin. I could see that except for those knowing her well enough, she could certainly be mistaken for Angela. But that didn't explain the use of the Company's aircraft, a flight to Naples, the Police alert at Anacapri, a house supposedly used by Angela, an official report about somebody either taking her place, or using her name. I had time at Rome to check that our aircraft wasn't at the field, and I phoned Truffo to wait for me.

I didn't mince words. His eyes slid away to look at a corner of the room. He seemed confident enough.

"The aircraft has returned, sir," he said. "The pilot is sure it *was* Miss Masters. I spoke to Verga—he went to the house with you—and he's gone back to search the place. If that report's wrong, it puts the Chief of Police with a silly face. He won't like it!"

"Miss Masters's got to be found. What's her address here?"

He wrote it, and went without a word. I didn't like his attitude, but I could deal with that later.

Angela's lodging wasn't far, and the walk was pleasant enough, through the park, and across the road to a large house behind a coach-gate. A porter, buttoning a green and black striped waistcoat, took my name in to Miss Clementina Dalziel. I hadn't the remotest idea how she'd look, but I never saw anyone fit a name so absolutely like a glove. She couldn't have been more than four foot, about the width of a little finger, white hair beautifully coiffed in a net with a black bow behind, a dress of grey velvet with a creamy lace cross-over in front, a band of black velvet about her neck, a massive pearl bracelet, and black satin shoes that managed to show their tips only when she walked, because her skirt just cleared the floor.

"Well, Mr. Trothe, how do you do?" she greeted me, in a tiny, tink-a-bell voice. "Do please sit down. What may I do for you?"

"It's about Angela Masters," I said, while a maid came in with a drink tray. "She's secretary, as you may know, to Mr. Paul Chamby, our Director General. I'm his deputy. He's away, and I've been away, and I wondered if Angela might be here, or if he might have sent for her, or if—"

Her frown stopped me.

"I was wondering, too," she said, bending her head. "She's a very punctual girl. But she hasn't been home since the day before yesterday, and she hasn't sent me a message, which I thought extremely odd. If she hadn't come in by nine o'clock tonight, I'd intended telephoning your office!"

"Very wise, indeed," I murmured, wondering how much I should tell her. "You said she was punctual?"

"Oh, yes! So was her dear mama, and her aunts. All pupils of mine. I retired before Angela was of age. Her mama wrote to me that she was coming to work in Rome, and I offered her rooms here. I've greatly enjoyed her company, and I was really quite distressed this morning. Quite distressed. Would you care to help yourself, Mr. Trothe?"

"Not for the moment, thank you. Did Angela ever appear the worse for drink?"

I thought she'd drop the decanter. I never saw a face so comically horror-stricken. She couldn't get a word out for a moment.

"But *Misss*-ter *Trothe!*" she whispered. "What a—what a *shock-*ing thing to say!"

"I'm really very sorry, ma'am. But you know, I'm not here on any casual errand. We can't find Angela, and it's been reported to me that she's been visiting night clubs and—ah—she's had too much to drink on occasion!"

She put down the decanter, looking at me, not a line in her face, though she was paler. She used her elbows to sit higher in the chair, and deliberately reached a lace-mittened hand to press the bell. In silence, I saw the flash of silver and crystal in armoires, blue velvet curtains, fruit under domes, a fine collection of cameos just behind her chair, and an enchantment of dolls' hats under a glass-covered table.

The maid tapped, and opened the door.

"Fernalda, you will call Maria and Gregoria, and Giuseppe and Pertacchi, and tell them to come here without a moment's loss!" Miss Dalziel said, calmly, staring over my head. "But hurry!"

The maid dipped a knee and ran. Miss Dalziel spoke the most perfect Italian I ever heard a foreigner use. I didn't comment. The atmosphere didn't lend itself to polite chatter. Her grey eyes held strange light. I could suddenly have done with a drink. She made no further offer.

One by one the women came to curtsey, and the men bowed as they might at Court, from the waist, nose to floor.

"Pay attention to me!" Miss Dalziel said, in that little voice, that cut. "I am informed that Miss Angela has appeared here, in this house, the worse for drink. That she comes home inebriated. Has she bad companions? Why wasn't I told? Pertacchi, you're at the gate. Tell me!"

From their faces, it was obvious that there wasn't a grain of truth in it.

Pertacchi shook his head, mouth well down.

Giuseppe, the older, used his hands, bunching his fingers, looking from maids to mistress.

"But Donna Clementina we're scandalized!" he falsettoed, and they all nodded and made sounds. "Miss Angela is the personification of the English. And I call on God, she doesn't drink!"

"Santa Maria, how stupid, how ridiculous!" an older woman said, in a fine contralto. "Don't I take care of her? If there was something, anything, especially drink, could we hide it? How? Who's got the dirty mouth?"

Miss Dalziel smiled suddenly, and waved a hand.

"That's all, thank you!" she said, looking at me. "I hope you're convinced, Mr. Trothe?"

"I am, indeed," I said, and got up to go. "I'm most grateful for a quite unexpected mass testimonial, as it were!"

"Is there something more I may do?"

"You might let me see her room. There may be some hint?"

"I'll take you," she said, moving to the door without appearing to walk, turning along the corridor, up a short stair, opening a heavy door in a pull, and pushing open a leather padded draught-stopper, standing with her back to me.

"This is the sitting room," she said distantly. "Beyond is the bedroom, bathroom, and terrace, with a private entrance. You have permission to examine any paper you please. I shall tell her, of course!"

I didn't turn the place upside down. They were two of the most agreeable rooms I've ever seen, in mint and cream, with a circular white carpet, and Angela had made the best of everything. She was as tidy here as at the office. I looked through the small files in the secretaire, but they were family letters, monthly bills, shoes, clothes, laundry. In the bedroom, I looked at the double bed under a pale-blue baldachino, almost ashamed of trespass, and opened the wardrobes. Dresses, suits, underclothing were all hung or folded, in order, with a perfume I couldn't quite catch. But in the compartment lined with about a dozen or so handbags in plastic wraps, I couldn't find the mate of the one I'd seen in the villa at Capri. One pair of shoe-trees were not in use.

"A fool's errand," I said, going back to the sitting room. "Thank you for your help. I shall let you know immediately if there's any news—"

She nodded, and led down to the hall, gave me her hand, and Giuseppe let me out.

I walked back in evening air quicker than I'd come. I had a most unpleasant feeling that something was seriously wrong. Angela wasn't the sort to go off without a word. A group of servants had plainly denied what the Police had presented as fact. Had there been the smallest error in her conduct, they were the type of peasant to dredge any detail in terms of moral outrage. But since she was innocent, they defended her with the positive fervor of the righteous, and I believed them.

But why had the story been concocted, why had Marlq' Ben Ab dangled a red herring, and, far more importantly, where was she?

I went up to find Lieutenant Truffo waiting in the anteroom.

"You will check your report in detail, Lieutenant, and be ready to explain how it came to be written," I said, without waiting. "It is incorrect where it concerns Miss Masters. If she saw it, she could sue for libel. Who instructed you to watch her?"

"Nobody, sir. I am in charge of Police, here. Anything affecting the staff doesn't require specific instruction—"

"But you're absolutely wrong!"

He didn't seem impressed. He had a habit of sliding his eyes down at a corner.

"We are used to expressions of disbelief, sir," he said, softly. "When this matter was brought to my attention, I put on a woman I trust. She provided the first reports. That was four days ago. We come to Wednesday. Miss Masters was taken back to her place from this office. Drunk. Then I decided to take charge personally. From that time, I, personally, followed her, with two assistants. Sir, that report is correct!"

I had to try another tack.

"The woman I saw at Capri this afternoon wasn't Miss Masters. Who is she?"

"It will be known by this time, sir. The Chief of Police in Capri has the matter well in hand. I wait for his report. It is all, sir?"

"I'm very worried. We've got to find Miss Masters!"

He raised large, knuckly hands, touched index to thumbtips, and drew a long line.

"Rest assured everything will be absolutely clarified within a few hours, sir," he said softly. "This case is what is called 'open and-a shut-a!'"

"I shall be here all night. Report the smallest detail to Apartment D if I'm not here."

When he'd gone, I had a drink I felt I deserved, and while I ambled about the room, I went back to Marlq' Ben Ab and his—as I'd thought—warning. Why had he put me on a false scent? What was the idea? How could a policeman of Lieutenant Truffo's experience be hoodwinked? How could he follow somebody he knew to be Angela Masters home, watch her enter, and be wrong? How could he direct me to a house in Capri, where, in fact, somebody very much like Angela happened to be—and where I'd seen a handbag I knew to be hers—and be wrong? I hadn't, at the time, said anything about it, because I judged that my going, and saying nothing created a sort of fool's paradise. At some time, that handbag's presence would have to be explained.

I went down to Paul's office, above Angela's, which was beyond, on a split-level, from the main accounts and personnel office, under mine, and the same size. Except for an air of disuse, all seemed in order, and I went on, down the narrow stair to Angela's office, a large room, with her desk and one for her secretary, filing cabinets behind panels, a couple of armchairs, and a glass wall separating the planning room, which held a large-scale model of the pipeline project, cine equipment, and a bank of retractable maps. The main office next door appeared peaceful enough, seen through the two-way window. The entrance gate was down, and the three control lights blinked with the electric clock to show that all was in order. Because of double windows I couldn't hear the traffic or anything else. The air seemed to press fingers against my eardrums. My hands were shaking. The vase I was looking at became three or four, and I failed to focus, frown as I might.

That Xth—the warning sense—took instant command. I went face-down on the floor and turned to crawl, grabbing a handkerchief to my nose, determined to reach the stairway and slam the door. It seemed to take an age, every limb trembled, every muscle tugged as leather, but I got to the small space, pulled at the jamb, managed to sit, reached for the button, and *thank God!* the door slid shut.

Air was clearer, and I went up, hands and knees, to the door in Paul's office, and on, up to mine, and clicked the partition shut, feeling a way along the wall to the bathroom. I didn't bother to undress. I turned on the shower and lay down, letting the icy pour numb me, head to foot. Pulling off my clothes made me a new being, and I towelled into electric warmth, went into the dressing room for underwear and a suit, and came out sensibly myself, most happily in a grinning temper, believing I knew exactly why poor Angela had appeared drunk.

That office still held the residue of an oxide gas. Fortunately I'd known the 'smell' though there isn't one, but the effect leaves a permanent scar in memory. By greatest fortune, in other days, I'd passed an examination in sights, sounds and smells, and the lessons weren't forgotten. Hands shaking, eyes refusing to focus, pressure on the eardrums, were signs of gas poisoning, and the air's always freshest near the floor.

Why should somebody want to destroy Angela? But in that office were the maps and pipeline routes, the sandbox model, and, in the cabinets, the reports of our engineers, and our diplomatic and commercial correspondence with the many governments taking part in the project. For that reason, we had three security officers on duty by day, and six at night, with a twenty-four-hour link to the Police and fire brigade.

Had anybody managed to get in? I didn't see what good it would do. Everything was in code, each piece of incoming paper was micro-taped and sent to Lausanne each night. The pipeline route was marked in detail, in maps and model, but only Paul and I knew the cipher, and it wasn't easily broken, even with a computer, because computers can't think.

It flitted across my mind that I ought to get in touch with Druxi, but I thought I'd stick to essentials for the moment.

I had a friend of long standing, a one-time Security Officer at Allied Command Headquarters, Agosto McGowan, Italian mother, Scots father, retired and living not far away. He knew everybody from the top down.

I switched on the scrambler, got his number from my book, and asked our board to put me through. A manservant answered, and presently Mac came on.

"Have you a friend or friends at the top, active or retired, and could you bring him, or them, here, soonest?" I said. "Hire a car with chauffeur and let him wait. I shall be delighted to see my old friend, Billy Whosis and his friend or friends of the Milk Board, or whatever. On?"

"Absolutely!" he whispered. "Thirty minutes. Oh, I say, what fun!"

Fun, yes, but Mac was no funster. When the lobby phone flashed, I went down to meet him, and two men I didn't know, though I hardly recognised him, smart fellow. He wore a real plaid suit, with a beret to hide his bald spot, and carpet slippers, and he leaned on the craggiest blackthorn I ever saw. He'd taken the trouble to put on a mustache, real or false is beside the point. His lines were deeper, his smile was of the tomb, and his voice phlegmed through the delicate coughing of one resigned to another world. I didn't get the names of the men with him, but I gathered—and so did the doorman and the night guard—that they'd all come to tell me of the passing of our mutual friend, Istogenes Hronk.

"Poor, poor Hronk!" I said and put my hands together. "Let us drink to his memory, gentlemen, and get out of this draught before we join him!"

We got up to my room, I locked the door, and Mac did a sword dance with the stick and beret. He introduced the others as Brigadier Toranzo and Colonel Perrine, both of Special Investigation.

I gave them Truffo's report to read while I poured the scotch, and then brought them up to date.

"I'll look into Truffo, first," Brigadier Toranzo said, and stood. "As to Capri, I'll have them rounded up inside the hour!"

"I'll come and see you in the morning," Mac said. "I'm away for a sly catch at those clubs. There'll be a fine expense account, of course!"

Gloom became them on the way downstairs. I might have been seeing off a hearse and mourners. I'd missed all Arturo's calls that day, but I was ready for Paul at two zero zero nine. WTHRU he sent, and I could almost hear him bellowing Where the Hell Are You? and I sent HIMPBZ Here On Important Business, and GBKSNT Get Back Soonest, and I got RO, Right, Out, which meant he'd be back before morning. Then I waited for Arturo in the emergency period, and he came on with GTSU Got to See You and URO Urgent, Out. I didn't want to leave the house, but he wasn't the sort to send that message without reason. I took hat and coat, and went downstairs. The movimeter's needle had warned the doorman that somebody was walking about, and he stood behind the closed grille, ready, smiled when he saw me, and opened the inner lobby door.

"How's Mrs. Galvani and the children?" I asked him.

"Ah, but very well, sir, thank you!" he said. "At what time should I expect you?"

"In an hour more or less," I said, knowing he asked because it was almost time for him to tip the switch and close the steel partitions over outside doors and windows till six o'clock in the morning. Only my key or Paul's, or an extra few degrees of heat—in the event of fire—would open them, with an alarm bell ringing outside and at three adjacent fire stations.

I walked down to the corner and took a cab to the Via Veneto gateway. The avenue was lit and crowded. I turned left, widened my pace to the turning on the right, crossed over, and went in a bar about two minutes' walk from Arturo's cafe. I got him after two engaged buzzes, and he said he'd meet me in the left-hand buffet at the main railway station. I drank a little of my beer, paid, took a cab to the terminus, and walked into that magnificent plate-glass façade with as much pleasure as if I'd never been there before, wondering why we, the sons of Trevithick, Watt, and Stevenson, inventors of steam transport, had nothing to compare, whether in terms of utility, architecture, or pride.

Arturo sat on a bench reading a paper. He looked like a respectable workman going home. He didn't "notice" me, and I didn't "see" him. I went on to the buffet, ordered a veal sandwich and a glass of beer, and knew he wouldn't be in for at least five minutes. He took longer. The buffet was crowded, and I enjoyed listening to a dozen robust accents, each a literature and history in itself, possibly unchanged since the days of the First Republic.

Arturo came beside me and leaned across the bar.

We were surrounded by loud voices, bawling children, and an intermittent bellow over the loudspeaker, followed by a tonal pus, serving as "music," and used, possibly, to quieten the nerves of an adolescent congregation, or, more usefully, to confuse eavesdroppers.

"Your caterer is in my pocket," he said. "The gardeners, the boilerman and the window cleaners, all straightened my way. One of your cleaning women, Emilia Rocco, she's no good. One of your night cleaners, Lorenzo Baldi, no good. I'll find out who they're working for. One of your porters, Ugo Vittorini, he's being paid, I'll find out who by. He's got a second job. Doorman at the Crop and Bridle Club. Night spot. He finishes at five. He ought to be on duty at your place at eight in the morning, but he gets there about eleven. Somebody looks the other way. You could find out who. That's all for the moment!"

"It's enough," I said. "Know anything about Miss Masters? She ought to be in charge—"

"I didn't want to mention it because I haven't made up my mind," he said, with a little finger joining one spot of beer to another on the counter. "One Miss Masters walks almost in the middle of the heel and swings her hands, thumb forward. It's a long pace. Bony hips, small breasts. There's another, looks like her, walks on the *in*-side of the heel, different shoe, more meat on her, three or four sizes, I'd say. One speaks fluent Italian. The other doesn't. I didn't want to say anything till I got it right!"

"You've done very well. Any idea where the first Miss Masters is?"

"Haven't seen her for the past two days!"

He drank the wine, put down the glass, buttoned his coat and walked out. Even those next to us would never have known we'd been talking. I finished reading the paper, left a piece of the sandwich, an inch of beer, strolled down to the coffee machine, changed my mind, hurried out of the station, and made a long pace toward the Grand Hotel. If anybody was behind me, he'd be breathing as hard as I was. I went through the foyer to the bar, and into an anteroom, across to the telephone, and called Miss Dalziel.

The maid answered, and asked me to wait, please, and what was my name?

"Twockenham," I said. "T-w-o-c—"

"Oh, now, that's such a mouthful for the poor girl!" Miss Dalziel said suddenly, clearly. "I'm sure I recognise your voice—"

"Then please tell me, when was the last time you saw Miss Masters, personally? Did you see her every day?"

"Oh, dear, no. She has her own entrance, as you saw. She lunched earlier than I. Didn't often dine in. So many friends. I think I last saw her to talk to on Monday evening. But the maid's been telling me she'd been a little strange—or unwell—lately. Angela's very much a creature of the light, don't y'know? Windows, curtains, always open. But for the past couple of days she'd been in the dark. Yes, and smoking, too. Angela didn't. And after you left, I made it my business to go into her rooms and make a thorough inspection. I found that she hasn't taken a single thing with her, even her make-up. Now, you know, that is *simp*ly not Angela. Shouldn't I write to her mama, do you think?"

"*Not* for the moment. I'll telephone tomorrow."

So far as I was concerned, that little talk tied everything in neat bows.

But where the devil *was* Angela?

I was suddenly frozen by the thought of her keys.

The map room, electronically locked. The project reports, correspondence, surveys. Any small item of it would be a gift to a competitor. Once the code was broken, a comprehensive listing, in other hands, could virtually put us out of business. What the original Company had done, before I'd joined it, the diplomatic soundings, the capital structure, could never be assessed in terms of money. But with those details known, and a slight rerouting of the pipeline and stations, plus a considerable cut in costs by ordering material from other, except our own European and American sources, our Company could never compete. We'd never be able to fight slave labor and a State-run—cooked books and nary a balance sheet—costing department.

We knew that our competitors were purely Russian, or a mixture of those working with them. We had three shadow-companies spotted, and others more umbrous, in constant report.

Which was responsible for the Angela Masters *coup*?

Coup it certainly was. It must have been known that Paul and I were away. All they had to contend with was an ex-police team on day and night duty, and an office staff coming in at nine A.M. and going off at five. Except for a night-call operator, everything shut down till eight in the morning. We'd been blind, slow. All keys, and the register, were kept in the police office, off the lobby. Angela signed for her set when she got there in the morning, signed them in at night, but nobody would question her working late, or going in after hours. She often had to. We all did. To find a girl to impersonate her wouldn't be easy, but it had been done. She hadn't been recognised only because neither Paul nor I had been there, and Angela worked alone except for her secretary, Estelle Greig. And where was *she*?

Gaps opened wherever I looked. I got a cab back to the office, determined to make my desk a battlefield. Dorandi opened the main door, smart in the blue uniform and scarlet facings. I went to the key safe in the police office. Angela's keys were in their compartment. I turned the pages of the keybook. The last two signatures for the keys, on Wednesday and Thursday were certainly not Angela's. They were a copy. I looked at the staff signing-in book. Estelle Greig hadn't been in since Wednesday.

"Find Miss Greig," I told Dorandi. "I want to speak to her. When your relief comes on, take a cab and go to her address. Bring her here. Understood?"

He bowed.

I went up in the Otis, unlocked the East Room, and put my nose round the door to sniff. I wasn't being caught again. All was in order, and I'd gone to the stationery rack for my favorite note-pad of blotting-paper, a yard wide by two-foot high, and Vox flashed.

"Captain Tustini, the Company's aircraft pilot, is here, sir, and wishes to speak to you, if possible?"

"Show him up!"

I didn't think it worthwhile holding a full-scale enquiry then and there. I asked him for the facts, and he said he'd been warned in the usual way for a flight to Istanbul and made routine preparation. He'd seen Angela once or twice, but never to talk to, and thought he recognised her, with three men, entered in the manifest as engineers, and another, older woman, down as a relief nurse. Instead of Istanbul, he'd been given Naples, and told to wait there for Mr. Chamby. At five o'clock that evening, he'd been ordered by flight control to pick Mr. Chamby up at Gallipoli, south of Brindisi. He'd waited till this afternoon, couldn't make contact with the office, and flew back on instruction from Naples.

"You're in the clear," I said. "But at any time in the future, you'll require an order signed by Mr. Chamby or myself!"

Captain Tustini, short, pale eyes, cropped fair hair, stared.

"The order is in that file, sir," he said. "You signed it!"

It wasn't a bad forgery.

"There'll be an enquiry later," I said. "Anything about those people excite your interest?"

He looked at his co-pilot, a younger man, wrinkling his eyes.

"It was a quiet flight," he said. "Nobody spoke except Miss Masters, and she spoke German. She said, 'Well, that's over' and the other woman looked at her. I saw her in the glass. Not a word after that till we got to Naples, and Miss Masters said wait there for Mr. Chamby—"

"Report here at ten in the morning. Leave the file here. You did well. Good night!"

Dorandi called when I'd almost finished my battle plan.

"I'm at the Misericordia Hospital, sir," he said. "Miss Greig's here. She's very worried, sir—"

"I'll meet you there inside the hour. She's not to worry about anything!"

I called the Company's physician, and found him at the house of a friend. He knew nothing about Miss Greig—and that was strange, since the matron downstairs would be on to any absentee —we nearly always had a dozen engineers and mechanics a day coming in from every village in the Mid-East, and they could all be carriers of one or other of the killer diseases—and she'd file a medical report in minutes—and I told him I'd meet him at the hospital.

Vox flashed blues for an outside call.

"Mac here. Who's Wayne Miles?"

"Our chief constructional engineer. Why?"

"He was at the Crop'n Bridle. Nicely tanked, apparently—"

"Spare time privilege?" I said, slowly, to restrain enthusiasm.

"There was a girl with him. Eurasian. We're trying to find out who she is, and where she lives—"

"The girl at the Opera?"

"Don't know. You can cross him off. He had a heart attack. He fell behind the table, and she mizzled—"

"Where's Miles?"

"In the city mortuary. Care to go round and identify him?"

"I'll warn his next of kin—"

"Edmund, there's something going on. The maître at the club's an old friend of mine. He said he knows your Miss Masters. She doesn't drink. He always mixed something special for her. She's never been carried out. He's putting the word round to other places. But he *did* say there's a girl who looks like her. In films, he thinks. I'll know tomorrow—"

"Find that Eurasian!"

4

The ride to the Misericordia was at least a breather. The nun on duty gave me Miss Greig's room number, and said Mama Guillermina was waiting there. I went by lift to the second floor, through white tiles and plate glass, and the faintest smell of iodine. Mama Guillermina—that's how she looked—stood, a black, ragged patch at the end of a shining corridor. I never saw a larger woman, or, when I looked into her eyes, lustrous with the mournful clarity of the peasant, a dearer. They were tear-y red—she reminded me of a beagle I'd once had—and she told me, in the Roman dialect, which takes a little getting-used-to, that Estelle had come home on Wednesday afternoon with what seemed a bad cold. She'd put her to bed with hot water bottles and aspirin, and the cold seemed gone by Thursday, but she was too weak to get up.

"Imagine how I felt!" Mama Guillermina whispered, in tremolo. "She's a daughter to me. But she *is!* She's part of my life. From the first moment, our hearts were together. I called the doctor. He had her brought here. But she'd never told me anything about herself. I didn't know where she worked. *E?*"

"You go home in my car," I said. "One of the girls will see you tomorrow to take care of expenses—"

"Expenses, whiskers!" she hissed. "I wait for Estelle!"

The Company's doctor nodded me in. I knew him slightly, but I didn't know Estelle Greig, though I was pleasantly surprised to see a dark-haired, brown-eyed girl smiling at me, with a nun holding her hand on the other side of the bed.

"I permit two minutes," the doctor said. "First, the patient was admitted with a gastric condition. Fortunately not very serious. If tomorrow's tests are satisfactory, she may leave in the afternoon—"

"Terribly sorry to be such a nuisance, Mr. Trothe!" Estelle said, as if she weren't. "There *was* something wrong in that office. I think it's the air conditioners. I couldn't breathe properly. Miss Masters got the engineers in, and it seemed better, but only a few minutes later I couldn't even stand. Well, I got taken home. That's the last I remember till I woke up here!"

"You didn't see Miss Masters afterwards? Haven't seen her since?"

"I don't think I had a clear thought about anything till yesterday," she said, and flashed a bright side-glance smile at Mama Guillermina. "I saw the date, but I couldn't remember where I'd been!"

"But what happened to her?" I asked, and an ice-cold balloon seemed to be inflating in the pit of my stomach. "Was she taken ill at the same time?"

She looked away, and shook her head, and the doctor held up a large hand.

"That's all," he said. "Tomorrow, at four o'clock, the patient may leave. Two days' rest, she will be well. Now, she will sleep!"

"Terribly sorry, Mr. Trothe!" Estelle said, contritely. "I can't remember anything after that American lady came in!"

"A moment!" I said, over the doctor's shoulder, almost chesting me to the door. "Which American lady?"

"She asked for you or Mr. Chamby. I tried to go out to see her, but I couldn't get up. I think Miss Masters saw her—"

"Was she unwell, too?"

"She was worse than I was, but she wouldn't give in. That's what kept me going!"

45

There wasn't much more to be said. I sent Mama Guillermina back in the car, and got a cab to the office. Mac had left a note that Toranzo had put on extra men, and not to allow the main office to be used until the Inspector had submitted a report. I went up to the East Room, and called Wilbur Kemp at the United States Embassy, from the sound of his voice, out of the sheets.

"This is scrambled," I said. "I'm looking for a warhorse of many names. The lady's been here in the past couple of days. About a hundred and thirty pounds, taller than you'd think, fighting out of Massachusetts. And very beautiful. Know her?"

"Betch. Been in and out of the Ambassador's place at Frascati. You won't get her tonight. She'll be here around ten tomorrow. Any message?"

"Just that I'd be more than grateful for a call. My apologies for dragging you out!"

"'s all right. I finally got to the stage where a good night's sleep's a penalty!"

I made an all-round inspection of the building, inside and out, surprised at the number of Police on duty, and the large sealing-wax blob on the main office door. All the time I was thinking of Angela Masters, wondering what I might do before Paul arrived. It wasn't like her to go off, ignoring Company Standing Orders to leave an address or telephone number where she could be found soonest. I didn't feel like going to bed. I put on pajamas and a gown, and I'm hanged if I didn't fall asleep in the armchair.

5

The day poured grey buckets. Paul hadn't arrived. He didn't come on the air, and neither did Arturo. I tuned clix to London for the zero-eight-one-eight signal. It came through clear, on the dot. I had a cup of tea, and sent down an order that all clerical staff were to be told to go home and report next morning. When I got downstairs, the matron was just leaving the doctor's office, a grey-haired, smart woman in white. She'd enhanced a wart on her left cheek into a beauty spot by a touch of black pencil. I like that sort of initiative.

"Why hasn't Miss Greig been shown on a sick report?" I asked abruptly. "Why isn't Miss Toverell? Where's Miss Masters?"

She wasn't in the slightest perturbed.

"All three are down, sir!" she said, in a Milanese gravel-voiced bellow. "They should have reported here for treatment, as I told them. They didn't. It's not in my orders to run after people!"

"In future, you will, and you'll be quite certain you know where they are, and what's wrong with them. Where's Miss Toverell?"

"At her *pensione*. She rang me and said she'd be in this after-noon. Miss Masters I haven't seen since the day before yes—it was the day before *that!* I sent her up to the terrace to sit down till the doctor came in. But she'd gone—"

"How d'you mean, gone?"

"She'd left. The man on the door said she'd been gone some minutes—"

"What was the doorman's name?"

Her forehead cleared, her teeth held the bottom lip, and she looked over blue spectacles at reflections across the lobby's marble floor.

"Dorandi, I think," she said. "It ought to be in the register!"

I didn't tell her it wasn't.

"Later today you'll have new instructions, matron," I said. "Meantime, don't leave until I've spoken to the doctor!"

I didn't wait. I'd just seen a yellow flicker, magnified in waxy brilliance, splash across the lobby floor.

I'm a fair hand at radio and communications generally, and I knew far too well, since I'd designed them, that in the Vox circuits, there was absolutely no room for flicker. When the On button was pressed, the pulse lasted so long, making a steady signal, which passed through a yellow or blue prism to flash the call. Paul shared my hate for bells or buzzers, and we'd decided to save nerves.

I stood in the doorway and waited. I'd looked at the time. The hands were on the hour. Moments dragged. I couldn't stand there without good reason. The Police and porters were glancing at me, and away. Vox was in the porters' office, two blue plastic boxes with an Out handset in red, and a yellow for In. Perhaps the light had been caused by a matchflame. But smoking wasn't allowed on duty, and anyway, the flicker wasn't that color.

I walked over to the Otis, and Dorandi hauled me up to my floor. I waited till his head disappeared, and almost sprinted for the East Room, got to my desk, and sat there, staring at In-Vox.

Moments went into minutes, while I thought about everything else, wondering where Angela was and determined to give her the wigging of a lifetime unless she had something remarkably watertight in the way of an excuse, and trying to imagine why Paul hadn't arrived, telephoned or radioed, and why Arturo hadn't come through, and on, till I'd almost forgotten why I was sitting there.

The flicker!

I almost fell off the chair. The hand of the desk-clock had just touched the quarter. That meant it was on every fifteen minutes. I leapt for the cabinet, and the folio of architect's blueprints, ripping the bows open, sliding everything out except the red-bordered print of the Vox system installed throughout the house. From roof terrace to garage there were twenty-eight points. I realized that only a point-to-point inspection would provide an answer. Without wasting time, I switched open my private safe, took out the micro-tool kit I'd made the original models with, and started dismantling the In-Vox. The plastic cover came off by taking out four plugs—my own invention, and without that special key, they couldn't be touched—and then came the copper casing, and six needle screws, again requiring a magnetic four-way key. To get at the innards and make a flicker by contact, somebody had to use that kit of tools, or break a way in, which would cause a short.

But then—something I'd quite forgotten—I saw the minute hole in the southwest corners of both the plastic and the copper casings, where the fine steel rod was anchored after the casings were on, and where an aerial could be fastened when the sets were used for distance work in the field. Somebody knowing a little about the layout might try sticking a fine wire down there, though just that one spot directly underneath would have to be touched.

That, certainly, would make a flicker.

I didn't try any tests that might have provided warning. I locked the office, went up the back stair to the terrace, saw that Vox sets weren't in use, and switched them off. Then to the other three on the same floor, and switched *them* off. In the rest of the building the only sets I didn't look at were those in the main office, and in Angela's. I knew they hadn't been touched, or the emergency alarm would have rung because the doors were locked. I didn't bother about the porters' or the police sets. There were too many people about. I inspected all the other offices, Mariotti's, and the rest, all in order, and switched them all off.

That left only the garage, and the storeroom.

A sudden ice-cold surge of excitement, such as I hadn't known for a long time, brought a pulse at the temples, and a heart-tip, it seemed, denting itself against my ribs. The garage ran the length and breadth of the house, lit by bare electrics. Across the space of swept concrete, with only a few cars and a couple of trucks in the bays, I could see Manzini and Tasso, two good men, in the porters' cubby, neither of them near Vox, on the farther table.

That left the store, a big place, once a wine cellar, running under the street.

It had two steel sliding panels, and I had the master key. I looked at the place in mind's eye. We knew too much about the Italian winter, and constant strike threats to gas and electric supplies, to trust in any one method of heating and lighting. In the event of strikes, we had our own emergency electricity supply, a large store of gas tanks for cooking and heating, the garage reserve of petrol, kerosene and methylated spirit, cut firewood, bags of charcoal, stacks of anthracite and coke, piles of sacks, sand, cement, planks, ladders, and the other small items difficult to come by when needed on the dot. I inspected the place now and again, but I hadn't been in there for a couple of months or more. There was no way in, except by opening those panels. There was certainly no other way out. The four vents in the cellar walls held pressure fans to take out the gases, and those fans operated on the closing of the panels, stopped when they were open.

I waited for the three quarters, and *again the flicker!* but the porters hadn't gone near the Vox sets.

I slipped my little friend out of the shoulder holster, made a pad of the index finger, and quietly slid the key in the lock, turned left, and the panels opened with far less sound than the whine of the slowing fans. Lights came up, glittered on stacked coal, glowed in piled scarlet barrels.

The place was like an icebox.

A movement to the left brought my friend at the point. The stores table, with the Vox sets, was hidden by sacks that seemed to rise, and then subside. The sacks were new, and the pile looked like a pale gorilla. I watched for a moment, and over the almost silent hum of the fans I heard a curiously high-pitched groan, and the sacks moved again. I went nearer, a step at a time.

A wrist, with a gold bracelet watch, was held over the table by the other hand. The hands were a horrid bluish color. I grabbed the sacks, felt a warm core deep inside, tried to pull them off one by one, but they were held tight. Head, arms, legs, and body had been pushed into sacks to keep out the cold.

Carefully, I pulled them off the head.

I knew the eyes looking out of shadow at me. They seemed old, very pale, without light or expression, and the icy draft had made deep wrinkles. Gently I pulled at the sacks, lifted them one by one off the head, off the arms, and then I saw that the right hand held a brooch pin wrapped firm by a sizable ball of white elastic. I got the last sacks off the head, and a silvery-blonde tangle of hair dropped across my hands and she fell against me.

Angela Masters, of course.

6

I carried Angela to the stores hoist and went up to my floor thankfully without seeing anyone. She was no tiny tot, and I was dry-mouthed by the time I put her down on my bed. She hadn't moved or made a sound. I put the eiderdown over her, got my breath, and called Miss Dalziel, asked her to come over with Angela's maid and bring a few clothes, and to call her physician, and I'd meet them in the lobby. I got on to Brigadier Toranzo's office, spoke to Colonel Perrine, and said I hadn't called the Police downstairs because I didn't want to alarm anybody. He agreed, and said he'd send a squad.

I looked in at Angela, but she hadn't moved. Oddly, in just that short time, the lines had left her face, but she was hollow-cheeked and the nose shone bonily.

I hadn't long to wait downstairs. Miss Dalziel got out of her car, followed by the maid with a bag, and without a word I showed them to the Otis. I closed the door of the East Room and nodded at the bedroom, and I must say I admired Miss Dalziel's sense of propriety. Without a word, she let the maid in, and the door snapped.

Nobody, so far, knew that Angela was in the building, and I didn't intend they should. I was fairly certain somebody would be keeping an eye on the storeroom, and I wanted very much to stick a couple of fingers down his collar. There's nothing like a question and answer session with a few yards of flex and a common or garden toasting-fork, lovingly wired for business. Even mutes become screaming gabblers.

I wasn't leaving Rome until I'd spoken to Angela. For every moment she'd suffered, I wanted to be sure that the culprit would screech for at least ten. Consuelo might have been in her place.

I switched on Vox, and instantly got yellows and blues. I took the blue, and found Arturo being somebody else, and played on.

"If it's a matter of buying and selling, all goes well. Fresh flowers this morning. Everything else satisfactory, except for two items, one who walks in the middle of the heel, and the other who doesn't. They haven't been seen for nearly three days—"

"It's been cleared, but keep watching!"

"The porter and the maid. They've disappea—"

"Picked up!"

"Somebody at your place is playing a game. About half an hour ago, I can give you the exact time, a man went in and came out with a brown attaché case. Wasn't in there half a minute. He went to the Bank of Rome down there on the corner, gave it to a girl, and she took a cab to Trastevere. I can give you the address. It's one of the most important drops in the City, and they pay money—"

"Drops?"

"Stolen goods, hot money, drugs, anything you like!"

"Who's getting the cash?"

"Don't know. Same girl comes out, makes a phone call, and then goes to the central Post Office and mails a letter. My guess, a money draft. Way they work, it won't take the Police long to nose 'em out!—"

"Anything else?"

"There *was* a Eurasian girl staying at the Cosmos the night the bomb went off. She had box H. Had her own car and maid. Went down to Ravello day before yesterday, sailed from Naples last night—at least, the maid and the car did—and I'm checking if she stayed on at Ravello. I can't pronounce the name. It's

M-u-o-h-y. You could get the details from the Cosmos. Only a couple of the night staff ever saw her. The owl type. Slept all day. Same two men always called for her. Germans, they think. No names. Went to all the best clubs. Spent a lot. That's all—"

"You did well. Call tonight. Out!"

The yellows had been persistent.

"Mr. Trothe? Mariotti. Good morning!"

"Hardly that. Well?"

"The library books for the Technical School at Ryadh. There's an urgent telegram—"

"I'm en route to London. Three o'clock on Monday ought to do—"

"But the director's waiting. I could come up im—"

"I said, provisionally, three o'clock on Monday!"

Dorandi gave me a list of calls from the porters' office, none important, and then I got Mrs. Balbi, the housekeeper, and told her I wouldn't inspect the building until the following week, and asked if there'd been any purchase of combustible stores.

"Yes, sir. On Wednesday, fifty liters of lubricating oil—"

"Who signed them in?"

"Zoppini, the garage attendant, sir."

"Thank you!"

Yellows flashed again.

"Matron, sir. The doctor's office—"

"Yes, is the doctor in?"

"Not yet, sir. I just saw Doctor Vivaldi go upstairs. Is there anything—"

"No, thank you. It's an old knee condition of mine. If he requires anything, I'll call!"

I opened the door as the Otis came up. Doctor Vivaldi wore black and stripes, a short black beard, and pince-nez on a black ribbon. He looked exactly the type of doctor Miss Dalziel would have to choose. I wasted no time, but took him to the bedroom, knocked, and from the way the door opened, Miss Dalziel must have been on a hair-trigger inside. I hadn't got as far as the desk, and she came out, sat in the nearest chair, folded hands in her lap, looking at me, eyes diamond-bright, nobody to trifle with.

"The child's been *starved!*" she whispered. "Not a *word.* Can't *move. What* am I to tell her mother? Because of course, I've *got* to telegraph, d'you see?"

"There's a cable-pad over there," I said, at the window table. "Be quite sure whoever's responsible—"

Doctor Vivaldi came out in shirtsleeves.

"I want an ambulance immediately!" he said, to himself, and took seven-league strides to the desk.

"Press the red button, and touch the numbers you require," I said. "Tell them to come to the garage entrance in the Piazzetta. I'll meet them."

"Papal physician!" Miss Dalziel barely whispered, while he made the call. "Wasn't I lucky to find him in?"

"Here in a few minutes," Doctor Vivaldi said, putting the links back in his cuffs. "The patient suffers from exposure and starvation. I don't think she'd have survived another day. As it is, she'll require most careful nursing—"

"You have carte blanche, sir," I said. "There's no danger?"

"But there's every danger!" he said, half-laughing with annoyance. "Women aren't elephants, you know. How did this happen? I must report to the Police!"

"Already reported. I'm going to meet the ambulance. Don't answer the door!"

I left them staring, switched on the lock and hurried down the back way. I didn't want anything known until Angela was well away. The steel panels were in place, solid, and I could hear the hum of the fans. Considering I mightn't have inspected that cellar for a week or so, I flinched from imagining what I might have found.

I strolled across the concrete, hands in pockets, saw that Paul's car and mine were in their bays, and all other cars were in except poor Miles', and thinking of him, I could smell Consular and other trouble. If the Eurasian girl with him was the catty piece at the

Opera, there seemed to be a link, though what use he'd be, except to pay the tab, didn't go in for the moment.

The ambulance came down the ramp suddenly and silently. I waved Manzini back to the cubby, and signalled the driver to turn round, and back down, so that the rear doors opened directly to the gates. The two men carried the stretcher in the hoist, and up we went. The corridor was silent, the Otis was below, and I switched off the lock, finding Doctor Vivaldi dressed, and I let him take charge. Minutes passed while I waited, but at last they came, and I signed to the doctor to cover Angela's face. I didn't want her recognised.

She was put in the bedspace, the doctor, Miss Dalziel and the maid got in, the doors shut, and the ambulance moved out. I hurried round to the driver.

"Don't use your siren till you're well away from the building," I said, crisping the hand with new notes. "If anybody stops you outside, say it's a man in there!"

He nodded, and moved out. I walked behind to the cubby. The shadow of the ambulance passed from the ramp. Manzini was lit in half-sunlight, talking at In-Vox. Tasso finished writing in the register and stood up.

"Add a note, the ambulance brought thermal equipment," I said. "Who's the call from, Manzini?"

"Miss Hurriyat, in Doctor Mariotti's office, sir. Wants a can of meth' to clean the copying machine—"

"Who's got the stores keys?"

He nodded at the glass-front racks.

"Up here, sir. The garage attendant's got to sign for them out' the police office. He isn't back, yet—"

"Tell him I'll probably inspect this afternoon, sometime!"

I knew I'd put a moggy among the pigeons, and going out of the garage and round the building to the lobby, I made up my mind what to do.

"Warn Dorandi, quietly, that nobody's to leave this building till the Police get here," I told Galvani, in the Otis. "Nobody means *no*body!"

He raised a hand, and went down in a heave. A ghost stood at my door, nearer to, a waiter with my elevenses.

While I poured the coffee I saw the police cars turn in the drive. I called Miss Hurriyat in Mariotti's office to bring up the Arab Womens' Aid Center report, and went back to enjoy the coffee.

There was a knock at the door.

An Inspector waited with a sergeant and two policemen. Behind them, Ferrani, a junior in Mariotti's office, held up the report, smiling, perhaps, through a lemon.

"I asked for Miss Hurriyat!" I said, over the policemen's heads. "Send her here!"

"But—uh—sir!" he wheedled. "She's not here. She went to meet her mother, going to the United States. It was so—"

"Who gave her permission?"

"Doctor Mariotti, sir. You were not here—"

"Ask him to come up!"

I gestured to the Inspector, and they all came in. I used my best Italian to explain what had happened, and while they went down to examine the stores, Mr. Thanotis, Doctor Mariotti's assistant, came in the open door, tapped the back of a negligent hand against the panels en route, and without waiting for me to speak, stopped by a chair. I didn't ask him to sit down. He was just below my height, a little paunchy, in a blue sports jacket, red and black checkered shirt, black silk tie—beyond a mourning period, I distrust black tie wearers, from experience, as mentally and physically indolent, spiritually non-existent, and therefore not to be trusted—and because so far, I hadn't had much to do with him personally—though his work was sound enough—I heeded intuition and played the fish.

"Miss Hurriyat's mother travelled to América for a meeting with her family, Meeztuh Trot'," he began smoothly. "They had not been in each other's company for three years. The poor girl was crying to me, so Doctor Mariotti had to say charitably 'you may go' and she will be here tomorrow, I hope. I am sorry if I have offended, but while Doctor Mariotti is away, I am the head of the

57

department. There was nobody else, and I am used to accepting any responsibility!"

The smug, pinky face reminded me of medieval tryptych lads enjoying a torture.

"Did you hear of anything going wrong with the air-conditioning system?"

He was a little off his ground.

"N-no, Mr. Trot', I haven't. Is it something the matter?"

"Passing enquiry, that's all. Did the couriers call on you this morning?"

"But not. The mail is brought to me by the clerk—"

"Very well. The library matter I'll deal with on Monday. That will be all, thank you!"

He hesitated, but my side-glance decided him. He went out, leaving the door open. I heard the buzz from the lobby floating up the liftshaft, and then the Otis filled the space.

Dorandi tapped, bowed, and shut the door.

"Somebody came this morning and picked up a brown attaché case," I said. "Who was it?"

"It's the doctor's office laundry, sir. Coats, overalls, sheets—"

"In an attaché case?"

"Brown plastic, sir. The laundry's own. Yesterday's lot comes back this afternoon—"

"Did you check what was inside?"

He began to squirm.

"Well, sir, the matron, she said she didn't want a lot of paws in there, and it's highly infectious, she said, so—"

"Against all orders, you let a package go out without checking, is that it?"

He nodded, and I was sorry for him.

"When the couriers come in, do they go straight to the mail office?"

He pulled in a shaky breath as if he felt himself reprieved.

"The morning man generally went to Miss Masters, sir, or if she was out of the office, to Miss Toverell. They separated the reports and sent the rest to the mail office. The night man's pouch generally came up here, or else Miss Masters took it if she was in. Doctor Mariotti's taken them lately—"

"But he doesn't see the couriers?"

Dorandi stared, looked away, came back to me in a shrug.

"They have a drink in his office, sir—"

"And of course, the matron often drops in?"

"Friendly with most of us, sir!"

"Thank you, Dorandi. Nobody's been allowed to leave the building?"

"The steels are down, sir!"

I nodded, and he bowed and went and I voxed the garage. I had that strange sense, that can't be explained, that birds have flown.

"Tasso, sir!"

"Are the Police down there?"

"Yes, sir. All in order, sir!"

"Have you had any cars in or out in the past fifteen minutes?"

"Yes, sir. The doctor and matron went out on a call, and Doctor Mariotti's gone to meet Mr. Chamby at the airport!"

"I suppose Mr. Thanatis went with him?"

"Yes, sir—"

I strolled down to the lobby and gave the Trastevere address to the Inspector, told him what had happened. His pucker, as if he might weep, amused me.

"Those idiots!" he groaned, holding his head. "All you have to do is show 'em the right badge. I'll call radio patrol. We'll get the lot!"

I felt rather pleased with myself going back to the Otis. The only sore point was Angela, but I was fairly certain that either Paul or myself would settle accounts sooner or later. I'd avoided a lot of unwelcome publicity, there'd be no arrests on the premises, and all guilty parties, by their own acts and volition had put themselves out of the running.

I radioed Lausanne to send out an urgent call that Mariotti and his entire staff were no longer part of the organisation, to cross the medical unit off the roster, and to withhold pouches from all couriers, and send all nine of them to meet me on the following morning. I was sure that those with something to fear wouldn't be there. Again, a painless amputation.

I had to wonder for what reason Mariotti and the medico could risk losing a well-paid job—and court arrest on serious charges —and what sort of organization was behind them. I couldn't believe that any company in the industry was responsible. This type of quasi-sabotage on a commercial front wasn't new—it was borrowed from war, and not at all strange to me—but the cost of keeping mouths shut, to begin with, had to be enormous. There, I saw a little daylight. All we need do was put out the word that we'd pay a high price for information. I made a note of that for Cairo in the morning.

While I waited, I skimmed through the field reports, relieved to find everything normal. Then I called Miss Toverell at her *pensione*.

"Oh, Mr. Trothe, I've been wondering what you must all think of me!" her voice came fraily over the wire. "Anyway, the doctor says I'll be fine tomorrow. But I've a bone to pick with that nurse, there. I wasn't all right by any means, but I could walk. But that injection she gave me, well, the cabman had to drag me in here!"

"That will be gone into—"

"I hope Miss Masters is better, sir? I had to carry *her!* She was in a dead faint. There was something very wrong in that office. They said it was the air-conditioning—"

"Everything's being put right, and we're only waiting for you to come back to your desk. Get well quickly!"

The only three women to be trusted had been put out of the way. The business of the air-conditioning plant had to be cleared up. I called Dorandi to send for the maintenance engineers, and he told me that Mr. Agosto of Strabo Insurance had just come in.

"Send him up!"

I went to the door to meet him, and though I'm never really surprised by Agosto, he made me smile, in a floppy black suit, dark glasses, no wig or mustache, the umbrella of all umbrellas, and a scarred papier-mâché case.

"Selling insurance," he said. "Almost got rid of a couple of policies downstairs. Well, Edmund, I must say I've never known such an astonishing melange as this!"

I held up the warning hand.

"Soft-pedal it," I said. "So far, we've come out very well. I must remind you this is a commercial undertaking. Our capital is inordinately sensitive. The smallest scandal causes trouble everywhere. What we have to do now is dig in. Reassess our staff, first of all. Protect ourselves. Though I don't know who or what from!"

Agosto hauled up a handful of trousering, and crossed his knees.

"I'm baffled!" he said, and looked it, holding up a couple of new red files. "You mean you're going to let all this happen to you, and you're not giving a cakie?"

"All relevant information will go to Interpol. The people concerned, whatever their aliases, are then on the list. It's not a pleasant place to be. So far as this Company's concerned, the main worry is protection of staff, and of course, day-to-day business—"

"You might look at these when you've a moment," he said, and got up. "To a certain extent, I agree. The Police'll take care of their own end. But you've had some atrocious types here, haven't you?"

"A little matter I'll have to go into with our I-Unit. What's really bothering me is who's behind it!"

"Wish I could help you," he said, and pulled mightily at the front of his trousers. They came off as if split down the back, and another jerk took the legs away. He wore a pair of fawn beneath. He opened the bag, took out a felt hat, pulled off the tie he wore, and snapped in a bow. He trod on the heels of the boots and took out a pair of feet in shining moccasins. He turned the coat inside out to a brownish broadcloth, stuffed everything in the bag, put the hat on at a boilermaker's tilt, slipped off the dark glasses, put on hornrims, footed the bag under the chair, and held out his hands.

A different man.

"What's this?" I asked. "Rehearsal for Gaudy Night?"

"I believe the chap who shot at you's outside," he said, taking the stuff from the inside pockets. "My own man's got an eye on him, I hope. We'll bag him if we're lucky!"

"Don't bring him in here!" I warned. "I'm not a bit curious!"

At a tap on the door, he turned smartly for the bookshelves. I trod on the foot-button, and Colonel Perrine half-bowed pleasantly, and came in with the Inspector and some policemen.

"I fear I have no good news," he said, and took a plastic folder from the Inspector. "Last night and this morning, we made a thorough inspection of the two offices downstairs. I have the result from our forensic laboratory—"

He opened the folder to show rows of green tape loops with bits of stuff hanging from them.

"These are pieces of wrapper from a microfilm not in general use," he went on, pointing with a pencil. "Each film takes fifty photographs. These are splinters of a small photoflash, quite new. The suction sweeper also picked up remnants of a nickel pellet. They held something that became a gas on contact with the air. We have samples from the filters of the air-conditioning. Fingerprints, other traces, nothing!"

"The Eurasian woman?"

He shrugged.

"A wig, some pencil, anyone becomes Eurasian, no? No new evidence!"

"Capri?"

He looked sorrowfully at Agosto.

"The adventure was unfortunately not in our hands sooner. The young woman and the older, and the two men, were joined by another man. They were all in the bikini and shorts, and they took a basket of food and wine, and went down to their launch to picnic at the Marina Piccola. But they didn't come back. There was nothing in the house. Everything they didn't take was burnt, all surfaces cleaned with kerosene. Not a sign of innocence!"

"And all they had to do was buy some longs and a shirt somewhere, and they could go anywhere," Agosto said. "No names, nothing?"

"Unfortunately, passports are not checked outside the hotels.

They paid for three months, but they stayed less than a week. The house agent and the maid thought they were German. Neither of them know the language. How can we be sure?"

"Truffo, Vittorini the porter, and the others?" I asked. "Anything useful?"

"The examining magistrate required more evidence, and let them out on a surety. None of them lived where they said they did, and apparently, none of them were who they said they were. Again, nothing!"

We three, and the Inspector, the sergeant and two constables, laughed together. It was all rather funny, except when I thought of Wayne Miles and Angela.

"The Trastevere address?" I ventured.

"They'd gone," the Inspector said. "Left everything in a confusion. But no paper. Landlord said they were foreigners. Might know more about them later today, but—er—I doubt it!"

Everyone seemed to be savoring the watery taste of a blank.

"Well, finally, there's this very serious Wayne Miles case," Colonel Perrine said, in a different tone. "The medical panel find that death was caused by nicotinic poison, and that's either a matter of suicide, or murder. Who administered the dose, and where? He hadn't been in that club more than a few minutes. Hadn't had time for a drink, and they were deciding whether to serve him because he had to be helped in. The woman with him pretended to be indignant about his condition, and left. Then they called a physician, and he was found to be dead. Unfortunately, the autopsy wasn't till the following morning. A very long lapse of time. We haven't been able to find the woman. She'd been there before, but she wasn't an habitué. We are trying to find her, but after all, what charge could we bring?"

"All the lumps and clumps of a case, but no glue," Agosto said, and took his bag from under the chair and gave it to a policeman. "I'll pick that up later."

"Coming with you," Colonel Perrine said, motioning the Police outside. "A full report will be ready in a day or two, including any late developments, Mr. Trothe. There's a lot here that needs explaining, but there doesn't seem a witness who isn't made of phantom indiarubber. And what is the reason? I see nothing. Not money, not anything!"

"Industrial secrets also have a value, Colonel," I said. "But we prefer not to advertise it. My compliments to Brigadier Toranzo!"

I shut the door and went over to sprawl in the armchair for a few moments. I hadn't liked Agosto's attitude, and I thought Perrine not evasive, but in a certain way, sly. Nothing worthwhile could have been photographed in Angela's office because all paper was in wall cabinets electronically closed. Any attempt to open them without the key would have caused a short-circuit which could blind a burglar, if it didn't burn him to ash, and at no great loss, since all paper was non-flam.

I went down the stair to Paul's office. The air was fresh, and on the way down to Angela's office I took all precaution, though there was no need. The place had been thoroughly aired. I opened the gates down to the main office, and went from desk to desk, examining drawers, files in work, and paper. Everything seemed in order. I went back to Angela's office and locked the gates again. Miss Greig's desk was swept clear. The drawers were tidily banked with files and office books. Angela's desk held one surprise. The top was clear except for the office-diary kept in a shorthand I couldn't read—that made two of us!—but in the main drawer, I was surprised to find a colored pamphlet that shouldn't have been there.

It wasn't so innocent as it looked. It purported to advertise the pick of the season from a seed and bulb company we controlled in Holland. It was beautifully illustrated in color, and of the five thousand printed every three months, only twenty—sent to members of the Board by courier—were.'different,' though it would take a gifted cipherist to find the changes.

The copy I held was one of the twenty, brought in by a courier for editing and last minute changes, and it should have gone back days before. I put it under my arm, inspected the correspondence racks, as I'd thought, untouched, looked in at the map room, untouched, and at the sand-table model of the pipeline—though it didn't look like that—and wished any photographer joy of anything he might have shot. It needed our wickedly devised code, first of all, and then a computer, though I doubt they'd have had anything like the enormous fun Paul and I enjoyed in putting it together.

I took the copy up to Paul's office, into the bathroom, and sat down with the magnifier and green salts. I dipped the copy in water, towelled off the residue, and sprinkled the crystals. In moments, on page after page, I found the marks of Angela's pencil, a few impressions of her gloved fingers, but miserably black and plain, at least two other sets of prints. Somebody idling through pages of pretty flowers? A policeman?

Or a photographer?

I went out to call Miss Toverell.

"Oh, yes, Mr. Trothe!"

"When you helped Miss Masters out, was anyone else in her office?"

"No, sir. Cassetti, that big porter helped me, and I told him to close the switch. I knew nobody'd ever get in without the master. Did I do wrong—"

"On the contrary. Can you remember if there were any papers about the place?"

"There were not, sir. I noted that. Both desks were clear. Whether they were locked or not, I didn't have time to see. I gave Miss Masters over to the matron—"

"And her keys?"

"Cassetti handed them in. I know he did!"

That settled that.

I took the catalog upstairs to my office, went over to the paper rack and interleaved the pages with blotting paper, put a wad top and bottom, and stood on it, pressing out the moisture. When it was dry, there was no trace of salts, pencil or prints.

Blues flashed over the ceiling.

"Miss Dalziel, here, Mr. Trothe. Angela's in Doctor Vivaldi's clinic, and quite comfortable. Nothing wrong, really, thank heaven!—"

"Four tickets to London are in your name at the BEA desk, here. Angela, yourself, the maid, and a man I'm sending with you to look after baggage and things. When you're ready, telephone and let them know. Mr. Chamby will be in touch during the day, and her family is being notified. There will also be out-of-pocket expenses, and the clinic's account should be sent here—"

"But that's a most unexpected surprise! London again? Shall I know it? Oh, Mr. Trothe, thank you!—"

Blues again, and the Hullo—even if I've always thought the word ridiculous—was Druxi's, at her Druxiest, and an absolutely peerless surprise.

"Paul tells me you've been painting the place white for us. What's the idea?"

"Wish you'd get out of Rome!"

"Going this afternoon. What's wrong? Tilt at the Mafia?"

"Couldn't be much worse. Edmund, listen. What's wrong with that office of yours? Do you have a laboratory there? Or some kind of a mash going? Look, I could send you a case of Jack Daniel's and save you some trouble!"

"On! What is it?"

"I went in, and I remember talking to somebody, but that's all. I came back here and went to bed. Don't remember another thing till this morning. I rang the number I was given, but I couldn't get a reply. I had to call Lausanne to get this. Any worries?"

"Plenty. When do we meet?"

"My car'll call for you in twenty minutes. He'll take you out to the flying club. I'll be in the red twin-jet. Left of the main road going in. Any more on the bomb job?"

"Not much. D'you know anything?"

"Know lots. Out?"

"Out!"

7

I was almost in the car when Dorandi came running after me.

"Mr. Chamby from Lausanne, sir!"

I doubled past him, and took the phone from Galvani.

"Edmund here!"

"Get up here as quick as you can, will you? I've got a few answers. Is Angela there?"

There was very nearly a break in that voice.

"She's here, and well taken care of. Tell you about it. I can catch
that Swissair—"

"Be down there to meet you. S'long!"

Paul's voice was a barometer. There was a lot more "spring"
in it, as if he were more at ease about things in general. I felt relieved beyond words that Angela was safe, if only for his sake.
That vocal slip told of feeling he'd never willingly show anyone,
except perhaps to laugh at it.

We'd turned off the autostrada, passing through a village, with
the high wire fence of the airfield shining just beyond. We went
down the asphalt path to a gate and stopped. Just inside, across
the cropped grass, a twin-jet cherry-red beauty made a back-
ground for Druxi in white overalls. She waved, got into the pilot's
seat, and the co-pilot got out.

"Hi, Edmund!" she called. "We'll just take a little run over the
sea, and back. All right, Bennett!"

She waited for me to strap, started a jet, watched the board, started the other, got a wave from Bennett, and taxied down to the loop, talking to Control. She took off in what seemed to me not much more space than a handkerchief, and sailed over a vineyard, the village I'd passed through, a hilltop, and the sea was in front of us, an amazing glow of blue.

"Are you able to resist the feeling that the world's suddenly gone plain crazy?" she asked, perhaps dreamily. "Serious question!"

"Seriously answered. No!"

"You're one of the few men I know—officially—who doesn't expect me to compare notes. Or'd ever ask a *pertinent* question. But I'm going to ask one, and then give you some information."

She kept her eyes on the board, or ahead, or she turned to look behind, all the way. She was never still. Considering the years I'd known her, and the life of violent unease she'd led, I thought, with Consuelo, what a marvelous woman she was. Her skin appeared perfect, with the slightest touch of sun, not a wrinkle I could see except the eye laugh-lines, but there was a real set to the mouth and chin, and her eyes, I knew, held the adamantine flash I'd once seen in a general's in mid-battle. If she looked thirty, that was about all. Except in the eyes.

"Have you been losing people, lately?" she asked lightly. "Not just the ordinary kind, but top men?"

"It's become a problem. Well-paid, good pension, work well for the little time they're on the job. Then they go. It's known we're careful in selection. But well-paid, good pension or not, they go. Can't get a sniff of the bolthole or we'd have a go at closing it. I believe we've lost twelve or fourteen. Over about three months or less. The really surprising thing is that though they're all quite well-known in their own field, we can't trace where they've gone. Most are family men. Who's paying them? For what? It's a lot of money, I can tell you that!"

"I'm losing some of mine. They disappear. And *that's* money, too. If you happen to get any kind of a lead, will you let me know? I'll reciprocate, depend on it. Now, the information—"

"Before we explore the vasty unpleasant, what did you do to

68

yourself since we last met?" I asked, deliberately putting her off-stride. "You were a porky old lollop, thirty or more pounds over-weight, boozing gin to beat Mother Camp, and I'd have said you were bouncing seventy. How d'you do it?"

She gave me the famous side-o'-the-eye smile, an ocular burnish.

"A clinic I know, plenty of exercise, no alcohol, lots of wonderful sleep, two small meals a day. Never felt better. And I've been flying this to keep my hand in. All helps, Edmund!"

"Indeed. And what's the information? The bomb?"

"We can start with that. The Cairo job was bungled. Five men in all were picked up. Riff-raff from one of the little sheikhdoms alongside Aden. They'd been paid to set off plastics in your office, the bank on the corner, there, and the insurance offices, down on the right—"

"With each of which, *en passant,* we're pretty strongly connected!"

"What wasn't found out, was why. Egyptian Police aren't a bit backward, you know. If the facts are there, they'll get them. In one way or another, and we won't go into it. But the men were let go for lack of evidence, if you please? Of course, there was some cash in the deal. Had to be. We had that information about three days before they flew into Cairo, but we couldn't find out who was behind them. That type of goon doesn't act on his own. And who turned the steam on up top? Now go to Rome. Three were sent there. We didn't know what it was going to be, bombing or assassination. All of them'd been in the Arabian mess since it started, so killing people's no problem. But who's behind them? It's got to be money. The man they blamed the Opera bomb on was an odd-jobber they must have paid. Probably an Arab of some kind or another. He'd been in Rome for years. He was found dead in an hotel he couldn't afford. But mark this. He was in the hotel a good half-hour *before* the bomb went off!"

"Police had nothing to say?"

Again that side-eyed smile.

"A cop takes orders, Edmund!"

"But, Druxi, you're not—you're never—surely you're not—!"

"I didn't say a word, Edmund. But if a Minister says it, things happen, that's all!"

She turned, in a long, smooth climb, levelled, and made for the coastline.

"Well, then, in the matter of your disappearing personnel, and mine. You had a man named Aubrey Shanklin, and another, John—?"

"Reeves?"

"Right. They were in Teheran last week, trying to knock it down. This boy who just died, Wayne Miles, was with them. They tried to tell him some kind of a story. But the girls with them must have got a little too rowdy. Well, the police came in just when he was getting near the bone. An Asiatic—that's all they said—an Asiatic with plenty of money—had made a deal, and they'd quit your Company. They just walked out. They were on velvet, and celebrating. Wayne got taken to his hotel in a police jeep, which I'd say wasn't at all auspicious. To say the least. But he spent all next day trying to locate them. Hide nor hair. That's not a week ago. He went back to Rome, and the same night, he's dead?"

"I was fairly sure we had somebody from CIA on the staff!"

"If you thought it was Wayne, you'd be wrong!"

"I accept that, and I apologize, of course. This mention of an Asiatic. There's a possibility that a woman at the Opera that night was also Asian. No proof, and we can't find her. But there was an Asian woman staying at the Cosmos—"

"Checked, and blank, for the moment!"

She took up the radiophone and talked to Control. I greatly admired the way she handled the aircraft. She made it all seem so easy.

"By the way, there's a big movement east to west, mostly by air, in gold bullion, jewels, and every kind of money, real and false," she said, holding the radiophone by the wrist-strap. "Enzo Mariotti—you know the name?—went to Russia with the Italian Army. Ever hear what happened to them? He'd be about twenty-or-so years older than your man, anyway!"

I watched the hilltop coming nearer.

"Somebody on our I-Unit's a little lax," I said, mildly, I hoped. "*Laches*, perhaps, is a better word. I can see there's going to be some fancy firing!"

Druxi smiled those beautiful teeth, and our shadow passed down the middle of the village's one street taking the houses in grey embrace.

"I wish I didn't have to tell you this," she said, and I knew—if I hadn't known before—what Consuelo had meant by "something 'cold and quiet' about her," and I was inclined to shrivel. "How long is it since you heard from our friend Errol?"

She took me absolutely at disadvantage. I could only sit there, staring at the approaching tarmac.

"Well," I said, at last. "Just before he left for Fräglechsaben. Same sort of business as mine. I mean, at that time!"

"He hasn't been seen for a couple of months," she said, bringing us in. "The bar he took's been turned into something else. No trace of him. But he's reported held in the East German prison of Hauer-furth. One of the most miserable dens ever. Political prisoners, mostly—"

I had to start thinking back.

Errol—we'd called him Yorick because of an apparently empty skull—was a most excellent friend and ex-colleague, one of the younger, brighter lights in M.I.6, or as some had begun calling it, Special Intelligence, though from my point of view, there wasn't anything specially intelligent about any of them, or it.

Yorick was different. Because of his quick-wittedness some months before, I was then and there sitting next to Druxi, a free man, and for that, I owed him a debt of gratitude. As it happened, I'd known Hauerfurth Prison in the days before East Germany was born, when we brought away something less than a hundred of all the thousands of Hebrews sent there to die. It couldn't have changed much. The keepers were little better, though now perhaps the prison surgeons used anaesthetics, and possibly the prisoners ate something better than pigswill.

"That's the worst news I've heard for a long time," I said, while we bounced along the tarmac. "No details?"

"I'll send on whatever I can get," she said, and swung to stop. "Just came across it, that's all. Think it's fact?"

"Barely. I'll get on the blower. In any case, I'm more than grateful."

"Don't forget he's a friend of mine. Of *ours*. If there's anything I can do, it won't take you long to find me. And do take care of yourself!"

"And please take your own excellent advice. May I hop in the car to the airport? I've got eleven minutes!"

"Oh, of course. He'll come back for me. All the luck!"

I got in the car, absolutely depressed, wondering, in a sort of fever, whom I could call to ask about Yorick, but far more to the point, trying to think what I could *do*. The idea of a breakout, of course, was a pipe dream. I had to get the facts, first.

I'd thought the chauffeur had worn a hard cap when we'd driven down. The man driving seemed younger, and wore a blue cap, without the stiffener, in a head-back air of brio. I'd barely thought it, and I saw we were going at speed approaching a fork. The right hand, I knew, joined the autostrada again, and the left went direct to the airport. We were veering for the right fork.

At about that moment, I saw the puff of smoke—I thought it was my cigarette—but it came from the speaking tube, and another puff, pale. I grabbed the door handle. It was locked from the front seat. So was the other. I smothered my face in a handkerchief, saw the driver grin at me in the mirror, and drew my little friend.

One shot smashed the off-window, a second opened the near door. The driver braked in a screaming skid, almost overturned us, righted, bounced, opened his door, and ran behind the car, throwing off the cap and coat. But I wasn't letting him get away.

I kicked the door open, took a split sight, and fired. He dropped and rolled. A man plowing a field a little way off stopped work, but made no move. I got into the driving seat, started up, and drove down to the In-way of the airport, parked in the visitors area, and gave the attendant a big tip, which meant no questions.

"Any enquiries about this car, give them this card," I said. "Had a little accident, that's all!"

I hurried across to the Departure side, gave the Swissair clerk my Air Cred, and he called a delectable girl to run me down to the Out door. There are few things prettier than pretty legs. Swissair, I've noticed, have their share.

And very good scotch, almost as I sat down, which was just what I needed.

8

Even the calm airs of Lausanne, which I'd always thought one of the pleasantest cities in the world to work in, didn't cool many of the ashes Paul and I had to share in the main office, up there, overlooking the lake. It took almost a couple of hours to go detail by detail through my report, and at the end we both thought we deserved a drink.

While I poured, Vox flashed blue, and Paul took it.

"Ah, well!" he trumpeted, up at the ceiling. "We've been looking for you!"

He cupped the receiver, and mouthed "Azil!"

"Yes," he said. "He's here. Look, would you meet him if he comes to Paris tonight or tomorrow? You will? *Wonder*ful! Where? One o'clock, your apartment? That's on. Yes, extremely important. We need a decision. Thank you so much. And we'll meet very shortly. 'Bye!"

I didn't show how happy I was. It simply meant I could fly to London for a few hours, do all I had to, and not a soul the wiser.

"That ten o'clock flight tomorrow ought to do it nicely," Paul said. "Now we'll start getting some news. All right, Edmund, my turn. Not much, but one or two points are significant. The two youngsters I'd hoped to bring with me've gone somewhere else.

Last heard of, they were in Trebizond. What' they doing there? How d'you get there?"

"By ship, I expect. Nowadays, they call it Trabzon. Which company's there?"

" 'bout time they all made up their minds how to spell places. I had a look in the register. Couldn't find anything in our line. Place like that, have to be a Turk in charge, I imagine. It's pretty nearly on the frontier. I don't suppose they'd allow anything else. I'm wondering if some of our defaulters went to the same place!"

"Hardly. The two were probably flown somewhere—south, perhaps—"

"Where? Both these lads are geologists. With all that ramification. I think we ought to get a man over there. Have a look round. One of us'd be the ideal, but I don't think it'd be too healthy. For the moment!"

"I agree. Pot-shotting tends to become wearisome!"

"Right. Second item. Tamm was insistent we ought to get a a team to go over the whole line again. Make sure we're where we think we are. He thinks our maps're all wrong!"

I could only stare. I couldn't argue because I hadn't been over the line's entire length. Ground detail had been left to the engineers and surveyors. Paul was in the same boat. We were office men. A theodolite, to me, was a handsome piece of tooling, but looked at against territory and distance, it was the heart and soul of our business. The slightest detail wrong with those readings, and we were seriously in the cart. I imagined the line wandering all over the desert.

"The start of a splendid nightmare," I said. "Fortunately, we can begin an immediate check. O'Brien's at El Humir. He could pick his own team. Free hand, and a bonus for all concerned!"

"That's a great idea," Paul said, too quietly. "Except that Mr. O'Brien's left us!"

"Dear me. When was this?"

"I asked Overton to see him. He cabled me. Gone. No forwarding address. We've got to get busy, Edmund. We haven't got

75

many O'Briens. We've got plenty of Overtons. Good as gold. Workmen. But they don't get the offers. It's the top men. We can't afford it—"

"Why not send Logan? Thoroughly well-grounded, a to z. Move Carmichael over to Beirut. Johnson takes over. He's worth promotion. But it's going to take a little time. Question of further building. If we stop, there'll be gossip. The market's nervous enough. If we don't, we might be going further out in the blue. How do we protect costs?"

"Talk it all over with Azil, tomorrow. He's the real power. But we're inclined to look stupid. We ought to have known what was going on!"

"Tell me how, and I'll agree. Ever since the first man ducked out, McIntosh, we've had enquiries going. You can't go much further than our own agents and the Police!"

"We ought to have got Azil on to it—"

"I'd like to bet you he won't do any better. He's flesh-potted too long. His Arabian brethren tolerate him because he can't go wrong in Europe. He's got the banks and the most expensive whores in his handkerchief pocket, and he's up to his navel in his own oil. But let him go just a mile east of Cairo into the real Meccan zone. Where he has to talk to the bigots!"

Paul nodded. He couldn't do much else. He knew.

"Let's get him on our side, and I'll feel more comfortable about everything," he said. "As to the bigots, well, we'll soon have to be talking to them, too. You know, Edmund, it pains me. I've been mixed up with them all my life. One kind or another. Since I was this size. Sundays, in my home town, you couldn't even change your mind. Blue-noses. Wowsers. Wherever you looked. What time d'you think we can call Rome?"

"As I believe I've said. I've got a call in for seven. What do we do about Yorick?"

I knew perfectly well he was thinking only of Angela. I sympathised, of course, but it's extremely difficult to talk to somebody on a variety of subjects, all of extreme importance, knowing that his mind, for the most and best part, is elsewhere. I had no room to complain. The better part of my mind was with Consuelo, two floors down.

Paul stood at the window, looking across water ruffled pale gold and grey in the evening wind. The office was so blessedly quiet that I could hear the ice settle in his glass.

"I don't know what to say, Edmund," he said crisply. "On the face of it, there's nothing much we *can* do, is there?"

"I thought of getting in touch with Melrose—"

"If you do, he'll promise you heaven and earth, and anything known around the Chancelleries in Bonn. You know him. And tomorrow morning, your name'll appear in the *Digest*, and you'll have the lot of them, from the Prime Minister down, wondering where you got the juice. Melrose made his name out of gossip. That's how he got to be First Sec'try. Going to give him another choice bit?"

"Suggestion, that's all!"

"Von Staengl owes me a favor or two. You could talk to him without getting a poignard in y'kidneys. And he's rabid about the Reds. He's in Paris—"

There was a knock at the door we both knew. I was nearest and covered ground. I switched the lock, and opened, in one wide move.

Angela, in a brown tweed suit, didn't even look at me.

"Paul!" she whispered. "Are you very angry? I'm here!"

Without seeming to move, he had his arms round her, his eyes were shut, she was wrapped tightly about his neck, and taking everything by and large, I thought it an excellent time to nip downstairs, Consuelo-and-dinnerwards. I made the smallest diplomatic noise in releasing the door handle. Paul opened one eye, I gestured downstairs, he winked, and away I went.

Consuelo looked even more wonderful in a blue mousseline affair that whispered a poem about all it hid. I never felt better than when I was close to her, my arms almost all the way round her, and her arms strengthily round me. We didn't have to talk for those moments. It was simply a joy on its own to stand there, and breathe her in. We were in my office, and that was about the only reason I kept my head. We'd been apart far too long, and that old one, about absence, is perfectly true. It does make the heart, and everything else, distinctly fonder. I loved her, deeply, absolutely, and I sparkled with it, standing there, for those moments, tempted blindingly to go further, warned by the smooth lines of Vox—for some reason—perhaps because it was part of the office and all I could see for the moment—not. An office was simply not the place. There was a magnificent carpet, and a sumptuously soft sofa. Any other girl, perhaps, yes. With Consuelo, no. And if I knew her, she'd probably acquiesce with all delight, and regret after, not because of what went on, but because of the place, the aftermath, the getting-up and pulling-together, the this, that, and the most important other, best—ah, but always gloriously best!— in a bedroom, and a king-size with or without the four posts, and a bathroom, with good old hot and cold, a fine big hunk of soap, and the more perfume the better, big towels, not those damned little ragged things, and all that. Consuelo, I knew, was very much herself, and liked to see any sort of business done right.

So did I, and though her mouth was softest, and dearest, I set the pace, and looked down at her.

"Dinner first, because the beast requires at least two courses, and what a pity there aren't any oysters, though I don't need them, and a glass or two of that claret."

"I want some of that *bombe profiterolle,* and a *drop* of Château d'Yquem. I don't care what you say, it's my favorite. And Turkish coffee without the grounds, and a dash of orange water, and a *sip* of your yellow Chartreuse, please!"

"Let's get moving before those two upstairs get a twinge of conscience, and invite us to share a sandwich. You could reserve a seat for me on the ten o'clock for Paris tomorrow—"

She looked at me in horror and loathing.

"Don't dare tell me you're leaving—" she began. "You're as bad as a sailor!"

I got the "bright" of my life.

I went around her to reach Vox, and got Paul's office.

There was a distinct, a most hair-raising pause. I knew that

Paul, Australian from the outback, one of the finest men I ever met, didn't, as he often said, go much on the lares and penates. He preferred what he called a good go, and clean up afterwards.

"'lo?" Paul rasped, at his out-backest. "I thought I cut this line out?"

"Except me. Would it make any difference if I went to Paris tonight? More rest in the morning—"

"Best idea of the lot! We don't need to meet again, do we?"

"If anything occurs, you could phone. I'll be back on Monday by that eight—"

"Don't overdo it. If I know Azil, he'll want time. Just let me know. Good luck, Edmund. Consuelo going with you?"

"If she will!"

His cackle flew all round the room. I couldn't look at her.

"If she *what*? Angela says don't spare the horses!"

"We're a fine lot!"

"We are, and we're legal. Tell Consuelo, when you get to the Rondpoint, think of us, and blow us a kiss, will you? That's the best luck of the lot. It's better than pennies in the fountain. It means we stick. We'll never come apart!"

"I never heard *that* bef—"

"Take my word. And listen. Got your clix? Be on at one one one four, and zero zero one four. Out!"

Since I hadn't unpacked, I had splendid time for another drink while Consuelo went off to her place for a bag. I was very happy about many things, but most for Angela. She could have been dead at that moment, and the more I allowed my mind to play on it, the more joy I promised whoever was responsible. It must have shown on my face when Consuelo almost flew in, bloom-cheeked, a couple of tendrils blown loose, bringing a little of the lake's cool air, standing hips out, arms out, *what* a good girl am I!

"Record!" she holloed. "There and back, changed, pack—"

But she wilted.

"Darling! You're scowling at me!" she baby-voiced. "Don't you want to take me?"

"I was thinking of Angela in that damn' place, and making up

79

my mind what to do to whoever locked her in there," I said, putting my hands under her coat and feeling that waist again. "I'm not sure what he deserves, but I'd love to get my hands on him for an hour or two—!"

She pulled away a fraction, a little surprised.

"But what would you do?" she asked, frown ready. "I thought the Police—"

"Police? You might have been down there. D'you think a little time in prison's punishment? I've got other—"

"Oh, no! There's too much horror in the world. I couldn't stand any in the family. In that, I don't think there's any question. Can't be!"

I picked up the bag, and held the door open.

"Family'd know nothing about it," I said, trying to lighten the mixture. "Strictly personal. That type can't be treated as human—"

"I disagree absolutely!" she said, going past to the lift. "Cruelty, suffering, misery. I feel sick if I think of it. I almost don't want to go!"

"Now we're mixing up one thing with a dozen," I said, wondering how to fish the baby out of the water. "Tying up a girl to starve and freeze to death, what's that? No real crime, so be merciful? A little time in a nice clean prison, is that the idea? Just a gentle tap on the wrist? Same 'punishment' as some poor devil who cooked the books? The swine who put Angela down there cold-bloodedly knew the place wouldn't be opened for at least a week. That would have been enough. Can you imagine us, at this moment, and she still down there—?"

"Don't, please!" she said, fingers to ears. "She told me a little. She can't remember being put in there, or who it was. She's blank. But she never wants to go back—"

9

"An urgent message from Lausanne, sir!" the air hostess said, at Orly, and read from a blue slip. "Please go direct to the apartment of the Prince Azil. Three directors of the Company arrived tonight from Bushire!"

I didn't have the heart even to groan. I knew those parties. I also knew too well I wouldn't be able to drink one small scotch. No drinks was order of the day when dining with our Arabian directors. They were all teetotal. Azil laughed at them. I couldn't. Secondly, transcending all else, it meant I'd have to forget dinner with Consuelo.

She rested on her left foot, hand on hip, and stared at a legion of macro-bogeys.

"Very well," she said, in an expiring sigh. "Take me to the hotel. It's not the first time I've had to look at a wall in this *hole*. You can't flank destiny. Or nemesis. Whatever it is. I was feeling *too* sinful, and this is what I get. I'll give you to midnight. After that, I'll go out on my own!"

I began to realise what I'd been missing when we got to the Plaza Athenee. We had adjoining suites in the Louis XIV style, with a wonderfully roomy bathroom, the soap I hope to die with, and towels that are bathgowns. I came out of the shower like Bul-bul, the baksheesh fellah, and Consuelo tapped and came in with my trousers and shirt, ironed beautifully clear of creases, tie pressed flat, with—of all things!—a maroon carnation.

"Pinched it from downstairs," she announced, and put the links in the cuffs, laid out socks, braces, a handkerchief. All I had to do was dress behind the bathroom door as far as the trousers, socks and shoes, and then come out to have my tie neatly knotted into a bow, put my arms in a waistcoat held for me, get into a jacket, and stand there to have the carnation pulled well down in the buttonhole, and the handkerchief flattened in the pocket.

I didn't know myself, but I liked it.

I kissed her, felt the yield. Christ, *that's* exciting!

"I'm going to tell Azil you're here," I said. "He's a sympathiser. I bet I'll be here by midnight. Be dressed. Don't forget, you've got an appointment at the Rondpoint!"

She looked at the bed, a handsome affair with a red and white silk coverlet, sheets turned down, lace pillows, a marvel of appeal, I must admit, to the lower man.

"I'll blow you a kiss from there!" she challenged. "And behave yourself with those Arab girls!"

The apartment was only a short walk towards the Champs. I saw the cars and waiting chauffeurs long before I got there. Again I groaned. If it was a full-scale affair, I wasn't properly dressed. If it was one of Azil's "nights" it didn't matter how I was dressed. I knew I wouldn't get away till morning. I'd had some.

A footman took my overcoat, and another escorted me to the lift. It was impossible to tell how many floors we went up. There was no movement, though from any window in the apartment there was a glorious view of Paris. When the doors opened the familiar smell of cigars, flowers, Egyptian cigarettes and perfume met me. I like it. Some profess not to. I believe they're merely envious of luxury.

About twenty men, mostly in lounge suits, were talking to a lot of girls, some rather older but still fresh, and a dozen or so mature women, all in long dresses, jeweled, soigné. Any girl invited to an Azil night, could walk into any *couturier*—or anyone else for that matter—and order what she pleased.

He saw me, and left his group without a word.

He looked not worried, but pensive, perhaps.

"My dear Edmund!" he called, which made a few heads turn. "You must think me such a nuisance to spoil your evening, no? But my brothers are here. They haven't good news. Paul told me you have a companion? Bring her, please, tomorrow. Maxim, one o'clock. Now, before I introduce, we talk our business. Come!"

He didn't seem to look anywhere or make the smallest sign, but when we reached the office at the end of the foyer, we hadn't sat down and the three brothers came in. The oldest, Habib, was principal shareholder and proxy for six others. The second, Fuad, and the third, Niz'r, were lesser lights, that is, if about thirty million sterling in shares between them can be called "lesser."

We shook hands, and sat down at the table in the chairs we'd come to regard as "ours." Mine was on the right of Azil's, with Fuad beside me. Habib and Niz'r faced me.

Azil and the others spoke Arabic which I love to listen to, and so nothing was lost. But when I understood they were talking of passing war stores and volunteers along our line as a short cut, I was a little appalled.

I thought I understood why our men were resigning, or simply disappearing. Any pump-station could come under attack from Royalists, if Republic forces held it, and vice-versa. It wouldn't matter which side was in or out. Anyone inside would "get" it.

But I was relieved to find Habib categorically, but quietly, refusing to permit the line to be used—officially—for any except the purpose we were building it for.

"Let them spend their own money and build a road, or better still, the railroad we always needed!" he said, as if from distance. "I don't spend my money to help wastrels!"

"How do you prevent them using any route they please, or attacking where they think fit?" Azil asked, smilingly. "They've been fighting for years, from the breasts of their mothers. What shall we do? Recruit a corps of gendarmes for the Company? How many men? Foreign Legionnaires? How much a month?

How much insurance? How many millions? To do what? For how long?"

"I shall order that our own people will not follow the route," Habib said. "This will prevent the line from being a constant target. It will not be a temptation to unruly elements—"

"Unruly elements?" Fuad asked, in astonishment. "We're fighting to survive!"

"Wasn't talking about us!" Habib said angrily. "We mustn't give them reason to destroy the one industry in the country that *could* become international!"

"Isn't oil?" Azil asked, in the same smiling humor.

"Oil's not an industry but an empire, and too few of our people are healthily employed in it," Habib said, and tapped the table with a stubby forefinger. "The only foreigners will be the men who teach. The rest will be our own people. Then *they'*ll teach. Why do you think I've spent money?"

"Very well!" Azil said, holding up his hand. "But this isn't fair to our friend, Mr. Trothe. It's not why we asked him here. Fuad, why don't you begin? Briefly, please!"

Fuad was darkest of them all, and obviously spent more time in the desert. Except for Azil, they were all black-haired, a touch of grey, crop-bearded in the Arabian style, withdrawn, even from each other, with a dignity uncommon in this day, and all three were desert-burned, which is different in tone from sunburn, and far less the townsman, whether in dress or manner. Azil tailored in London, the others possibly in Paris, or Beirut. The cut, the cloth was different, gave them another sort of appearance, little more than urban, not of the city.

But there was no hint of the rustic about them. They were, in hard fact, some of the shrewdest brains, financially or politically, in the Middle East.

"Mr. Trothe, I speak in English, because I know what I say, and you understand," Fuad began, showing fine teeth. "We have known for a long time that we have a new power working against us. I do not speak of recent events. It is new. We have the evidence, but nothing to show who it is—"

I had the strangest crawling sensation in the back of my neck. What I'd been thinking—or thought I'd been dreaming—seemed to be coming out in words.

"It is first something which takes away men," he went on, with a fingernail lifting a wide, roseleaf-tipped cigarette out of a gold box. "We lose our chief men from the oilfields. From the docks. Most of them Europeans and Americans. Where do they go? We don't know. We thought they drink too much. It's not the reason. Many don't drink. We thought they are afraid of war. It's not the reason. The war is not near them. We pay well. Makes no difference. They go!"

He lit the cigarette and the smoke that reached me smelled so good, I took one. I could have done with a drink, but not there.

"Three months ago, my land agent, an Englishman of the first class, with me and my family twenty years, his own house, everything, he is gone," Fuad went on sadly, I thought, looking at the ash. "We made enquiries. He could be in hospital. No. He took a plane to Pakistan. He went. No letter. Nothing. The Chief of Police tried to find him. Nothing. But this is when we hear of others going. No trace. Now, it happens with this Company. Mr. O'Brien has gone, why?"

"I don't know," I said. "I was told only today. I saw him not a week ago. He was perfectly happy. Everything was in order—"

"Very well," Fuad said. "But in the course of our enquiries, two curiosities. Well, I think so. First, in four cases, they are in towns in Iraq. They are with foreigners, not European, not Russian. I have spoken to the witness. She is the only one. She is a buyer of prayer mats. She goes from town to town. Iraqi towns are not big. Word soon passes. She heard of these men. You see how it happened? She knew them. Because in the houses where they live, she had sold mats to them to make a pretty color on the wall. But when she tried to see them she is refuse' and they go away. The second time she hear of them, it is different men. She say nothing. She only look. The men do nothing. They wait two days. Then, this woman say, they go. But the man, the payer, was not Iraqi or Turco. Not Russian, not of Europe. Not *giaour—*"

"Not, in other words, like me," I said. "Could he have been Indian or Parsee? Ethiopian? Somali?"

Fuad shook his head.

"A mystery," he said. "I sent two good men to Tabriz to enquire. There is a register of her name in the hotel. Not of the men. Not of the man who paid them. And my men were not allowed to stay in the town!"

He nodded, mouth in an arc.

"Power, this is what I mean," he said. "Somebody has the power to close the mouth of these people. Pay. Who? American? What for? They don't throw away money. Russian? They are not fools. Our own people? All the enquiries, everywhere? *Nothing!*"

"What currency do they pay in?" I asked. "If they buy the currency of the country, they've got to have other currency, or a draft. Don't any of the banks know?"

Azil pointed his finger at me, and looked, eyebrows up, at the others in turn.

"You see?" he said. "Highly practical and very necessary, Mr. Trothe!"

Habib rested his elbows on the table, widened his arms, and opened his hands, looking at me over his cheekbones.

"Tell me, Edmund, how will you do this?" he invited. "I am a great wonderer for miracles!"

"May I make a call?" I asked Habib.

He held an open palm toward the battery of telephones under the window.

I waited for the operator and asked for Information, London, all charges reversed.

"The Canal Banking Syndicate Ltd.," I said. "I believe there's a night staff—"

In moments, Dillon was on.

"Sir Chapman's at the Cocoa Tree," he said. "I'll get him and he'll ring you. Won't be two ticks!"

"Please say I'm sorry to disturb his game!"

"Oh, it's not that. He's taken up petit-point to improve his nerves, that's all!"

I tried to imagine the panelled comfort of the Cocoa Tree club in subdued glow of reading lamps, and the formidable Sir Chapman Ryder, in the depths of a leather armchair, stabbing a needle into a circle of jute, and gave up.

"Hello, Edmund!" he bellowed. "What are you doing in that miserable sty of a place?"

"Wondering if I might spoil your Sunday, or see you early on Monday morning—"

"Oh. I'm—uh—I'm lunching rather distantly tomorrow. Monday, breakfast, seven thirty?"

"Excellent!"

"Give me a little idea—?"

"Iran, Iraq—"

"Yes?"

"Odd, or unusual amounts, brought in for purchase of national currency. From sources possibly not European or from the Americas—"

"What a *very* tall order!"

"Any sort of information gratefully snapped up—!"

"I'll see what I can do!"

I went back to the table. Habib smiled almost painfully. Azil was openly jubilant, and in passing a cup of coffee, winked, a slowish closing of the left eye.

"If you have success, I shall be so happy!" he said. "But that is only the first part. The second is more serious. Mr. Bowles was buying a railway at Ismailia, and some other *materiél*. He had no chance. Yes?"

"That is correct. Have you heard about him?"

Azil nodded at Fuad.

"Continue!" he said, and sat back

"A great deal of our information, naturally comes from our friends in Government and relatives in various positions. It is a circle very close, and everybody helps. We knew about the railway and told you a long time before anybody. But we lose our chance to buy very cheap? It was secret information. How does anyone else know?"

87

I was aching to ask him about the alleged Yemenis, but I held on.

"I went to see men I have known from a child, at the University. I married the sister of one. Habib married her older sister. Mine is better!—"

"Opinion!"

"Naturally. Everybody's. Well, they told me—it was the same answer—it was a sudden decision from high. But very high. Take up the railway. Use troops. But where is it going? Where have the ships gone? Nobody knows!"

"Get the names of the ships. There's Lloyd's Register—"

"No, Mr. Trothe. We were before you. I had good men at the docks. They could pay. Not one word. In Port Said?"

"In other words, ships were loaded and got away without anyone's knowing it, and those who did were paid a fair sum—as a bribe—and also threatened, is that it?"

Fuad nodded.

"But more surprising, even my friends had nothing to say!"

Niz'r hadn't spoken a word, but he tapped his cigarette as if calling attention, and took a diary out of his pocket.

"It was the twelfth when the woman saw these men in Tabriz, and it was the fifteenth when the ships sailed," he said. "Did the men also go on the ships? Is it the same people?"

"Fair question," I said. "I'm surprised you had no luck with the Port Said pilots. They're a steady lot. Wouldn't get far with threats or anything else!"

"The ordinary pilots and stevedores were not used," Fuad said. "It was the naval docks. Naval officers to guide the ships. They are different from politicians. They don't talk. For money or not!"

"There's got to be *one!*" I said.

"You find him," Fuad said, biting it off. "I don't want a firing sqaud. Neither do they. For answering a question?"

"Where do you think the ships went?" I asked, taking another tack. "When and where? Israel?"

They shook their heads, not more than a small sorrowful shake, but still a unanimous no, looking at me with that curiously minus expression of pity and disgust which most Arabs seem to wear at sound of the unmentionable.

"We have all information," Habib said authoritatively. "They did not touch the eastern Mediterranean. We do not know the ships, but we know the type of ships' stores taken on board. It is the only real information we have. Rice, salt, vegetables, beef, chickens, live pigs. They were supplied by the chandler in the partnership of a friend of mine. The stores were enough for three months for a crew of twenty for each ship. It was paid for against a Greek bank in Salonika—"

"Let me have details of the draft," I said. "It might lift the lid off—"

"Copy of the papers, and the draft," Habib said, opening a briefcase, and taking them out one by one. "Eight pages of items. They bought electric clocks, fountain pens, ball pens, soap, all of them not very common. For the officers? Five cases of soap? French perfume? Cigarette lighters? What is this? Contraband?"

I put the papers in my pocket without looking at them. I'd just seen the time.

"You don't think it is important?" Habib said, a little irritated.

"Too important to run over here," I said. "It requires close study. By analysis, we'll arrive at the people best able to help us. If they took on this type of stores elsewhere, they mightn't have been so secretive. Is there any feeling that the people behind this are anything to do with a Communist government?"

They were all quite still. Only cigarette smoke whorled, broke.

"It is why we are here," Azil said. "We wish to find out how we should think. A railway thirty years old, some other things, it is nothing to us. But how are they taken, against our wishes, contrary to the word of our friends? Now, this is important for us. Who *is* it? Another company? We can put in ten times the capital. Another country? Who, and where?"

"What do you want me to do?"

"Start from the first day," Habib said, suddenly, louder, taking command. "You have complete freedom. We are told it will become worse, this pick, pick, pick—"

"Who told you?"

"In Beirut, in Damascus, in Teheran, they told us," Habib said. "In Cairo, we saw for ourselves. How can we make business with men disappearing?"

"But surely, a few isolated events here and there aren't going to affect the running of the Company?" I said, deliberately playing it down. I didn't believe they'd told me all they knew. They didn't convince me. They weren't the sort of men to scatter. "Who were the Yemenis arrested in Cairo?"

"Those men were not Yemenis!" Azil said, with the first sign of nerves. "They were from the slums of Basra. From the hills, north. Entrails, no more. Not worth a bullet!"

"Anyway, I could talk to them?"

"There were eight," Fuad said, stubbing the cigarette in the ashtray. "A little time ago, you could interview them all, I suppose—"

"In hell!" Azil said. "They no longer exist!"

"Pity. Good evidence there. Gentlemen, there's something more, but you're not anxious to tell me. Am I permitted to suggest another Arab—let's say—movement? Anti-royalist?"

"I don't hide it was our first thought," Azil said. "We are quite sure it isn't. Those ships wouldn't have left Cairo. You seem to forget, also, the words of the woman. The man, the one who paid, was *giaour*. Not Arab!"

"He could be paid by an Arab movement," I suggested.

"Out of the question!" Habib said, openly annoyed. "I assure you, we would know. It is foreign. It is a power. It has money. It has great influence in Cairo. It is *not* Russia. This we know also. I have many good Russian friends. As they have said, they have their own ships. And what would they do with Europeans and Americans?"

"You believe they were shipped off somewhere?" I asked, and I was just a mite startled. "How can you be certain?"

"Because—saving further exacerbation"—Azil came in, calmly —"we have enquired, and we know that none of them are in an Arab country. Not in Pakistan, or India. Not in any African country we have approached. I don't believe they will dock in any European port. Our agents are waiting everywhere—"

"Have you an agent anywhere in Albania?"

They all smiled as if at a child.

"We are well served in Albania," Habib said, and left no room for doubt. "It is almost like a dream—five ships? *P-w-f-o-o-f!*— Nothing!"

"Why are five ships significant?"

"About forty to fifty thousand tons of shipping isn't insignificant," Niz'r said. "It's a small fleet. It's money. It's men. Which power do they serve?"

"Why are you so insistent upon a 'power'?"

"I answer you in a word," Azil cut across everybody. "Cairo!"

"Or we could not have been ignored!" Habib said, slamming the cigarette box shut, though it didn't make a noise. "Many millions smell in this. In funds for the Government. Credits. And in pockets. *Canaille!*"

"Therefore, somebody, somewhere, isn't getting his share, and for the right sort of reward we might be presented with a gift," I said. "It's always the same. The missing men, for example. Somebody, somewhere, knows perhaps one of them, or where he went. Somebody's going to get an offer, perhaps. Make it easy for him to tell us. Let's make it known we'll pay a year's salary. Or five years. What we want is information we can act on—"

"Five years salary!" Azil said. "Make it worth a dishonest word!"

The others nodded.

"But 'act' in which way?" Niz'r asked, sceptically. "I think these people will destroy what we have done. They may try to destroy the oilfields. Either by sabotage or fighting a war that doesn't end. So many fools are ready to kill each other if they are paid and fed. What would you do?"

"Destroy the brain," I said. "It follows. No brain, no money!"

"So we find the brain?" Fuad almost hooted. "How?"

"I always found a little patience more than necessary," I said. "Well, then, gentlemen, I shall go back to think a little—"

"You have just time to take the lady to supper!" Azil said waspishly. "I shall look forward to meeting her tomorrow at Maxim. One o'clock!"

10

Paris is a wonderful place for a night out, but so is London, or Budapest, or New York, or anywhere else if the mood's right and money's no object. Night clubs were never my choice of entertainment. But with the right girl there's a lot to be said for that extra "bubble" in the air, a sense of being somewhere else when you ought to be at home, listening to music you've only read about, watching the "entertainers" of the moment, crowded among people you may have seen on TV, or in the papers, and trying to drink if only the waiter could find his way to your table.

We went to the *Follies* and got the excellent late show, to the Lido for an even better one later, and after that we went to three clubs, one after another. The difference between the audiences at the *Follies* and the Lido was simply that the Lido's looked more affluent and less honest, but the clubs, the bands, the turns, might have been the same. I loved watching Consuelo's eyes, restless, ruthless, glinting at the jokes she didn't want to admit she grasped, measuring, accepting, rejecting. At the clubs there was too much noise to talk, and not enough room to dance. The majority on the floor simply doubled their fists, moved their arms in a sort of sleepy shadow boxing, slid their feet from here to there and wagged their bottoms. When it was over they dropped into chairs, lights went down, and comedians either commented on politics, or girls came on almost naked, and went off nude. After a couple of hours the night stayed in memory as an unsteady film of white bodies and paste jewels, wonderful breasts, black fringed eyes in pallid glitter or warily seductive, legs, thighs, bare rumps, champagne not always cold, whisky that never knew Scotland, and a drumbeat that seemed to dig down in the base of the brain and stay there. With all, there was about as much real excitement as in any country pub. The only girl I remembered had a large mauve love-bite on the inside of her left thigh. I couldn't keep my eyes off it.

A little after three o'clock, the cigarette girl offered Consuelo a large, fluffy black and white spaniel, which she took in such an embrace that I was jealous, and had to buy it for a ridiculous sum, thinking of all the starving children it ought to have fed. But they were both looking at me, and I hadn't the moral strength to say no. In any event I wanted to keep that look in Conseulo's eyes.

"The most supinely idiotic extravagance of my life, darling, but I suddenly *wanted* it!" she whispered in the foyer, while I waited for my coat. "Besides, the girl looked at my dress and almost dribbled. I know that feeling too well. So she got a commission, and I got my guardian angel. Isn't he an utter darling?"

"What are you calling him?"

She looked up at me, the same look, velvet-mouth, and in some way, somewhere, I sensed the yield.

"I'm thinking," she said, at her most dangerously innocent. "Either Ed, or Eddie!"

She knew my dislike, even hate, of the diminutive of Edmund.

"I'll buy another," I said, pretending to move. "We'll call her Connie!"

"So long as you love her, I shan't mind, and they'd look so comfortable on a bed together!"

"Falling in with the general form—"

"We should have been there hours ago. But I'm not sorry. A tiny bit. I've seen what I expected. If I never see it again, I shan't be disappointed. But aren't the girls a little brazen? Even for these days?"

Too innocent.

94

"I liked it. Nothing wrong with the female—"

"But so *much* of it!"

"A little for everybody. Nudity whets!"

"I noticed you were fascinated!"

"As an esthete, of course—"

"That girl with the enormous bust!"

"Wondering how she kept it all up without a keeper-upper. I prefer the champagne glass type—"

"You're going to be disappointed!"

"Wonderful. Second glass always improves the first—"

Consuelo's frown stopped me. Her eyes looked up at a corner. Above the chatter I heard my name over the speaker.

"Here," I said, giving her the cloakroom ticket. "Let's see what *this* is!"

I went to the little hatch where the cashier sat counting the notes, and asked him where the voice came from. He trod on a button and a piece of the wallpapered panel opened. In the inner office, the head waiter flipped through a pad, and another man held a mike.

"My name's Trothe," I said. "Somebody calling me?"

"Ah, yes, sir. The concierge, Nicol, at the Plaza Athenee, would like you to speak to him. It is very urgent!"

I picked up the telephone as if I'd just heard a death sentence, wondering whether to ignore it and go to another hotel, and wait for the morning. But I couldn't.

"Ah! Mr. Trothe? Yes, sir. His highness the Prince Azil el Nur—"

"Yes? What does he want?"

"Sir, his highness requires your presence immediately. It is most urgent. He ordered the police to find you!"

"The police?"

"To help, sir—"

I called Azil's apartment. Three telephones were engaged. I waited.

"Oh, Edmund? Please come here now! There is a terrible— please come here. I wait for you!"

Fortunately, the Plaza Athenee was just around the corner from

Azil's apartment. Consuelo made no comment, either in the foyer, helping me on with my coat, or in the cab. I didn't feel like talking. I couldn't think what might be wrong.

"Try not to be *too* long, darling!" she whispered, when I put her in the lift. "I'll be awake whatever the time is. And damn dear Az-i!"

I felt like saying more than that, but a job's a job, even if I thought things were getting a little out of hand. There seemed more cars than ever in the street, but I was unprepared for the Force Mobil uniforms at the doorway.

I gave my name to the sergeant. He seemed to be waiting for me. He pushed through a crowd of photographers in the foyer, shouldered me into the lift and slammed the gate on the faces and the shouted questions I didn't catch.

"What's happened?" I asked.

He turned his face to me, one direct from Mars, pulled into another shape by the chin strap, and shook the helmet.

A footman took me through the drawing room, crowded with people, all whispering, turning, silent, to look at me. We went through the library, to Azil's study. The footman knocked, listened. I heard nothing. But he opened the door just wide enough to allow me in.

Azil sat in the red leather armchair, white—but white—in the face. Fuad had been weeping. He stood at the window. He simply looked at me, and turned away.

Azil beat his hands together, turned his eyes to the ceiling.

"Habib has been kidnapped!" he said, through a strangled throat. "It is forty minutes. Not far from Les Deux Magots. He met friends. At a dinner. Old friends. They saw it. Three other men from the street. In front of everybody. They saw. Ah, my brother!"

"What action by the Police?"

"There is an alert. Roadblock. Airport. Railway stations. Garages. Such absurdities! With a careful plan, what need to leave Paris?"

"No warning of any kind?"

"Paris is our second home. We never had warnings. Never a small breath. Now see what she does!"

"But not Paris!" Fuad shouted, tears in a run again. "Somebody. *Assassins!*"

"Has the warning gone over the radio?"

"They promised—"

"Buy time. Put out your own advertisements. Give our postbox number in Lausanne. All cable charges paid. Pay them what they ask—"

Azil stood, a little unsteadily.

"Edmund, I was sure of you," he said, and he was far weaker than I'd thought. "Please, take charge here. My doctor's waiting for me. Excuse, please. Fuad, come!"

Fuad took my hand in passing.

"You will find him for us!" he whispered, gulping, dabbing his eyes. "Our brother is so dear to us. We would give our blood!"

I was touched by a display of affection that might have been comic, but was far, far from it.

I began by calling everyone I knew on the newspapers and then the TV boys, though most had gone home, but hadn't arrived. That done, I called Lausanne. It took time to find Paul. He was in bed. But not in his apartment. I wish, sometimes, my sense of humor were a little more malleable. After all, I hoped to be in the same place quite soon. For the same purpose. Then why did I consider him indiscreet? His voice changed from impatient grunts to a clear, lungy bawl.

"He's what? For God's sake? My word—"

"I think you'd better come here—"

"Be with you soon as I can get a plane. Don't leave till I get there. Carrying a gun?"

"Yes—"

"Right. *'Voir!*"

A tap on the door, and Captain Launceville, police chief of the district came in, slapped his hat on the desk, and stood there, nodding at me, mouth down. We were old friends.

97

"Another Barka case, eh? Poor man. There isn't *that* much anywhere!"

He measured an nth of a fingernail.

"It wasn't his car. That's in the garage. The chauffeur says he was sent home. Plenty of witnesses. It happened—zut!—and some say he was pushed into an old black Panhard. Others, a Daimler. A Cadillac. You show them photos of various makes. They're all wrong. Cretins!"

"Sure about the chauffeur?"

"He's at headquarters. Seems all right. But we'll make sure. We want a list of his friends, here—"

"That's simple. His social secretary's on her way—"

Which reminded me, if I needed it. I called Consuelo. She took her time, and my heart was suddenly in my throat.

"Oh, Edmund, darling! I fell asleep. On our doggie, dear Eddie—"

"Dress in your plainest. I'm sending a car for you. Nothing over the telephone. Not even blasting, biting disappointment!"

"Ten minutes. Fortunately, I didn't cream. And it's lovely waiting, isn't it? I'm going to *boot* this dam' dog!"

I asked Launceville to send two of his men to the hotel to escort her.

"If we're lucky, it'll only cost them a fortune," he said. "But they'll be luckier if he's anything but a corpse!"

The social secretary, Mme. Marie-France Belac came in, early thirties, quite lovely, but she *had* creamed, and hadn't got in the corners, and she was in between a thorough weeping fit and eyes-full. I took care of it.

"Get your lists of friends and acquaintances of all four princes," I said, chopping it off short. "I want them all telephoned and asked the same questions. Here they are. We may get just a little information—"

Consuelo came in, cool, perfectly lovely, in a black suit, no make-up, and the sort of attitude that brought Mme. Belac over on her side. We might never have met. I introduced them and told them to work in the study. Consuelo began on the list of people outside Paris. It looked endless, but then, I had to wait for Paul. The office seemed the best place for me, but when I got there, it was full of people. I asked Launceville to usher them out, and while the footman cleaned up, I phoned London, and found Ulla Brandt Ben Ua in her Upper Brook Street house. As a girl, she'd married an Arab oil millionaire en route from her home in New Zealand, had a most beautiful palace in Muscat, property in Beirut, a house on a beach near Tobruk, another in Hammamet, and one in Tangier. Between them and all her friends, she knew as much about Araby as any, and far more than most.

"Oh, Edmund, what terrible news—!"

"Look, Ulla. Do you know of any 'new' movement anywhere? Heard anything? Never mind what. We're looking for crumbs. Desperate, in fact!"

"I know. I wish I could help you. The only thing I've heard was in Muscat. I don't know what it's worth—"

"Let's have it!"

"Well, somebody was buying out people. I didn't hear all of it. Just somebody using a lot of money and buying out technicians, that sort of people. Not Arabs. Just the foreigners—"

"Nothing affecting Europe? France in particular?"

"No—"

"Nothing moving among the younger Arabs? Students—?"

"They'd get their heads cut off!"

"Not a small whisper about attacking, let's say, the ruling families—"

"Wait a minute! Let me remember. I was at a party at Baholi's place. He's a man I've known for years. He said one of the Trucial sheikh's sons had been missing. Quite recently. The young man was in Vienna, at the University. They've hunted all over. Not a trace. His bank account hasn't been touched. And when the old man got there, he was given a note to hand over a million cash. Or he'd never see his son again. He had a heart attack and died—"

"I saw that. I knew him. I didn't know about this, though—"

"Listen, I'll call Baholi. He's got the details. Cases seem similar—"

"Reverse charges, and I'll—"

"You and your charges!"

Not that it had got us very far, but it was a start. I didn't know the Viennese Chief of Police, but I *did* know Interpol's, and called him, and pulled him, a little sleep-thick, out of bed.

"Yes, we know of the case. There is no trace of the young man. It's very strange. Arabs are not easily able to disguise. He cannot walk normally in the street without recognition. He may be hiding. But why? He is extremely wealthy, and his woman friend is beautiful, intelligent, and also wealthy. She is desperate. Why should he hide? No evidence of mental instability. A first class student. Economics. The Austrian police have been diligent. Naturally. A truly colossal reward—"

"Nothing on Prince Habib, yet?"

"Nothing. I shall keep you informed—"

"My apologies for disturbing you—"

"Please! You know me by now!"

Marie-France turned up the first crumb with a call to one of the friends who'd been dining at the restaurant, and went home before the others. He was tired out after hours with the Police, but he said that Habib had been in very good humor, except for worry about his uncle, Abdullah, who was in a clinic in Switzerland, and not expected to live. The chauffeur had been given a message to go home about an hour before they left, because Habib was going to play cards at the Count de Stefan's place in the Champs de Mars, only a little way down the street. Count de Stefan was also with the Police, and so were the others and the chauffeur, and he thought there were fourteen witnesses to the fight. Three men had knocked down the Count de Stefan and George Fonisca, the other partner, both elderly, and Habib was bundled into a large black car, and driven off. Nobody got the number, which in any case, may have been false.

"The three men were Europeans?" I asked.

"I believe so. They used small iron bars. De Stefan has a painful shoulder—"

"Was the restaurant table reserved?"

"I believe, by de Stefan."

"He told them who the guests were?"

"I think, yes. Habib was a patron of many years. So was his father—"

"It's an Arab meeting place?"

"N-no. But many Arabs go there—"

"They employ Arabs?"

"I'm sure they do—"

"Thank you. You must be tired—"

Launceville had been listening on the desk line. He called his Inspector, and began putting on his coat.

"Listen to me," I said, when he was almost outside the door. "There's money in this. Those men must have been paid a wad. Anyone bringing information that leads to Prince Habib's release would earn ten times whatever sum those men were paid—"

"What guarantee?"

"Name it. Cash. No questions. Come on, Launceville. Spread it!"

He nodded, back to me.

"I have to convince somebody it's not a trap!"

"Tell them to make their own terms. All we want is Habib, alive. He won't talk. We won't. Name the figure!"

I watched him walk through the dark lounge. His men followed him from the shadows. For no good reason I was glad I'd remembered to wear my little friend. The library lights were on in niches. I turned them all on. Two policemen stood in embrasures. I told them to conduct the two women to the hotel, and report downstairs.

Consuelo drew a line through another name, and started to dial. I pushed the bar down.

"No more this morning," I said. "That's it!"

"Oh, but I've just begun!" she complained, and in truth, she looked fresh as a daisy.

"Bed," I said. "Both of you. Two policemen are waiting to escort you. Don't come here before three o'clock tomorrow. Grethe will be here with the office staff in a little while—"

"And what are *you* going to do?" Consuelo asked. "When do *you* sleep?"

"The moment Paul gets here. You've both done a wonderful job. Marie-France, let me have a list of all the women the Princes might have met or entertained in Paris—"

She pressed both lips between her teeth and drew a breath, inclined to refuse.

"We rule out nobody and nothing," I warned. "A woman might well be in this!"

"It is the holy of holies!" she said. "If they were known, you have no idea of the immensity of the scandal—!"

"I can well imagine. Let me have the list!"

Marie-France took keys from her bag, and left the study.

"A fine excuse!" Consuelo whispered. "More telephone numbers than any Soho madame!"

"What do you know about Soho?"

"What you like, how you like, very nice, very sweet, not much money!" she whined, in fair imitation of a pimp. "Darling, when *are* we going to be quite, quite *alone?*"

"I'll be there when Paul comes in, I give you my word—"

Her smile brightened all existence, but Marie-France's heels tapped in warning, and she came in with a thick leather folder, with about thirty pages of names and addresses.

"Those with those little red marks are, let us say, tried and good. With two red marks, they prefer to work with another girl instead of alone. With three marks, they like to play ha*reem*—"

"Who wouldn't be a Prince!" Consuelo said. "Am I a one, two, or a three-er?"

Marie-France gave her a brief, clear, upward glance.

"You will never be more than a one, my dear," she said. "Like me, a healthy *one*. If my husband knew I did this work, I don't know what he would do!"

"So you're a Mrs.?" Consuelo said gladly.

"With three children, and I work to keep my family. In a certain position. With a town house, and a country house, and one at the sea. And the cars, children's school—well—some of us use one thing, and some use only the head, you see? My husband is a farmer. We lost our home in Algeria. It isn't enough to live on a potato, you agree?"

I could see she'd gone slap into Consuelo's good books.

"Off you go," I said. "Both of you call me when you're in your rooms. I'll give you exactly fifteen minutes!"

I saw them to the lift. Consuelo's kiss was in her eyes, my kiss in mine, but we were both flat-faced, and I was positive that neither Marie-France nor the liftman knew we were anything more than what we pretended to be.

The entire place was quiet. I'd never seen it without people before. I was surprised at its size, which hadn't been so noticeable. Neither had I realised what a wealth of art decorated walls and floors. Without the furniture, and the vases of flowers everywhere, I could have been in a museum. As it was, I thought it the most quiet, luxurious, as well as the richest, bachelor's quarters I'd ever seen, or imagined. It wasn't neo-American, and except for some lovely rugs, no sign of Arabia, but someone had designed the rooms in an entirely European style which I appreciated for the first time. I hadn't realised there was such a thing.

A door opened quietly on the further side, behind two columns. I went a few paces forward. Azil, in—of all things!—a long, white nightshirt with lace at neck and wrists, stood in the doorway. He'd probably taken a sleeping pill and didn't know where he was. I don't think he recognised me.

"Habib?" he whispered. "You are here?"

"Go back to bed," I said.

He sighed a moan—like a small boy—and turned, walking slowly along the passage to a lit room. In the quiet I heard a whisper of bedclothes. I walked over and closed the door. I suddenly realised there was nobody else. I was alone. Not that I minded. But I knew that Azil kept a night staff. Inspection was in order, and I went on a tour of the rooms, turning lights on and leaving them on everywhere. I was suddenly aware of size, area, floor space, wall space, every room an art gallery on its own. One smaller room I hadn't seen before I particularly took to. It was like walking into the first century A.D. The four walls held panels which must have come from Pompeii or Herculaneum, painted in the Roman black, orange, and oxblood, with damsels cavorting in a surprising manner with fawns, half a dozen nudes from the Golden Age of the Greeks, some alabaster and marble bas-reliefs of a bacchante's wedding, and a group from Etrusca, in *flagrante delicto,* all staring those grim, slit-eyed smiles that through centuries carried on to Giotto. I was looking at the Aphrodite, and wondering how the Greeks, supposedly without edged tools of any hardness, were able to get that surface on marble, and I heard the hum of the lift, just down the corridor.

I stood flat to the wall, and waited. The doors opened. A footman got out, profile to me, took a pace forward, bending a knee to look into the lounge and signed "Come on!" with the right hand. If that weren't enough, his uniform was baggy, and he lacked a cravat. Two men came out of the lift, wearing felt hats and overcoats. One, bearded, carried a black bag. They whispered for a moment. The "footman" signed through the lounge, to the left—Azil's bedroom?—and the two were about to move when I walked on.

"What is it you want?" I called, in fair imitation of Arabian French.

"Ah!" the beard said. "I am the private physician of the Prince Azil. His highness sent for me—"

"Then you will kindly wait until the major-domo announces you. Who is your friend?"

The friend looked like a bruiser. The "physician" seemed nervous. He hadn't taken his hat off. The footman looked from me to the two, back to me.

"Go to the pantry, and bring a bottle of wine and a cheese tray!" I ordered. "Where have you been? We've been ringing for you for the past hour—!"

The fellow had a sloppy blue eye. He looked up hesitantly, pathetically at the other two. Almost as one, they hurled themselves back in the lift, the doors slid shut, and that should have been that.

It wasn't. The big black button in the wall on my right worked the burglar alarm, which rang in the police station, and in the police boxes in the street, flashed the red lamp in the apartment entrance, stopped all the lifts in mid-floor, and activated one which came into use in the foyer.

It wasn't long before it came up with a sergeant and three policemen, hard-eyed, and ready for trouble. They barely waited for me to explain. The red button under the sergeant's thumb brought up the trapped lift. The other three, without a word, drew heavy .45s. As well they did.

Both the "physician," and the bruiser held automatics ready. Their eyes died.

The footman dropped on his knees making noises.

The unarmed sergeant jerked his thumb, and out they came. Looking at those policemen's eyes, I don't think I'd have tried anything, either. Without a word they gave up the automatics, and as if they'd done it all their lives, put their hands up, walked to the wall, as the thumb told them, and stood, waiting. The footman was hauled to his feet, and thrown there. Both automatics swung from the sergeant's little finger.

"Got a permit for this?" he asked the "physician," and looked at the bruiser. "You?"

Both barely shook their heads.

"That will be the first charge," the sergeant said flatly, and pulled out his book. "Right. What's your name?"

"You can find out," the "physician" said. "I want to see a lawyer!"

"You've been living in the cinema," the sergeant said, and looked at the policemen. "Take him in there, and look through his pockets. Careful. He might have another gun!"

Two policemen grabbed him, and almost lifted him out. Bruiser opened his coat.

"All right," he said mildly. "I don't want any trouble!"

The third policeman went over him in the most thorough frisk I ever saw. He unbuttoned coat, jacket, waistcoat, shirt, trousers, underpants—long, grey—and singlet. His booty was quite astonishing. He had two small bars of gold, a small leather bag of good diamonds, a thick package of one thousand franc notes, a smaller of five thousand, and rolls of lesser notes, all of them new. He also had a flick knife, a length of nylon twine, rubber gloves, a swatch of skeleton keys, a long aluminium box filled with something like clay—"plastic!"—the sergeant said, sniffing it—a small rubber sac of detonators, a roll of black material, and a tin box with a syringe.

"My God!" the sergeant said, and looked at me almost jovially. "A master of arts, hn?"

From the grunts and slaps in the other room, and the general bundling about, there seemed to be another master-of-arts being painfully shorn. A policeman came out at the same moment, as a fist *smacked!* into flesh, and a body fell against the wall and shook some of the statuary.

"Take advantage of good nature," the policeman complained, and put a pile of items down, one by one on the broad seat of the chair. "He had this taped round his guts—!"

It was a foot-long, wide band of new chamois leather, sewn in small pockets. The diamonds were first water, all the size of my middle finger nail. There were rubies, and other stones that rattled in the sergeant's palm. I didn't try to see the rest of the stuff.

"A pair of notables," the sergeant said admiringly. "And you were just paying a call, were you? Physician, eh? These your tools?"

He unrolled, and held out a kit of drills and bits.

"Probably a ground plan of the place," a policeman said and showed a penciled sheet. "They got a car in the garage round here, I see. Probably there's some more stuff in there?"

I suddenly saw a parcel in striped paper with a red cord in rough tie. I couldn't believe my eyes. My astonishment was so wordless that the sergeant turned full about to stare at me. He must have thought I'd gone mad. I thought I had.

One of the turquoise studded handles of Angela's handbag had split the package.

"Something wrong, sir?" the sergeant said, and went toward the chair.

"That handbag was stolen in Rome!" I managed to say. "No doubt about it. It was a New Year's gift. Special design—"

"Then that's the second charge!" the sergeant said, with great satisfaction. "Armed, without a permit, and theft. The rest we leave for the clerks. I'll send the Inspector up to get your deposition, sir—"

The two had to take their overcoats off to button themselves. In a sudden move, the sergeant pounced on the footman and began ripping his jacket off, shaking him like a bag of laundry.

"Thought you'd crawled with it, did you, my tulip?" he grunted. "Tip yourself out, quick!"

The footman might have stripped himself, but a policeman found a lump which he outlined with both hands. The sergeant put a thumb-tip under the man's chin to force his head up.

"Now tell me," he said, smiling dreadfully. "What's this? A tumor?"

He tore the shirt apart, opened the undershirt, and while the footman half-shrieked, stripped the tape, black, the sort electricians use, and held out a package knotted in a handkerchief. The foyer clock struck the half hour. Under the chime, I heard another, more melodious.

"That's a watch," I said, pointing to the handkerchief. "It's gold, has the moon, planets, stars, bells, everything!"

"How do you know?" the sergeant asked, unknotting. "Is it yours?"

"It is the Prince Habib's. He was kidnapped tonight!"

"A-hah!"

The sergeant didn't look at the watch. He pushed it into a broad pocket, got to his feet, and started filling his other pockets with the stuff on the chair. It all went in. He didn't look any bulkier.

"Right, down they go!" he said, and turned to me. "I'm leaving a man downstairs, sir. You'll be all right—"

The men were shoved bodily in the lift, and down they went. It would have been no use my asking the sergeant to question any of them. He was an old-timer, a real icer.

I almost ran to the telephone. I was late. I rang Marie-France, first, got a sleep-fractious "I am pair-fect-lee ohl-right, thank you, sair!" and rang off.

Consuelo was on the line before I was ready.

"A fine fifteen minutes!" she began clearly, crossly. "It's light outside—"

"Listen, we've found Habib's watch. It could only have been taken off him tonight. I'm hanging on for the Inspector, now. With you soon!"

"I heard that yesterday. Now it's today. I suppose I'll hear it tomorrow. Dam'!"

She slammed the phone down, just as light flashed in the foyer, and lift doors opened.

Paul came out among half a dozen policemen, and a couple of civilians.

"Edmund!" he called, hurrying. "Had a hell of a time getting here. Old friend of yours here. Any news?"

"Not much—"

"Remember Inspector Gauffure? He wants to talk to you. Only you. Quietly!"

11

I'd known Gauffure as a policeman long before he was transferred to the political branch in France after the Algerian tragedy.
He didn't look any older, and the handshake was a blacksmith's.

"A few minutes, no more," he said, in his diffident way. "I am
retired, as perhaps you know—"

"I didn't—"

"Three years ago. I went back to my garden, bought a field
next door—well—I do a good business. My son is a sergeant, on
special investigation. Elite. At half my age he's almost my rank.
These young men of today, they have opportunity, eh? But I
keep my friends. I am informed, you know, of this and that.
I don't get my knowledge from the newspapers!"

"You want to discuss Prince Habib—"

He held up the flat of both hands.

"We should understand one or two matters, sir, you forgive
me? My son was telephoned tonight. He came to see me. You
understand his position? He's young, ambitious, naturally. He
knows his world. I trained him!"

I nodded. Gauffure had been known as a walking register of
all the criminals in France. He knew where they were, what
they were doing, what type of crime they specialized in. Within
a few minutes of any "job" he would make out a list of names

to look for. He was rarely wrong unless it was new blood, in which case he added another name to his list. If his son had the same talent, his rank was no surprise.

But the father was taking plenty of time. He crushed a cigarette as if there were no such article as a clock. He might have been out in his garden. The cigarette had stuck to his bottom lip. He crossed his knees, folded his hands, leaned on his left elbow, looking up at the Crivelli.

"This abduction can only be something a few would try," he said, suddenly. "We know—my son and I—that field. We made enquiries. That boy works. He reminds me of myself at that age. He has a nose. But you know, it's dangerous. From the men themselves. They could be guillotined. So they shoot. And it's dangerous from up above. There might be politics. We don't like to interfere, eh? Modest policemen, with a wife and babies, it's always a risk!"

I knew he was going to pause there. He wanted it to sink in.

"I have a lot of money available," I said. "No risk to anybody—"

"If this man, this Prince, were—let us simply hypothecate—released somewhere, out in the country—"

"It doesn't matter where—!"

"But how is the money to be paid, and who to, and at what time?"

"I shall pay the money, to you, to your son, to Launceville, to anybody, when I see Prince Habib on his feet and ready to accompany me!"

"And supposing the Prince was put out of a car outside Notre Dame Cathedral. How would the money be paid?"

"In cash, old notes, whatever *you* say. And wherever—!"

"In this, you have confidence in me?"

"You wouldn't make a fool of yourself!"

"Others could. I must be sure. What sum will you pay? You see, others also require to be paid. It's not a one-man business. The official reward, of course, never reaches the men who do

110

the hard work. The real work of enquiry, finding, arresting, fighting, if necessary. Risk also has a price!"

"What do you suggest?"

"Half a million francs!"

"Agreed!"

He turned his head in half-surprise.

"You have the cash?"

"Of course—"

"And if I said a million?"

"You prejudice your case. Half a million in used notes isn't simple to put together. A million?"

He waved his hands. And stood.

"We understand each other," he said, wiping the inner side of his hands. "Half a million, cash. Later today, I shall telephone—"

"How was the Prince's watch found on somebody else?"

He turned, shaking his head, half-amused, half-wry.

"They sell a watch for a few francs, they spend money found in a wallet," he said, making gestures. "They light bonfires. Which can only lead to them—"

"A moment, Inspector," I put in. "Do you suppose the officials —I mean the Police, here—will make an arrest on the evidence—"

"They won't, because they haven't any. By the time they have a case, the man's buried. Look, sir. Somebody wants him out of the way. Somebody above. With money. The three idiots who made the pinch, they were supervised. Of course. They do their part. They're paid. They rob, first. Then the man is taken in hand by the real professionals. Where do you find *them*? You think the three idiots can tell you who employed them?"

"Then how's it going to be resolved? We want the Prince alive!"

He made a soothing gesture.

"When we're quite sure who we're dealing with, a lot more can be done!" he said, pointing to the ceiling, almost as an evangelist in frowning certainty. "That's why I came here. To do all I can. Why should young men work for nothing, and see their hard work disappear into other pockets?"

He pulled down the revers of his overcoat, and pressed the hat a little farther on.

"Nobody else will know of this?"

"Nobody. Not even Mr. Chamby—"

"We spoke only about my employment as a private investigator, you and me. Isn't that so? I named my terms, you accepted—"

"Precisely!"

He bowed, took off his hat, we shook hands, he put on the hat, tried to open the door the wrong way, shrugged a half smile, and went out.

I sat down to think. Paul came in and stood, looking down at me.

"This isn't the time to talk, I can see," he said. "You're beat. So am I. You go back and rest—"

"I'm expecting a call at the hotel at nine, or just before. I don't raise any hopes."

"Had any time with Consuelo?"

"No. Dinner. That's all—"

He laughed, head back.

"I'm taking Angela to England," he said. "Meet her family. We're at the George Cinque. I just know I've got something so wonderful, so—well—I've got no words. No words. She's wonderful!"

I was suddenly a little sad, or disappointed with myself, or envious of him, I'm not sure. But I wished I felt as he looked. Thinking of Consuelo—only a passing thought—of her sleeping under the red and white coverlet, a note in her voice, the warmth of her knee, that smile, was enough.

I pushed myself out of the chair, and stretched till bones cracked.

"Grethe's coming in with a troupe of secretaries any moment," I said. "These are the telephone numbers we want called. Those are the questions to ask. We want to know who's seen Habib since he's been here. Somebody knew he was dining at that restaurant. You can't put that sort of plan together in a couple of hours—"

"Wouldn't be any of his uncles, would it?" Paul asked, pulling the curtain aside to look out. "He isn't too popular, you know. He's a lot too radical. Do you know, Edmund, he'd actually, old Habib would, make peace with the Israelis!"

"I didn't know that!"

"New light, eh? My word, it's a gay ball, isn't it, really—"

"In the present state of things, not unlikely. Well, I'm off. I'll be bathed, shaved, and reading the Sunday's at ten or so—"

"Good-oh, Edmund. What I love about you is the *abandon*. That soupçon of go-and-have-a-game in everything you do. It's fantastic the way you sling yourself about. 's Consuelo found out you sleep with your hat on?"

"She's about to, I hope. Good morning!"

I found a policeman beside me in the lift, and out in the street. There was a distinct whistle in the morning wind, the paving still shone from a night rain, and the deep blue dawn sky held a ragged edge of gold in puffy clouds, slowly breaking, grey, crumbling, wisping by the top of the Eiffel Tower.

"More rain coming," the policeman said. "I'm sick of it!"

"Freshens things up?"

"You ought to do a few nights on the beat. See how your corns feel!"

That shut me up rather nicely, and I went into the hotel agreeing with him. The night concierge was just going off duty, but since the porters were cleaning, and he and I were old friends, he took me up.

"Is it true that Prince Habib—" he began.

"True—"

He was silent for a moment, watching the floors indicator.

"I don't know what's happening to us," he said, not looking at me. "I mean, to the world. It's no pleasure to open a paper. Poor people taken off the street? But who'd dream of it? I'm ashamed to go home and tell the wife. He was only here, what?

—two—days ago. Gave a dinner. They made a lovely scene downstairs. From Arabia, India, ah, yes, China—"

I seemed to burn from the feet up.

"Look, Nicol," I said, and took out the wallet. "Get me the names of all the guests—"

"Twelve or fourteen of them. Many women—"

"Get me their names. And addresses, if possible. But *now!*"

He nodded, I got out, and he went down. I couldn't wait to get to my room and the telephone. But in my hurry, I must have made a lot of noise. I'd just got on to Paul, and Consuelo came in, adorably half-awake, hair in tangles to her waist, and holding the dog in both arms.

I patted the bed beside me.

"Paul? In the desk drawer, there's a letter folder with names and addresses. I didn't have time for a real look. See if there's anyone from the Far East. Remember the piece at the Opera?"

"On!"

"I'll be back to you—"

I turned to meet open mutiny.

"You're going *back?*"

"After I've bathed. And shaved. And got into pajamas—"

"What are *they* for?"

"So that I don't catch cold—"

"Eddie will keep you warm—"

"You wouldn't?"

Eddie went sailing overhead in a two-handed fling and landed with a thump against her wall, fortunately. We went back in a rib-breaker, across the bed, kissed for moments. In a sudden stopping of the senses, almost of breath, I felt the strength of heartbeats, the slow tracing of a tender hand at the nape, and wished that living held nothing more, nothing less.

The buzzer made that sound.

She lay back a fraction, staring.

"The Police?" she whispered. "I'm always found out. Oh, damn—!"

I got up and went to the door. Nicol gave me a menu, and a folded paper.

"One address I can't find, sir. I'll have it from the day man, and he'll send it up. Good morning, sir!"

Two names on the list were perhaps from Malaysia, three were Chinese, one French woman, one Italian male.

"Checking the laundry?" Consuelo asked.

I picked up Eddie and threw him at her.

"You get into that bed, to begin with. I'm going to use the phone for a moment. Then I'm going to bathe, shave—"

"Don't shave. You're wasting time—"

"If I don't, I'll scratch your chin off—"

"Scratch it off, I don't care. We're wasting time. And no more telephones!"

I had instant thought of Paul.

"Right," I said. "No telephones, no shave, or anything else?"

"And I'll scrub your back. Might just as well go the whole hog—"

12

The dressing table clock said ten to ten. I looked up at angels flying in and out of darkness across the ceiling. The telephone snur-r-r-ed beside my left ear. A small lamp winked with the snurr-rr-snurr. I never heard a more snobbishly restful sound. It seemed to say "If you've got enough money to stay here, then you can afford to ignore me. Press the white button, I'll stop, and you turn over. Why not?"

Indeed. Consuelo was marvelously warm beside me.

But I suddenly came wide awake. Gauffure, of course.

"Mr. Trothe? I disturb you?"

"Yes, Inspector. You're late!"

"Ah, if you knew! Well, in one hour, at eleven o'clock, please be at Notre Dame. If you are at the center door, look to the left, on the corner of the railings across the road. Two men will recognise you by raising their hats. You will raise yours. One of them will be my son. A man will then approach you as a beggar. He will be wrapped in a sheet of transparent plastic. He will offer a beret, very old, worn in a curious manner, for your contribution. He will walk toward the right-hand side. After a few minutes, you will follow. When he reaches the corner, he will turn to the back of the Cathedral. But you will cross the road opposite you, to the right-hand corner of the railings. When

you reach the corner, a car will stop in front of you. It will be—
you call it a station wagon?—with the windows plastered in paper.
At the moment the rear door opens, the beggar will come behind
you. Two women will get out, with a child. Behind them will be
the Prince Habib. He will have a blanket round his shoulders.
When you see him, give the beggar the money. Have a car somewhere near, but not on that stretch of roadway. To your left,
along the street—the long leg, as you approach the Cathedral, on
your right—you can leave a car. It's not far to walk. Do I make
myself clear?"

"If you've got him, why not bring him here?"

"My friends don't like the zone. It's alive with metropolitan
Police. We are not in their area!"

"All right. I'll be there—"

"At eleven? On the point!"

Eleven o'clock on a Sunday morning outside Notre Dame
didn't sound very dangerous. But there's nothing like taking care
of details. I kissed Consuelo's silken shoulder, got carefully out
of bed, showered, and shaved. Before I dressed, I took an extra
refill for my little friend, and as a precaution, I dislodged three of
my little stickers from the flap of the briefcase and clipped one
inside the right-hand pocket of my raincoat, one in the left, and
one to the inner leg of my trouser, at the ankle. Since it was
raining, I'd chosen flannels and a jacket, took an umbrella,
looked for a long moment, and sent a kiss among the hair spread
over the sheets, turned out the light and went downstairs. There
was still a drizzle.

"How long will it take you to find a cab?" I asked the porter
outside.

"In this, sir? Private hire's best. Where are you going sir?"

"Notre Dame. And wait for me—"

I went inside to call Paul, and got Grethe instead.

"Mr. Chamby went out for a shave, Mr. Trothe. So far, nothing
very new. All the people have now been called. Nobody had
anything to say, of course. It's in all the papers. The radio. Who
wants to be involved, after all?"

"Tell Mr. Chamby I ought to be there about eleven thirty. How is the Prince Azil?"

"Very ill, sir. Not to be disturbed. His brothers aren't much better. The place is full of visitors. Nobody, not a single one of the staff to do anything!"

"Where're Prince Azil's own personal servants?"

"Police've got the lot, sir!"

An Isotta-Fraschini turned into the carway, and the porter lifted his cap. I got into solid leathern comfort, and sat back, ready at last to think of Consuelo.

I'd never known anyone like her. I thought I'd had a fair acquaintance of women. I found I hadn't. I was more than astonished that I could have worked closely for almost nine years without knowing the first thing about her, except that in the office she was in a class of her own. She'd been in the early twenties when she joined me. That, in itself, was an additional barrier, because I held to the principle of no familiarity with junior staff. I'd known nothing about her till she'd resigned from the Civil Service when our Department closed down and went to study for a degree. She'd come to visit me in my new quarters at Whitehall, I'd taken her home, and from that moment I'd realized she was more than a paper-chaser. If she hadn't told me first, I doubt I'd ever have been able to tell her that I loved her. Those words had always stuck in my throat. I'd never liked showing feelings. But that's a matter of training. Perhaps. Training or not, Consuelo was more honest. That I wasn't made me honor her the more, and so far as I'm concerned, love's very much a matter of honor. There's precious little without it. Apart from that—with a marriage behind me, a married daughter and an older son—I was really terrified of making a mistake. For her sake. She was far too fine a girl to make a fool of, and with the sort of temperament that in passion gives without thinking, it's always too easy. I hadn't her sort of honesty. It takes some facing. A god-that-was begins to crumble. I had to see that, and admit it, first.

In this hippie day it ought to be enough to take any girl to bed if she wants, or if *you* want, and think no more about it. All very well, I suppose, when honor's a joke to some. But not Consuelo. So far as I was concerned, not. Not that I was above it, or any stuff like that. Not the type, that's all.

We were going up the right-hand side of the square in front of the Cathedral. It was eight minutes to the hour, and there weren't more than about fifty people walking to, past, or away from the side door. The center door was shut. Two pairs of lovers talked in the shadows, which I thought felicitous, since lovers rarely have time for anyone else. I wished I was back in bed. I'd never had such a couple of hours. I'd known passion in women before, but not the tender, all-giving strength of Consuelo's, that clung, gloried, and drained. I felt hollow, and I ached quite pleasantly. And I'd have given anything for a cup of coffee. I realized I'd have to keep my wits about me.

Before I was quite ready, the beggar was at my side. He was wrapped or bound in a dirty sheet of transparent plastic which made him look like a Michelin man run to seed. I couldn't see his face for a shag of hair, but the beret in his palm had been creased in rings and hardened, perhaps with soap, like a jelly mold. I gave him some money, and without thanks he crammed it in the depths, and dropped the beret on top of his head, a three-tiered mini-crown, the last size of a small bun. Even the lovers gave him some money and smiled at the turn-out. Two men walked to the corner on my left about a hundred yards away, stood talking, and looked over at me. They waited a moment, and as one, raised their hats.

I raised mine.

A blinding flash that wasn't in the day, and a thunder clap nobody else heard hit me together. I stood there, absolutely dazed.

I'd forgotten the money. It was in the bottom drawer of the commode. I could see it.

The beggar had gone. The two men were walking across the street, away from me. I couldn't warn anybody. The plan had been carpentered to the smallest detail, that was clear enough.

There was no room for a thirty-minute pause while Mr. Trothe raced back to open a drawer.

Gauffure's son and the other man were looking to their left. The beggar was the tripwire. I walked to the right, and looked round the corner. He was a fair way down, facing the turning in front. Obviously, he was giving a "clear" to the car coming up— and into—the one-way street in front of the Cathedral. In despair, cursing and hoping, I crossed the street, pacing slowly, and stopped on the opposite corner, looking over at the center doors, wishing I'd had time to pray. I had a feeling that in this, prayer wouldn't help. Any notion that my carelessness could rob Habib of a quick return to his family, or put his life in balance, made me feel ill. Ah, Consuelo, I thought, it's nothing to do with you!

The beggar was crossing toward me at a corn-and-bunion hop, which hardly let him put one foot flat before he picked it up and put the other down with a kickety in between, a fair performance if it was an act, or if not, then a lovely bit of the current scene. Almost before I'd finished looking at him, the car crossed a yard in front of me, windows plastered with *Le Temps*, *Figaro*, and *Match*, mud-spattered, with clay still hanging from the undercarriage. One of the men in front got down, key in hand, and opened half of the rear door.

Two women bent to be helped out, a child in pink wool was lifted and set down. The younger woman jumped, the older was held for a moment and found her feet, the child was taken by the hand, and the three walked, blowing out breaths and filling their lungs, straight in front, without thanks or a look. The inside was rank with the fumes of petrol. The man with the key looked round at me. There wasn't anybody else except the beggar. I could still smell that petrol, and understood the women wanting fresh air.

The other half-door swung out. The smell of petrol was stronger.

Habib in a brown blanket, saw me.

I shall never forget that look, of scalding hope.

I didn't hesitate.

"I haven't got the money, but we can settle that—" I had time to say.

The man slammed the door he'd been holding, reached for the other. The beggar—from the corner of my eye—flung himself at me. But that's always a silly thing to do. I caught him fair on the nape with a downward chop, and as he went forward I gave him another crack on the beret with my little friend. The man at the door barely had time to see it when I had the barrel in the small of his back.

"Get in and keep your mouth shut!" I said. "Your highness will be safe in a very few moments. Lift up your heart!"

"Ah, my friend!" I heard him say, and I slammed the door.

The car went in gear and began moving. I ran to the front. Luckily the window was down, and I jumped and hung on with my feet dragging.

"Brake!" I said. "I'll spread you—"

Wise after his fashion, he put both feet in. I opened the door and sat down.

"Listen to me!" I said. "Drive direct to the hotel Plaza Athenee, Avenue Montaigne. That's where you pick up the money!"

"It's outside my orders. We'll be in trouble in a couple of minutes!"

"How?"

"We're watched all the way—"

The man was really frightened. I could still smell petrol in the interior. In all probability, they meant to burn the car afterwards. A shot in the right place could burn it now. We wouldn't stand much of a chance. Especially if there were a banana or two of dynamite, or some other prime help to disintegration.

"Turn here!" I said, on the corner.

"It's one way—!"

I slammed him across the eyes, kicked his foot off the button and grabbed the wheel, pulling down. We were about halfway over the fairway, but we turned sharp, almost ran into a car coming up, stopped a moment, and then I found the button and went on down a couple of hundred yards to my car. Cap back, head on the seat, the chauffeur was dozing. Somebody was shouting behind us.

"Get out!" I said, and took the key. "Walk round the front where I can see you. Don't fool, eh?"

He did as he was told, walked in front of me when I got down, and I threw him the key.

"Open up!" I said. "When the Prince is out, you get in. Tell Inspector Gauffure to call on me for the money at three o'clock—!"

"You're not going to lock me up in there?" he pleaded. "No, listen. I've got my family—"

"Behave yourself and all's well," I said, pulling the leaf open. I put a hand in, and felt Habib's trembling clutch, helping him into the light. But the fool inside proved himself by trying to jump me, and at the same moment, the driver thought he'd help. But though Habib was near the sixties, he hadn't fought all his life without learning a few tricks. He ripped his hand out of mine, and with a snarl any tiger might have envied, he stuck two straight fingers directly into the man's eyes, almost drove the eyeballs into the back of his head, and went for his throat.

With his teeth.

The man next to me was ill-advised. He was still teary from the knuckle-slap, and misjudged his punch. I had the right-hand leaf still open, and all I had to do was slam it against him, and follow with a kick square in the mouth.

I reached in to pull at Habib. I thought he'd been hurt. But it was the other man's blood. He almost fell out beside me, and I held him round the waist and scudded him the few yards to my car. The chauffeur was awake, licking his mouth, a little startled.

"Come on!" I said. "Quick!"

I put Habib in, and through the glass divide, saw three men running down next to the railings, on the inside of the parked car. I got out and ran to meet them.

"Which of you is young Gauffure?" I shouted.

They pulled up, but instead of wanting to talk they came out with .38s, crouched, left hand and gun hand pointing toward me,

122

ready. I didn't wait. I put a round on the paving between the three, merely as a warning.

My little friend—as I'd got used to calling him—was different from ordinary firearms. It was doll-sized, fired a bullet not much larger than a small vitamin capsule, made about as much noise as a quiet sniff, worked on a rocket principle, and for its size did unbelievable damage.

The paving stone the bullet hit leapt in a thousand chips, spraying all three, drawing instant blood. They dropped the .38s. One of the men had a nosebleed.

"You're giving yourself too much trouble," I said. "Tell Inspector Gauffure I shall expect him at three o'clock. Are these two in the wagon friends of yours?"

Nosebleed nodded, lapped the run.

I threw him the key.

"Let them out, and behave yourselves," I said. "If I have to shoot again, there'll be more than one funeral!"

Nosebleed waved the key in denial.

I went back to the car, nodded to the chauffeur, and while we pulled out, watched the three go down to the station wagon. We turned a corner. A police car was parked farther down, and on the corner of the first turning, another.

"If there's trouble here, hold tight," I said. "I'll shoot through it—"

"If there is plenty of blood, it is in perfect accord with my present disposition," Habib said, sitting up, calm, ready. "I am a little tired, a little hungry. Couldn't we stop for something?"

"We stop at the Prince Azil's apartment," I said firmly. "It's a fortress, with the best kitchen in Europe. Seven minutes!"

The police didn't even look at us as we passed.

Habib leaned over, offering his hand, smiling in a lift of one side of his mouth. We shook, and he sat back, closing his eyes. He was unwashed, he wasn't in his own clothes, and the rope-soled rags he wore showed a big toe among the drying clay.

"They didn't ill-treat you?" I asked.

"Twice I thought I was going to die," he said quietly, without opening his eyes.

"They wanted money?"

He shook his head.

"I offered them money. Anything—"

"Who were they? What sort of treatment?"

"I was pushed in the car and thrown on the floor. Hands and feet tied. Something over my head. Three heavy men. We stopped. I think it was the quiet place at the end of the Boulevard Raspail before the bridge. But I'm guessing, from the way our car turned. I was pulled out and carried to that truck I came in. We ran for a long time, an hour or more, to another car. On again. I slept. Then I was carried. They cut the string on my hands and feet. When they took the bag off, I was in a dark room, only a lamp shining in my eyes. Somebody put down a bottle of whisky. I asked for milk or lemon water. There was none. A man with an unusual voice, asked me to accept his apology for such an interview. I said if he wanted money, to ask, and give me a piece of paper—"

"What sort of voice?"

"Not French. I don't know. The words had a slippery sound—"

"Slippery?"

"Not, I suppose, not sharp. How many people know the share structure of the Company?"

"Well," I said, a little surprised. "Let's see. Board of Directors, Paul Chamby, myself, Miss Masters, Miss Furnival—perhaps—McGregor, the accountant, two or three more in his office, possibly. Why?"

"Isn't it a close secret?"

"Yes, it is. Are you suggesting it's not?"

"How could it be known that forty percent of the stock hasn't been issued?"

"I don't know—"

"Well. He wanted that forty percent, and half of all the remaining stock in the name of my brothers and myself. That would mean absolute control. The stock would be owned by a Swiss company. All contracts would be considered in abeyance until the new Director took charge. Then he would decide which contract should proceed, and which terminate. In any case, all to do with *materiél* of any kind would be cancelled—"

"That would mean millions in damages alone—"

"Yes. But, he pointed out, I would be alive to enjoy many things—"

"Meaning you mightn't be alive?"

"Or my brothers. Or my uncles. We must have a strong guard at the clinic—"

"How could this operate?"

"I couldn't ask anything. Only he spoke. How could they? It would be found, never fear. I couldn't sign papers, on oath, if it wasn't true. I had also to sign a letter to my uncle and my brothers, and another for the other Directors. Mr. Chamby and yourself, and many others would be paid and sent away. All this time the light was shining in my eyes. I saw nothing except that light. I couldn't move. But I could smell. She was on the other side of the table. It's a perfume I know. I don't remember the name. She seemed to be helping. I didn't hear anything from her—"

"What did you decide?"

"No."

It was the quietest No I ever heard. In those moments, while it hung, it seemed to hold some of the quality of Fiat Lux, echoing through the reign of time to voids undreamt, though meanwhile filling me with respect, and gross anger, that he'd had to go through it.

"Were you threatened?"

"I was told I would stay in the same position until I agreed. I was not allowed to go to the lavatory. Or drink. Or close my eyes. My back hurt me—"

"How were you brought here?"

"There was a fight. It was very serious. Many hurt. I had this blanket thrown over me. I was put in the car, and that's all.

I shall fly to Lausanne this afternoon, and home tonight. It will be a long time before I come to Paris again!"

"I'm sorry to hear that!"

He reached out a hand as the car stopped under the awning.

"Without your help, I couldn't say it. I couldn't think of this afternoon or tomorrow. I am grateful, Edmund. I shall meet my brothers, and bath my tired body. Let us say, in two hours, we meet upstairs? But what are all these policemen doing? I am so important?"

"No, sir. They probably heard about all the girls up there!"

13

Consuelo was dressed when I went in, but it didn't take her long to undress—and I understand the appeal of the strip tease, since it holds a world of promise that's never kept—and by the time we thought of looking at a clock, it was too late to lunch decently. Neither of us liked the idea of hurrying through a meal, or for that matter, anything else. And we hadn't.

"The really nice thing about being in love is that it hasn't a timetable," she said, lining an eye. "And it's no use trying to look innocent, is it? Look at me!"

I started under the small curls at her neck and kissed all the way down the pale hills of her spine, with two smackers for the warm white cushions.

"That's the correct answer," I said. "A little plate at the Relais, and I'll just have time to get there by three o'clock. It's extraordinary, but I've almost lost any sense of time. I don't like to think it's anything to do with you. But between you and the clock, there's simply no choice!"

"Glad of that," Consuelo murmured. "It's hours since you kissed me!"

I took care of it, and called Paul.

"Edmund, my word!" he began. "You're tremendous. Listen, first. There's this Inspector Gauffure, he's looking very umpty, waiting here for you. Says you've got something?"

"Correct. I'll be there at three, or he can come here now, and get it. How's everybody?"

"There's been such a ruckus here, I can't start to tell you. Everybody was cheering and crying and laughing, all at the same time. Azil's up and almost himself again. Habib's in bed with a roomful of girls. They're really fond of him, you know? It's the diamonds. Anyway, I've had the reports from everywhere except El Humir. I'm 'on' all the time. Everything else is normal. Nothing went to Lausanne about the reward. The newspapers don't know he's free yet. He's leaving on the four o'clock. I've got a dozen heavyweights for a bodyguard. I'm leaving on the eight tonight. Be in Leicester tomorrow morning. Come back Tuesday, midday. What's your program?"

"An appointment with Chapman Ryder at seven thirty to-morrow—"

"Seven *thir*ty? What, in the morning?"

"Early bird. Back here about six tomorrow. All right?"

"Keep in close touch with El Humir. I don't like it—"

"Agreed. Heard anything from Rome?"

"Normal. Oh, wait a minute. What's the matter with me? In addition to Mariotti, and the others—there's no trace of them—Truffo, that Lieutenant feller—he's been found dead. No details. You'll be there when?"

"Thursday, en route to Cairo."

"Where do we meet?"

"Tell you at three o'clock. We've just got time for a sandwich—"

For a little something to eat, I don't think there's anywhere to touch the Relais Plaza. I don't know why. I always found the chairs a little small, the tables so close that at times you can be mopping up the other chap's gravy. But that's all part of the atmosphere, though I couldn't describe it beyond the mirrors, the many-bottled bar, the staircase, and of course, the world's most beautiful women—of all ages—at any time. It's simply that an ordinary ham sandwich isn't ordinary at the Relais. Consuelo ordered eggs benedict, which I thought a contradiction under the circumstances, and I had a favorite chicken liver and eggs, with a white wine. I told her what had been happening. Her eyes were almost the size of the plate.

"I didn't for a moment think you'd be in *any*thing like *that,* darling!" she whispered. "And I was sleeping—!"

"As well—"

"But supposing—my God, how selfish—!"

"You couldn't have done anything."

I saw Inspector Gauffure before he saw me. Fortunately, I'd finished. I nodded toward the small door into the hotel, excused myself, took the bag from under the table, and followed him. He didn't look a bit happy.

"Here," I said. "Before you say anything, count that!"

"Ah, but not here!" he said, in a bad-tempered mumble. "We are not entirely in order, sir. Things were not done—"

"Everything was done and it's all settled!" I said. "Now start counting, or I'll get the cashier to do it. For ten percent!"

I led him into the lounge facing the Avenue, that always looks so ready for a coffin. He sat in a corner armchair, put his hat on the floor, and opened the bag, a plastic shirt-cover, and took out the first bundle. They were all sealed in amounts of 100,000 by the Bank. He looked at the seals on five, and began to smile.

"I knew I could trust you, Mr. Trothe!" he began, pleasantly enough. "My son—"

"Tell me the details," I said, putting another chair directly in front of him. "Please remember I know the facts on the other side—"

"But this was not the bargain—"

"It was, certainly—!"

"We said nothing of details. You said if I produced evidence to show who were the instigators there would be a further half million!"

"True. Who are they?"

He put the money carefully—lovingly is perhaps the better word—and there's something a little sickening about the way a pair of scrawny hands fondles money—back in the bag, put it between his feet, straightened his tie, reassumed that air of diffidence. Which disappointed me. It wasn't a natural characteristic, but stuck on like a false nose. That meant I had to watch for other falsities. People do so give themselves away.

"Well, now, the three who did the job in the street were controlled by the driver of the car. When the Prince was carried to another car, the three original idiots were paid, and went away. One drank too much in a bar, and one of his men got on to my son, and then we knew who the three were. They were paid a large sum, and they had a rehearsal every night, at the same place and time, for the past three weeks. The information came from the waiter at the restaurant. He telephoned the garage at the moment the Prince and his friends went off. No difficulty. We have the man. Not the second driver, yet. But when the Prince was transferred to the other car—ah! who was the third driver?"

"Who?"

He raised a hand. He was enjoying the story.

"We put the garage attendant in a doubtful position—or at least—my son did. In garages, there are tools and electricity, and sensible men make up their minds very quickly—"

"I understand. Go on!"

"The driver is a student, a young man, not quite a playboy, but he likes money to spend. He talks to the girls. Girls also talk. And so, when the Prince was taken out of the station wagon, he went back to his favorite cafe, and he talked. My son received a call from a girl, and he was taken for questioning. Since he is more intelligent than a garage mechanic, he spoke faster. He gave us an address in Neuilly, and spoke of a fellow-student, a girl, who introduced him. It was an anti-war movement, to give the Prince Habib certain terms which would bring the Arab states to the conference table with Israel. The Prince would never meet them. They took other measures—"

"Indeed!"

"We went to the girl's house. She told us—I think innocently—that she'd done nothing wrong, and didn't know that a man was to be taken off the street. At this point, her father, a banker, demanded she tell everything or he would whip her raw. I believed him, and so did she, and she directed us to a house further away. Again, a large house, with many cattle. We saw the station wagon, and many other cars on the other side. About a dozen or more. We had ten men with us. We made sure of the men on guard outside. When they saw the uniforms, of course, it was enough. They were all police pensioners. We entered. In the room on the first floor we heard a meeting. Somebody was talking. I went downstairs—what a stroke of fortune!—and found two men watching the Prince. They were also pensioners—"

"Good. Then they can tell us what was said—"

"They didn't understand a word. One of the pensioners served in Tonkin. He said they looked like Tonkinese. He could swear to it!"

"How were these pensioners employed? Who paid them?"

"Well, now. A man we didn't arrest found them all in the agency, here. They find odd jobs for police pensioners. They pay very well. That man was a Frenchman. The others also spoke good French—"

"Nobody else there? Just the pensioners, and two men?"

"They said at least four other men stood at the back. But it was dark—"

"No women?"

"No, no women. I asked. In these cases—"

"Yes?"

"Where you find Arabs, you must look at the possibility of blackmail—"

"Is that all you have to tell me?"

"Well, we arrested eight—"

"All pensioners?"

"Yes—"

"But you're sure the Prince won't press charges against any of them because—?"

"He said that before we left. He didn't want anybody held—"

"But still you hammered together that nonsense at the Cathedral—"

"There was a reward, we must remember, Mr. Trothe. If the Police in this zone knew, do you think we'd have got through? After all, they also would like a piece!"

"They'd have kidnapped him again? Get along with you!"

"They'd claim the reward! Of course. And hold on till it was assured. And us? We'd be disciplined, at the least, for going out of our district—!"

"I don't believe a word of it!"

"Mr. Trothe!"

"How do you expect me to? Who were the people talking *up*stairs?"

"A meeting of sympathisers for the Viet Cong, and all that sort of activity. Most of them students. More than forty people up there—"

"A man had been kidnapped, and you let them all go? How much were you paid?"

He was looking at me in what he hoped, I suppose, was glacial distaste. Instead, it made him appear undernourished.

"The Prince particularly requested us not to make arrests," he said. "He didn't want any court appearances. He wanted to leave the country peacefully this afternoon—"

"Why the business at the Cathedral?"

"They thought they'd be caught by Launceville's people, here. The reward—"

"You've been paid. Now. Who were these 'Tonkinese'?"

He took a sheet of paper from his pocket, unfolded it, and held it out.

"These can be checked," he said sharply. "The house was rented for six months. The owners of the farm live in a smaller house about a kilometer away. The people who rented it paid six months in advance. They were there not quite five months. They had many well-attended meetings. Anti-war in Vietnam, anti-war in Israel. There was a lot of printed stuff. Most of the people were young. Good families. I'm sure nobody knew what was happening down below—"

"Which is the woman's name here?" I asked, looking at the

list. None of them was more than Parisian telephone book, well-worn European, two French, one with a touch of Belgian. "Where are the Tonkinese?"

"They have the names of their French fathers," he said. "How many thousands had French fathers? There were no women!"

"*You* check them," I said. "Addresses, who they are. Prince Habib was under considerable nervous strain, remember. His brothers are stamping for action. There's an ambassador here. You're not going to appear in a good light, Inspector!"

"I have these three in custody at my old station," he said, without a blink. "Question them when you please!"

"What will you charge them with?"

"My son will do as I tell him. If they answer questions, they can go. If not, their visas are not in order—!"

I got up, feeling I was in the middle of a charade for mental invalids.

"I'll send a friend of mine to see your precious three," I said. "If he finds any one of them of use to us, and gives us the information we want, you shall be paid. If not, nothing. Four o'clock, here, in the foyer?"

"Who is this man?"

"Chief Superintendent Lucien des Vosges. You may remember him? He was famous enough!"

I'll swear he changed color.

"Ah, but, naturally! I shall be honored. You will see if I have earned my money or not. You don't believe me, but you'll believe him? Ah, Mr. Trothe!"

I was unmoved by the reproach in his eyes and voice. I had no evidence he hadn't told the truth. Crime and criminals were nurtured in the sub-realms of the unbelievable.

"Come up to the Prince Azil's apartment with the Superintendent when you've finished. I won't mention money in his presence. What I want from both of you is the name, or names, of the people who kidnapped the Prince Habib. Is that clear?"

He half-bowed.

"We shall be there, never fear, sir. And you will pay me there, later?"

"On the spot, *if* you have the stuff!"

I found Consuelo in the foyer. She looked at me and turned away, took my arm, and we walked out in the pour under my umbrella. I went over what I remembered of the talk, and at the end, she laughed.

"Sounds just stupid enough to be true," she said. "Look at that Post Office train robbery. All sounded so romantic till the Police told the story, didn't it? I saw some of them in court. You'd never believe any of them capable—"

"This is a little different, surely?"

"I don't see why? There's somebody using people. Same thing!"

"Doesn't hang together. What *does* tickle my interest far more, is this mention of Tonkinese. Anything to do with this Asian will-o'-the-wisp we've been chasing?"

"Has the Inspector that sort of imagination? Tonkin was a French colony. Why would he mention it? And why tell a tale he knew you'd check? He knows what sort of—of *horror*—you are!"

There were policemen in the foyer which prevented my immediate reply, and one of them had to come up with us. He tried not to look at Consuelo, and since neither of us looked at him, he stood there and stared at her, and I knew what he was thinking. So did she.

"One of these days, a man's going to look at me like that, and I'll pull my clothes up!" she whispered, walking through the lounge. "That'll learn him!"

"Case of rape!"

"That sort? Never!"

Paul waited for me in the small study. Consuelo took away a pile of reports, and we looked through the week's journal first, and set the work for the week to come.

"El Humir's still not coming on the air," Paul said. "I'm worried. I sent Logan over there with a squad of paratroopers. If there's anything wrong, they won't drop, and we'll know about seven tonight from Ryadh. We ought to have a parachute plane of our own. Always useful. I'll talk it over with Habib. About time he appeared—"

"Among all this, what can we do about Yorick?"

He put the pen down and clasped his hands.

"I've thought about it, off and on, Edmund. I don't like to think we might be able to do something, and pass it over because it's too much trouble. See what you can pick up in London. And don't forget Von Staengl, here. Wait a minute. Let me call—"

A footman came in, and bowed.

"His highness presents compliments to Mr. Trothe, and waits his convenience, if he pleases!" he almost bellowed. "This way, sir!"

"Good luck!" Paul said. "Ask for a rise. Me, too!"

Habib, in a double-breasted grey flannel, white buttoned-down shirt, blue tie, cropped head, henna-tipped beard, freshly shaven, looked a little peaked, but fit. Azil, in flannels, and a green jersey didn't seem any the worse for a night on pills, and the other two, in long white burnous, held out their arms and embraced me.

"Edmund, we pay tribute as a family," Habib said. "If not for you, I am not here. I am sure they meant what they said. I would stay there. I would never sign. You know the meaning of never?"

"I have an idea—"

"We have made a decision among ourselves," Azil said, offering me the box of cigarettes. "It is our opinion that perhaps my uncles planned this conspiracy, that is to say, my father's brothers. Perhaps. We don't know. We don't wish to know more about it. Not one word. It is our wish. I shall do what I please to do. I am no longer part of this pipeline project. I never wish to hear the sound of those words again!"

"It is also my wish," Fuad said. "Without a pipeline, I am still a happy man!"

"For me, I wish a pipeline only to people who don't like horses," Niz'r said. "I am flying tonight. I don't come back for years, and when I do, I bring my own bodyguard!"

"That's how I think, for the moment," Habib said. "Perhaps the moment will last for years. I am homesick for my family. Azil, the proposition, if you please!"

"Edmund, we are grateful, more than words, more than blood," Azil said. "We have our brother. It's enough. Here is a paper we have signed. So far as we are concerned, it is legal. But call the lawyers. We want to sign immediately, if you agree—"

"But, your highness, gentlemen," I said. "You haven't told me. Agree to what?"

They collapsed as if it were the joke of all time. They pointed at me, themselves, the paper. They were bent double, trilling, coughing.

"You think we are mad?" Habib said, wiping his eyes. "No. Only very happy. Look, Edmund. I pass in your name, my shares in the Company for ten years. In ten years, you return fifty percent, one half, to my sons. That is, one half of the shares as they are in ten years from now. No money. Only shares, so that what the market yields in the eleventh year, is theirs, conjointly, and thereafter. You will be a co-guardian, I hope—"

"Sir," I began, fogged. "Um—I—"

"My shares entirely, for the same period, same arrangement," Azil said, looking out of the window. "I am already twenty years younger!"

"Mine, of course," Fuad said, through a handkerchief.

"And, naturally, I am with my brothers," Niz'r said, taking a sweetmeat out of the bowl and chewing over the words. "I have business enough with horses!"

"Further, the unissued stock will go entirely in your name for ten years, and fifty percent will then revert to us, again conjointly," Habib said. "This is fair, I think? Considering I shouldn't be speaking except for you—"

"And we would give ten years, a hundred times more, to have those dogs in front of us!" Azil said. "Unfortunately, in this country, it's not permitted—"

"We don't think about it," Habib said, with an impatient gesture. "Well, Edmund?"

136

"You're giving me com*plete* control of the Company?" I asked, on the ropes. "With your shares and the forty percent I outvote everybody—"

Habib showed pink palms, and raised his shoulders.

"But, Edmund," he said, quietly. "There isn't anyone else. You own the Company—!"

"Together with holdings, and the et ceteras," Azil said. "I can show you what you own!"

"You accept?" Habib said.

"What will be Mr. Chamby's position?" I asked, thinking forward, through a blazing hedge. "His contract has eighteen months to run. He doesn't want to continue after that—"

"It's for you to decide," Azil said. "You're the—what do you say?—boss?"

I couldn't look at any of them. I could barely breathe. But one thought stuck.

"I don't want Mr. Chamby to know about this, if it can be helped. He'd never remain, knowing he was virtually second to me. We need him. I'll accept, if this proposal remains strictly among ourselves, for the time being. There's no need for anyone else to know, is there? At any rate, for some time to come?"

Azil started feeling in his hip pocket. Habib turned to look at him, very much the older, benevolent brother.

"That's right!" he crowed. "We had a bet. He said you'd accept, and make the 'diplomatic' approach. I said you'd say exactly what you did. Edmund, you are our brother-*manqué*. Pay, Azil, pay! Pay up, my boy!"

14

Being a millionaire takes a little getting used to.

I must say I enjoyed it from the first moment. My "riches" were only on paper for the most part, but I knew more or less what we had as cash reserves, and that, added to the vast credits we'd been granted, brightened a far rosier future than I could ever have imagined. But I couldn't tell Consuelo. For the moment.

The team of lawyers made little enough of it, and at about four thirty, I was asked to see Azil again, and we signed, drank a loving cup of a nectar I'd never tried before, made from pomegranates, and I was called back to the office by Paul. He'd thought I'd been with the Police.

"You're having quite a time," he called. "Here's Lucien des Vosges!"

We all went into the office and shut the door. The Superintendent wasn't tall but broad. And he'd lost his waist since we'd last met. His head had always been shaven, but he'd let the hair grow in a grey mop of short hooks, which gave him a surprisingly youthful appearance. With a French face—long nose, rather fruity, and small grey eyes—he wasn't a man to forget. He sat in the old way, leaning forward in the chair and holding his ankles with those plowman's hands, the more noticeable because he kept them white.

Inspector Gauffure nursed his hat. He looked sat on.

"Your Tonkinese are only French-born Cochinese," he said, without a howd'y do. "Two are shipping clerks up here for the weekend from Le Havre. The other's a bill clerk in the same company's Paris office. The three are in this anti-Vietnam War movement. The fares of the two from Le Havre were paid by check. We shall find out the account tomorrow. It's unfortunate I wasn't called before. The Inspector, here, was operating in an expressly forbidden area. He has some questions to answer, I must say. And he let everybody go except the people we might have wanted!"

"I had the victim—" the Inspector began. "Was I asked—?"

The Superintendent raised a flat, fending hand without looking round.

"Half a case," he said, from distance. "A victim? But your business is the criminal, naturally. However, we're not entirely lost. The people who rented the house have a collection of souvenirs. I'm going there at five thirty. The three Cochinese don't want to go. They're going to be recognised, I suspect. In addition, one had a hat check from the Hotel Bristol. What's a bill clerk doing there? The manager's a friend of mine. He's off till tonight. There are other little fantasies. For example, they all had more than fifty thousand francs each. Equal sums? Where from? Savings, of course. Gifts. Fifty thousand in a clerk's pocket? Three together? The income taxers will have to know. Not that I like to feed them, but they can help us, here—"

"Inspector Gauffure's report to me, in effect, was correct?" I asked.

"Perfectly," the Superintendent said. "Under cover of a legitimate movement to collect funds for the Viet, and to bring the Arabs and Israelis to the peace table, other types of eggs have been hatching. I suspect drugs. The kidnapping of a Prince could be an attempt of other types to extort money. He won't press charges? He could be made to!"

"I believe there's a movement higher up," Paul put in, deferentially. "There are Government influences here—"

"He's flying in thirty minutes," I said. "I don't think we'll see him or his brothers for some time to come!"

"We're not interested in the criminal?" the Superintendent said, in small surprise. "But *we* should like to make his acquaintance, I assure you!"

"All we're really interested in is the name or names of those involved. We think it's a conspiracy against our Company. Other attempts may be made—"

"I've provided Mr. Chamby and yourself with a sufficiency of bodyguards. They'll be beside you wherever you go!"

He stood. The Inspector looked like a child beside him.

"I'll get out there, and leave a report in writing," he said. "I'd like some petty cash for eventualities—"

I gave him the envelope I'd prepared, and walked with him to the lift. Paul came behind with the Inspector.

"You pay him nothing, you understand?" the Superintendent whispered, pointing behind. "He got into this under Launceville's nose, and very nearly cooked the barn. Launceville was late getting there because he had to book the other people. Who gets the reward?"

"Launceville, of course!"

He opened his hands, looking up, beaming.

"Ah, but now, Mr. Trothe, you make yourself a *corps* of friends!" he said, as the doors opened. "I'll leave my report—"

Inspector Gauffure bent his head in passing, and down they went.

"Funny lot," Paul said. "Now tell me what *you* make of all this!"

"I wasn't going to worry you with it," I said, a little uncomfortably. "We've had an afternoon getting Habib off the peg. Now he can go. But what do I make of it? I think it's part of the same job. Cairo. Rome, everything. Same people. Same touch. Next stop, one of us. We've got to be damn' careful!"

"I intend to be. Angela's not coming back with the Company. She raised hell, but I won't have it. I still don't understand why she was put down in that place—"

"Give them time to use her keys and look the place over, I should think. Then they galloped. What I'd like to know is, where to?"

"Perhaps the Prince Abdullah could tell us. He and his brothers are dead set against these lads here, Habib, Azil, and the others. The old man hasn't got a cent in the Company. They wouldn't let him in. I said at the time it was bad policy. The brother of the ruler of the country, and his entire clan and hangers-on against you? This kidnapping business looks just like them. Money buys anything. Except!"

"If they'd chosen better people, they'd have been home and dry. The man at the top doesn't speak the language well enough. He couldn't say exactly what he wanted, and he didn't want to say too much. He had to rely on inferior brains. Money's no good, there!"

We went in the small study, and began to sign the pile of paper Consuelo had left for us.

"It's about time these stores were loaded, isn't it?" Paul said, looking up from a manifest. "The tubing ought to be out by now. What are we going to do about Intelligence?"

"Unless they've got a solid answer, sack the lot!"

"I'll get some names from Barrett—"

I shook my head. That Xth sense again.

"I don't trust anybody in M.I. these days. There's the Commissioner of Police. Try his office for a few top-drawer men. Good head, steady, sound knowledge. That's what we want—"

An idea exploded like a burst of stars.

"Are you absolutely decided once for all that Angela's not coming back to the Company?" I asked gently.

"Nothing's going to change my mind, Edmund," he said, without looking up. "I've had a home all my married life. It's something I'll always be grateful to Moira for, because I've missed it. I hate hotels and bloody apartments. I want my own house. She's going to find a place and furnish it. That's going to take all her time. It'll be a couple of years till it's the way we want. She doesn't have to work, anyway. And when you take over the wheel, watch me beeline!"

"In that case, just as a stop-gap, and because I don't want her in any more Cairos, how about Consuelo taking over Intelligence? She knows it inside out—"

"I'll buy that!" Paul said, and put the pen down. "That's a solid step, that is. I've been worried about her, and a couple of the others. She'd be as safe as houses. Cut out for it. Let me have a little talk to her, will you?"

While he'd been speaking, I'd had the most extraordinary series of notions, quite new to me, and not altogether agreeable. I'd suddenly realised that he was no longer Director General, except at my whim. I was his employer. He no longer had a word to say about anything, anywhere. Not even by contract, since I could dismiss him, pay him, have done. I didn't even have to tell him. All I need do was pick up the telephone and instruct the Company attorney. I began to appreciate the discipline of spirit and will required by wealthy men if they were not to appear as small-souled monstrosities. I choked the phantoms, and went back to signing my name in full, so that Paul could write his initials as guarantee that my decisions were his, and in order.

Before we finished our pile of manifests, doors opened, voices clamored, and the brothers went off together in a crowd of girls throwing flower petals, singing and laughing. I saw only their hands waving to us in the lift over the heads of a dozen beauties crushed in with them. Those left behind shrieked for the other lifts, pounded the doors till they opened, pushed in, went down.

We were left, in silence. Perfume, and strewn flower petals stayed.

"That's the lot," Paul said. "Funny you can run a business like this, isn't it? They don't give a damn, Edmund. Women and horses. And the oil bubbles up moment by moment. To fill those barrels full of lovely lucre. Perhaps they're right? If you had the money, would you work?"

"Not sure," I said.

"I *am*. I've worked all my life. For somebody else. And they weren't worth it. I haven't done what I've wanted to do. Wasn't allowed to. When my time comes round with the Company, at least I'll have the satisfaction of knowing there's an industry in operation that wasn't there before. It's building the thing, that's what I like. We're lucky it's an easy build. The market's ready. All we've got to do is get the line from one place to another. If conditions stay half-stable, we're set. If anything happens to stop us, I mean, a war we couldn't do anything about, I'd simply go home—"

"What else do you see happening?"

We were walking toward the study. Paul looked at an Aubusson tapestry covering the wall.

"Took years of heart, and art, to make that, Edmund. A time when people thought about themselves. They were nationals, but not units. Not numbered voters. Fingerprinted. Crook-galleried, front and profile. They were people. We're not. I see a lot of things happening. I believe some of the Arabs are going to wait till we're almost finished. Then they'll start as they did in Aden. Taking advantage of the good old Christian. So-called. Soft-hearted is what we really are, you know. Just like the rest of them. Nuisancing first, and then shooting. Far's I'm concerned, they've started!"

"You don't think we'll finish?"

"Perhaps. Then they'll start a real schemozzle. They'll take over in their own sweet time. Haven't you ever thought so?"

"Because it's Arab-owned, no."

"We'll see. Let's try El Humir, again. After all, wasn't everything, Aden included, Arab-owned? Of course, now they've got to make it work themselves. That's a little different!"

He went slowly along the band of the radio. There wasn't a sound.

"That's a powerful station," he said worriedly. "Three good operators? What's gone on, there? If we don't hear by midday tomorrow, I shall have to go. Can't understand what's happened to Logan!"

Consuelo came in with the last sheaves.

"Let's have a little talk, shall we?" he said to her, and stood. "Out here's fine—"

He went out, Consuelo looked eyebrows-up at me, I blew her a kiss, got one back, and she shut the door. I finished signing paper, and leaned back, deciding where I'd take Consuelo to dinner, whether we ought to marry, however hurriedly, in London, if she ought to work at all, or if I shouldn't get someone in my place, leave Paul as Director General, and take my position as Chairman of the Board and virtual owner.

The idea of power has enchantment of its own.

Instead, I tried clix, and London's signal was clear, but Arturo in Rome didn't come on. I put in a call to him by telephone, but too late I remembered it was Sunday and the cafe was closed. I got Lausanne in moments, and the night operator reported many calls for Miss Furnival, otherwise normal.

"Who were the calls from?"

"Two from Athens, four from Rome, three from Beirut, one from Tallid, one from Cairo, and seven from London—"

"Give me the numbers—"

"They weren't taken, sir. I think they were our offices—"

"Before you accept any calls in future, verify the number. That is an order. Miss Furnival will be at the London office from Monday. Miss Frazer will take charge till I arrive—"

I got on to London, and found Hines on duty, a good, solid ex-C.P.O. in Royal Naval Signals.

"Yes, sir! Been trying to get you or Mr. Chamby since this morning—"

"What is it?"

"We had a fire, sir. Don't know how it happened. The firemen got it under fairly quick. But it burnt a lot of furniture. And the records. The staff's been in all day trying to save something. They just went home—"

"I'll be there about eight thirty or so in the morning—!"

I hadn't thought of fire. I was thinking, of course, of Consuelo. She wasn't going to be as safe in London as I'd imagined, and this was fair warning. Or might it be an accident?

Paul came in looking pleased enough.

"Settled!" he said. "I told her London'd start being a more important base because of the little troubles we've been having—what's up?"

"Hines just told me they've had a fire there—"

His eyes went from surprise to anger.

"Give up that office!" he said. "The building's too old, anyway. Not our style. I'll find something else—"

"*Not* Onslow Close?"

"Well, I thought it'd do for the time being—"

"First of all, Consuelo wouldn't go. She doesn't like the place. Secondly, I wouldn't. I sold that house because I never wanted to see it again. I refuse to go back there for any reason!"

"Right. Find some office space in—where?—Mayfair? Belgravia?"

"Leave it to Consuelo. She'll have the time. Anything more to add to the memorandum for the coming week?"

He shook his head and I wrote T&D—type and distribute—closed the pen, and stood.

"What about Yorick?" I asked.

"You'll have to see what can be done. We're in too much of a tight one of our own to do much. And Von Staengl, by the way's in London. Been there some months. Do what you can, Edmund. That's all!"

I finished signing the reports and letters, and he came to the doorway.

"Lausanne, six o'clock, Wednesday," he said. "Take care of yourself!"

I heard him call to Consuelo passing the office, and then she came in with a footman carrying a silver tea service.

"Thought it time for a breather," she said. "I've just been talking to Angela. She's livid Paul won't let her come back. And *what* do you think? She wants him to buy Onslow Close. She thinks it a beautiful place and quite wasted on the Company!"

"That's a pretty switch—"

She poured tea, and sat on the arm of my chair.

"Did you think Paul looked well?" she asked, suddenly. "Wasn't he rather—quieter—than usual?"

"Oh, I don't know—"

She held up a plastic phial, a pale bluish tube, with a label inside from Boussaf, the Cairo druggist.

"This must have rolled off the desk," she said. "Pick-up pills?"

"Not Paul—!"

"His name's on the cap, and the office address's on the label. That's what made me ask. But these aren't really pick-up pills. It's heroin—"

15

There's a wonderful five minutes after waking up at the Savoy, in London, and seeing the Thames a little way over, deep blue, with the Embankment parapet black, a long curving string of yellowy lamps still alight, perhaps a tug going by with a couple of barges, and lights scattering emerald blobs in the water.

Consuelo tapped and came in, wearing a jersey and riding breeches, with a kerchief round her head.

"Had an early call," she said. "I wasn't letting you go off without your breakfast—"

"Don't want any—"

"You're going to eat what I've ordered. You're supposed to be married—except here—so behave yourself, and strengthen your inner man against this clammy brute of a morning. I'm going for a gallop. First for months. Then I'll go home—"

"Bring your mother for a theatre party tonight—"

"Oh, wonderful! I'll choose the play. And we'll dress?"

"If I have time. You two can, anyway."

"What could make you late?"

"How do we know?"

She put her arm around me, soap'n all, and held tight.

"I get the most horrible feeling something's going to happen!" she whispered. "I'm not a bit comfortable, here or anywhere else. I suppose you *must* keep on with the Company? Nothing rather more relaxed or—"

"No," I said.

She squeezed for a moment, and went to let the waiter in, with what she called an "English" breakfast, which I've never in my life eaten, never mind what the doctors say. I had my usual cup of China tea, and orange juice with a lemon, and watched her ladyship put away porridge, eggs, bacon, and the rest of it, till I looked at the time, kissed her, and bolted.

Just as I was leaving, I heard my name, and the porter hurried with a letter.

"Gentleman 'brought this's over there, sir—"

It was Paul's fist, and he was introducing Bilat Khan. He wrote that I might find him useful somewhere, but he wasn't sure where, and hadn't raised any hopes.

Bilat Khan was a good-looking man, late thirties I judged, well dressed for that hour, and darkly Indian.

"I'm off to keep an appointment, but come here about eleven thirty, and let's have a talk," I said. "Just back from India, aren't you?"

"From other parts, not India," he said, almost free of accent. "Mostly all of the Middle East. But I know India, of course, and Pakistan. If you're thinking of sending me to either place, I resign here and now!"

"Eleven thirty here," I said.

The taxi put me outside the Canal Banking Syndicate's modest offices at five minutes before time. I've noticed that the wealthier the company, the dingier their offices, and the bigger the bucket-shop, the more ornate.

Sir Ryder's office, however, corrected any impression of imminent bankruptcy. It was panelled in teak, furnished with a partner's desk, silver and crystal everywhere, with the finest collection of sailing ships I ever saw. I could have spent hours there. Sir Ryder was one of the world's greatest authorities on sail. He knew I was a buff, and it always took a little time to get down to business because he always had something new.

"Well, then!" he said briskly. "Let's look at our muttons. You set me a fine task, didn't you? We raked, and we combed. But I believe we turned up one small trump. There haven't been any large drafts going about. We looked at the commercial stuff first, of course. But our people there'd been taken by an appearance in the gold market of people they didn't know. And since it was currency they wanted, they left themselves open to enquiry. As a consequence, I got the names of eight companies, and two men. The two are from Hong Kong, and Macao, across the water. There they are!"

I could have gone through the ceiling.

Huan Chen Muohy, the first name, was the woman's in Rome. The other I didn't know. But the company in Paris was that which the arrested clerks worked for.

"I believe you've done the trick," I said.

"There *have* been certain expenses which I'm sure we'll be able to recover?" he said, cocking an eye. "For example, item, a return air ticket—"

"Whatever the expense, it was more than worth it," I said. "You might send my secretary a chit. That takes it away from bookkeeping!"

"So glad to've been a little useful," he murmured, on the way to the door. "I hear you're having a little trouble?"

"We'd like to know where from!"

He looked over my head.

"There's a very nasty war situation from several directions. On Thursday or Friday, our representative gets back. He'll have a report. If there's anything there, I'll call you. At Lausanne?"

I went down to the car feeling a little worried. The talk with Consuelo had been more effective than any report. She wasn't the girl to say a word, much less express any emotion, unless she was sure of her ground. The bare fact that she'd thought of my leaving the Company said quite enough. Sir Ryder, the last man on earth to be unsure of himself, was most unsure. He was far from being the man I'd once known.

The "something" Consuelo feared was in the air.

I got to the office just after eight thirty. Hines was on the board, and taking calls. I waved him down, and walked about the offices, through paths cleared of debris, looking at damage. People wouldn't be able to work there for many a day to come. There wasn't a dry spot in the place.

"Telephone everybody," I told Hines. "Stay at home till Wednesday. Call here on Tuesday evening. We'll have other office space—"

"Fire assessors were here yesterday, sir. Be here at ten to see Mr. Gilbert—"

"Ask him to call me at the Savoy at noon. I want to see everybody. Assessors, insurance people, so forth. How did it happen?"

"Brookes was on duty, sir. He said it just went up. He tried to do what he could. He's in Willesden General Hospital, sir. Bad burns, he's got—"

"He'll be well looked after. So will the rest of you. Who was on last night?"

"I was, sir."

"Weren't you on yesterday?"

"Yes, sir. I kipped on the table out there. Wasn't nobody else, sir. Somebody had to hang on, here—"

"Where was Wilkins?"

"He wouldn't stay, sir. Dead afraid of fire, he is. He chucked it in—"

"You get fifty pounds as a little present from me, and triple wages for the month. Put any calls you think're mine on to the Savoy. Talk to Miss Furnival, or myself. Nobody else!"

"Thank y' very much, sir. That'll get done!"

I went down the street to the shipping brokers, and had to wait for the man I wanted to see. I hadn't met him before, and didn't catch his name. My card gave him mine.

"Ah, yes, yes," he said, getting out of an overcoat, hanging it, and slapping a bowler over. "Sorry to've kept you. Traffic's terrible. Well, I'm afraid we're unlucky. That ship's been bought for scrap. Nothing we could do. The owners had the right. We've only just heard—"

"You got another ship in her place, naturally?"

He stared across the paper on his desk. His secretary was untidy. So was he.

"You know we have a full cargo waiting—?"

"Ah, yes, but an agreement with one company's not an agreement with another. Terms have to be ratified—"

"Is there a ship available?" I asked.

"'fraid not. For the moment—"

"What do you call a moment?"

"Might be a month or so—"

"Thank you. Don't bother—"

"But, look. I don't know who you are—"

"There's no need. Good morning!"

I went out boiling. In the clearing mist of the street I recalled Lars Elef Petersen, an old friend of mine, and dialled the Norwegian Embassy.

"Hej, Edmund! Where d' hell are you?"

"About ten minutes away—"

"Coffee's on. Come on!"

It took us exactly seven minutes to find a ship, the Verschoyle Castle.

"If you want to buy some good tonnage cheap, now's the time," he said. "Have your own ships and crew. Best way. The men like a good, safe berth. And the captain and agents between them can always get her the cargo—"

He answered the telephone, spoke Norwegian, which I hadn't heard for years—that always seems to bring the smell of the sea, tarred rope, and the sting of rum into the room, legacy of days I languished on a destroyer, sick as a cat for the most part—and looked across at me.

"You heard of a projected dock strike in Liverpool?" he asked.

I shook my head,

He spoke again into the telephone, and looked over.

"I trust this fellow," he said, lifting the receiver a fraction. "Couple of days is all you've got. Where's the cargo?"

"Birkenhead—"

He spoke, and listened, wrote a note, said goodbye.

"Here's a port on the east coast, south of Harwich, used a lot in the last war. If you can get the cargo there, it'll be loaded without trouble. Local men and the crew. Where will you find enough transport? It's on the other side of England, bai God!"

I had the answer to that one. I called George Raikes, another friend of years, who'd left the Transport Ministry to found his own truck company.

"Tubes in bundles, yes, crates, of course, listen, it's no problem," he said. "Let's have the tonnage, where it is, where it's going to, that's all. Don't tell me where it *is* going. I don't want to be blacklegged. I'll let you know when we're loaded. Then we could meet. Nothing on paper!"

I didn't argue. Another day or two in London suited me down to the ground, and there was only Cairo that needed handling, but wasn't urgent. I went back to the Savoy on the dot of eleven thirty, and found Bilat Khan sitting like a maharajah, waiting for me. I said I'd be down in two moments, and chased upstairs, just in time to get on clix to Paul. CMEUO—Call Me Urgent, Out, I sent, and got R. I waited, and got on to Arturo in Rome. He came on in a long burst of U's. I sent CGNO—Calling Now, Out.

Consuelo came in with some letters. She looked simply lovely. She'd been to the hairdresser, and wore something peachily breathy I could see through.

"Get Arturo in Rome for me. Then get your bonnet on. Find an agent. We want new offices—"

She clasped her hands in a half-swooning ballet turn.

"Isn't it what I was dreaming?" she whispered, picking up the telephone. "I hated that horrid, dark place over there. Now we'll have something we can all enjoy getting out of bed to go to. If that's possible!"

I went through the letters, found one from my son, Frederick, one from the Reverend Doctor Tomsett, his mentor, one from Doctor Norris, his physician, and one, which I put in my pocket, from my black son-in-law, still trying his damnedest no doubt, to make me a grandfather.

"Rome, *sir!*" Consuelo said, handing me the receiver, with a tart's moué. "Arturo!"

"Ah, Mr. Trothe? I am so pleased! At the office nothing except the Lieutenant Truffo dead, Vittorini gone, Lucia Rocco gone, Dorandi gone—"

"Dorandi? What was that? When?"

"Nobody knows where or when, sir. Wife and two children. House empty. If the robbers got in, he let them. He was head porter—"

That explained a great deal.

"All right. Now, the rest of the staff?"

"All well, sir. Miss Toverell, Miss Greig, both well. Both in here for coffee and a party tonight. Pertacchi, the porter for Miss Dalziel, gone. I think he was very fright'—"

"Anything else important?"

"Very important sir. Is why I call!"

"What is it?"

"Your friend, sir, Mr. Agosto McGowan—"

"Yes?"

"He was found dead in his apartment last night—"

"Mac?"

"There was a big fight. Everything is smashed. I was there with the first. His apartment is not far from the cafe—"

"Who found him?"

"An American lady came with the Police. He was at her dinner. At Alfredo's. She said he had no drinks. The body was found by the cook at five thirty o'clock. He was flying to London at seven—"

"Anything else?"

"Nothing, sir. In order!"

"Thank you. Come on as usual."

I was shocked. Obviously Mac had found something going on in the night clubs he'd visited. I'd known he had hundreds of friends in the underworld. In all probability he'd got on to somebody and they'd got "on" to him. But I wondered what he was doing with Druxi. She, obviously, was the American lady, and I hadn't a doubt she'd warned the Police.

I called the United States Embassy in London and Rome, and her house in Washington. Nobody knew where she was.

I left the calls in.

"I'm going down to talk to a chap for a few minutes," I told Consuelo. "Try to get El Humir—"

"I've got to go home and get Mummy, remember!"

"The car's ready when you are!"

"Don't *snap* at me, darling!"

"Snap? I'd eat you. If there was time—"

I'm not a worrier. I've always acted on the principle that only a clear mind, free of all worry and fear of consequence, can make an appreciation of given data, and decide what to do. But in whatever the Company was doing, I seemed to smell death. It was an absurd thing to think, of course, but I *was* the Company. I've smelt death. Once that stench has blighted one's soul, it rises at times, without volition, for no reason. One's reminded that we're all walking about by the Grace of God.

I was hardly in a mood to meet Mr. Bilat Khan, but there was nothing else to do.

"Now then, what did you want to see me about?" I asked him, in a corner of the lounge.

"Mr. Chamby thought I could be of use in one of your Middle East offices," he said, as if he weren't at all sure of it. "I speak Hindi, Urdu, Pushtu, Bengali, Tamil and Arabic with, I am sure, the same fluency as English. I also speak German, French, and Russian—"

"But what a pity," I said, dreamily. "I'd thought of sending you to Finland—"

"A difficult language, sir, but I could pick it up in three months. I have a facility—"

"Do you also ride a bicycle?"

He laughed without sound across the room, straightened his face.

"I would like very much to work with you, sir. My father worked for Mr. Chamby in the Sudan. He was Indian, and so was my mother. I went to school in Delhi, and at St. Matthews, here. Then to Cambridge, and the London School of Economics. I went to India before Independence for an oil company. I was there with a steel company. Then with accounting machines and cash registers. Lately for insurance. But in that area, nobody lives long enough!"

"Why?"

"Because everybody undercuts. Soon there is only paper, but nothing to eat!"

"Why did you leave your job?"

"Restlessness of the spirit, mostly, sir. Desire to do more. See more. Make more money."

"You don't by any chance speak any Chinese languages, do you?"

"Mandarin wouldn't take me long to learn, sir. Cantonese. I had a Sumatran mistress in Africa. She spoke many dialects. She taught me many things. Oh, a sly little package, sir!"

"How?"

"Opening the company's correspondence. We wanted a contract. We didn't get it!"

"They undercut you?"

"By millions!"

"How did you find out?"

"I had a man in every Ministry in my pocket. It's usual. One of them reported a couple of facts and figures that could only have come from the papers in my safe. None of my staff could know. At that time, it was no use getting up early. The offices opened late. I worked late. That is the first thing. Second, it is easy to trace a letter. Go the the Post Office. Put the man in charge in your pocket. Take all the letters as they come in. Read them. Reseal. But first, put in a good pinch of sneeze-powder. There, they make deadly stuff. Then wait till you hear the postman in the morning. Early. She took my keys. I saw her. I got up when I heard the sneezing!"

"What did you do?"

"Thrashed her. Got her visa taken away. She had to go!"

"Draconian?"

"She had very good revenge, sir. She became a decorative part of the entourage of an ambassador in a country nearby. Then I lost *my* visa. *I* had to go!"

"An eventful life. What can you do, apart from spanking mistresses and talking ten languages?"

"Accountancy, certainly, sir. Management, of any kind. I have no color prejudice, as you see!"

I had a feeling he'd be very useful indeed.

"What do you really *want* to do?"

"I would like to work at something which would indulge my artistic side, sir. I wish to flatter my undoubted commercial acumen, and at the same time earn a large salary, with a free car, and a commensurate expense account. That is, to begin—"

"I want you to go away and bring me back all this in writing so that I may check your antecedents," I said. "I would start you at fifteen hundred pounds a year, a car when on Company business, an expense account at proper times, and plenty of opportunity for promotion. What were you doing in Kabul?"

He was staring at me as perhaps only an Indian can. It's not grief that weighs their eyes at those times, by any means, but, as it were, an eternal sadness, induced perhaps by contemplation, momentary but ineffably clear, of the human scene. Atavistic, yes, but new as coursing blood, conscious of all suffering, whether joyous or tragic in past generations, luminous with the shock of the moiling moment, prescient of the future's mischief, an infinitely gladly-sorrowful acceptance of all that man has been, is, and will be, with no reviling, no regret.

He shifted in the chair almost uncomfortably.

"Well, sir, first I shall accept in case you forget your offer," he said, blinking like a hen, surprisingly—nerves, perhaps?—in that "flat" English raddled by the distinctive Hindu accent—"I am a little overcome by your generosity. My mind is a holus-bolus. For the moment only!"

I know the feeling but I'd never be honest enough to admit it or say it.

He sat up, smoothed the hair at his temples with flat palms, and fingers like bamboo slightly bent backward, and grinned all his teeth, which from the effect, might have been twice the normal human ration.

"I was selling insurance as I told you, sir, and also second-hand armaments of any kind, old Indian Army stuff, Russian, Chinese and American," he said, in his normal accent, which was perfectly good. "I also gave lessons in English in the morning to Russians, Baluchis, Afghanis, Afridis, and others. In the afternoons I gave lessons in Russian to Americans, English and Europeans generally, most of them commercialists. At night I had many clients for a massage—"

"Massage? You mean ordinary—"

"Not ordinary, sir. I took the old Hindu system, and improved it by certain techniques taken from the Chinese that my mistress taught me, sir. It is most efficacious in times of debility, or for a rejuvenation of the muscles and blood—"

"Never had any great faith in it—"

"For a man, it is certainly necessary, sir. We suffer because of our arteries. But I practice exclusively with women. No men. Only women. There is no drug which gives the spiritual afflatus of the female body supine under the hands. It is maddening, but gorgeous, immeasurably a joy!"

He didn't seem to be pulling my leg. He meant it.

"If I ever find you practicing on any of our staff, that's *all*. You understand that, don't you? No discussion. You go!"

"But, sir, when food is scarce, then the devil smiles. Kabul is a cold city, sometimes. Hot food, money, *and* female flesh, sir, have their several appeals. I found it irresistible. Especially the food—"

"And which race of women do you find most appealing?"

"Women have no race, sir. They are bodies only. The same. Ah, sir, a fat Afridi girl—!"

"Why did you leave Kabul?"

"I had the opportunity of a passage by air, sir. I am also a pilot. I couldn't afford to choose. I flew to Bushire. From there, by ship as a purser, to Muscat. A long trip by road to Aden. I sold rice, cattle, sheep. In Aden, I became the manager of a petrol station. Until it was blown up—"

"With the books and takings, of course?"

"We could save nothing, sir. It was a source of great sorrow to me. Then I took passage to Dar-es-Salaam, and sold everything I had bought in Aden. With that money, I bought a truck and ran the blockade into Rhodesia. For five months. I sold the trucks—I had eight, then—for considerably more than I gave for them—I am also a mechanic—and I bought tobacco and sisal. I ran it into Luanda, and sold it for many times what I gave, plus the expense. I bought a farm. The second night, notwithstanding my agreement with the marauders—I paid them well, sir—the farm was burned down, the cattle driven off. I was in my trousers, and nothing. I worked as a mechanic, and I began a shop for spare parts. After a month or two, I had enough to buy another truck. I started the ferry between South Africa and Rhodesia. Unfortunately, I incurred the enmity of a tribal chieftain on the way—"

"Massage?"

"It is strange to them, sir, to the women, I mean. It is a new form of tickles. And the word, you understand, in these backward places, penetrates swiftly. However, I reached Capetown after some trouble—"

"How do you find apartheid?"

"It doesn't need to be found, sir. It is part. One accustoms oneself. I don't like prison. I prefer the ugly look to indifference. Indifference is one's own death before the proper time. Those whites, to me, were all dead. Through them, I saw their graves. They became shadows. I lived. Again, I taught English and arithmetic. Then I became a storekeeper in the docks. One night, I had the luck to be on a ship coming here. I got off at Tilbury. I was taught the ancient game of Crown & Anchor on board. I managed to make enough money to keep me for a little time. But your offer reduces me almost to the salty globules of gratitude—"

"Come here tomorrow at noon. I shall have a job waiting for you. Need any money?"

A pageboy came to say that Mr. Paul Chamby was calling on Trunks. I shook hands, and hurried to the callbox.

"Edmund? Listen. Gilbert—in the London office—just told me Shepworth and Grey left two days ago—the day of the fire—and haven't been seen since. They're both married men, but they were both packed up by the same removal company. Their stuff went to Southampton, the Reston Manor, *both* going to Sierra Leone. What d'you make of that?"

"Has the ship sailed?"

"Same night. But they and their families went by air to Marseilles, and caught a French cargo-liner, the Balintin, yesterday. I want you to put the best men you can find on tracing them. Try and find out where they're going, who meets them, where they go after that. We've got to start breaking things apart, Edmund!"

"Entirely in agreement. Heard anything about the dock strike?"

"What dock strike?"

I told him what I'd done. He was quiet for a moment or two.

"Well, that's *one* thing wasn't planned *at* us. Still, I'm glad you tackled it. That tube's going to cost us something. Heard about Rome, and Agosto?"

"Curious, I thought!"

"More than that. My word. I've been on to Lausanne, Cairo, Athens and Baghdad. Nothing new. Heard anything from El Humir?"

"We're on all the time. Nothing yet. I think I shall take on Bilat Khan. I believe he'll do well in Beirut—"

"Good place for him. That's a laddo. Be useful. Well, Angela's fine. We'll be buying Onslow Close from the Company. It's quite near. By car. I met the family. Most of them don't have to die. They're already on the wall. How's Consuelo?"

"Wonderful. I'm waiting to hear the tube's loaded, then I'll meet Raikes. We have an engagement for six Wednesday—"

"Out! What about after you come back from Cairo?"

"Right—"

Shepworth and Grey had been, I'd thought, a tremendous strength to our I-Unit. Both had been with M.I. for many years,

Grey with Allied Headquarters, Europe, Shepworth with Central Intelligence, Middle East, and neither were the sort to leave without notice. That's what astonished me. We weren't exactly friends, but we could always have a drink together. I wondered what sort of offer could attract them from a well-paid position which they'd find difficult to match elsewhere, especially overnight. I didn't think either of them had anything to do with the fire. Both were the serious type, essentially studious. I didn't know what to think except, of course, if they *had* been playing a double game, it explained a lot of our misfortunes. Their going seemed to mean that they knew the game was up.

Consuelo had gone when I got upstairs. She'd left the dog, with a note round its neck: "I am looking after you till my doting mistress gets back. Eat a *good* lunch, and no sandwich nonsense!" I went along the band looking for El Humir, but though the air was live, there was no signal. I heard our station in Ryadh talking to the pump team at Bayakh, but it was the daily reading of pump dials. I was glad to listen to something normal.

I spoke to Grethe in Paris, gave him the name of the ship going into Marseilles for a thorough check, owner, crew and passengers. He said everything was quiet, nothing yet from the Superintendent.

The reports brought in by the courier took a little time to read through. I didn't skim. At the end I was relieved to see that everything seemed to be going as well as it ought. But on the way down to the Grill for luncheon, I was a little annoyed—I'm not sure why—by Paul's attitude. Taking two or three days off was all very well in a period of no stress. But in our position I thought he ought to be in the thick. I didn't quite see what he could do except go from office to office, supervising the work being done, and taking the necessary measures when whatever-it-was came up. I wondered if, had I still been second-in-command and nothing more, I'd have had the same feeling. A little voice said I was being unnecessarily affected, zealous, too big for my boots, overweening.

I put it out of mind, or I tried to.

But it didn't quite go.

16

The telephone took me away from the map.

"Mr. Trothe? I do hope I haven't disturbed you? I'm Gillian Roule—"

"Oh, yes!"

"I've just come back from a—a holiday. I'm in London. Downstairs's a matter of fact. I met Patricia the other day in Tangier. She looked really very well indeed, and asked me to give you the usual messages—"

"*Please* come up. Love to see you—"

She'd been my secretary for a short period when I'd belonged to H.M. Civil Service. Consuelo had once told me she was probably the best agent we had—"not pool stuff, like the rest of us!"—but I'd reserved judgment. I also had cause to know she was rather more than friendly with Yorick.

I went out to meet her.

Patricia hadn't broken my heart, but she'd left a distinctly numb area by marrying a Negro—millionaire or not made no difference—without my consent. That he was indeed a power in most African states didn't hide the fact that she'd refused to attend her mother's funeral, hadn't invited me to her wedding, or given me a kiss before leaving on the honeymoon. And I hadn't heard a word since, except a shattering telephone call, when she'd accused me of murdering poor Mel, which, when I didn't want to think of it, brought that numb feeling.

Miss Roule came from the lift in the shadowy light of the corridor, moving with all the grace and weight of a feather, dark-haired, wearing a felt hat on the back of her head, in a flowing tweed overcoat that reached to her knees, and made a frou-frou as she walked.

"A delightful surprise!" I said, shutting the door and looking into clear, cornflower-blue eyes, whereas from memory I'd have sworn they were not merely brown, but black. "A cup of London's best tea—"

"Nothing, thank you," she said, and sat down, undoing the overcoat. She wore a spun-silk dress, which explained the frou-frou. She didn't wear lipstick. I couldn't see any powder. She looked thoroughly scrubbed, lit from the inside, shining.

"First, Patricia. She's going to Paris for her baby. In about two months or so. She looked wonderfully happy. And she said she's writing to you. This was two days ago. I—er—I called Consuelo. She'd called Mummy. She said I'd find you here—"

She fell against the back of the chair, and broke into helpless tears that shifted the chair on its castors.

I felt slightly off-level.

. She wasn't the sort.

Suddenly, angrily, she sat up.

"I don't know *what* you must think of me, Mr. Trothe! But I'm at the end of my little string. I don't honestly know which way to turn. I'm terrified. We can't find Errol!"

"Start at the beginning," I said, dry.

"You know he went to Fräglechshaben just after you came back from Regsmund"—she gathered herself, sat straighter, looked away, into the light of the window—"it was after you left the Department. Well, I left in the following week. I had him on clix twice every day, till midday of the twenty sixth, two months ago. That night his signal didn't come through. I tried everything on the band. I dared not stay on, of course. I scoured all the bands for days, weeks. I reported to London, naturally. They had no news, either. Then I had a breakdown, and Daddy took me to Tangier. I got back yesterday. Still nothing. Quite suddenly, Mummy said, 'Go and see Mr. Trothe. I'm perfectly sure he's the only man in this world who can help you.' I-I've lived in Church. I've burned candles. I've prayed, prayed, *prayed!*"

I felt like saying Alas, Poor Yorick!

"What, exactly, does London say?" I asked.

She shook—shrugged—looking for another handkerchief.

"Nothing. Nobody even wanted to see me. The Blur pretended he was out!"

We both knew the Lord Blercgrove and his manner of being. He directed the entire Service as if it were his own property, and Parliamentary control were merest fiction. If the raising of a little finger would in the slightest discommode his lordship or any work he might have in hand, then rather than move, the finger might rot.

"Has anybody been to Fräglechshaben?"

"I went there more than a month ago. Daddy's been there. We went as tourists, of course. Errol had two very good men there. One was his barman. The other supplied a lot of the food. Ham and sausage, and things. Well, they've both gone. But what's quite—well, horrifying, really—the farm *itself's* gone!"

"What farm's this? How, gone?"

"I mean, in so many words, where the farm *had* been is grass. No sign of anything. But it was a comfortable old place. It's all gone. I thought I was mad. So when I went back home, Daddy went. He couldn't find it, either. The bar Errol had, on the corner, was a fairly big place and they did a lot of business. Now, it's two shops. Of course, I couldn't make many enquiries as a tourist. I couldn't go to the Police. What highly unlikely tale could I tell our Consul if he had to rake me out for acting in a suspicious manner? And the nearer the frontier, the touchier they are. That's why I'm terribly afraid they've somehow managed to send him across. It's not even ten miles—!"

"Why would they do that? And how? His passport's West German—"

"A forged passport doesn't stand up. The Germans aren't idiots. Someone got 'on' to him. Somebody, somewhere. Of course, the Blur hadn't much time for him. It would have been so easy—"

"We oughtn't to think like that. You haven't any other information? Beyond the bar, which he'd bought—I knew that—the barman and the farmer? What were their names?"

"No idea. He told me nothing!"

"The clix'd be the best evidence they'd have. The wristwatch would be a most unpleasant thing to explain—"

"It was a pencil, not a watch. Here's mine—"

It was a cheap, well-used ball point, and the top turned—only if you knew how—to bring in a signal. It would have to be taken to pieces, and even then, the micro-set and flat capsular battery could easily be missed. Unless they'd used X-ray. I turned it on. Air was live. But no signal.

"That's what I've been doing," she said. "In the name of the Holy Mother, I *wish* you could help me, wish, wish, *wish*. And I've been such an *utter* nuisance!"

I was a little shocked, though not disagreeably.

She got up, buttoned the overcoat, set the hat, hair, began to put on the gloves.

"You haven't told me if you will or not!" she said, in a voice about that far from a quiet shriek, at odds with a raised chin. "Please, Mr. Trothe, I *must* know!"

"I have one or two things to do. But I'll let you know—"

She turned to me, smiling, weight on one foot, gloved hands under forearms, eyes in bluest shine of whites almost as blue, and an air of trust that almost made me put my arms about her, as if she'd been a child. Before I was ready she tiptoed and put a smudgy soft-lipped kiss on my chin. Something inside me rattled like a bag of old kettles, though thank heaven, without sound. I'd been used to the notion that a kiss led to other things. Not this time. I've always thought that women's lips and poetry are much the same piece, though I don't suppose I could explain that even to myself.

"Burn those candles," I said. "The light reaches a long way!"

164

I walked with her to the lift. She used the handkerchief, put it away as the doors opened.

"Errol told me," she said, in barest whisper. "That's why I came here. Thank you!"

Again that sense of shock, as if some other, newer nerve had been touched. I knew what Errol had told her. Before he'd left he told me he was becoming a Roman Catholic because of her.

"I've been greatly torn because really I ought to be orthodox Hebrew, because of my mother," he said. "I've been brought up as Church of England. Never thought much about it. My mother said she'd had an agreement with my father ever since I was born, almost. She wouldn't interfere, he wouldn't, they'd let school go by—he said I'd catch hell in school—and let me choose when I came of age. I never even gave it a sniff till Gillian said she'd marry me only if the children were brought up as Romans. What does one do?"

I felt it time to tell him that the eldest sons in our family had been brought in down the generations, as I had, immediately after leaving school and before going up to University.

"On Thursday, you'll be ready to join me for a trip to Paris," my father had said, those years before, in after-dinner candlelight. "I want you to look at this book!"

It was raw-leather bound, smooth with age. Our crest had been tooled on the front. Inside were pages of fat vellum, one name, an eldest son, to a page, with a date, beautifully illuminated, all in Latin text. My father's name was last but one. My own name surprised me in amethyst and blue, with gold and white scrolls, but no date.

"Our family was Roman till fat Henry destroyed the Church," my father said, over his cigar. "Onslow Trothe, our senior kinsman at that time, saved the family lands, this house, the village, and many a head including his own, by letting fall he'd joined the Protestants. But a priest lived in the Hole upstairs for many a safe year afterwards. Until sanity came. From Cromwell's time—that porringer of mealy-mouthed sanctimoniousness—to William, there've been candles burning, and a Latin prayer in this house every morning. Our family survived, name and Faith intact. You're next. What objection have you to offer?"

"None, sir," I said, and strange, though I'd never wasted a moment on religion, the idea seemed part of me, not in the least alien or odd. We'd gone to the Vatican to see the cardinal, I'd had excellent chance to practice my Latin, there'd been a lovely service, candles everywhere, and I'd been Roman ever since.

But in all that assault of memory, I knew myself pierced through, pinned to the Timber.

Errol was brother-in-the-Blood, and not to be denied.

17

I called Frederick at Doctor Tomsett's for the fifth time since the morning, still there was no reply, and Doctor Norris was at a conference in Harrogate and wouldn't be back till Friday. No news isn't always good. I wanted to hear the voice I'd known since its infancy. Without having to see him, I'd know from the tone exactly how things were. He had examinations in a month, and he'd have to present himself for a final interview with the magistrates on the tenth. I had it ringed in red. If they gave him a clean sheet, I intended to offer him a job on the pipeline, on a pump station in the desert with no town for a couple of hundred miles. That, of itself, could be make-or-break.

George Raikes called after lunch and said the fleet would be loaded that night at ten and the drivers would be at Norwich about six next morning.

"Choose your own route," I said. "Are you coming here?"

"About nine thirty? After dinner? If you're not there, just leave a slip. Place, ship's name—"

I went across the park to see James. I don't know why I thought of seeing him first. Yet I did, of course. If I was going into a prison I had to get out. The only way was to blow something up or down, and James was one of the greatest explosive experts—one of the few times a man deserved the word—I suppose, in the world. I went up to his bare office, shadowy on a rainy afternoon, with colored plates of hunting dogs on the wall, a photograph of his family on the mantelpiece, waxed board floor, damn-you-sit-up chairs, and a gas ring and tea things in the corner. The only "staff" I saw was a rather fat girl in a cubby. I don't know what she did. Yet he was a nerve of the Service, earned a large salary, lived in a gem of a house, went to and fro in a Daimler, and ran a string of successful race horses in his wife's name.

We spoke of small matters for a few moments, while he made tea in the corner. He knew what I was doing, asked no questions, talked with affection about Arab friends we'd known, and said he'd give anything to know that real peace was restored between them and the Israelis.

"Enmity between fraternal peoples is quite horrible. It's like ourselves and the Germans. It happened. One still doesn't understand how, really, it was ever allowed. One does, yes. But for the ordinary individual, it's a hopeless business. I was never able to ask you. How did you find things in West Germany?"

I was grateful for the question. It was the opening I'd looked for. He knew I wasn't there merely to gossip. He also knew I'd never broach a crucial subject without encouragement. Because of that, I knew he was sympathetic and might help. It's the straws that show.

"I managed to destroy a nest with the help of your little stickers," I said. "It was put down to a short circuit and a gas explosion. Unfortunately, while it put a few out of the running, it didn't do much else. The rot's creeping. That is, nationally. Whether they're going to be the menace they were, I don't know. But if they won enough elections to control the Government, we'd have to start counting the days. They'd have nuclear power sooner than the French. Heard anything of Yorick lately?"

He poured the tea, and brought a cup over with the sugar bowl. It made a pregnant break.

"I'm told he's not answering on cue," he said distantly. "His father was a school friend of mine. One of the reasons I'm here. A truly *great* man, I always thought. Errol has every gift of his.

Plus a something from his mother. I'd stop at nothing, literally nothing, to help him. I want you to be quite certain of that!"

It was sudden, and—from him—a quite unusual demonstration. I hadn't expected it. But since he'd taken me so far into his confidence, I felt I could show cards.

"It's reliably told he's in Hauerfurth Prison. East Germany. Not far from the border. The Wall."

"Oh?" he said, without feeling. "What put him there?"

"I have an idea that somebody on our side blew the gaff. He was trying to do what I'd done. Chaps in these Nazi lodges had been getting rid of witnesses who'd been useful at Nuremberg. His father, of course, was one. All very clever, the way they killed so many. Errol went there for a few targets of his own. I believe he had a fair success, too. The bar he took was under the club. Most members had a drink there, and he supplied the bar upstairs. He knew who'd been in this country recently. If they'd been successful in killing their man, their lodge brethren gave them a party. Errol waited his time, and gave *them* a little party. One little drink. They didn't live long. Somebody must have informed. But why take him into *East* Germany? That's a puzzle to some of us—"

He brought his cup to the table, and sat down, carefully turning the handle to the right, putting the spoon at its proper angle, looking into the tea as if he saw an answer. He reached for the telephone.

"Alison, ask Mary Tompkins to see me when she can, will you? Take a note for Mr. Jolliffe, and Mr. Hendrison. I want the answers before I leave!"

He sat back, picked up the cup and saucer, and sipped. The tea was hot.

"Hauerfurth," he said. "Even worse than our Dartmoor. Can't have changed much, either. I was there for a couple of days, before the Russians advanced. They had a rocket site there. I'm told they've done some rebuilding. And that forest's gone. I'll know more in a couple of hours. What do you want to do?"

"Get him out!"

He smiled.

The telephone ting!-ed.

"Yes? Mary, look here, you've got a file on Hauerfurth Prison, and there's a very good model somewhere—"

He listened, nodded, and ting!-ed off.

"Come and have some coffee at eleven tomorrow," he said. "We'll have what's known, and we'll see if we can't boil something up to go with the cabbage!"

It was an old expression, and it meant he was going to prepare an explosives chart to take care of any eventuality. Which was exactly what I'd wanted. But I was perfectly certain that had it not been for Errol, no bribe, no appeal to sensibility, friendship or anything else would have done.

I had a feeling, walking back, that Errol had one leg out of that damnable place, and I felt I ought to call Gillian. But I thought I'd leave it to Consuelo, simply because the right sort of friend at the right moment carries a special sort of emotion for a long, long time.

But seeing the trees of St. James's Park in fine mist, listening to taxi-horns along the Mall, smelling the soaked earth, safe and warm in my overcoat, sure of a good drink at the hotel, I thought of Yorick, wondering what he might be going through, or if he was still alive, and what I had to do to find him, first, and then what, to get him out.

I heard Gillian's voice filled with that prayer.

The first problem was to get into East Germany. Gillian was absolutely correct. A forged passport may be all very well, but it doesn't stand a moment's official scrutiny. I had sets of other men's papers in my deposit box which had been of use on occasion. But this called for another form of attack. I had to enter a prison, and then leave it, and the country, with somebody else, all, preferably without "embarrassment."

What excuse could a foreigner have for wanting to visit one of *our* prisons? Not *any* prison, but one of maximum security. Unless he was somebody highly important, he wouldn't stand an earthly.

Even then, the Home Secretary would pick and choose. Far worse in East Germany.

Consuelo hadn't arrived when I got to the hotel. I poured a drink, thought of Yorick, and called Von Staengl at his home. A manservant answered, and went to find him.

"Ah, Mr. Trothe! Paul telephoned this morning. We had a short conversation. Is there perhaps somewhere we might meet? I am taking my companion to the theatre. Could we meet before? The theatre is on our way—"

"Seven thirty at the hotel?"

"Oh, splendid! Of course—"

That Paul and he had spoken—that "short" conversation told a great deal—and that he wanted to meet before the theatre meant that he had something to say. I felt a hope.

I went through the courier's pile on the desk. Everything still seemed to be going very well. I got on again to El Humir, but never mind how carefully I went up and down the band, there wasn't a sound. I couldn't understand it. It was a big place as desert camps go, with a pump station, warehouse, garage for trucks, wagons and cars, workshops, sleeping quarters for thirty with a bathhouse, kitchens and offices, and a compound for the ordinary labor. Logan should have reported, but there wasn't a word even that he'd gone. I ripped off cables to all offices asking for any information soonest. Clix was quiet.

About then I started dressing, and Consuelo came in, pink from the drive, beautiful because she was, and not to be kept from kissing my lathery face.

"Mummy's down the corridor, and not in the least perturbed that I'm next to you," she said. "We've got an hour and a half. I'm starving—"

"Eat something with your mother. I'm seeing Von Staengl downstairs for a moment—"

"I know your moments. I'm coming to get you!"

"Do. He's theatre-ing too. With his wife—"

"Not if I know *him*. That's *the* golden-bushed wolf. He's tall— he's not handsome—he's beautiful, fair as Siegfried on the loose—"

"You know him?"

"*Of* him. My brother knew him. They served together in Germany—"

"I'm going to keep *you* away from him—"

She stood at the door in her 1908 musical comedy version of Pah! A Lot I Care!

"Far more sense if I kept *you* away from the girl *he's* with. He has *the* flower!"

"That's what I'm worried about!"

She put her tongue out, and turned to open the door for a pageboy with a couple of telegrams, one cable. He looked at the tongue, and me. I was still in a towel, shaving brush at the ready.

"There's some change over there. Read them, will you?"

She gave the page some silver without looking at him, and tore open the cable.

"From Geneva, sent at four fourteen. Message 'We all hope your first day as our youngest brother was an enormous success and we wish for all other days the same generous blessings. Our uncle was particularly happy because now he thinks you will sell him at least a little of the holdings we jealously kept for ourselves. We warn you he is difficult and impossible and hopeless. But a few shares of the unissued parcel would be a gesture and could preclude more El Humirs. Please send your reply to me. A most affectionate embrace. Your eldest brother Habib.'"

Consuelo glanced at me in her What-Sort-of-Game-Is-*This?* look, and opened a telegram.

"Burton on the Rise, five sixteen. Message. 'Just back from fox hunting. Didn't ride but broke my leg again—'"

She started laughing, swallowed it.

"'—by falling out of the dogcart. Laid up a day or two. Angela's family won't let me move. And we didn't get the fox. Take care of things. Splintily and plastered both ways, Paul.'"

She opened the other. "Birkenhead, four eighteen. Message. 'Dockers won't allow cargo loaded on trucks. Strike called midnight. Wire instructions urgent. Ship Hotel. Raikes.'"

I picked up the telephone.

"Get me the Ship Hotel, Birkenhead. Person to person, George Raikes. Urgent!"

"Go and dress," I told Consuelo. "I'll go on downstairs. I can't go to the theatre—"

"Oh, darling! How could I sit still?"

"I'll meet you for supper—"

"All right, youngest brother. I suppose you'll be dyeing those whiskers red, next—?"

The telephone stopped the move.

"Mr. Raikes on the line—"

"Mr. Trothe?"

"What's the trouble, there?"

"Very ugly indeed. Worst I've ever seen them. Rough lads best of times. My lot don't want to go in there again. The fleet's still inside the dock—"

"Think an offer of fifty pounds a workman, that is, a docker, cash, would do it?"

"That's *it!* *Cer*tainly! Just the right medicine. Where do I get the cash?"

"I'll bring it up. Expect me in three or four hours. Before, if I can—"

I called the air taxi firm while I brushed my hair.

"Weather's fairly clear, sir. If you're at Gatwick in an hour, you can be there by nine, easily. And return, sir?"

"Please. Is that a jet?"

"The jet's a higher tariff, sir!"

"That's what I want!"

The great thing about running a business as cock-o'-the-walk is that there's no need to ask anybody what you may do. Had I still been second man, I'd have had to find Paul, or the accountants might have raised the devil.

I rang the manager's office and asked if I could have five thousand pounds in pound notes.

"With pleasure, sir," he said, as if I'd asked for a glass of water. "I'll send it up—"

It suddenly dawned that if I'd been in any other, except an

hotel in that group, I might have been in a pretty pickle. Five thousand pounds is no ordinary sum in pound notes.

Seven thirty chimed as I reached the foyer, and Von Staengl was coming through the swing door. He was, indeed, a remarkably handsome man, about thirty-something, and he moved like an athlete.

"I left my wife in the car," he said. "It's a little blowy in that courtyard. How do you do?"

I knew he was "sizing," and so was I. He had a good grip and a dry palm.

"I haven't got time for a drink," he said, as I turned to the bar. "I'd like to post a letter—"

A pageboy came over at a nod, Von Staengl sorted the letter out of his pocket, tipped, and the boy went toward the box.

"You might ask the porter to look through the mail," Von Staengl said, buttoning his overcoat. "We're leaving in the morning for The Hague. A call there wouldn't be wise. If you're in London in the next ten days or so, I'll be at that number if necessary. We'll meet another time, I hope. Goodbye—"

I went over and bought a paper, picked up the little bouquets I'd ordered for Consuelo and her mother, and went to the lift pretending to read, but keeping a weather eye for anyone who might have been interested in our meeting. Von Staengl had been covertly nervy. I didn't blame him. Possibly, if he hadn't liked the cut of my jib, he wouldn't have "posted" the letter. Paul must have given him a bill of goods. But he was taking a risk, and I was grateful.

Cousuelo's mother was a quieter edition, very much like my own mother as I remembered her, and she dressed in much the same way, black, sleeves one saw the arms through, a diamond necklace, a gold net bag which I hadn't seen for years, and long gloves, hands out. I helped them on with their coats, gave them their bouquets, and saw them downstairs.

"I'm flying to Liverpool," I told Consuelo as we waited for the car. "Back tomorrow morning. I'll take you both for luncheon. Promise!"

She said not a word. Her mother got in. Consuelo looked at me.

"You *will* take care, won't you?" she whispered, and kissed my cheek, a nothing. The porter closed the door, and I saw her glove wave from the rear window.

I suddenly felt lonely. I didn't want to go to Liverpool. I wondered whom I could send. There wasn't anybody. But that tube had to be on board that ship, and she had to sail on time.

I went up to the bar, and called the hall porter about the letter addressed to me and put in the box by error.

"Often happens, sir. I'll have it to you in two ticks—"

"To my room, please!"

I went up to change. I'd poured a drink, but not the soda, and the porter was at the door. He went off happy, and I tore open a typed letter addressed to Edmund Trothe, Esq. By Hand.

The sheet was without address or signature.

"M and D. We know E suffers glandular disease, swelling of limbs, slow movement, excess weight. Verify medical sources. Held on political charges not yet published. Help unlikely. Good luck!"

I couldn't imagine Errol as anything more than the lanky clothes-prop he'd always been. "Slow movement, excess weight" meant that any remote notion of cut-and-run had to be dropped. M and D? Memorize and destroy.

It seemed to me that before I caught that plane, I ought to find a church. A candle's light, so far, appeared to be the only answer, but while I put a match to a corner, I had a feeling we both —poor Yorick!—had about as much chance as the paper.

18

It was years since I'd been in the hurly-burly of a dockyard. The last trip on the *Queen Mary* brought back the roses and cheers. Tonight was slightly different. There were thousands of men under the lamps, black shapes in greenish clouds of breath and tobacco smoke, waiting. They made way for the car, but slowly, hands in overcoat pockets, taking their time. I saw their faces, their mouths, their eyes, the several masks of root British stock, that has nothing in common with diplomacy, drawing rooms or niceties. They were the faces I remembered of troops going into battle, resigned, almost passive, docile, and murderous.

George Raikes sat in front with the driver. Twice he stopped the car to talk to the men who might have made a wall, and twice they gave way. But then we came to a turning where the rail tracks looped to follow the road. The driver braked hard. Oil barrels and timber blocked the quayside, with a crowd standing behind. We stopped. We heard the shouts. It was no welcome.

"They'll put us over the side for two pins!" George said, turning to me. "I've never seen them like this. D'you think it's worth it?"

"Let me talk to the man in charge," I said.

"Don't get out!" George warned. "They might set about you.

You're too well dressed. And you've a toff's accent. Anything like that, they hate!"

A heavy man in a cap, with a label in his buttonhole, walked across the cobbled space, hands in overcoat pockets, pressed into the groin.

"What d'you want here?" he called, and stood in the headlights. The driver switched off.

"You know me," George said, out of the window. "Raikes Transport? Listen. Come here. No larks!"

The man came unwillingly. George got out to meet him. He talked for a minute or so, and turned to me, jerking his head.

"He wants to see the color of it, first!" he called. "Show him!"

I got out, opened the briefcase, and the man looked in at the bundle.

"Handle them," I said. "They're healthy. Are you a Union official?"

"I'm the steward in this basin. I do the talking. All right. How do I know you won't sue after? Make some sort of bother? Illegal payment, and that sort. How do I know? I've to be right careful!"

"Not with Mr. Raikes. Or with me. We want a job done—"

He stared. I never saw a more expressionless face.

"I wish they was all like you, guv'nor," he said. "All right, George. Just give us a couple of minutes. I'll send a few blokes with you to bring the lorries down. Might smack 'em up, else!"

We waited while he hurried—as if his hips hurt—back to the barrier. He went in the darkness behind the lamps. We heard him speak without hearing what he said. Suddenly, a murmur, then a shout, and a hard-edged cheer that went on, and then cut.

That, in all truth, was British.

Half a dozen men came at a run. I got out of the car, and they all piled in without a word, and the driver turned and left us.

"The ship's behind this warehouse but she's no crew," George said. "Funny business altogether. Cargo's at dockside, ready. Shan't be long, now."

The Union official came back with a couple of others and turned invitingly. We followed, through the barrier, along a lane of shadows. I didn't see a face. We went between two warehouses. Ships' lights were at left and right. On the foredeck of the ship in front, a white spot shone on the lines of tubing and crates. A lamp under a mobile crane spread softer light. Men were folding their overcoats, rolling sleeves.

A hand at my elbow offered an enamel mug of tea, which I very gratefully took. It was *real* tea, hot, sweet, and I began to realise I was frozen. The lorries came in before I was ready, but at the other end.

"Quick, wasn't it?"

"Oh, they don't waste any time," George said. "Watch this lot go on. Take you longer to pay out, I'll bet you!"

I timed the load-on by my watch. The Union official put a box at a makeshift table, and I started paying the men who'd finished their load just as the last lorries eased in for the final lot of crates.

"I was told sixty-five men," I said. "I've paid only forty-eight—"

"That's all right, guv'nor. That's how many it took for the job—"

"Then, look here. There's the extra seventeen men's pay as make-weight. Thanks for the help. I employ a lot of men. They've all got families. This stuff's going to keep most of them in work. They'd say thank you, too!"

"I don't doubt it," the man said, putting the notes in his overcoat pockets. "If they're all like you, you're a lovely lot. Wish I was with y'. But, sitha. Tha've the secret. Ah. Secret it bloody is, that!"

"What's the secret?" I asked, locking the briefcase.

"It's an easy one, as most of 'em ha'n't got," he said, and lifted the mug. "Pay 'em. Nobbut that. Pay 'em. Good health!"

Two men stood on the car's running board, and we went through that crowd without a sound, out of the gate, and down the road, passing the long line of the loaded lorry fleet. I took out the map I'd marked, and gave George the ship's name, berth, the agent, and his check.

"Strike's called for midnight," George said. "That's why they're all out. If we hadn't had those lads with us—well—I'd never have gone in, to start with. If I may say so, you've been very smart. You've probably saved weeks. And far more money. You're not worried about flying? I can't take one foot off the floor!"

"But you weren't worried about going in there? Where you might really have gone in the ditch?"

He looked me in the eye.

"Mr. Trothe, when you've got the money, everything else takes care of itself," he said. "If I had reason to trust you before, I've got a lot more now. Enjoyed working with you, sir!"

19

On the bumpy flight back I was thinking of Yorick. I slept till we
got on the flat, thanked the pilot and his co-pilot, made a note to
bring our own plane to London, and walked across the tarmac
into the lights of the airport building, and the warmth of Consuelo.

Those are times when you take a woman in your arms, to the
exclusion of all other thought, and all else in the world, not even,
in those moments, with thanks unto God for one dear, sweet soul,
but only, selfishly, thanking your stars that you found her, you're
loved, you have a place, a woman of your own.

There isn't a more wonderful feeling.

"I brought some sandwiches and hot coffee, and the same
whisky flask," she said, in the car. "I went down to that e-*nor*-
mous kitchen, and the chef ran rings round everybody to make
a collection—he made sausage rolls in moments!—of all sorts of
sandwiches. I had a marvelous time!"

"Turn them out. I'm hungry!"

"Don't be impatient. When you're hungry, you're inclined to be
a piggie. Well, now, *what* do you think?"

"What?"

"I got on to El Humir!"

"No!"

"I spoke to Mr. Logan. There'd been a sandstorm for days, that's why he couldn't drop. It cleared this morning. The station aerial was blown down. The water stopped. They had no electric light. But it might have been even more serious, because they'd been threatened with a burn-down. A lot of soldiers from somewhere became—he said—a threat. He didn't know who they were. They'd gone this morning. But the casual labor doesn't want to stay, twelve of the Europeans have gone, and only five want to stay on. The rest want to go at the end of this week. That won't leave enough men to keep the place working—"

I saw I'd have to sell a few shares to his highness, dear Uncle-once-removed, Abdullah.

"Anything else?"

"I've found a lovely suite of offices in St. James's Square. It's ideal. I took them—"

"All right—"

"Angela's handbag—?"

"Ah, yes! Isn't there some mustard?"

"Darling. Staring you in your simply charming face. Handbag. Two men have been identified by Interpol. They were the two who tried to get into Prince Azil's apartment. Both are wanted everywhere. They're both murderers. Both escaped prison. They were paid—you'll see the report—to kill Prince Azil. Three others were paid to get hold of Prince Habib and take him to that house. Well, these two—the murderers—didn't believe what they were told. They were paid half in notes, and stones and *lingotes*—I can't remember that word in English—!"

"Of course you can. 'Ingots.' Donkey—!"

"Watch the hooves, *haji!*"

"You're running up an account!"

"Wonderful. Well, they said the people who paid them were small—they weren't very tall—and they didn't speak a single word. Somebody else spoke for them. It was in the dark. It was in the Gare du Nord, on the platform at the end of the main line, going to Boulogne. It's *very* dark. I know it. I can quite believe they wouldn't see much. Well, the two didn't believe the offer. They were given an address to go to. Guess!"

181

Halfway through a delectable sausage roll, about the size of my little finger, I went over the ground. I couldn't see much. I crunched, savored, poured a cup of excellent coffee.

"Don't know—"

"Our office!"

"Was Grethe in it?"

"He paid them!"

"Has des Vosges reported?"

"Well, of course, he tore the entire thing open. Grethe can't be found. His house is empty. The two men said they were given a plan of Prince Azil's apartment. They were told there wouldn't be anybody there except an English clerk—"

"Wait till I find Grethe!"

"They were going to give Azil another pill—"

"All right. Angela's handbag—"

"It was in this bag Grethe took the money and other things out of. One of them took a fancy to it, and Grethe said he could have it. He wrapped it up, and that's that—"

"Could Grethe have been in Capri?"

"If you look at the travel desk, you might think he could have been!"

"Check all travel vouchers. Let's see where they've been going. We'll have to plan a system for issue of tickets. That's the worst of a block permit. I'd never have thought Grethe could have been got at—"

"Worse to come!"

"Can't possibly be much worse—"

"Gilbert's no longer with us. The records that weren't destroyed he must have taken. There isn't a single piece of tape in the ashes, and there's not a reel in the library. Apart from that, the inter-office cipher book's not in the safe. He couldn't do much more harm if he tried!"

"Shepworth, Grey, and Gilbert. And possibly Grethe. Get the files of all the people who've gone. Lay them out systematically. See where they touch—"

I didn't want her to know that I was far more interested in

Yorick. The notion of his being stuck in a cell in that stone tomb wasn't one that went well with the warmth of the car, the taste of coffee, her perfume, nearness. Some of us have too much.

There was a sheaf of messages, cables and telegrams on the desk when we got upstairs. I got ready to start a day's work backward, and Consuelo went to see if her mother was safe. The cables and telegrams were all normal enquiries, and the answers went off one after another. Two telephone calls, one from James. The other, from Paul, I thought I might leave till later. But the cable I almost didn't see had come in just after I'd left for the airport. It was on a salver by the door.

"Send invitation before morning or make no complaint. Habib." Sounded brusque, indeed.

I got out the shares folio and looked things over, and after some pencilling, I decided that five percent of the unissued stock would be a fair offer. I sent off the cable, and got thankfully into bed. Not two hours later, the telephone woke me. I hate being jerked out of sleep.

"Geneva, sir. Urgent. Message. 'Twenty five percent or nothing and a seat on the Board self or proxy. State price. Regards.' Message ends. Signature Azil—."

"Just a moment. Take the reply. H. H. Prince Azil. Lake Palace Hotel. Message. 'You may with pleasure buy ten percent of remaining unissued stock for twenty million sterling, cash, but without seat for yourself or proxy until as a shareholder you prove your worth to the Company. Accept by noon, or offer withdrawn. Signed. Edmund Trothe.'"

The missing cipher book worried me. It was a secondary cipher, but still important for business reasons. We weren't doing much in code except for the innocuous stuff sent to Lausanne each night more in the nature of practice. But when we began working the pipeline, then daily figures, sales and reports would have to be safeguarded. That apart, the files and references already in code would be worth more than a prize. I wondered if the book could have been stolen before the attempt in Rome. If it had, then it explained the break-in, photography and the rest. Those photographs, and that book, with men like Gilbert, Shepworth and Grey to decipher, would give a partial picture, not a lot, but enough to cause us a great deal of damage if that was the idea.

I tried to imagine for the hundredth time who, or which organisation, would run such extraordinary risks, pay large sums of money, and transport men and apparently their families somewhere or other.

For what?

I turned over to sleep. While I'd dictated the telegram, an idea had nibbled. No more than nibbled. But I slept on it, as I always do with an idea not fully formed, confident that in sleep, the missing bits of jig—would fit itself to the—saw.

20

A cable came up while I read the morning pouch.

WHAT DO YOU SUGGEST WOULD PROVE WORTH TO COMPANY TO OBTAIN SEAT FOR SELF OR PROXY? ABDULLAH HASSAN EL HUDRI.

I sent off SEAT FOR YOURSELF ONLY AND NO PROXY EXCEPT HEIR IF YOU PREVENT INTERFERENCE THROUGHOUT ARABIA AND WHEREVER YOUR INFLUENCE HOLDS. PEACEFUL CONDITIONS AND CIVILISED DEALING CAN QUINTUPLE OUR INVESTMENT IN FIVE YEARS. REGARDS.

If Uncle-once-removed had decided to appear personally, then either he'd quarreled with his brothers or his nephews, or else something far more important was in process. But it didn't interest me as much as the idea I'd-almost-knocked into shape about Yorick.

My third call to James got him at a few minutes after nine. "Could you manage to be here in half an hour?" he said.

"Certainly. What's—"

"I believe I've got at least one of the answers, and possibly two!"

"Expect me!"

Paul came on while I shaved.

"Tried to get you last night. There's a mess in Paris—"

"Dealt with. You heard about London?"

"Consuelo told Angela. That handbag business knocked us over. How'd it get there?"

"We'll have des Vosges' report pretty soon. He'll squeeze it out of them—"

"How about the tube, and stuff?"

"At sea, by now—"

"Good. What are we going to do about London?"

"I'm seeing Farqhuarson. But every applicant's going to be vetted from the skin out!"

"True. What's he? Commissioner's Office?"

"Divisional Superintendent, CID Records. That's at New Scotland Yard—"

"How about that cipher book?"

"We're lucky it's not the main cipher. But I believe we'll have to change the lot. We'll have to knock skulls—"

"Been thinking about it. I've got a couple I've been nursing. Few small snags, though. My math isn't what it was. You're due in Cairo, when?"

"Not any longer. I've had a good talk with the Swiss Consul. All in order—"

"I can't get about till Friday—"

"Sorry you didn't get the brush!"

"Scent, that's all. A dogcart, my word. Angela's never stopped laughing. They're really heartless, you know? They pretend they're in love. They just wait to cackle at you!"

Gillian called while I was dictating.

"I don't intend to waste time by saying how I feel, Mr. Trothe. Consuelo told me of your decision. Lady Imbritt would very much like to say one little word to you—"

"Some other time, especially if her Ladyship happens to be passing. By the way, isn't there a gymnasium down there?"

"A gym—oh—you mean—yes, there is!"

"That skating floor, down there. There were special skates. Larger wheels. Collapsible. A sort of ski-get-in. Held firm, but quick in and out—"

"I know exactly what you mean!"

"Choose the best. I want two pairs here—"

"We'll bring them together. Anytime?"

"Absolutely!"

Consuelo gave me her freezing Now-What-Are-You-Up-To? look. I brought together any last rags of innocence I happened to have, and looked back, blithe as a button.

"I'm asking no questions of any kind," she said, with ominous delicacy.

"As well—"

"I simply don't want to hear you're up to some nonsense, again—"

"Oh, but you won't!"

"I insist you think of me, for a change!"

"I rarely think of anything else—"

"I believe what I told Gillian had some nefarious meaning—"

"But you'd never think Gillian and I—that I was—"

"Goating again? Oh, no. Gillian's like me. I'm talking about Errol—"

No use joking. She meant business.

"I'm going to try to help in a certain way," I said. "No risk of any kind. You're worrying over nothing. But if I were in Errol's place, wouldn't you prefer to think that my friends were helping me? Instead of accusing me of 'goating'? A fine expression, I must say!"

She had her back to me.

"Fits you, too!" she said, putting something in the cabinet, and giving the drawer a shove that almost put it in the next room. "I *hate* your being taken away from me. *Hate* it. I'd *never* allow it!"

The telephone brought blessed interference.

"Cable, sir, Geneva, ten sixteen. Message. 'Accept your offer. Draft now in mail. Shall earn my seat. Wish to see you when next in Lausanne. Quasi-avuncular compliments. Felicitations. Azil for Abdullah Hassan El Hudri. End.' One more, sir—"

"Ready!"

"Geneva, ten twenty. Message. 'Ah, what a clever little boy is in our family. We love our new brother. Come here soon. An embrace. Azil. End.'"

"One other thing," I said. "When this sort of cable comes in, they should go in my private file. They're not Company's business. In other words, I don't want Paul to see them. Nothing behind his back—"

"Wouldn't it be far better to tell him before he finds out? Angela's not by any means a woolly one—"

"And you're not? Isn't that what you're hinting? What do you deduce from the little you've heard?"

"*Little?*" She put her head on one side. "I was 'on' this morning, and I heard Niz'r or Fuad telling somebody in—it must have been El Khadye—that they had nothing further to do with management. It was all in your hands, and to get in touch with you, here!"

"Great god of wars!"

"And don't forget Paul's got his own set with him, and Angela's never off it. You know that. She really runs things—"

"Don't you?"

"I'd like to!"

"Then do. It's a little defeating. I don't want Paul to leave. He's needed. When Angela calls, tell her I want to talk to him—"

"She's already been on, and I told her six tonight's the best time—"

"I think office kisses are the original forbidden fruit—"

"This isn't an office. Come round to St. James's Square at about four, could you? You *must* see your suite. And mine's a dream!"

"Those office suppliers were pretty slippy, weren't they?"

She put her hand to the back of her head, and lolled. I thought it provocative.

"They're getting double-time, and I chose the furniture yesterday. No trouble at all. *And* I got four Sergeant-Majors from the Brigade of Guards. They're giants. And terribly strict. I warned them about bombs and all that sort of thing—"

"What did they say to that?"

"They asked what time their lunch hour was, and if it was free—"

21

Watching the clock, at three A.M., I put a call through to the "Blue" number at the United States Embassy, and told the officer I wanted to speak to Druxi, in, of course, her maiden name. I didn't have many minutes to wait. I heard her a long way off. Then she came in clear.

"But what a coincidence! I was wondering where *you* were!"

"Yorick—"

"Yes. Just tell me. We're quite safe—"

"That little jet of yours. The red one—"

"It's in Belgium."

"May I borrow it?"

"But of course. You'd have to repaint, change numbers—"

"It'll be well-covered, insurance, so forth. Any idea where I can get the repaint done?"

"Did you ever meet Red Pusey? He's really tops. Knows Europe inside out. He's the best man. Organised. You'll find him at Pusey Instruments Incorporated, Brussels. Or he could meet you. Better—"

"Have you a pilot in mind?"

"Yes. But I'll talk to Red, first. Anything else you want, ask him. I'll call him. Then he'll call you—"

"Never be grateful enough—"

"Oh, come on, now!"

I went back to sleep, perfectly happy, with a full half of the jig-saw in place. I seemed to be filling silver pots when the waiter put the tray down, with the newspapers, and should have pulled aside the curtains. Instead, he looked at me, and shuddered.

"What is it?"

"Shockin' day, sir. Bit of a fog, rain, cold. I mean, give you the aches'n croggles looking at it—"

"How do you get here?"

"Tube, sir. Nice and warm, down there. Anything else, sir?"

"You might drop this in at eight twenty eight—"

"Lady's gone out, sir. She was called at six thirty—"

I wondered what her ladyship could be doing, and then remembered we'd moved the radio set to St. James's Square. I had to look in my book for the number.

I was answered by a rumble, and a clatter.

"Hello?"

"Did the place fall down?"

"Oh, darling! No. It was a carpet layer. They've almost finished. The main office furniture's piled on the stairs. The Sergeant-Majors are simply wonderful. Why aren't you asleep?"

"I wanted to talk to you—"

"I'm sitting on the floor, perfectly comfortably, and here's nice Sergeant-Major Harrison with a *basin* of tea. We've got to get cups—"

"Heard from anybody?"

"Everybody and everything's absolutely quiet. Mr. Logan managed to pacify everybody at El Humir. We're not losing anybody. A Mr. George Raikes rang late last night and said the ship sailed late because of this awful fog—"

"Is it foggy?"

"Not very, here. Superintendent Farqhuarson's sending some people at ten. Will you be here?"

"Of course. Did your mother go off?"

"Yes. Ecstatic. I'm going to bring her down next week, if I may—"

"If I still had a mother, I wouldn't ask—"

"I love you more than any words—"

"I love you without any—"

I went through the courier's pouch, signed, counterinitialed, finished a stack, and wondered why Paul hadn't called the night before. I had no business reason to call him. But I felt I ought to call him to find out about the leg. Which, I thought, I should have done before. But after all, Angela was a secretary employed by the Company. *She* should have called me. Childish nonsense. There's no protocol in friendship.

The number didn't reply. I tried again. No reply. It was a big house. Another fox hunt? But there were servants. I called the local Police, and a sergeant told me he'd look into it.

I sent the tubes of maps to St. James's Square, a number of them, of various countries, to confuse any issue there might be in some minds. Those of use I'd studied until I could have drawn them from memory. But I still had to "see" the area from the frontier to the prison, and back. Yet, the nagging thought was constant.

I had to persuade the East German authorities to allow me into the prison.

I couldn't go as myself. I not only had no valid reason, but I was a suspected foreigner. As anyone else, I was equally vulnerable. Apart from that, I knew Errol would be a marked prisoner. That he was in there at all pointed to it. Hauerfurth Prison was only forty-two miles from the border. My constant fear was that he'd be taken somewhere else if he were named before I got there. I knew plenty of people in the West, but few in the East, except those who knew me, and that would be fatal.

The telephone called me back from the door.

"Mr. Trothe? Gillian Roule, with a small parcel, and somebody else. We can come up the side way—"

"Do. I'll meet you!"

I went for a slow stroll down the corridor. Gillian came from the emergency door on the stairway, and held it open for a veiled woman in a long grey coat.

"Here's the parcel, Mr. Trothe," Gillian said, breathless. "We came up in the lift to two floors below—"

"Mr. Trothe!" the veiled woman whispered. "Only a second. You must know how I feel?"

I took a firm hand, kissed, and held it.

"I don't make more fuss of you because I'm sure there are people who'd like to know you were here—"

"We didn't come through the courtyard," Gillian said, still holding the door open. "Nobody saw us, I'm perfectly sure. I'd kill anybody I thought—!"

"Gillian!" Lady Imbritt scolded. "Darling! Mr. Trothe, my prayers—"

"Both of you take care of each other, say nothing, do nothing, till you hear from me. Gillian, keep off clix. *Off!*"

She nodded, took Lady Imbritt's arm, and let the door close on its spring.

I walked back with the parcel. Absurd, in the middle of London, to act in such a way. But Gillian didn't think so, and in fact, I didn't. Whether we liked it or not, there were eyes. The telephone was ringing when I got into the room.

"Sir Roland Ainsworth's secretary, sir. Sir Roland's been on the Continent for the past two days and he's flying to the United States tomorrow—"

"I'd very much like to see Sir Roland if only for ten minutes. A consultation, but not personal. Advice is what I very badly need—"

"One moment, sir, please—"

I held on. I could have seen others, scores of them, but Sir Roland was *the* physician of his day, with a world-wide reputation in glandular disease.

"Could you be here in thirty minutes, sir? Sir Roland has a patient at the moment, and can't speak—"

"I'll be there!"

I got a coat, hat, and umbrella, and ran. It was grey foggy, with about thirty yards visibility. My driver went up and down alleys I didn't know, but we weren't stopped for traffic lights or anything else, and when we pulled up I only had to walk round the corner. But he wouldn't wait. I had to pay him, and damn his rear light. On a day like that, the Harley Street house was murky enough to serve as staging place for a cemetery.

"I know, I know!" Sir Roland said, in creased black and stripes. "I'd like to move out. But Harley Street's Harley Street. They get here, they're almost better. When they get the bill, they're quite recovered. Or dead. Sit y' down. You don't look as if you need me!"

I'd written Von Staengl's message, and I passed it over.

"If you got that from a source, let us imagine, you respected, what—perhaps—would you diagnose?"

We'd known each other too long for explanation.

He looked over at me, fingers threaded on the table, spectacles down his nose.

"No hope of seeing the exhibit?" he asked gently.

"On the other side of the Wall. I want to take medicaments, drugs, whatever's called for—"

He shook his head.

"Worse than useless without examination—"

"What could it be?"

"That's wasting time I don't know. On the face of it, it could be myxoedema. But aren't there physicians where he is?"

"They may be using him as a guinea pig—"

"Then nothing's going to be of the slightest use, is it?"

"I was wondering if there's anything that might put a little life in him. If it's only for fifteen minutes. Half an hour. To get him away!"

He leaned back, laughing quietly, looking round the room.

"Just let me think this over, and I'll let you know this evening. At the Savoy?"

"You don't hold out much hope?"

"As you said, they might be experimenting. What's a few minutes treatment going to do?"

"I mean, as a momentary reviver. Till we get him away—"

"If you do, I want to see him—"

"You shall. He won't be the least important of your patients—"

I had a most gloomy walk back. I hadn't quite thought Roland would bring something out of the hat, exactly. But at least, I'd imagined he'd have an answer, give me whatever was needed, and that would be an important part of the business over. I didn't like to think of an overweight Errol. I couldn't quite imagine it. Our departure, as I'd planned it, would be a sharpish nip, and away.

But I had to get there, first. That was the worrier. The idea that'd nibbled hadn't put its teeth in hard enough. I couldn't seem to attract it into growth.

I had to assume another identity. It had to be foolproof. I had to enter East Germany as somebody able to ask for a permit to visit the prison, not with a delay of days or weeks, but then and there. Or the timetable wouldn't stand up. Moreover, I was asking permission to see *a* prisoner, and not merely gape at what they wanted to show me.

They could be fully aware that Errol was only son of a late head of our Secret Service, and by no means an amateur. They might also have got him across the border because they knew. In which case, willy-nilly, they'd never let me see him.

But they might want to find out a little more about his visitor.

Which meant one of two things. Either the identity I adopted, and the papers, must be immune from momentary enquiry, repel any immediate suspicion, or else I'd join Errol without a hope of seeing daylight again. With nobody to appeal to.

The idea that had nibbled was quite good, but not as good as all that.

22

I got to James' office while the fat girl was taking a plastic cover off a large, square model on the table.

James gave me a cup of very good coffee and a biscuit, and nodded at the model, of grey, flat walls with air ducts at the top, no windows anywhere, a high, wide gate, and a flat-topped water tower affair in the middle of the four buildings, diamond-patterned inside.

"I believe you'll have to forget anything except the entrance and adjacent rooms," he said, munching. "That gate is thirty feet high, twenty-four broad. It's backed by a steel grille. There's a peep window in this postern. The grille has to be raised to a man's height when people enter. It's lowered after they're through the postern. The whole thing's worked from the watch tower. It's also the generator house, et cetera. When the door guard gives the signal on this board outside the gate, the guard up here works the switch. Clear?"

"Perfectly. Once you're in, you won't get out till the procedure's gone through again in reverse—"

"That's it. And it takes an appreciable time. About four minutes!"

"They only need a fraction of that, and we're dead!"

"Well, let's say, in normal circumstances. That's *not* what I have in mind!"

"Love some more coffee, please. It's excellent!"

"Alison makes it. Well, now, it's off the road, as you see. The main road's just over a half mile away, up this absolutely flat, straight approach. The surrounding land is part kitchen garden in the rear, a cemetery, as you see over here, and a sort of stores and barn affair here. The rest, all the way—that's about three miles—is flat terrain, rough pasture for the most part, but sown with tens of thousands of tree stumps. This little river's the local devil. All this land is bog. It runs almost up to the prison garden. But it breeds mosquitos, midges and God knows what other type of pest. Must be hell to live there. Especially now. Sun's getting warmer every day—"

He pointed to the large aerial photograph.

"Those clouds are chemicals they've been using to keep them down. They can spray oil, of course, but it's the bog among the tree stumps they can't reach. The wind, as you see, is fairly stable in this direction, from this corner toward the prison buildings. I don't know if you remember the evidence given at Nuremberg? That wind was the inmates' greatest friend. It blew away the smell—"

"Some of us don't know we're alive—"

"That's what I'm thinking about, here. It's mostly for political prisoners, you know that. And they're not likely to leave for any reason. That cemetery's grown more than two hundred percent in three years. Even though they're also buried in quicklime. Not always one by one. Without markers—"

"They haven't learned much—"

"Well, then, you've been taken by car to this point on the approach. You turn in here, and the guard takes the keys. If you've got a driver, he stays in this shed, here. You walk the rest of the way. If it's raining, you're given an umbrella—"

"Can't be—!"

"—sheer old-fashioned capitalist thoughtfulness. It *will* creep out. You now come to the gate. The guard gives the password. The peep window shuts. A pause. You hear a loud, sustained roar. That's the grille going up. A longer pause. The small door opens. You enter, and a guard—you don't see him—asks for your pass.

You present it in this little letterbox. You're told to go forward, and stop. The grille comes down behind you. You're locked in the prison—"

"A portentous moment—"

"You now—if your pass is in order—reach this space, enclosed by high walls, without foothold or windows. The door in the main building opens, and you're invited to enter by a guard. You are taken into this entrance hall—"

He pointed to the plan on one side, and a colored sketch on the other.

"It's panelled in elm made in the prison. On your right is the cloakroom. There, you leave hat, coat, umbrella—"

"—that's how they get it back?"

"—briefcase, galoshes, whatever other rubbish you may have brought in that's not an essential part of your person. You're now taken next door. It's a waiting room. You stay there for ten minutes or so, while they check your pass with headquarters, and go through the things in the cloakroom. Take block chocolate and cigarettes. The guards appreciate them—"

"They take them out?"

"It's not 'taking.' It's 'finding.' You're not supposed to bring them into a prison. But they then know that *you* know the game, and they play accordingly. The waiting room's sprayed to kill the pests. You'll find out the moment you get out of the car. They're like a cloud. Then you're taken to this room to see the assistant governor, possibly. You make your request. If it's to see a prisoner, and HQ's given permission, he'll send you to the medical inspection and operating complex, here. You notice all these rooms lead off this part of the entrance hall? This plain, polished door here, goes into the prison. You won't go in there. Unless you make a mistake. In which case, you won't come out!"

"I'm drinking a lot of coffee this morning—"

"The weather for it. Splash of whisky over there—"

"Not before six thirty, thank you—"

"Same school. Very well. Now, kindly note. You haven't at any time gone more than a few yards in any direction. You're enclosed in a solid cube of reinforced concrete. Unless the prisoner is brought from the prison, through that door, to the medical inspection room—it's disinfected—they're afraid of outside infection—in his medicated gown and cap—he wears nothing underneath—you won't see him. There's *no* way of getting into the prison proper. Behind that plain door, there's a grille and a cage. The cage is operated by remote control. I won't go into it. You, I take it, want to do something in this entrance hall?"

"It's a general idea, that's all—"

"'General' fits splendidly, I think. Well now, notice the construction of this entrance 'cube.' It's a square, built out from the main building. The inner walls are simple concrete blocks. The doors are elm. The outer walls—there aren't any windows—are reinforced concrete, but nothing much. Nothing to compare with the main building. Your obstacles to any escape of your own timing are first, the main grille and main gate. Then the automatic steel door into the entrance hall. Well, you'd be very silly to tackle any of those. But you *could* make a hole in this wall, here, in the waiting room, and providing you raised enough hell in the hall itself, you could be in the open air in moments. Going where?"

I could have kissed him.

"I believe I have the rest more or less marked out," I said. "Do we know when they spray for pests?"

"Yes, we do. On five consecutive days of each month, from April to October. The twenty first to the twenty sixth. Sometimes there's a day or two's difference. Why?"

He was looking at me, I dared to think, puckishly, though it wouldn't ordinarily have sprung to mind. I'd never have thought there was any Puck in his character.

"It occurred to me we might, let us say, 'help' that spray if we mixed something with it. Somehow—"

"We might indeed!"

He flipped through a looseleaf book of plastic holders, and held up a picture.

It showed a stretch of country about a couple of miles by three, seen from the air. Most of it was covered in thick white mist.

He opened a drawer, and took out a can just a little larger than a tin of lighter fluid.

"This is what did *that*," he said, holding it up. "Doesn't kill. But you don't see or hear or eat very well for a couple of days after, and you won't use your arms and legs for a day or two longer. A nice little breath or two, that's all. I've got the mask, and the antidote pills. Do you think you ought to work something out, and come and see me again?"

"Tomorrow? About five? Why not come to the Savoy?"

He shook his head.

"All business on the premises, please. After all, the management at the Savoy would be most annoyed if we knocked a wall down, wouldn't they?"

23

I have a fairly extensive knowledge of radio and electronics in general, and had I not gone into H.M. Civil Service, I might have made a fortune. Might. It's one of the things I often think about before I go to sleep, often while I shave, and on railway journeys with nothing else to do. But it had always been of great use. I'd fixed many a device for doctor friends, especially in the shock treatment of depressives. I didn't follow it. I find any mental disorder frightening. It's an easy "out," but that's how I feel. I'll help, but I can't be interested. Among the men I'd helped, Leon-art Graeffe was possibly the best known. We'd met in Tangan-yika-that-was. He had his own makeshift hospital there, and first I put in electric light, then a generator for the operating room, and after that, the minor refinements. He was an extraordinary man, and I suppose he'd "cured" more "mad" people than any other dozen. He was loved by his patients and we got along very well. More importantly, he'd once told me that a relative of his was in an East German prison. I couldn't remember which. We don't take all that notice. Hebrews seem condemned to live without sym-pathy. But it was worth trying.

He'd opened a clinic in West Germany, where many East Ger-man bigwigs went for treatment. That was part of the idea which had first nibbled. But it didn't go quite far enough. I hadn't made up my mind who I was supposed to be.

Without telling Consuelo, I booked a seat for Bonn, with a stop at Brussels, and left the date open. The Company's aircraft I'd already sent to Handley Page for a repaint, to be ready in London for Monday, and I'd given orders for a flight plan to Brussels, and Wildesheim, which was almost due west of Hauerfurth.

The nearest airport on the East German side was at Geldern, about twenty miles to the northeast. The nearest fighter airfield was another fifty miles or so away, east, and one further south. But the fighters could be airborne in four minutes, and they flew at well over Mach-1.

Which meant that from the time of warning, I had four minutes, and not more than a few seconds' grace. I knew too much about German pilots to think of luck. It had to be split-second timing, and I still had to find a hiding place over the West German border. The fighter on my tail wouldn't worry about geography.

In the new St. James's Square offices that for-once bright morning, I added the minor details, and at the same time, took care of the Company's business, signed the directives, talked to all the offices, except Cairo which wasn't working. El Humir was in excellent form, and the exploratory team reported that so far, the pipeline was correctly orientated.

"I can't think what's happened to Angela," Consuelo said, just before lunch. "When I see her, I'll have a few choice words—"

I went to great trouble in finding a shilling and putting it, with fingery ceremony, in the middle of the blotter.

"Bet you," I said.

"Let me get a shilling. I can just afford it!"

She rummaged in her handbag and brought out two sixpences.

"What are we betting?"

"Angela heard that message or some other. I'm betting you one shilling they're both in Geneva, and Paul's raising hell—"

She picked up the sixpences.

"No bet. I asked BEA. They were both on last night's late flight. They'll have seen Azil by now. He'll be up. Habib's in Damascus. Fuad and Niz'r flew to Cairo yesterday. Prince Abdullah—I suppose the only one you have to worry a little about—is going in the nursing home at Gstaad-Brö, apparently with hepatitis, for at least a month—"

"I'm sorry Paul didn't come to see me—"

"Why *should* he?"

"Point's well taken. Book me to Geneva, now. Telephone Azil I'll be there in time to disturb his post-prandial—"

"If that—what's her name?—that French girl's with him, you'd better not!"

"You're coming with me. We'll confront them, nude, if necessary, together!"

"No other woman's going to see *you* in the nude!"

"Not in question. I was talking about *them*—"

"I wouldn't let you see her—"

"That's selfish—"

The telephone rang.

"Mr. Halloran Pusey to see you, sir."

"Immediately, please!"

I went out to meet him, redhaired, shortish, thick shoulders, grey eyes, sunburned, a good chap to be beside in a scrap.

Consuelo brought us a coffee tray, and indicated the new china service by a lifted eyebrow. Mr. Pusey held up a cup, looked at Consuelo, and at me.

"Coalport? Boy, my mother ought to be here. She'd love this place. Then the Coalport? She has a collection. I just bought her some Sèvres in Paris. I'm still bleeding!"

"Prices are getting out of hand. But we'll never get any more Sèvres. That's why. You may speak absolutely freely. Miss Furnival has no secrets!"

"Well, fine. I'm only here for a moment. I'm just going to drink this, and blow. The aircraft's in my hangar. Top condition. What color d'you want her?"

I didn't look at Consuelo.

"Something that might confuse a gunner on her tail?"

"Visual confusion's one thing. But radar's another. I think a leaf job—"

"There's forest, yes. I'll be in Brussels tonight or tomorrow—"

He put the cup and saucer down, stood, looking out of the window. Consuelo went out.

"Beautiful place to work. Peaceful. All history. I have that feeling when I'm in Brussels. I love it!"

"Have any problems with staff?"

"Less than in France. I get along fine with the Belgians. They train like shelling peas. Especially the Walloons. I didn't know about *them* before. Told you're going to want a pilot?"

"I'm all right as co. Not as captain—"

He stretched until the fashionable blue suit threatened to part down the back.

"I hear the trumpets again," he said, picking up his overcoat. "I know all that country—"

"If you take off from less than fifty miles over the Eastern border, where do you hide on the Western side with a squadron of fighters behind you?"

He laughed up at nymphs in plastered gambol over the ceiling.

"I'll take a coffee on that one. See you in Brussels tomorrow, when?"

"Seven, the Metropole?"

"Fine. But don't book in. I have a house—"

Consuelo stood at the stairhead when I took him down to the car, and she was still there when I went up.

"You're quite determined to do something?" she said lightly, though I knew her too well.

"Whether I am or not, is moot. Are you ready to go to Geneva?"

"No!"

"Why not?"

"I'm not going to do anything to help you to—to commit suicide!"

"Will you please pull yourself together? You're being hysterical—"

"Not in the slightest. I'll do everything I can to stop you—"

I turned about and walked downstairs, without hat or coat, passed Sergeant-Major Briggs on duty, through the swing door and into a freezing wind, turned left, walking fast to warm up, and into Pall Mall, across the road to the Royal Automobile Club. As I reached the doorway, somebody in smart pace caught me.

Sergeant-Major Briggs held out hat, coat, muffler, umbrella, and gloves.

"Compliments of Miss Furnival, sir. You forgot these!"

"My compliments and thanks. I shall not be back this week!"

I went down to the snackbar but I was in too much of a fury to eat. I had a glass of wine and asked Daimler Hire to send a car to take me to the airport. I hadn't known I harbored such a rage. But I cannot stand disobedience, or any pretense of threat or blackmail, whatever it may be. I didn't give Consuelo, or for that matter anyone else, the right to dictate to me where I had decided, and neither did I wish to listen to any advice. Not that I'd suddenly become a nabob. Very far from it. I'd been trained to obey without question. I'd watched that tradition eroded until any whippersnapper could cock a snook at all authority, and not merely be patted on the head, but applauded by a generation which should have known better. There were not many of them, seemed to be the excuse. Unfortunately, those small lesions spread into a lasting wound. I was not, for one moment, going to permit that spirit to gain ground in my own Company. Both my children had defied me, though outside my knowledge. It was not to happen in my office, and certainly not with a woman I hoped would be my wife. I knew why she rebelled. She'd lost her brother not long before. She knew that to avenge him, and others, I'd gone to West Germany those few months ago, and had, indeed, more than levelled the score. She wanted to marry, settle down. So did I. But not at any price. She had to learn one simple lesson.

A man has his job, and woman hers. We're all in trouble when we mix them up, decide each other's problems.

I was having none of it.

The soprano voice of a pageboy called my number. I ignored it. When I reached the airport there was a message at the arrival hall, and at the airline desk, and on the plane. I took no notice of any of them.

A lesson learned is a lesson in hand.

24

Of course, the moment I reached Geneva, I telephoned her.

She'd gone out. I left a message that she was to telephone me. I was sorry for the flare-up, wished I could hold my temper at such times, but I've never been able to. The best I can manage is to turn, walk out, wait till the pouting period's over, and then go back and apologize, if, that is, I was in the wrong.

Our offices in Geneva were the best we had. They were on the last three floors of a fine building in white stone, parquet floors and plate-glass, spacious, air-conditioned, fire and burglar proof. My office was next to Paul's on the top floor, with the conference room on the other side, and the offices, used till then, by the Princes.

I walked into my office, hung up my hat and coat, and saw a note on my desk: *Consuelo told me you were due here, and I'll be waiting next door. P.*

I went over, tapped, and heard his "Come in!"

He sat in a glittering metal wheelchair at the window, with a tray on one side, a pile of reports on the other, more on the floor.

"Glad you got here so soon, Edmund," he said, his old self. "I was flying back on that five-something—"

"I'm going to Brussels. Paul, there's a matter—it happened easily enough—but it's difficult to put in words—"

He held up both hands, laughing.

"I talked to Azil and Prince Abdullah. They gave me the entire story, and I want to tell you how grateful I am—"

"Entirely misplaced, Paul. Allow me to explain. I'm stepping down. Not out. I won't be active in the Company for at least a month. Perhaps longer. I'd very much like you to pick a second-in-command—"

"What're you going to do?" he asked, in a Head-One-Side-Mouth-Twisted-Don't-Like-the-Sound-of-It stare. "Errol? Now, listen, for God's sake—"

"There's nothing to be discussed," I said, choirboy style. "I'm simply saying I shan't be dealing with Company business for at least a month, and when I come back, I'm going to devote my time to the social problems along the line from Beyfoum, west. Neither of us'll ever have time to get at them. But they're piling up—"

"I have to go along with you, there. But I decided to resign, Edmund!"

"Absolutely not. What happened had nothing to do with me—"

"Why didn't you tell me on the spot?"

"Put yourself in my place—"

"But you let me go off—"

"If I'd told you then, you know perfectly well you'd have resigned. Nothing on earth'd've prevented it. We'd never have got you back. But we need you, Paul!"

"The perennial one-leg? Look, Edmund, you know how losing the old Department hit me. Well, this was just another of the same sort of blinder. The whole therapy of this position is that I was my own man. Nobody ahead. Nobody to ask. Nobody like—the Blur—"

"—I'm no Blercgrove. You'll never get an instruction from me. Everything's the same, except that I'm no longer on the staff, and you have five percent of the unissued stock. Your seat on the Board carries over while you hold it. One stipulation—"

"Knew there was a catch!"

"Not even that. If ever you feel you want to sell, you offer to me, first—"

He rolled himself back and for a few inches by the wheels.

"I have to smooth out a bad mood, Edmund," he said, at last. "I saw red. Angela got me here. She had a talk with Consuelo. Couple of real witches. What's Consuelo think of this Errol nonsense? You're going to wind up a *real* Yorick, don't you know that? You're just handing them your skull to quicklime it!"

"Pretty thought—"

He reached down for a telephone message slip.

"That might explain this," he said, holding it out. "The designation's familiar!"

Please change appointment I. Eight ten. To three o'clock Thursday, and acquaint Alison.

"How did you get this?" I asked.

"Sent on from London in the pouch. Mean anything?"

I suddenly had a curious idea. I felt it would be dangerous—for some reason—to say anything. Even one word.

"It's a file I wanted, that's all," I said.

Yellow flashed. Paul answered, smiled at me, listened.

"Consuelo's in your office. She's got a tray waiting for you. Prince Abdullah'd like to see you. He's on his way. She's got to run. No flowers in your office or his!"

"Or yours—"

"Angela's trying to straighten things downstairs. Gilbert and that lot sent through some funny stuff—"

"Nothing important?"

"They didn't have enough time. As it is, we'll have to change codes, ciphers, every damn thing—"

"All right, Director General. I'm due in Brussels at seven. I'll be back tomorrow after I've seen about a new weather-radar for our aircraft—"

"We'll get along fine without you. I've got an idea for the new code. You could bring back an edition of Leonardo da Vinci's drawings. Preferably with the mathematics—"

My tray was on a side table by my desk. On the pad, where I couldn't miss it, a tumbler full of dwarf anemones brightened things. Consuelo's kiss. I ate an excellent brawn sandwich and drank two cups of coffee, read the reports just in from Baghdad and Damascus, and I was smoking a cigarette when the door opened.

Prince Abdullah stood there.

I knew him from his portraits, and they didn't flatter him except for age. He must then have been nearly eighty. There were no details in Who's Who. He didn't look sixty.

"Mr. Trothe, we meet here or in the conference room?" he asked, in a deep voice, from the timbre, trained in public speaking. "I am late!"

"I think your own office is the best place," I said, and opened the door of the conference room, crossed it, waited for him to follow, went through Azil's office, through Habib's, to a room we'd never used, furnished with pieces sent from London and Paris. It looked less like an office than the drawing room of a Georgian palace.

"The chair was especially built for your highness," I said, looking at the blue leather near-throne. "I was very glad you accepted—"

"You're lucky I did. I don't like to be left out of business which affects my country. His Majesty didn't understand it. We wish only to help and protect—"

While I pushed a chair to the table, I had the opportunity of looking at him without staring. His hair was short, grey, touched with henna, and so was the clipped beard. He wasn't dark. He didn't spend much time in the sun. His eyes were deeply sunk and blackish—hepatitis?—but the pupils were black, bright, if the whites appeared bloodshot, with deep wrinkles at the sides. He wore a wing collar, grey cravat and pearl pin, white vest, and a grey frock coat, the first I'd seen for many years. What really surprised me was his command of English. I hadn't been prepared for it.

"That was my main object in allowing you shares," I began, prepared for argument, or discussion.

"On my nephews' excellent advice!"

"That, yes—"

"Then let us confine ourselves to essentials. When my older brother dies—God protect him!—I shall succeed to the throne. I may not live much longer. My successor is not the type to be interested. But his advisors are. They are able men. They have capital. They do much as they please. I believe a great deal of your difficulty has been due to their influence. They work through intermediaries. In these days, a large sum will buy almost anyone. I think you would be surprised what political influence they have bought. We must outbuy them, or when we reach certain countries in Europe, we shall find we are helpless. The prospect pleases you?"

"No, sir."

"What have you to suggest?"

"Let me have the names of the men. Cash has to pass through channels—"

He shook his head, smoothing the bristly grey mustache under thumb and forefinger.

"Not cash, or anything but gold," he said, and took a capsule from a box on his watchchain, swallowed it without water. "Gold can be bought by agents. No names. Giver and receiver remain unknown. The same with jewels. The market is free. And anonymous. Well?"

"Obviously you've used the same methods—"

"Of course. That is exactly why I asked. How will you answer this campaign? Which, I must assure you, will grow. This is why I am here. I have had a talk with His Majesty. He is sympathetic to my side. But he cannot choose between brothers, naturally. And my brothers' advisors are loyal to the royal house. This is all-important in these days. There is a so-called republican movement. It is in the highest degree dangerous. To the country, and to us. Is there a way of coming to terms with my brother's side?"

"From what you say, if they got an inch, they'd take a mile—"

"That is the fact—"

"Fighting them means weakening the royalists?"

"A schism is always a weakness—"

"Why don't they apply for shares?"

"They haven't until now, because Habib and Azil even refused me!"

"Why did they do that?"

"They knew I would soon control the Company!"

"I hope you've decided to put that out of your mind?"

"For the moment. I shall see what *you* intend to do!"

"First, I'm going to find out if those men had anything to do with trying to kidnap Habib—"

"No. Nothing. I will guarantee that with my life!"

I stared at a Corot, a countryside in fading sunlight.

"Then we *have* other enemies," I said. "That's not what I'd thought!"

"That, which you put so simply, is why I applied for shares, and why I suggest we come to terms with my brother's advisors. We are foolish to work against each other—"

"That's not what you began by saying!"

He laughed, folded his hands, and leaned back.

"I had to meet you, first!" he said. "I believe between us we would be a strong partnership. But we have, as you say, other enemies. We all know it. We all know it's not our republican enemies—"

"How do you know?"

He sat up, forearms on the chair, fists on the table, looking out at the lake.

"Habib would never have been found," he said, beyond attempt at argument. "I have you to thank, but inexpressibly. No. Neo-republican followers don't descend to such methods. Their fight is in the country itself. Secondly, they know Habib and Azil, in particular, are sympathetic to them. It is a matter of great pain to me. But to people who would parlay with Israel, what do you expect?"

"I want to know what evidence you have of 'other' enemies?"

"Nothing I can put before you in the way I'd like. I would like to say A, B and C. But even my 'A' is a small cripple. When the Court was informed of the attempt, His Majesty was in a most—"

He waved the back of his hand in front of his eyes.

"—ah! Such a violent fury. His nephew treated with indignity, and nobody to punish? Everybody had to present themselves. Now, you see, nobody can lie at such a time. Therefore, it was not anybody to do with my brothers. In addition, the leader of the republican side—but remember, an enemy—sent a message personally, that nobody on that side had any hand in it, and, I suppose to provoke more trouble, professed great friendship for Habib and Azil, and promised them their lives and property when the republic is in being. Imagine the scene!"

"I can well imagine. But what's the—"

He nodded, eyes shut, impatiently.

"We all had an opportunity of a talk together. Extra-officially, of course. They accused me of several acts. But I knew nothing of them. They spoke of people in their oilfields—we have our own in many parts—taken away—"

"Bought?"

"Perhaps. Engineers in charge of construction, and a chemical laboratory, I remember. Of course I knew nothing of it. Habib and Azil didn't. Then who? Freighter ships sunk. Ferries with hundreds on board. Men in charge of public works. But as Afad al'Aram, the republican leader said, these are the very men they need to put their program into force—"

"He had no ideas?"

He breathed in, pushed back the chair.

"I asked him if it was the Russians. Of course, the Russians are always a threat. But in the past few years they've worked more through commerce. Banking. Some of the works destroyed have been Russian-built. They're not madmen. They don't destroy their own property. Or buy their own men!"

"Communists? Other than republicans?"

"The republicans are not communists. It has become a word to use when there is nothing else. No. Not republicans. Not Russians. Not communists. There is no evidence of any sort. Except that a great deal of money is being used—"

"You said your brothers' advisors were using money—"

"I know. They are, and they have. But there is nothing to connect them with any of these extraordinary happenings. Except the internal damage. It is true they have sent men to attack the pipelines. They would like to buy the Company's contracts and responsibilities. They know what the profits are going to be—"

"And if they are allowed to buy shares?"

He smiled, turning his eyes sideways to me.

"Of course, they will pay a high price. But they are not paying these men to leave. I am sure it is the truth, because I have seen the banking statements. His Majesty, of course, must see everything. I had the opportunity—"

"Then where on earth *do* they go?"

"I am always in daily touch with all my agents. Those men could fly anywhere. Now I have the airports watched. But only in my country, of course. They can fly to Cairo—"

"I thought we had absolute right of way in Egypt?"

He nodded.

"I sent Niz'r there. I want to know who permitted those contracts to be countermanded. I must tell you I also tried to buy. I shall find out who was able to summon ships which didn't exist. Our only informant reported they didn't fly a flag—"

"Very strange. And officers of the Egyptian Navy commanded—"

"Again, wrong. They had nothing to do. The men and officers were in uniform, yes. But not Egyptian. I am also sure of this!"

"A 'power,' you said. Not Russia. Nothing to do with communists. A neighboring country?"

He shook his head, eternally sure.

"We would know immediately, and we could stop it immediately—"

The taps on the door were Consuelo's. She brought in a cable. Her dress was a demure triumph in black.

"For his highness," she said, without looking at me, yet I sensed the appeal and loved it.

"Thank you, my dear. Ask for my car, if you please—"

He took the paper knife and sliced along the edge. A neat man.

The cable was two strips of print, and he took a monocle from the top right-hand waistcoat pocket.

"Where is Durres?" he asked, putting the monocle back. "D-u-r-r-e-s—"

"It's what we call Durazzi, I believe," I said. "A port in Albania—"

"The ships called in there last night. They took aboard thirty eight passengers between them. With some industrial machinery from Poland—"

"What did they unload?"

"Apparently nothing. They sailed this morning. He doesn't know where—"

"Albania? They're not overfriendly with Russia. Not many friends anywhere—"

He got up, put the cable in his pocket, and buttoned the frock coat.

"Perhaps they have not," he said, pushing back the chair. "Unfortunately, I believe we have less. There will be many cables for me. I give you permission to reply. I shall not see you for at least a month—"

"You don't want visitors?"

He laughed rather tiredly.

"If you bring your secretary, I shall be charmed!" he said. "Illness is a nuisance. Death is a state of mind I haven't cultivated. Sir, we are well-met. Good morning!"

25

Brussels was rainy, but in spite of delays, I met Pusey on the stroke of seven and we went in the comfortable bar at the Metropole. Pusey didn't drink—which surprised me—and we decided on a split champagne.

"I can drink this, or a beer," he said. "Just one, that's all. I'm going to take you home and get you settled in, then I'm sorry, but I have to leave. Something's come up in Brunswick. We have a factory there—"

"Suits me splendidly. I have to be in Geneva tomorrow—"

"Only if you promise to come back soon. Druxi'd murder me!"

"Afraid of her?"

"Who isn't? Let's get one thing set first. Going to let me in on this? Pilot? Don't say no, else I'll clobber the aircraft!"

"I'll be more than happy. But you've added up all the could-be's?"

"Done all the figuring. Comes out to one hundred percent—"

"That's that. I brought some maps with me—"

"Come home, and I'll show you a few—"

Home wasn't far, in the older, more fashionable part of the city, and the moment I went in, I knew Druxi had stayed there at some time. A woman leaves her own perfume in any house she's loved. It was fifteenth century, with additions perhaps every hundred years or so, and a touch of the present in some of the oils and sculpture.

"I'm a bachelor for the moment," he said. "What's surprising the hell out of me is the size of this market over here. Why didn't anybody see it before?"

"Stuck in medieval bird-lime—"

"Superiority complex? I think they lost that. It's kind of a jealousy syndrome. And they still have peasant's ideas about gold—"

"It's not a 'peasant' idea, if you'll forgive me. Peasants are the solid base of all civilisation. It's very much a dingy little middle-man's idea—"

"You mean de Gaulle?"

"The original plaster of Paris—"

He opened the door to a room that had been added. One long window showed a flood-lit garden. The other three walls were tacked with maps.

"That's my factory, there," he said, nodding at the far wall. "In Brunswick. This is the one that'll interest you—!"

He touched a spring I didn't see, and the wall parted to show a map of the West-East German border country, far superior to anything I had, with the prison clearly circled in crayon, only a few miles over the line. The fighter airfields had been flagged.

"You've been doing a little homework," I said.

We stood there, looking at it in the light of two spots.

"What's the plan?" he asked. "You won't have time to undo your collar button, you know that, don't you?"

"I'll be able to tell you more next time. Roughly, I want to arrive at the prison by car. Hired. Then I want to be in there not more than a few minutes—"

"How do I fly in? Where?"

"Along the driveway. It's asphalt. Three lanes. Very little traffic—"

"Right. What do you use for keys? That's quite a gate!"

"D'you know the place?"

"I was there before the Russians—"

"Good. I'll take care of the gate—"

215

"I'm told the guards in that tower have automatic cannons. That's heavy stuff—"

"If they can use them—"

"How many are you bringing out?"

"One—"

"That's three of us. I'll turn her when I touch down. Come out on engines."

"He's heavy. Perhaps two hundred or more pounds—"

"We're lightweights. No baggage. She lifts like a dove. She's the best in her class—"

"Is the door wide enough for a *fat* man? A *clumsy* fat man?"

He looked at me in sudden thought.

"Let me make a note of that!"

"How high's the step from the floor? Do we need a small ladder we could throw away?"

"I'll test tomorrow. I've got a couple of real fat gals at the factory. Boy, they'll get a workout!"

"The sentry or sentries at the arrival hut. You'll have to keep an eye—"

"I've got a Thompson-sub. She's old, but she still puts 'em where they're wanted—"

"I don't think you'll have to shoot a round—"

"While this's going on, where are you?"

"Inside. I got there by car. Remember?"

"Then you come out, plus fatso. What do I do? The guys in the water tower, and the others in the shed—"

"*If* they get the opportunity—"

"You mean, all I do is wait there?"

"With your mask on. All that's set. Once we're up, we shan't need them—"

"Going to gas 'em? How about international law?"

"No proof!"

He rubbed his hands, stamped his feet.

"Happy days are al-l-l-l-most!" he crooned. "I'll make a flight plan for getting there and back. And I know just where to go—"

"We don't want 'incidents.' This is a quick, clean, in-and-out, barely anybody the wiser—"

"That's why I want in. I have a family. Property. Comfortable life. But I go for the whole idea. I have to see you come out of that goddam' gate. When's this to be?"

"Don't know, yet. Fairly soon, I hope!"

I never got along better with any man I ever met. We talked over Common Market problems on the way to the airport, said *au 'voir* in the huge vault, made an appointment for the following Monday, and I went off to my jet, and he to his.

My appointment with Leonart Graeffe was for nine o'clock. I got there early, but there was no pain in riding about miles of forest till it was time to enter the gate. I've never felt any "mystery" in trees. They've always seemed friendly to me. I really believe my only enemies on earth are the brutes earning a living by cutting them down without replanting. There's no cemetery so horrible as a slaughtered forest.

The clinic, so far as I could see, was a series of blocks, whitish in moonlight, with a lake in distance, two swimming pools in green light, and a long line of lit windows. A young, rather pretty nurse in a smart pale blue and beige uniform took my card down the corridor, went into a double door, and appeared in a moment to smile, and hold out a hand toward the room.

Leonart came out in a rush. He hadn't aged a moment. His mop of white hair almost stood on end. His laugh was the same, there seemed no extra wrinkles, his skin was like the nurse's, and his grip was a cracker. We spoke of everything and everybody over a tray of excellent little sandwiches and meat jollies with a Riesling, and I began to wonder why I ever bothered with dinner.

"I have to work at night," he said. "I don't like plates of this and that. A little, a good taste, it's enough. Very well. What? Speak. We have no ears in these walls!"

"I want to get into East Germany. Into a prison. I want to interview one particular prisoner. Any ideas?"

He chose a mustard and cress square, doubled it with a smoked salmon, bit an arc, and raised his glass.

217

"Always the surprise!" he said. "The last time, wasn't it an interview with Patrice Lumumba?"

"He was on the run, and you were the only possible means of talking to him. Same thing, now!"

"His death was stupid as the Kennedys' or King's. I'm honored you come to me. Let me brush my thinking cap. Mr. Trothe, do you intend to go as a private person? A relative of this man?"

"No. I don't even know his—prison—name!"

The sandwich stayed at the halfway, between chest and chin.

"How do you propose this?" he asked, staring sombre pale blue eyes.

"I thought you might possibly be able to present a case for me to appear. He's suffering from something that might be a disease of the glands. He's gone to fat. Slow of speech. Movement—"

"Eunocoid, possibly. No clinical reference of any sort?"

"None."

"Guessing is worthless. Are they treating him, or using him?"

"I'd like to find out!"

He poured coffee and spooned a lot of sugar.

"I need it," he said. "Sugar is a good friend. A little idea presents itself. I owe you a great debt. No, no. You know very well. Now I shall pay back a little. It will take two or three days, though."

"Perfect. I shall be an electronics specialist of some sort—"

"Please tell me. How does one become that? What *is* an electronic specialist?"

"One who uses electronic apparatus—"

"And supposing they ask you to demonstrate?"

"With the stuff I'm taking with me, I'd give a fair show—"

"And the patient?"

"Wouldn't touch a patient—"

He brushed crumbs off a white blouse, retied the necktapes, poured more coffee.

"You're staying here tonight?" he asked.

"No. I'm going to London."

"You could be here on Sunday?"

218

"Certainly—"

"Please come in the early afternoon. I must be in Prague that night. I shall introduce you to two men. It is also better you say nothing of Egypt. Nothing of electricity or any profession. They will think you are a physician here. An impression only. Your name is Reinhardt Stautz. Your name will be on the door. You will take a cardiograph reading for one and an encephalograph for the other. I know you are competent—"

"Entirely—"

"They both leave next Wednesday evening. They are considerably better than when they came. But they won't live long. They work under mental pressure worse than the Americans. They condemn themselves to death. We make two things clear. Your German has a Russian accent. Accentuate it. If they speak to you. You keep a clear picture that you are a dedicated communist. You work here to perfect your knowledge. If they speak Russian, you have a French accent. Therefore, you are a Frenchman. If *they* speak French, they *know* you are a German. Clear?"

"Perfectly—"

"Secondly, and more importantly. The first man is a high official. You will not know his name. You will not speak unless he speaks to you. The nurse in attendance will speak. Then she will leave. He will be on the table with the electrodes taped. You will be at the controls. I shall have injected him thirty minutes before. When the pulse slows, you will suggest in your best German-Russian that he will sign a permit, make all paths quite open for you to enter the prison for the purposes of making an important experiment in glandular therapy. Those findings will be made available to the Department of Glandular Pathology at Magdeburg. You will make the suggestion over a period of fifteen minutes, in the same words, in the same tone of voice. Write them, learn them, say them positively, as an order. Understood?"

"Yes—"

"You will see the pulse waves returning to normal. At the moment they do, you will say nothing more. He will come to himself in a normal way. When he is almost at waking point, you will press the button and the nurse will enter. He will probably barely notice you. The second is also a high official of political police, intelligence, anything to do with detention or suppression. A most horrible ape. He is a far more difficult subject because, after years of treating people as Pavlov never treated a dog, he is virtually without feeling. *Without!*"

He poured two liqueurs.

"We have had a most difficult time with him. He looked normal, worked well, and his appetite was ravenous. For underdone meat. But he couldn't sleep, and he couldn't remember. Even where he lived. Where he came from that morning. Or what he signed yesterday. Thought passed through his mind without leaving impression. Or, that he could recall. The past was blank. He was a robot of the future. We shall put him back partially to that state. You will then, exactly as before, watch the dials for a change. You will then in *French*-German tell him you want a permit to enter the prison at a time, and a day, for the purpose of seeing this prisoner—so and so—to make certain electrical experiments which can be of great use in certain phases of memory lapse, schizophrenia, depression, sleeplessness. You'll have at least forty minutes. I suggest you write out exactly what you want. Speak at a slightly slower rate than ordinarily, but in the tone of voice he'll remember when you meet him. Do you follow?"

"Absolutely—"

"When you enter their offices, they won't recognize you physically. But your request, in the same words, *will* evoke a recall. We shall hope. What is the name of the prison?"

"Hauerfurth—"

He sat back, looking up at a large moth butting into the lamp, apparently without damage, making me wonder—not for the first time—why insects at speed can survive the most painful thump time and time again, but a man-built craft smashes at touch.

"You know, Mr. Trothe, I envy you so much!" he said, in a different tone. "Years ago I should have gone to America. Instead of coming here. But it's for a purpose. There is always purpose. When

I heard you say Hauerfurth, I can't believe it. It is always in my head. It is in my soul, this horrible word!"

Tears were falling from the sides of his eyes in silvery paths to the tops of his ears, into the white hair.

I was too shocked to say anything. I realized that when a man of his experience could feel enough to release tears, a nerve had been touched in some distant oasis of the mind, rarely visited, even perhaps unknown. But the language which explains the working of our mentality hasn't been put together. We're only permitted to guess, and sympathise, and for want of any rational act, remain mute, stupid though that may be.

"I do not apologise for this disturbance," he said, and sat up. "I believe that my son has been in that prison for the past five or six years. Imagine. It is twelve years, four months since I saw him. I came here, not to be near him, but I hoped to be able one day to appeal to somebody of sufficient authority. The days go. Months go. Years go. Neither of these men you are going to see has the authority to release the man you wish to see. Through them I couldn't hope to visit my son—"

"But couldn't you use much the same means?"

He threw out his hands impatiently.

"You think I haven't studied every facet? What could either of these men do for me? Neither of them could sign a release. And who makes a travel permit? Where is the border pass? And then, if there is an enquiry, do you suppose it would take them any time to find out how it was done? Who suffers? For what? Ten minutes of speech? And the hell of leaving him? I remember his eyes. He was more his mother—"

"Why is he in prison?"

"No charge. He was arrested as a student. I tried to get lawyers. Impossible. I hear he is still alive—"

"Is his name the same as yours?"

"Ah, no! His name is Levi Bar-Dav. That is my name. Leonart Graeffe is only another skin—"

"I'll add that name to my command. If it works for one—"

He fell forward, clutched my hand, kissed the knucklebones.

"Just a moment!" I said, and pulled my hand away. "How do we know it's going to work?"

His smile was a marvel of the trusting heart. I felt my own Faith warm.

"I didn't come here for nothing, Mr. Trothe!" he whispered. "I am not given the means for nothing. My knowledge is not for nothing. These two men are not here for nothing. You didn't save my life for nothing. I am not grateful for nothing. There is a purpose, sir. It is why you came to me. There *is* a purpose. There *is*. I *know* it. You *will* bring my son to me. I *know* it. You *will!*"

"With God's help—"

"But who else?" he shouted, and flung out his arms. "Come, let us light candles—"

He swung round on me, almost in a snarl.

"You think I'm mad?" he almost sobbed. "Why do you look at me in such a way?"

"Wish I'd thought of it first," I said.

26

As I'd thought—and hoped—Consuelo reached London before me, and I'd barely got to my room when her knock on the door—the mere sound of it—made me feel drunk for those moments. We stood wrapped and enrapt, still.

"If only we were always like this!" she whispered. "You're so far away from me!"

"It'll be like this till I'm a dodderer," I said. "I'm never *so* far, you know?"

"I don't *feel* you near. You're going to do this nonsense in Germany. I don't care *who* it's for. I don't *want* you to—"

"But you know perfectly well why, don't you? Doesn't it make a difference?"

"I'm not the abnegating type. I'm me, and I want what's mine, and I want *you!*"

"But supposing—"

"I'm *not* supposing for a moment!"

She stood away, hands clasped, cold.

"Why should we marry?" she asked, without feeling, an office matter. "What's the use if I'm a widow in the next couple of weeks?"

"Not if I can help it!"

"You're not even trying!"

"That's relative—"

She turned to me, eye to eye. For the first time I was made aware of the true rock of her character. As I looked at her, I tried to put into words what I felt. But the light, the sharp light that isn't sharp at all, but only the awareness of a clear moment, that light in her eyes, dried any thought of joking, and stopped all notion of trying to explain to myself why she couldn't agree with me, wouldn't accept what I considered to be a duty. I didn't even think of trying to explain the religious side. I thought she'd simply hoot. We can "feel" all sorts of emotion, that we could never hope to explain, religious feeling among them. We can, indeed, "feel" them, know that we feel, certain that we believe. But in words they embarrass, they itch, they don't convince except in a church, where we have to sit still and listen, and we can't argue because the words belong to the place. Outside, in the arena, they bring that ridiculous desire to deny, argue, play the yahoo, or writhe almost in a blushing stupor.

"Look," I said, in quite sudden desperation. "We've got to be honest—or I've got to be—anyway. Or we'll never get anywhere—"

"I think that," she said gently. "That's why I'm determined not to let this happen—"

"It doesn't matter what you've determined. There's such a thing as friendship. There's loyalty. There's a hatred of inhumanity. Cruelty. There's also duty—"

"I'm aware of it. But I don't see—"

"Allow me to finish. Errol's a Roman Catholic. So am I. It doesn't make us comrades of any 'party.' It isn't any link at all. Unless we think so. And I think so. I don't want to think of him in that hellhole and not do anything to break him out. Not only because he's Errol, and a friend of mine. Or Yorick we all made fun of. Till we learned better. Simply and solely because he oughtn't to be in there. It's not our way of thinking. And doing nothing isn't our way of being. It's a question, purely and simply, of being what we are, and doing what we know we must. Or else we're only a damned lot of factory-made turnips, or worse. Aren't we?"

Half turned away, I saw by the line of her cheek that she smiled.

"I suppose I couldn't expect you to say anything else," she said, in an Ah-Well-That's-It voice. "But I'm a little surprised, I must say. I'd never have thought—after all—I never saw you go to church, except once. And that wasn't Catholic!"

"True. I'm not the practicing sort—"

"There must be a lot of us!"

"Surely!"

"I was brought up in convent schools. I'm simply lazy. That's a compliment. Or I don't believe enough. Not like Gillian. She goes to Mass every day. I suppose I ought to start!"

"Doesn't do any harm—"

"Your daughter isn't?"

"Unfortunately—"

"You think it makes *such* a difference? Why? Aren't people more, sort of—"

"What's called the stuffed-shirt mentality? Discipline, tradition, duty? 'Dirty' words, aren't they? But what is there without them?"

I was suddenly tired. Perhaps confession saps energy, or renders the mind limp. I wondered, for no good reason, if that were the secret of brainwashing—a term I've always detested as an ignorant label for a terrifying process—depending which end of the lens is being looked through—and I tried to summarize what I felt, though whether physically or mentally, I wasn't sure. I did, in fact, think I felt "better." I wasn't sure why a few words would have such effect. At some time, I'd have had to tell her, using perhaps different words. But it would have been, I know, far more awkward. Errol was a red-blood excuse. Again I wondered why. If I'd had to tell her I was a bolshevist of the old school, with a bomb in my bag, then there might have been reason for hesitation. But to confess I was Roman Catholic was surely no disgrace. It was simply silly. Yet silly or not, that's what I'd felt. I tried to summon a vision of my ancestor, Onslow Trothe, brave kinsman of three hundred years before, at the moment he realised he was in danger of having his head cut off, with his family and all the village people loyal to our House. It took time to realise one horrid fact, that Roundhead troopers would, indeed, use their sabers without mercy, certain they were cleansing the Earth of Satan's Own. No judge, no jury. Only the light of a Catholic head, and *chop!* In these days, impossible to imagine. But fact. In gravestones.

"Time you had dinner!" she said, in a brisk turn. "I saw my nice chef downstairs. I'm a freeman of the Savoy kitchens—"

"The greatest honor—"

"So I'm told. He's cooking a shoulder of lamb, with new peas and potatoes. The sommelier has a Charmes-Chambertin—"

"Ready!"

"Then you'll kindly sit down here and read the paper till the waiter comes. You look absolutely worn out!"

"Don't feel it—"

"You will please not argue. In the office, you're one thing. But here, I insist, I'm the madame!"

"When do we make an honest woman of you?"

"I can't see how a piece of paper makes one honest—"

"Paper's been an authority for a long time. With the right marks. Did Bilat Khan get his passport?"

"Brand new, no snags. His sisters are darling. One's a nurse—"

"If he hasn't a telephone, send a wire. I want to see him tomorrow. Nine o'clock. Get him a visa for Yugoslavia. I'd like him to be away for a week or so. Tomorrow night, I want to fly to Cairo. I shall probably be gone for a couple of weeks—"

She dialled, looking away.

"Will that be the Errol business?" she asked.

"No."

"Then can't I come with you? Hello? Mrs. Khan? Oh, Mrs. Khan, this is Miss Furnival. The office. Will you please tell Mr. Bilat Khan to be here at nine o'clock tomorrow morning? Thank you—"

She looked round at me, covering the mouthpiece.

"Why can't I? Doesn't matter about the paper. Yes? Mrs. Khan? You'll let him know? Good. Thank you. Good night!"

She put the receiver down.

"Do you really trust Paul?"

It was like a fiery arrow in a straw roof. I had long made it a rule never to disregard what a smart girl has to say. They—because of their sex—see more, feel more, in a way that may seem bizarre, but in truth often has wide base.

"Why do you say that?" I asked her, pretending to read the headlines.

"Why do you think Moira divorced him? Moira's a very strong woman. I mean, strong in everything. I can imagine a woman of her age being completely destroyed when the man she loves falls in love with an Angela Masters, twenty-six, beautiful—and she is—very well-connected socially, wealthy, everything in her favor. I can see that. But not Moira!"

"Why not?"

"Moira's twice or twenty times as wealthy. Socially, well-founded. Really beautiful. Full of life. Friends everywhere. Why did she give up without even trying? Because, although I like Angela, I'd never compare them as women!"

"Then why?"

"Moira knew something. She went back to Australia without any warning, didn't she? And you can't tell me Paul's the man *he* was!"

"Couldn't that be Angela's influence?"

She laughed at me.

"Are you the man you were?" she asked easily. "Have I altered you?"

"I think you have—"

"I don't think Angela's done anything for Paul, one way or another. She's flattered him, perhaps. Of course it's flattering for a man to have a wife as decorative—"

"Jealous!"

"Oh, no! But don't forget who her father is—"

"What's that to do with it?"

"He's quite a powerful man. Whether as Under-Secretary, or as he was. He's been a director of how many oil companies? In Arabia or Iran or the Middle East generally—"

"I don't quite see what you're getting at—"

"Who put Gilbert, Shepworth in their jobs? Who put the rest in? Of the men you've put in, how many have gone? Two. And both of them are accident cases, and they'll go back when they're better!"

"I think that's being unfair—"

"Isn't it? What about the entire Rome business? Why would somebody want to murder a girl? For a set of keys? Who put all those people in their jobs? Who vetted them? The I-Unit. Gilbert, Shepworth and company. Who put *them* in?"

"What's all this leading to?"

She looked down at me, *the* Miss Furnival.

"Do you—*really*—trust Paul?" she said.

"But, Consuelo, darling!" I tried to say.

"He was very sure of bringing you in—"

"I can't believe for a moment—!"

"—to make a wonderful scapegoat of you!"

I slammed down the paper, and stood, and she stepped away, a little frightened.

"How?" I demanded. "I hate listening to this. Paul's been a friend for years. He—let me remind you—was almost killed by that bomb months ago, almost before he started this Company—"

"But it could have killed Moira!"

"Oh, now, darling, please! Let's get things right—"

"I'm getting things right. I'm protecting you. I'm not interested in anyone else. He pretended to resign. Angela told me. Don't forget, we *talk*. You wouldn't let him. He didn't insist, did he? He'd told the Princes he was going to resign. They let him—"

"Look, this is sheer twisted—"

"But it's not, Edmund. He may be a sick man, but he's a very clever man, you know that, don't you?"

"Sick?"

"He's mentally sick, certainly. Don't you feel it? How could he put Angela in that place?"

"But, listen, that's simply an atrocious—"

"It's not! She has a faint memory—"

"He wasn't even there!"

228

"Really?"

I stared at her, certain that she knew what she was talking about, and I was beginning to feel cold.

"You might at least find out where he was," she said, quietly sure of herself. "Miss Toverell could possibly tell you. She's a very direct type. She's Scots, you know. Not impressed by anybody. That travel order to Naples, for the aircraft, was supposedly signed by you? A forgery? She's the supervisor, including the travel department. The original order for that flight was signed by Paul. He paid the hotel bills of the girl who took Angela's place. He took Angela to dinner several times with her. He called them Scylla and Charybdis. She's Austrian. I don't think she had any real idea what she was supposed to be doing. She hasn't really a brain in her head—"

"When did she get hold of that handbag?"

"Angela gave it to her. In the nightclub. She told me—"

"Ah, no!"

"Ah, yes. Paul took that house in Capri. Miss Toverell's got the receipt. There are many things I can find out about—now—that I couldn't before. So can you!"

"I can't believe he'd dream of harming Angela!"

"If you hear she's left him, you won't be surprised, will you?"

I was absolutely thunderstruck. That's the only word. Everything she said sounded plausible, and in the ultimate sense of the word, impossible.

"All right," I said, and straightened my tie, pulled down my jacket, prepared for the worst or best. "Where could he make me a scapegoat? Under what circumstances? Or, in other words, what's his general idea?"

She sat against the table, which showed the line of her long, beautiful legs, arms loosely folded under her breasts, smiling at me as at a noisy three-year-old.

"You didn't resign from the Civil Service," she said. "You were, to put it delicately, removed. If it hadn't been for Errol, you might still be in prison on some trumped-up charge or other, involving security, official secrets, and that rubbish. The case would have been heard *in camera* for the most part. Because of that, if anything else happened, you're the dog with a bad name—"

"What could happen?"

"I can't remember your exact words, but I just finished typing your report to the Board. You said, in view of the enormous capital outlay, that 'any information about projects, in any sphere, given to another company would be a grievous loss of hard-earned knowledge, which, in certain circumstances might even be a death blow,' didn't you?"

"Not quite like that, but it'll do!"

"Well, supposing another company—or somebody—gets that information? And went on getting it. Supposing our pipeline *isn't* where it ought to be? How much would it be worth?"

"Well, I suppose—a great deal—"

"And if it *was* known. If every move were reported. Let's imagine the Company code were broken. Couldn't they ruin us? Who'd get the blame? Who's had charge?"

"All right. Let's suppose. What next?"

"Your contract was signed in London. If you were sued, what defence could you offer?"

"Sued for what?"

"Selling information—"

"But that's nonsense!"

"Is it?"

I had to wonder if I was dreaming. I've many times had the feeling that I wasn't part of what was going on. I've often had to ask myself why I was where I happened to be, or if it was necessary. So often, I've felt I was dreaming. Or ought to have been. Of course, it's an infantile denial of reality. Or a puerile defense mechanism going into action. Or any of the other pretty excuses.

Looking at Consuelo's warmly stony eyes, I had to assume two items, one, that she knew what she was talking about, and, two, that I'd been complacently blind. It had happened before.

"What proof have you?" I asked, without much confidence.

"Call the Bank. Call Miss Toverell. Send for Angela!"

It was a little late to call the Bank, or Miss Toverell, and I didn't feel like talking to Angela.

"We're going to have dinner," I said. "Then we're going to bed!"

She stretched both arms widest, and diverted her hips in a quivering arch, a sudden springy-rubbery, muscular cat.

"I'm hungry!" she whispered, but it was more a moan. "For lamb, certainly not!"

27

I try to see things as they are. I try to say what I mean. I have a reputation for being objective, a pragmatist, with a flair for seeing what's to come.

In matters concerning Paul, I didn't want to "see" anything. I certainly didn't want to say anything, and I turned away from what the future might bring. He was a friend of mine. I could hardly ask our I-Unit to vet their Director General without his knowledge. I couldn't make a move anywhere, without telling him. I didn't choose to make a move. But at the same time, I had a duty to my shareholders and to myself, and moreover, I was in honor bound to recognise any danger to the trust which the Princes had vested in me.

I put in a call to Moira, and the operator said there was a twelve-hour wait, which meant I'd have to be in the office at about ten that night. The I-Unit worked in a separate suite at the back of the building, and when I went in, the staff was still sorting the debris from the other place, except Johnson and Berry, both ex-Superintendents of the Special Branch, C.I.D. We'd worked together before, and I knew that both were top in their class.

"Found a lot of 'mistakes' in some of these traces, sir!" Berry began, with small-circled gold spectacles on the end of his nose.

"We've got a line going to Interpol. Ought to get some answers in the next day or so."

"I want all dossiers checked in detail. Just in case any other 'mistakes' crept in. Especially office staff in charge of others. Start afresh. New files. You've checked the cipher book?"

"All in order, sir. But some of the last messages weren't accurate. The code was fouled. Nothing important—"

"Regard everything coded as important. It's mostly practice at the moment. Except the operational reports. And they oughtn't to come here. They should all go direct to Geneva. Get on to anything that doesn't conform—"

"How about orders from the Director General's office, sir?"

"Let's have a working arrangement. You alone will be responsible to me. Anything you find not in conformance with my orders, you'll confide to me. Understood?"

I caught that upward look from grey eyes alert in knowledge, hidden in service, old in duty. Without having to be told, I knew he was "on" to something, and wanted to tell me. But I didn't want to know. Then, at any rate.

Walking out, I knew perfectly well I was doing less than my duty. I felt that a little time would be well worthwhile. I intended to warn Paul in a way he'd recognise. I didn't want to be anywhere near. I didn't want any discussion. He might well be perfectly innocent, in which case, the warning would go for nothing. But I was worried that I'd been stupid enough to say anything about Errol. There were so many ways of botching the best of schemes. If he wanted to get rid of me, there was no better way than to inform the East German lads. Obviously, knowing what I did—which was virtually nothing except gossip— though I was banking on womanly intuition—I had to talk to Druxi. He knew her almost as well as I did. I remembered what she'd said about her "contacts."

Consuelo seemed to have found every piece of paper in every archive in creation. I signed through lunch—a sandwich—and read back reports, surprised again that all seemed normal. With the second cup of coffee, my desk was clear, I had a bird's-eye view of our entire panorama, and taking all in all, I wasn't unsatisfied. At two thirty I put on my hat and coat, took an umbrella and walked over to James' office.

The fat girl took me, not upstairs as I'd expected, but down, and down, and downstairs, through concrete tunnels of cold air, lit by a glarey bulb now and again, and I realised I was in the old Defense of London Headquarters, a warren of a place that went for miles.

James sat in a small office of concrete block walls, the same whitely glaring electric light, a wooden table with iron trestles, chairs made for people without backsides, and the same china cups. I'd hardly got in, and he told Alison to make tea. There was a tap and a sink in the corridor.

"All I was able to do was chalk out the ground plan, put up these carton walls, and put this wall here, simply to give you an idea of the place," he said. "It's exactly drawn to scale. There's only one very large 'perhaps.' That's where they choose to let you see him—"

"Them!"

"Oh. I thought it was one—"

"Gone to two—"

"Let's hope they're brought in together. If it's one by one, there's a serious time-risk. There's the distance between the medical room and the waiting room. It's twenty four good paces—"

I looked at the square, carefully chalked out, with the side rooms divided by brown carton.

"There's the door you came in," James said, pointing behind me. "To the right's the place where you leave your hat and coat and whatever impedimenta you happen to be carrying. Remember chocolate and cigarettes. They'll help. You then go into this room—"

It was about five paces long, and three wide.

"You'll wait here till the prisoners are brought down. They'll be taken over there. You won't see them, because in all probability, this door will be locked. The door opens. You are either invited to walk across this space—the entrance hall—to the medical inspection room, or, less likely, the prisoners are brought to you. The great 'perhaps' is whether they're brought in together. I'd say ten thousand to one, they won't!"

"—wouldn't take the bet—"

"Then, you see, if one's brought in while the other waits, it's well on the cards that the man you see first will be taken back to the prison while you're talking to the second—"

"—won't do at all!"

"Then—depending who else is in the waiting room—you'll have to be at the door. If there's anyone else in the waiting room, you can either hope the gas comes in quick enough, or else you'll have to deal with them—"

"—deal with the lot from outset—"

"Good. Then, let's go back. You arrive. You put your hat and coat in the cloakroom, briefcase, umbrella, a few kindly words, and you go into the waiting room. But just as you enter the outer door, before you get to the cloakroom, you drop one of these—"

He gave me a flat greenish rice-paper disk, fat in the center.

"You drop that, and two more, as you take off your overcoat. Tread on them. You've already taken your pill, and you pretend to blow your nose on the way to the waiting room. It's a special handkerchief—here are a package of a couple of dozen—put them in all your pockets, and give a couple to each of your friends. The air will be charged within seconds. The air's perfectly clear. Let's say the prisoners are brought in. They're generally punctual. Your companions—if any—in the waiting room are fairly well under the effect. They won't be able to move. Neither will anyone else, except, of course, the guard or guards, coming in with the prisoners. That's why you must be at the door. The moment you see them enter, you press this to the outer waiting-room wall. Look at it—"

"It" was an oblong of what looked like dull silver, about eight inches by six, with a wide copper strip in the middle of one side, covering a smaller oblong about an inch thick. The other side was flat, with eight shallow rubber circles.

"Now press the suction caps to that wall," he pointed. "Just a little below waist level. Press. Now stand aside. About a yard, flat against the wall, face turned away!"

He moved as I pressed. I stood about a wide pace off, shoulders jammed to the wall, hands flat, face in my shoulder away from where I'd been. The wall trembled. The place filled with dust. There was barely a noise. I've heard the same sort of p-sh-ssst! in laundries when steam operates a presser.

"Look!" James called from the grey clouds at the end of the room. "There's a gap there. Go through it!"

It was more than a gap. The ragged hole was about two yards wide and the concrete seemed to have powdered, floor to roof, for about ten feet. I stepped over a pile of rubble and I was on the other side.

"What you have to do now is run across to your friends, grab them, and run them through that space," James said, and I still couldn't see him. "Nobody's going to stop you. What you have to be most careful of is the effect of the gas on your unprotected friends. Otherwise, you might find them incapable of movement!"

"If they've taken too much before I give them the handkerchief and the pill, how long will it take them to get moving?"

"Three or four days," James said, from the corridor. "Come out here. This stuff's going to blow away. That's the only other problem. A, are they coming in together? B, will you see them? C, do you set off your charge *before* you see them, or after? D, do you use these gas disks as you enter, or wait till you cross the hall? You must remember that if the plane has sprayed the place with your little tin of APD-2, then everybody's feeling it as you arrive. The disks are a security device. You mightn't need them. But if the place is air-conditioned—and best information says it is—the guards might be very wide awake. I suggest you'll have to rehearse, and take your chances—"

"This thing goes off in about three seconds?"

"About that. Don't for heaven's sake stand in front of it!"

"The handkerchief gives full protection?"

"Completely. The pill can be swallowed. Then you're quite safe—"

"The air outside's loaded with that AP-et cetera—"

"Won't worry you. Anybody outside in the past ten minutes is only a sleeping beauty!"

We had another cup of tea to smother the dust, and James gave me a package in green plastic paper with the wall-breaker, the package of linen squares, the explosive stickers I'd used before, the disks, the two tins of APD-2 for use with the airplane spray, and a tube of pills.

"Did you build this especially for me?" I asked him, looking at the wall.

"That part, yes. But unfortunately, we were given a very large order indeed, which we've got to finish tonight, haven't we, Alison?"

"Yes, sir!" she called, from out in the corridor.

"So we weren't able to do as much as we'd have liked. But I happen to know that if those goodies are put to proper use, I don't doubt that circumstances will prove amenable, shall we say?"

On the way back, by bus, I wondered how many of my fellow passengers would have guessed what my chaste little green, shiny parcel contained, or what they'd have thought about a gift of taxpayer's money in time and goods. I was comforted by a thought that Errol paid more tax than almost anyone else in the country, and had never accepted a penny for his employment as a Civil Servant, or, indeed, his father before him. That came to a few million sterling.

I found that Druxi had been on twice as Mrs. Callaghan Birne of Rayswood, New England, in answer to my call, and Moira was coming through from Melbourne at seven o'clock. Consuelo had left a note to say she was seeing her mother. The other paper I didn't look at. Hines was on the PBX outside the I-Unit office, and he put the Druxi call through to the waiting room, a small soundproofed place, beautifully panelled and furnished in Hepplewhite, which I thought a waste.

"Edmund? What's going on?"

"You sound as if you were on the moon. Teeny-weeny. Can you hear?"

"Now I can—"

"About Paul Chamby—"

"What about him?"

"I didn't exactly tell him, but he knows about Errol—"

"Oh, my God!"

"You know?"

"Don't know a thing. Do *you* know?"

"No—"

"What *do* you know?"

"Only what I'm told. And bound to disbelieve!"

"All right—"

"I *must* think of him as a friend—"

"I know all that. I'm just playing the hand. Follow?"

"I think so. You'd prefer somebody else told me—"

"That's one way. But if I had the aces, you don't think I'd hold on to them, do you?"

"Druxi. What *is* the mystery?"

"Look, Edmund. Paul's a friend of mine, as well. He's a great guy. Always was. But people just seem to go funny in the head. Did you ever talk to Gillian? Why don't you—?"

I went upstairs absolutely miserable. The more I thought about "talking" to Gillian in the manner of a man far her senior, whether in age or accomplishment, the more traitorous I felt. I wanted to find Paul, and have it out. Never mind the consequences.

Blues flashed.

"Melbourne, sir," Hines said. "Put the lady through, sir?"

"Please!"

Consuelo had made a wonderful room in a couple of days, with my own pictures and some of the furniture and rugs I'd stored. The rest was all her. I wished, achingly, she were near. Silence had never bothered me before. I wanted to hear her voice, the whisper of her skirts, the most lovely sigh of silk when she crossed her knees.

"Hello?"

"Moira? Edmund!"

Her voice came in as though she were sitting opposite me.

"Oh, Eddy! Oh, my lord, you make me homesick!"

"Then come on back. We're all waiting for you—"

"I'm tempted, I'll tell you. It's been wonderful to get back here. It's just marvelous. I'm solid gold all over. There's really *sun* here!"

"You're making me envious. What we've got is icicles. I wanted to talk about Paul—"

"What about him?"

But what a change of voice! Guarded? Defensive? Sullen?

"There's something wrong I can't penetrate—"

"Eddy, don't waste your time. He's just no good any more!"

"Couldn't you please explain that?"

"I don't want to. I don't wish to discuss it—"

"Moira, listen to me, please. This could balloon into an international scandal. There's a lot of money. He's responsible for—"

"He's incapable of any responsibility!"

"Then tell me—"

"Eddy, you know what he meant to me. We had twenty four years of wonderful marriage. He was *the* most wonderful man, that's why. We've got five children. You ought to see them. I'm so proud, I can't start to tell you—"

"I'm very happy for you—"

"Thank you, Eddy. Of all the people we knew, I always liked you best. Always. Eddy, listen. How can I help you?"

"Couldn't you hint at what's wrong? I understand your reluctance—"

"Reluctance? It's plain disgust—"

"With what? Not—er—Angela? You see, Moira, I've got to try to force it out of you!"

"Not necessary. And Angela? Oh, Eddy! Yes, I'll admit I was blindly jealous for a long time. I acted like a perfect fool. No. Not Angela. Very clever. Perfect secretary. Edmund, one night, I was at home—in Davies Street—and I was giving a party for some

239

of our friends. Paul didn't show. This was after the accident. He was on sticks. This is five—six—months ago—"

"Yes?"

"D'you remember Otto Worbel, the engineer? Very nice couple. He's a brilliant man. He planned that desalinization business—"

"I remember him—"

"Well, they came in, and he said 'What's Paul's car doing outside our apartment?' That's down there in Charles Street. Well, I said, probably he's seeing somebody. I didn't think any more of it. But he didn't get in till next morning. This is the first time in all the years we'd been married that he hadn't come home when he was in London. He wasn't drunk. Wasn't noisy. Wasn't anything. Of course, I thought he'd been with Angela. Next thing I know, she's on the phone, frantic. Where is he? He's supposed to see Prince somebody-or-other at whatever time it was. No show!"

"Yes?"

"I asked her if he'd been working late the night before. She said no, he went off the previous afternoon. He didn't keep an appointment with his doctor that evening. I asked her why she hadn't called me. Know what she said? Paul had told her never to call the house for any reason—"

"Where *had* he been?"

"Well, don't think I didn't get busy. I got an enquiry agency, and gave them the Charles Street number. He'd been paying the rent of the apartment for *four* months!"

"Angela?"

"Oh, no! Angela's just a front. I always knew I was stupid to think about her. But you get like that, Eddy. I tell you, you don't even know *what* you're thinking. Mind, if I'd been sure it was Angela, she wouldn't be quite so tall, I'll tell you that!"

"What did you find?"

"He's been living with this half-caste. Still is. Won't give her up. I went there. I caught them. We took photographs. I just turned my back, and I caught the next plane here—"

"May I ask, what type of half-caste?"

"Her name's—wait a minute, now—Muo—something like that—"

"Could you send me a photograph?"

"I tore them up!"

"Could you send me *any* details?"

"They're not in Charles Street or London any longer. I believe they're in Rome—"

"Rome?"

"That's what I heard. But listen, what really killed me. Imagine, Paul? Hooked?"

"Hooked?"

"The most abysmally horrible thing I ever heard. My Paul. Oh, Eddy!"

"Well, tell me!"

"You'd never imagine it. Never. I called my doctor. He saw him. It's heroin and LSD. Can you believe it?"

"Moira, put the phone down, now. Just rest. I'll let you know all that's going on—"

"I wish I'd told you before. I couldn't!"

"I understand. Moira, I'll call you again—"

"Any time, Eddy. Wonderful talking to you!"

Curious, but subconsciously, or unconsciously, I'd known all the time. It had to be put in words. His way of talking, the eyes, the color of his hands. That fall from the dogcart—had it been? —on the day of his non-appearance was entirely suspect.

But the half-caste was my problem.

I called Berry at his home.

"It's a nuisance, I know, and it's late to come all the way back here. But could you?"

"I'll be there in just under the half-hour, sir!"

28

I had a very good talk with Roland Ainsworth just after lunch at the Club. He gave me the latest news of Frederick which I found most comforting. The boy was getting along splendidly, and expected to pass his finals without trouble.

"Of course, Doctor Tomsett's a Classics scholar of thirty or forty years ago. First class, and a wonderful fellow to talk to. If I had more of his sort as helpers for all my patients, I'd be well ahead. As it is—"

"I suppose Paul Chamby isn't one of them, is he?"

His eyes had suddenly gone brightly impersonal.

"I'd like to tell you he was. He's not. Why?"

"I'm told he's an addict—"

"He's very soft-headed. I'm telling you—since you mention it—because he's trying to use your name—"

"*My* name?"

"To get prescriptions. Your Company physician's very worried about it. I think you'd better talk to him. I'm telling you so much because he got the position, as you know, because of my recommendation to you. He's a most capable young practitioner. I don't want to see him in trouble. May I depend on you to look into it?"

"Of course. I'm a little shocked—"

"Every right to be. That's the only reason I've said a word. It could also save Paul. Which is far more important!"

"How do I go about it?"

"Exactly as you did for Frederick!"

"But I didn't. If you'll remember, he was arrested with half a dozen or so friends of his, and all of them were remanded in charge of various people—"

"Paul could also be 'arrested.' He could also be put under treatment—"

"But he's far from being a minor—"

"With his record, no magistrate would convict. Call on me!"

When I got back, Berry had asked to see me. Consuelo called him, and left us.

"Mr. Chamby, sir," he said, and tidied a few pieces of paper. "He's had three flats in the past eight months. His own Davies Street house is let for two years to an Under-Secretary of the United States. The first flat Mr. Chamby took—without his wife— ex-wife—he had to leave because the tenants complained of noisy behavior!"

"I find that hard to believe—"

"They got a judgment summons, sir. The second flat he had to leave because of nuisance. Left a bath running. Ruined two flats downstairs. More than three thousand pounds damage. The flat he's got now, it's got eight rooms, counting the kitchen, he's got three girls staying there—"

"Only three?"

"Two from Singapore, sir, one from the Philippines—"

"What are they?"

"The porter there said they were very nice, but they brought in a proper slit-eyed lot!"

"Don't doubt it. Now, did you find out how this can possibly happen?"

"Yes, sir. He generally goes there of a Wednesday afternoon, and he leaves about six o'clock of a Friday. Then he flies either to Beirut or Geneva—"

"Where's Miss Masters living?"

"He's got another flat, sir. Much bigger. In Grosvenor Street. That's where Miss Masters stays, sir. Nothing goes on there—"

"Good. When does he stay *there?*"

"Been there eight times in the past three months, sir. I checked the porter's register. Miss Masters' always there, except when she goes off for weekends. Generally alone, or with her older sister—"

We looked at each other, he with those small-circled gold spectacles on the tip of his nose. His eyes were a policeman-grey, pale, in the exact meaning of the word, inscrutable.

"All right, Superintendent," I said conversationally. "How do we deal with this? What's the underlying reason? Mark you, I know!"

"Yes, sir. So do I—"

"What?"

"Been known some time, sir. I've been on to the Drug Squad. Wouldn't be too long before he got pulled in. He's got two doctors. Both bad reputations. The three girls just give parties. Nothing much wrong with them. They're not whores, from what's known. They don't take men there. Lots of girls—"

"What's the best way to put a stop to it? I want Mr. Chamby under treatment—"

"Have to get a warrant, sir. Go there, let's say, one of these nights. According to information. If he's in a drugged state, send him to hospital. Certify his condition. Charge him!"

"No!"

"The only way, sir—"

"But if it's known, why isn't something done about it? Why's it been allowed to go on?"

"He's not the only one, sir. Not by long chalks. But he's a man of position. He's got a lot of money. Friends. If I were still at the Yard, I'd move very carefully, I can tell you. A policeman can get sued for thousands these days. They'll wait. The longer it goes on, the more careless he'll get. Sometime or other, he'll have a lot of stuff on him. They'll know it. Then go in. They've got him and whoever's with him, plus a lot of additional evidence—"

"How can we prevent that happening?"

He scratched his head with the end of the ball pen.

"He's there now, sir. Why not talk to him? If you can. See for yourself. Tell him to go somewhere else. Here, he's going to get it sooner or later—"

"How was it found out?"

"Sort of people he goes about with, sir—"

"Who's this woman he's staying with?"

He smiled down at the pieces of paper.

"One of the three, or all of them, sir, perhaps?" he said. "In the divorce case, a half-caste woman was cited. But she got away. They had the witnesses and the photographs, all right. Heard in Sydney, Australia, it was, sir. Divorce was granted on misconduct—"

"There's no one particular woman?"

"Not that I know, sir. I can enquire a little further—"

"I wish you would!"

I'd already made up my mind to go to the place in Charles Street. I didn't want anyone with me. I was fairly certain there'd be embarrassment enough, without witnesses to make things worse. And I wanted Paul to go on with the Company. I wondered what the devil could have got into him. He'd always been steady as a rock. That was when Moira was still with him.

What an anchor a good woman is!

But I wondered how Moira could have "lost" him so soon. In months.

I signed the afternoon's pile, and when Consuelo came in with the late pouch, I asked her to call Angela.

She hesitated.

"She's not a bit well," she said. "I'm worried!"

"Don't be. I'm about to put things in order—"

"Super-doc'!"

"I'm very good for *you*—"

"I think I'll stay. On grounds of self-defense. She's distinctly willowy—"

"You may scarper—"

245

"Yes, sir. If I drop in rather suddenly with early tea, it's because I can't hear anything through the keyhole!"

There was one nasty little surprise in the pouch. Logan reported from Beyfoum that the pipeline was eight degrees off rhumb, but at the time of dispatch he wasn't sure how far it went. I looked at the map, and used the plastic arc. The line was going straight to the very border we didn't want to go anywhere near, much less touch, or cross. I sent Logan a cable telling him to dismantle and start again, and repeated the official figures. Then I cabled Finlayson at Beirut to fly to Beyfoum, check the dismantling and reorientation, and report direct to me.

Angela came in while I was making sure on the map.

"Do sit down," I said, going on being busy. "What's the matter with Paul?"

She stood, looking, not at me, but at the desk. She was too pale. She'd always been slender, but now she was thin. Consuelo was right. She was more than willowy.

"I'd hoped I wouldn't have to speak about it," she said, no life, a lot of crackle in the voice.

"I'm leaving Company business, as you know. I want everything in order. Where is he, today?"

Her hands moved, and then she put them behind.

"I don't know, sir!" she said, but still without looking at me.

"Not at Charles Street?"

She turned her head.

"Perhaps," she said. "You know about it?"

"Of course. I want the keys. Go and get them. And look here—!"

She swung round. I'd almost shouted. But her expression hadn't changed.

"Don't telephone, don't attempt to leave a message of any sort. Understood?"

She nodded. She didn't show any feeling at all.

She'd hardly shut the door, and Consuelo came in.

"Did you ever expect to see Lot's wife?" she whispered. "I never saw anyone look more like a pillar of salt. Nothing like herself!"

I was about to say something, but managed to hold it.

Angela looked drugged. Perhaps she'd taken a calmative of some sort. I gave Consuelo the cable, and a kiss. Since I was no longer a part of official business, I felt I might relax the habits of years. Before, any notion of a kiss in office hours was my conception of the unplumbed immeasurable.

"Take her to dinner tonight, see her home, and—I don't say tuck her up—but see she's all right before you go. I'll probably be late, but I'll come in and see you—"

"You're flying to Germany tomorrow at two fifteen. You have an appointment on Monday at Gstaad-Brö with the Prince Abdullah at eleven o'clock. At five o'clock you have an appointment here with Mr. Joel Cawle—"

"What's *he* want?"

"He simply said he'd like to see you at the earliest—"

"Don't like *that* very much!"

"Neither do I. But it didn't sound as if it had anything in particular to do with you—"

"Can you tell that from a voice?"

"I think I can tell anything if it's anything to do with you!"

Angela tapped and came in. She held a ring with four keys.

"The garage door up to the flat," she said. "The side door on the terrace. Back door. Front door—"

"Have you been there?"

"Once—"

"Oh. Only once?"

She nodded, looking away with that curiously "dead" stare.

"Have you dealt with any of the business connected with the rental?"

"All of it, sir—"

"Is it rented by the Company?"

"Yes, sir!"

"I see. What other expenses is the Company paying?"

"Most of the accounts, sir. Food, clothing, entertainment—"

"Entertainment for whom? Business?"

"Foreign representatives. Their wives—"

247

"Are these expenses accepted by the accountants?"

"So far, sir, yes—"

"Does Paul live alone at this flat?"

"He has friends there—"

"What sort of friends?"

"Prostitutes. As I am. I thought I was buying a marriage—"

"But you've just taken him to meet your parents, surely?"

"I found out there. At home. We all thought he was drunk. When he broke that leg. All so funny. But Doctor Lennox told me—"

Quiet, too quiet, no feeling, still that stare, the sag in shoulders and breasts, lax knees.

"I've known for months something was wrong," she said, in a sudden deep breath. "I thought the flats were places where he held the conferences. And the Princes' parties he'd never let me go to. He never used the old office. Wanted a more 'friendly' atmosphere. We had a flat in Grosvenor Street. I thought we were going to marry and live there. But then I had to go to Charles Street. He'd taken it in your name—"

"In *my* name? How did he do that?"

"He used your name and the Company notepaper. Your daughter had sent you a message through her husband—"

"What's that got to do—!"

"Her husband's company owns that property. He thought you were the tenant of flat G. He left a message there. An envelope. The porter got on to the administrator, and he got on to me. That's how they found out you weren't the tenant. My fault. I didn't think anything was wrong. I told them it was a mistake. I went to Charles Street to get the envelope. It was about six o'clock. It was full of women. From the gutter. Paul was in a bedroom, absolutely in a coma, nude. They were painting him—"

"Where's this envelope from my son-in-law?"

"Probably still there. I walked out. I haven't had a chance of speaking to him. I'll go when I have—"

"I want you to try to think of Paul as in need of all the help we can give him. I'm quite sure there are times when he really doesn't know what he's doing. Will you help?"

Again that sudden, deep breath. She shook her head. I reached across the desk for the bell.

"You're going home with Consuelo. She'll take care of you. And you will *not* take any more pills. Understood? If I find you disobey me, I shall first talk to your father, and then to the Police. Get that in your head!"

She put her chin down. I saw that she was no longer taking care of that lovely ashblonde hair.

"I'm no good," she said. "I'm like the rest of them!"

Consuelo came in. I frowned to her to take Angela away.

"It's understood you go home with Consuelo, now, without further nonsense. Everything else will be set right tomorrow. Off you go!"

Consuelo rose-lipped a kiss to me, took her by the shoulders, and literally pushed her to the door, closed it.

It took a little time to find Roland, but when I'd told him, he was all for it.

"I'll get on to a friend of mine at Scotland Yard," he said. "The patient will be put in my keeping. No publicity. Best thing that could possibly happen!"

"I'll have you both picked up where?"

"The Athenaeum, eleven thirty?"

I told the Sergeant-Major to have a car ready to meet Sir Roland Ainsworth and a friend, and to come to the Savoy for me.

I didn't want to think about it. But I had to wonder what sort of savage sickness could have attacked Paul. An opium-induced sleep, with LSD phantasms could be about the furthest experience that any human being might endure. It said a great deal for the state of his mind that he could have succumbed, he, perhaps the coldest thinker, the best brain I'd ever met. I was also unhappy to think that he'd sent me to Madrid merely to pick up a packet— obviously of drugs—to relay to him in Stockholm. That wasn't like Paul.

The telephone rang.

"Hall porter, sir. Mr. Bilat Khan to see you—"

"I'll come down—"

I'd forgotten him. He was sitting in the foyer, watching the lift, and came out of the chair like a dog from a racing gate.

"Oh, sir, I think I got the day wrong!" he began, yards away. "Really, I am most foully apologetic—"

He fiddled with his hat.

"Sir, I think I have boggled my passport. When I came in, it was not, to tell the plain truth, candidly, quite right in the style of entrance—"

"You went over the side?"

"Not exactly, sir. There was a ladder—"

"But no passport officer?"

"No, sir. It was too early in the morning. It is quieter—"

"Let me see it—"

The passport was Egyptian, waterstained, out of date, no photograph, not his, obviously, and God must have sent it.

I stood there, almost in a dream. If the idea hadn't nibbled hard enough, it bit a chunk out of me, now.

"This is very, very serious," I said. "This could be a couple of years in prison, you know that, don't you?"

He looked at me, waving his head from side to side.

"My mother said it, sir. My sisters both. They will be thrown out of the country. I am a detestable thing. I bring trouble to others. The innocent others!"

"Could very well be true. Do you place any reliance on my word?"

"Ah, sir! I put myself in your hands with utmost completion!"

"I'm going to give you two month's salary. You're going home, and you're going to stay there, d'you understand?"

He waved the head harder to one side.

"Ah, but very perfectly, sir. Out of the way!"

"That's it. Keep out of sight. If—for any absurd reason—you should fall into the hands of the Police—"

"Ah, sir, oh, my God, my graciously good God!"

"You give them the office address. Say you are a contracted employee, and resting, and your passport is in the safe—"

"Contracted employee! Oh, my God!"

"I am very strict. If you disobey me, I shall kick you out. And this passport, of course, goes to Scotland Yard—"

"What a holus-bolus!"

"You must respect your contract, understand that?"

"I am confoundedly apologetic again, sir—"

"Come over to the cashier and sign a receipt. Remember, you won't be telling a lie if you say your passport's in the office safe. A new passport. Just a moment. Go along the Strand, here. Buy six passport pictures. Come back when they're ready—"

I almost didn't need the lift. I could have floated upstairs. The passport was genuine. There wasn't a forgery in it. I went over the pages rubber stamp by rubber stamp. I knew exactly where the owner had been, possibly a businessman. There were two Parisian telephone numbers scribbled in the back page, five in London, two in, of all places, Dublin. I had to find out if the owner was alive or dead. There was only one place, one office, one man.

Cairo, the Central Police Commissariat and my good friend, Nasr Khefi.

29

I was a little worried about Joel Cawle's wanting to see me. The last time I'd seen him face to face, I was ready to kill him, and others, to get out of the country. Errol had—God lift him—saved me. Joel wasn't an ordinary sort. He was fairly high up in M.I.6. These days, apparently, they'd found another name for it, and I suppose that in the Department there were other terms, other cant, but I thought of it as it had been when I'd had a number. Officialese, jargon, thieves' backslang are all the same, all in service of dishonesty, the sly dig, the dirty eye. If Joel hadn't been of the Service, I'd have put him down as a bent piece. Still, he could be dealt with.

Everything that had to be out of the way before I went to Cairo, I cleared. My desk was bare. I couldn't stand the thought of dinner. I had a steak sandwich in my room, read the evening papers, pretending I enjoyed the quiet, knowing perfectly well I needed, wanted Consuelo. I couldn't get my mind off that luscious realm above her knees. She called—I knew it was!—and I took off the receiver, waiting.

"Hello? *Edmund!*"

"I was waiting for a kiss—"

"Oh, you frightened me! I thought someone—well, here's your kiss—Angela's asleep. She's in the most awful condition. She's simply a long twist of string. She hasn't been eating. I got on to her mother. She's coming down. I didn't say much. Just that she had fever. She's bringing a maid—"

"Excellent! No more pills!"

"I found *eight* bottles! I've got the lot—"

"Bring them here. Do you think you ought to come back?"

Slight sounds. I don't know what they were. Adjustments of the bra, twitching of stockings, all amounting to hesitation, perhaps, or a searching of the conscience. Nice to listen to. A girl, thinking.

"Would it be very wrong to leave her?" she asked tentatively. "She's really *very* fast asleep—"

"What d'you think?"

"I'd *much* rather come back—"

"Why?"

"Because *I* like sleeping with *you*—"

"That's what I wanted to hear. Come on back!"

"Darling!"

But we didn't have very long before the car was announced. She looked quite startled. The room was warm, and her negligee was simply lace. Which I like. I told her where I was going, and she became *the* Miss Furnival again.

"You'll take great care, won't you?"

"Of course. We're with Scotland Yard—"

"Doesn't do anything for *me*. I'm thinking of those women!"

"Ah. So you know?"

"She didn't talk about anything else. They're all Oriental. Highly inflammable—"

"Except to me!"

"I've heard about those missy chinky-woo's—"

"I've got the best chinky-woo of the lot. Stay here, keep warm, and don't open that door till you hear me—"

"As if I would!"

Chief Superintendent Hockley seemed hardly to have changed his tie. He wore the same overcoat I remembered, a thick muffler, and a bowler hat that looked too big. We talked of everything, and the night's news.

"I just wanted to tell you, sir," he said suddenly. "We're not going on any tourist lark. There's a big ring involved, and if the right people are in there, I shall go in with a squad. We never had the luck to get hold of the keys *and* a good excuse. If everything's in order, we'll raid on Warrant. We've been after them for a long time—"

"Why don't Customs get them coming in?"

I felt his eyes in the darkness. We were going through Berkeley Square.

"Not this lot, sir. Most of it's homemade. It's not too difficult. You can buy the apparatus almost for nothing. No trouble. There's a tremendous market. Plenty of money for it. The raw stuff's smuggled. Opium, heroin, that stuff. Small harbors along the coast. Motor launches from European ports. Very hard to catch. Well, it all boils down to two or three big points. Here, in the Midlands, and Scotland. This place we're going to's the top o' the shop. You know it's in your name, don't you?"

"Yes—"

"That's why I'm glad I'm here!"

I was gladder.

The chauffeur stopped at a lit entrance. There seemed not a soul in the street. We could see to the end by lamplight. A night porter came down the stair and saluted. We got out, followed him to the lift. Nobody said a word. We got in, and the porter pressed the eighth floor button.

When the lift stopped, we could hear the noise. Quite a number of people. Shrieking laughter.

"Everything ready, Inspector?" the Superintendent said to the "porter."

"All doors covered, sir. Squad's waiting, sir!"

"Don't let the front door close—"

"Got rubber corks for the hinges, sir—"

"Stand by for my signal!"

We simply walked in. Nobody met us. Nobody looked at us.

The big room was full of people, more women than men, most sitting or lying on the floor, most of them undressed. Those sitting were swaying in a strange way. Two or three went over, prone, while we stood there. Just at the edge of sight of my right eye, I saw the Superintendent's hand behind his back angle at the wrist, pointing up and down. The "porter" took a small radio from his tail pocket, and spoke. The lift door closed.

I didn't wait. I stepped over a dozen or so women, a couple of snoring men, with more on the left, down a short passage. A large bathroom was full of people talking, laughing, drinking. In a bedroom next door, more. Nobody looked at me. They all seemed well-dressed. A number were drunk, but they were all in excellent humor. Laughter, nothing but. Men and women were asleep against the wall in the passage, pushed there. I opened a door and looked in. The room was dark, though from the breathing, a dozen or more slept. Light from the passage showed the shape of nude bodies.

Suddenly and coldly, I didn't want Paul caught in anything like it.

I looked in two more rooms, more breathing, more bodies. Next was a small boxroom, barely a wardrobe, where a couple had gone to sleep, he without trousers, she without skirt or underclothes. I opened the last door, at the end of the passage.

One lamp, by the window, with a woman's girdle and stockings over it lit the double bed. Paul lay in the middle under a red bath towel. I counted six women asleep with their heads on cushions, sprawled on the carpets. In the large bathroom, two youngish men slept almost under the basin. Five women lay about the rest of the black-and-white floor, with two in the bath. They were all asleep, but it wasn't a drunken sleep. I couldn't hear anything except fairly heavy breathing. The noise came from the drawing room down the passage.

The window slid in three partitions. I got over the sill on to a small terrace that went round the corner, down one step, to a space where laundry flapped pale in darkness. There was a kitchen down at the end. People still laughed. Glasses were busy.

Nearer me was a locked door. I opened it by trying the keys. It led to a back stair, and a service lift.

I was fairly certain the Police would hardly overlook it. Even as I listened I heard them coming up. Not much noise. Just a whisper on concrete steps. I went back to the window, got in, locked it, pulled the curtain. I turned out the light. Paul hadn't a stitch. I couldn't see his clothes. I hurtled across to the bathroom. Sure enough, behind the door, a couple of towel robes hung. I took them both and put one inside another. But that wouldn't be enough. I took out my penknife and slit a hole in the middle of the heavy blue blanket. I got him into the robe, tied it about his waist, pulled the blanket over, pushed his head through the slit. I'd heard the police trying the partitions. They couldn't see through the curtain.

I went to the window and listened. They'd gone. I went over to the bed. Paul lay like a corpse. Barely a breath. I picked him up in a fireman's lift, surprised he was such a weight. I opened the window, made sure everything was quiet, and got over the sill. It wasn't easy, but my balance was good. I paused at the corner. People in the kitchen were still talking, laughing. Round the corner, touching the wall, to the stairway door. My keys were out in moments. The second skeleton opened it. I went down a flight, stopped to listen, down another. In that time the service lift had gone up. I brought it on to the sixth floor, got in, went down to the basement.

I got out, sweating. Through the firedoor I knew there'd be the garage. I didn't know if the Police would be in there, or if I could pay the garage attendant enough to keep his mouth shut. I opened the door quietly. One light at the end glittered in polish and windscreens. I walked through lines of cars, careful of Paul's head. I saw the nightman almost as he saw me.

"I'm upstairs," I said. "I'm taking my friend away. Got a car here? Cab? Fifty pounds, not a word!"

"You're on, guv'l!" he said, instantly, and went across to a grey van. "Get in here. Where'y'want to go?"

Where, indeed. I hadn't thought of it. I saw the telephone,

took my one-shoulder dead weight over to the van. Strong hands pulled it off me, on to the seat. I had just enough strength to shut the door quietly. I stood for a moment getting some blood going. I went over and dialled the Savoy, asked for my room.

"Yes? Hello?"

"Consuelo. Listen. Go to Grosvenor Street. You've got the key. Wait for me!"

"Ten minutes!"

The garage man used his head. He went up the ramp without lights, looked about, saw the police cars to the right about fifty yards down, and turned left, for Park Lane, turned again, and we both heard the police car behind us. He pulled in.

"Where you off?" somebody said.

"Going down the other garage, get the diesel. Boiler fires. Why?"

"Anybody with you?"

"Pal o' mine, that's all. Help me with the barrel. What's this? A hold-up?"

"No, it's all right, mate. We was told you'd be going. Who's y'pal?"

"He's here—"

I took my hat off, looked out, well in shadow.

"Last time I help wi' no barrels, I tell you!" I said, at my theatrical roughest. "What, 'n get done?"

"All right. Report to the Inspector down there when y' get back. Might be some trouble—"

"Well, I didn't ought to be going—" the garage man began. "They might—"

"Dead right!" I said. "Ought to get back—"

"No, now you're out. Get it, but don't go in. See the Inspector, like I said. Any'the party's cars in there, is there?"

"Full of 'em. All 'the left hand side—"

"That's it. I'll look out for you. Where you say you was going?"

"Rutland Street. Our other garage—"

"That's right. That's what we was told. Go on!"

Paul snored in the most extraordinary way, once, long, a true sawmill arpeggio. I cleared my throat in a raking hawk, and spat out of my window, and the garage man step-danced on the starter. We were moving. I had the blanket over Paul's mouth.

"'s matter with this bloke?" the garage man asked. "All right, is he?"

"Up there with another girl. His wife came in. So I did the necessary—"

"Happened before. Funny lot. Go out all hours, they do. But they pay. And that's it!"

"Think I'm one of them?"

He kept his eyes on the blue street, lamplights, traffic jewels, green, amber, shot it on red.

"Don't matter too much what I think, do it?" he said. "All I want's fifty quid. But I' give you a straight tip. Don't go there too often. We been expecting this for the past couple of weeks—"

"Bad behavior?"

"Not what you might expect round there. The row they kick up!"

"I'll have to give you a check—"

"All right with me, guv'—"

"Not worried?"

"I know where you come out of, and I'll know where you're going. You're going to do the worrying. Not me!"

We were there, and so was Consuelo's taxi. She stood in the doorway. She'd opened the door by the time I'd levered Paul off the seat and out. I put him down in the lobby. Thank God, there wasn't a night porter. I took out my check book and wrote against the wall. I felt shaky, walking outside. But cold air does wonders.

"Thanks," I said, through the window. "Good luck!"

"Thank *you*, sir! Pleasure's mine!"

I went back to the hall. Consuelo held open the lift door. I heaved Paul on my shoulder. I felt like the Ancient Mariner. Up we went, and Consuelo still hadn't said a word, hadn't looked at me. She was pale. She unlocked a massive oak and we went into a really lovely room, long, broad, high ceilinged. I put Paul

on a leather sofa, covered him, and went across to take her slack
—very slack—hands.

"Come on," I said. "We've had enough!"

But then I groaned. Consuelo stared frightened eyes.

"Are you hurt, darling?"

I had just enough strength to shake my head.

"No. Not a bit. But damn it, I didn't think of Patti's letter!"

30

Fairly early next morning, I moved to the apartment over the offices in St. James's Square. Consuelo went to Grosvenor Street and found Angela looking after a still-sleeping Paul, and I telephoned Sir Roland. He was in bed.

"Sorry to have given you a great deal of trouble. Your patient's waiting. Is there a hospital you recommend?"

"Yes. I'm going there this morning. St. Emery's Clinic. It's on the corner of St. Emery Street. Just behind Belgrave Square. Can't miss it. Tell me something. How in God's name did you get away?"

"Down the backstairs—"

"Hockley swore that's what you did—"

"Was he *very* angry?"

"Oh, no! He laughed. He was in the most excellent spirits. A number of arrests. And half a dozen of the people they've been looking for. You'll probably hear from him—"

Sergeant-Major McClintock sent an ambulance, and Consuelo called from the clinic to say that Paul was admitted.

"Angela's going home with her mother. I'm clearing up the paper. There's a lot you ought to see. I'm bringing it. I've put the Charles Street position in order. But the Police took all the paper. They're retaining what they want and the rest will be at the office at twelve, noon. Your envelope among it, I hope!"

Inspector Ferris gave it to me, a little creased, and of course, opened.

"The Chief Superintendent was sorry about this, sir," he said, as if he weren't. "Could I take your statement, sir?"

"What statement?"

"Rental of the premises in Charles Street—"

"That's a matter for the Company's Legal Department. You'll find Mr. Robarts downstairs. I'd never been there—"

"You were there last night, sir?" He was writing, and it was an innocent question. But I never suspect the Police of innocence, and I gave him no time to talk.

"I went there in company of Chief Superintendent Hockley and Sir Roland Ainsworth, the neurologist. I saw that the premises were being misused, and having no further business there, I left—"

"How did you leave, sir?"

"On foot—"

"You didn't take a cab? Car?"

"No—"

"You went back to your hotel on foot, sir?"

"No. By cab—"

"But you just said—"

"I'd gone round to Grosvenor Street to meet my secretary—"

"Miss Furnival, sir? And who was with you?"

"Miss Furnival was with me—"

"Nobody else, sir?"

"We were unaccompanied. We reached the Savoy at a little after two—"

"You didn't meet, or see, Mr. Paul Chamby?"

"Yes, I did. At Grosvenor Street—"

"I see, sir. He was there, was he—?"

"He was. He was taken to St. Emery's Clinic this morning—"

"I see, sir. Something serious?"

"You'll have to ask Sir Roland. He should be there by now—"

"Right, sir. Could I see Miss Masters?"

"I'm afraid she's gone back to Leicester—"

"You don't know the address, sir?"

"Miss Furnival will give it to you. Why?"

"She signed the lease in your name—"

"How could they possibly accept my name as hers?"

"Signature's E. Onslow Trothe, sir. She had your power-of-attorney—"

"How about the Company's seal and that sort of thing? What about the check?"

"Check was issued on the Scottish Overland Bank. Signed by E. Onslow Trothe, sir—"

"It's not my bank—just a moment!"

I asked Consuelo to get Bruce Gorleston at the bank. In front of the Inspector, I asked him about the account.

"Miss Masters opened it. She holds your power-of-attorney—"

"For Company business, in my absence—"

"You were in the Middle East. She put fifty thousand in funds—"

"Fifty?"

"—and that was followed by another fifty, and the account has since been incremented—"

"I must warn you it wasn't my money—"

"Wasn't your—?"

"The account was opened without my knowledge or permission—"

"Wha-a-at?"

"Close it. Impound any further checks. Mr. Robarts, of the Legal Department's coming to see you, and Mr. Simmons, our Chief Accountant. I believe the bank's absolutely in the clear. But I fear the Police will be interested—"

"I really am profoundly shocked—"

The Inspector went off happily—from his bland expression—after dropping his stick of bombs—and Logan came through from Beyfoum to say that his team was working well, not too much damage had been done, and he hoped to have everything in order by the end of the week.

"We put up a couple of people last night, sir. Said they were Greeks. Telopadoulos, I think his name was. I didn't get the other.

He was sort of helping. This Telopadoulos asked me what I'd want to go and work for them. They had a plane waiting in Badashah—"

"What did they offer?"

"Twice what we're getting, with a down payment, gratis, of five thousand pounds—"

"Get the details, and I'll pay you five thousand each—"

"*Each*, sir?"

"Each. I want to know the name and base office of the company, names of all officials, field supervisors, engineers, and where, and how you'd get there with your family. Get me those details, and it'll earn you five thousand pounds—"

I took Consuelo to luncheon at Claridges. In the middle of a delicious steak, she was called to the telephone. I attacked the Brussels sprouts and fried potatoes, took on more endive, watercress, and tomatoes barely larger than a thumbnail, each a ball of sugar, and really enjoyed my appetite. I was glad I had, because Consuelo was away rather longer than I'd have thought, and when I saw her face I knew I'd finished lunch.

"Sir Roland wants you to go to the Clinic. Paul's awake. He's threatened suicide. They're going to give him the sleep-therapy, whatever that is. He thinks you ought to talk to him before—"

"You finish your luncheon," I said, and got up. "I'll go on to Heathrow—"

"One of these days we'll have a little peace all on our own. I wonder when?"

"After we've earned it. With Paul out, we're in poor condition. Cheer up!"

It was a nonsensical thing to say, but then, most of what we say *is* nonsense. I had a feeling that Paul hadn't been really at work for some time, possibly for weeks. As second-in-command, with areas of action clearly marked, it wasn't easy to see what the Director General was or wasn't doing. Deliberately I hadn't had a look at his desk or files. I knew that I must. But I thought I'd get the Cairo business off the slate first. Then I decided to put Logan in charge of Middle East, and find somebody to take over my position. It wasn't the ideal because Logan was an engineer pure and simple. He had a good head, and heart, and that was far more important than static knowledge.

St. Emery's Clinic had been a ducal townhouse of many rooms. Inside, cool shadows made ghosts of nurses in dark green uniforms and flowing linen headdresses. I was taken in a box of a lift to the second floor, along a wide corridor to a room without light, except for a small spot on the bedhead showing a temperature board, and a pencil in a clip.

Paul looked at me with truly enormous eyes. I'd have said he was dying. He breathed quickly, slightly. The eyes were palest blue. They seemed like lamps on their own.

"Edmund! So glad you came, boy—"

"All right, Paul. Everything's all—"

He tried to move, but the nurse put a hand on his shoulder.

"Look, I've been mad for months. I know it, now. I've got to tell you. Remember that I—"

Sir Roland came beside me, tapped my shoulder in warning, moved to the other side of the bed.

"It's all right, Paul, talk away," he said, soothingly. "That's what that little needle was for—"

"Yes, well, it's hard to keep my mind on one thing. There's so much. Listen, take care of Angela. I don't care what happens to me. I was getting her the same way. But she put up a fight. I didn't. I thought I was doing something clever. Listen, the dreams—!"

"It's the events leading to the dreams, Paul!" Sir Roland said clearly, almost loudly, bending over him. "Hold on, now. Start from the beginning. Come along!"

"Yes. Yes, the beginning. Tamm's friend—"

"Georg Tamm's?" I asked, quickly. "Stockholm?"

"That's right—"

"What's his name?"

"*Her* name. She's got this club. I owe her some—"

There was that sudden, long drawn snore again.

264

"That's all for the next forty-eight hours," Sir Roland said, and made way for the nurse to settle Paul's head on the pillow, arrange the bedclothes. "Did you get anything of use?"

"I think so. We'll have to see—"

I'd always wondered what Paul's visits to Stockholm were for. Georg Tamm had a great name, and had done some work for us, though I'd never seen any report from him, but that wasn't surprising since it wasn't my business. One way or another I had to fit in a few hours to fly to Stockholm. I knew Tamm. I had a feeling he might be of help.

I got on to Gillian.

"Did you find out?"

"Yes, I did!" she said. "Don't forget I have friends among the files, too. Pencil and paper? Name. Ugo. U-g-o. Primondi. P-r-i-m-o-n-d-i. His number's one one eight seven. Bar-Dav is four zero one two. I've also managed to find pamphlets printed by Magdeburg University Medical School, and three reports on patients in the prison—"

"That's wonderful—!"

"—and a certain Aunty Sam friend of ours is getting more—"

"I knew she'd be there, somewhere—"

"She got most of this. She's *the* flash *and* banger. Hottest part of the rocket—"

"Send the details over. They're the trump cards—"

31

The flight was cloudy and bumpy, a mixture I don't like, especially in a jet, and I was very glad to get into a car—which bumped far more over a country road—and reach the Graeffe Sanitorium. Leonart waited for me, and led into his study, away from the main building. He mixed a fair pink gin, a drink I don't like at teatime, but it was too early for a whisky and soda, though after that flight I could have done with one. Curious, I can drink in the air, but not on the flat.

"Show me what you are going to say," he said, sliding a crepe mat under the glass.

"I've memorized a piece for both. What's your son's name again?"

"Levi Bar-Dav. What's your friend's name?"

"Ugo Primondi. Italian, of Algerian origin, from the town of Constantine. Not exactly *pied noir*, but near. The family had a bar. It was bombed during the trouble. The mother was German. She took the son and two Arab girls to Echstatt—"

"Where is she?"

"Dead. Four years ago. Then Ugo went to Fräglechshaben, and bought the bar."

"No relatives?"

"So far as he knew, no. The father and two sons died in the bomb attack."

"The Arab girls?"

"Went back eighteen months ago—"

"And he was taken—?"

"Can't find out. How did your son disappear?"

"He was at Berlin University. Very happy. Hard working. Suddenly, no letters. For weeks. I went there. Nobody knew. I went to his lodging. Everything gone. The Police made faces, nothing else. I waited. About seven years ago, a repatriated soldier reported he was in Hauerfurth. That's all. The West German Government has done everything. Your men have been injected. It is time you put on your coat, please. This way—"

A different man from the time before, cold, metallic. His tone of voice hadn't changed from speaking of his son to warning me of my patients' readiness. He went into a warm, white-walled room, darkish, blinds drawn, with two operating tables, one against the wall, one nearer the controls of a cardiograph unit. A nurse made a movement of the stiff white cap in greeting, and rolled a large chair on castors near a more technical-looking board of dials.

Leonart snapped his heels, I snapped mine, and he left. I tried the dials of both units, and both worked. They were new, but I was familiar. Everything has a basic principle.

A tap on the door brought in a nurse and a large man in a white gown. So far as I could see, he was about fifty or so, white haired, blunted features—like a healed prize fighter—and small eyes, in that light, black. The nurse gave me a card, with the patient's room number, and nothing more. He was the cardiograph subject. The nurse put him on the table, scrubbed chest, arms and ankles with alcohol pads, fastened the metal tabs, dropped a knee, and she and the other nurse went out.

I switched on, watching the dials for a moment. From the needle's pattern, I saw that the injection was working. I waited. I didn't look at him. He stared at the ceiling. When I was sure he was well under, I went over to him.

"In ten days or so, I shall ask you to permit me to visit Hauerfurth Prison, to take blood samples, and send them to the Pathological Institute at Magdeburg. This is work of highest national importance. For that reason you will help me. Permit. Hauerfurth Prison. Blood samples. Pathological Institute. Magdeburg. Highest national importance—"

I spoke clearly, slowly, loudly, and had time to repeat about a dozen times, till I saw the needle wavering. I went back to the controls, stood in shadow, knew by his breathing when his senses were alert, switched off, and pressed the button.

The nurse came in, took off the straps, helped him to sit, and stand. He looked at me, half-smiled, half-bowed, and went out with his arm round the nurse.

The second man was a type I recognised, tall, thin, hair cut short lifelong, still dark, widow's peak, grey eyes in heavy pouches, fine, long nose, thick underlip, deep creases in the cheeks, large ears. The nurse sat him in the chair, and put the copper shell on his head, fastened the other electrodes, and gave me the cords in a bunchy cluster.

I plugged in, tested, ran the current, nodded to the nurse, and she went out. I listened for the click of the lock. The needle began to show the saw-tooth tower pattern, and then the flattened mounds and shapeless looping I waited for. The man seemed quite comfortable, sitting back, eyes closed.

"In ten days or so, I shall apply to *you* to see two prisoners in Hauerfurth. Their names are Ugo Primondi and Levi Bar-Dav. I *want* to see, I *must* see, and you *will* sign a *permit* for me to see, *in person,* Ugo Primondi and Levi Bar-Dav. I shall take blood samples for the Pathological Institute in Magdeburg. I am applying for a permit to enter Hauerfurth Prison. You *will* give me that permit. You will *not* question. It is work of highest national importance. You *will* sign a permit for me to enter Hauerfurth Prison—"

I said it, facing him, speaking slowly, loudly at first, and then as I might if he sat in his office, emphasising the key words, shouting, dropping back to the conversational. I was wet through when the needle began to spike. When the normal pattern began, I rang for the nurse.

Leonart came in after the man had gone—without a look—and rubbed his fists against his cheeks.

"If it fails, I take a broom, the rest of my life, I clean the floors!" he said, exultingly. "Your accent is a marvel. What is it?"

"One they won't forget. Listen to me. We're building castles. If I fail—and there's always that *if*—I want a few grains of something. For the three of us. Because we'd never have a chance. You know that, don't you? You know how they'd treat us?"

He nodded. Suddenly, he was old.

"I give you something gentle," he said. "Don't swallow, if it isn't the last possible thing. It is quick. No pain."

I took off my white coat, looked once about the room, and in all that whiteness, and aseptic cleanliness, wished there had been just one small candle to light, one bright flame to heal, and bless, and fortify.

32

Professor Georg Tamm waited for me at the hotel. He hadn't changed much since we'd last met. He was grey—fair, tall, heavy, sharp-eyed with knowledge, and obviously apprehensive, half-inclined to turn away.

"Paul Chamby is very ill," I said, when we'd sat down on the terrace. "I'm in charge of things, and I'd like to know what monetary arrangement he had with you, so that our accountants—"

He opened his eyes in surprise.

"But Mr. Trothe, I have no arrangement!" he said. "I was paid for a report. That's some time ago. I was also trying to find two mineralogists. They went to another company—"

"You don't know which?"

"No. I haven't heard from them—"

"Well, I'm glad there's nothing outstanding. Did Paul stay here during the time he visited you?"

"Visited *me?*" Tamm sat back, straight, staring blue suspicion. "When did he visit me? Last time, possibly six months ago, for twenty minutes. A question of sand-shift—"

"My information's a little out, apparently. Isn't there, or wasn't there, a club of some sort?"

"The Round the Corner, yes. I took him there. An English-woman owns it. Why?"

"He said something about money. If it's owed, I'd like to pay it—"

He clasped his hands, looking at me, not exactly underbrow, but still accusingly. He was very far from being a fool.

"How could he dare send his account to me from that club!" he said.

"Why should he?"

"I introduced him. Of course, I am responsible—"

"You didn't get in touch?"

"He didn't reply to my letters—"

It was my turn to sit back. This was as much unlike Paul as to be someone else. Paul was straight as a gun barrel. I'd have banked my life on him. On occasion, had.

I nodded to the waiter. It's one of those little things to do when words fail.

"Do please join me?" I appealed. "We both need a drink. You know perfectly well we do. Something's very wrong!"

He tried not to smile, and relented. He gave the waiter his order, I gave mine, and we looked at each other.

"All right," I said. "Cards on the table. What *is* it?"

"My wife is in that car coming now over the bridge," he said, looking at dozens of headlights. "When she gets here, you permit, I shall leave. I have time to drink with you. It is because I am sure you know nothing. First. I met Paul Chamby in the war. An extraordinary man. After, I heard from him. About ten years ago he was in Africa. Then in Geneva. I attended a conference. I met him with his wife. A month or so later, I was invited to Beirut. I went. I agreed to do a study. He came here. Naturally, he is a man of life. I entertained him. The Round the Corner was a good place. He was excellent as a companion. Then he didn't come for some time. In this time, this Round the Corner was no longer for people in a position—"

"Why not?"

He made a pursing motion of his mouth.

"A different sort of people, yes, a lower kind. Everything. Of course, drugs. I was told he had parties there. Without coming to see me? I thought it impossible. For such a man. But when I was sent this account, I knew it was true. I wrote to him, I think four times. It was a large sum. I went there in the daytime. I spoke to the woman who owns the place. Her name is Curly. I don't know her other name. She is the worst. She threatened to go to the University with her girls, and her man-girls and her girl-men. I paid. But I found he had his own girls there!"

"His own?"

"His own women. Ah, but something, you can't imagine!"

"Doesn't sound like Paul!"

"I assure you, Mr. Trothe, I was amazed beyond the word. But I paid. Then, about a month ago, I was sent the copies and translations of articles from our Foreign Service public relations. They were sent to me because I am the authority. I knew it was my confidential report to your Company. Under Paul Chamby's name as author!"

"I'll wager any money he never had the slightest thing to do with it. How about the Police?"

He drank, and stood, waving over the balcony.

"The Police here are the same as in other countries, Mr. Trothe," he said, agreeably enough. "They wait. They strike. I don't wish to be struck!"

"Drugs, you mentioned. Where do they come from?"

He looked out at the harbor, deep blue, with light shining on white buildings, quivering in water, showing masts, rigging, colored funnels.

"It's a port," he said. "Rats come and go. Who sees them?"

I followed him, like a wet dog, to the foyer and waited till he'd got his hat and coat.

"These women," I said. "Anything in particular about them?"

"They seemed only to serve him," he said, quietly, thoughtfully. "They were all on a Hong Kong visa, I found out. Of course, I have friends, too—"

He turned at the top of the stairway, hand up.

"One thing, Mr. Trothe. The figures in the articles are quite wrong. Did your Company proceed on that basis?"

"Till I've seen them, I don't know—"

"Please examine my original report. Mr. Trothe, please ask yourself. It seems to me you really don't know. Is Mr. Chamby working for *your* Company or another? For *your* country, or another? I think you must consider, Mr. Trothe. I am not the only one with this idea!"

He went down the stairway, and I watched him get into a car.

I don't think I've ever been more in doubt, of myself or anybody else, and more miserable. Or sharper for a fight.

33

It was too early to go to the Round the Corner club. I got a room, ordered dinner, booked a flight for London, and turned on clix at exactly the right time. Arturo came in from Rome, WTSURRO. Want To See You, Urgent, Out. I sent SUSTO. See You Soonest, Out. But I was waiting only for Consuelo, and when she came in at sixteen minutes, I could have gone, then and there, to the airport, and to hell with everything.

DLGILYNHEXLNGO, she sent, Darling, Love You Nothing Here Except Longing Out, and I sent ARGAMLNGCHKWOM-TMKLLPTSNSETCWFLO, Arriving A.M. Longing chinky-woo Meet Me Kiss All Points North South Etc., Wonderful, Out, and got back three spaced dots for More the Merrier, or any other meaning suggested by three short dots, agreement, emphasis, hurry.

I ate some excellent fish, drank a light beer, and lay on the bed. I woke at a little after eleven, sponged my face, and went downstairs. It took a long time to find a cab. The hotel service had changed a great deal. There seemed nobody at work. I didn't ask any questions.

Socialism, or whatever it was, in a very few years, had changed Swedish attitudes. That hotel had been among the world's very best. I'm not sure where it all ends. If I pay for something, I want it. If I'm willing to pay to have my bag carried up to my room, I want it carried up. I'd had to carry it up myself. But an hotel is that, and if Socialism, or whatever it is, prevents the proper functioning of an hotel, or any other business, then there's something wrong with it. So far as I'm concerned, Socialism is only a hint away from anarchy, a state of mind where somebody is everybody, and nobody is anybody, and Tom Rot will sit, and let somebody else feed and house him, until somebody else sits down and lets Tom rot. It's coming.

The cab took me to the older part of the City, which I always was fond of, especially for some of the restaurants. The club was down a small street. I paid the cabman and walked a few yards to the only light. A doorman watched me go down the stairs. I gave hat and coat to the woman behind the little counter, and pushed aside the red velvet curtains. I don't know what I expected to see, but no tomb was ever deader. The folds of cloth about the wall flattened sound. It was still early. A guitarist abused the instrument on a small stage. I saw the silhouette of about a dozen couples in a room that might hold a hundred or more. A girl in net stockings and very little else came out of the night, and hung a remarkably buoyant bosom over me, and said enough to let me know she wasn't Swedish.

"A bottle of scotch," I said. "And a baby polly—"

"Polly, no, sir," she said, in plainest Cockney English. "Soda, yes—"

"And I'd like to talk to Curly—"

"If she's here yet, all right. I'll see—"

She went away, the lummox on the stage plucked, bellowed, finished as if it were all too much, got off the chair, and made room for a pianist. The girl came back with a bottle of Johnnie Walker, Black Label and a siphon.

"Curly'll see you in a minute, when she's got her teeth in," she said, and broke the seal. "After you've had your little tibby-tabby, would you like me to sit with you? Bad night tonight. I've only got another couple of days here. Hearing you, I'll be glad to get back—"

"Been here long?"

"Ten days, altogether. I changed with my off-number. She's in London. I' be so rotten glad when she gets here!"

"Still something to be said for us?"

"Ooh, you don't know!"

"What's the trouble?"

She looked over the room. I tasted the "scotch." It wasn't. I didn't say anything.

"I don't know, honestly. They're full of sparks, I'll say that. They talk English better than I do, a lot of them. You know, like the books. But I can't understand half they say, and they don't dig me at all. I don't see how you can go to school and learn a language, and yet not say much. I mean, what I can get. Listen, want me to sit with you? I feel like a bit tonight—"

She couldn't have been more than eighteen or nineteen, and a quite, I suppose, pretty girl. At least, in that light. Patti's age.

That sore wound again.

I could see her better, the creased sheet, three lines in handwriting so much like Mel's, Mel, dead, unbelievably, in the churchyard, Patti, incredibly, married to a Negro.

Darling Daddy, time to think, hours to regret. I know so much more, now. You'll soon be a granddaddy. Chocolate milk? Plain black? 'alf 'n 'alf? It's all the same, isn't it? It's a new life. And I love him. I wish you'd meet him and talk. Then me. Love to sit in your lap again. Feel rather frightened. But happy. Please write and forgive. Kisses three. Patti.

I'd sent off a three-page cable.

A man came out of shadow and waved to me.

"Curly's going to see you," the girl said. "I'll sit here and look after the bottle. And go home after? Ooh, I do, I proper fancy you. Bit o'tweed, that's me, tonight!"

I followed the man through the curtain he held apart, to a small, warm, half-office, half-boudoir, fragrant with a mixture of perfume and alcohol, plus some years of cigar smoke.

"Cor-rly, a wisitor-r," the man said, and pulled the curtain in a rattle.

She sat at the make-up table, looking at herself in the light of about two dozen electrics framing a mirror, a large woman, with an electric green scarf round her head. A pale pink satin wrap showed a variety of tires, bumps, mounds until the final puff on the stool.

"Christ, you get a proper mess my age, don't you?" she said, in a man's voice, either to me or to her reflection. "Look at that. I mean, *look* at it. 'Course, I'm bald's a bastard under this lot. Spent a fortune this afternoon in the beauty parlor. Thought I was coming out the Queen of Sheba. I didn't half. Got more wrinkles now 'n when I went in. What can I do for you, dear?"

"Mr. Paul Chamby had an account here," I began.

"Quite right, dear!" she said, to my reflection. "Owing a time 'n all. Couldn't get a hold of him—"

"So you went to the University, and got someone else. Is that it?"

She pulled a face at herself, and began plucking hairs I couldn't see out of her eyebrows. Diamante borders on the wrap sleeves twinkled.

"We all got to live, y' know," she said softly. "That man Chamby, he disappointed me. I never knew he was that sort. Promised the girls everythink. Leave his friend to pay—"

"You knew where he was? Where his office was?"

"'s use of that? London's London. Here's here. Here's where I want my money. On the table, dear. Didn't ought to let him go. But he always paid before—"

"How much was it? Just give me the figures. I'll repay Professor Tamm—"

"Oh. So you *know* he paid? What's the idea 'asking me, then?"

"Your figure and his ought to tally—"

"My figure, dear? Know the dirge, do you? Everythink I had is gone. How about some champagne?"

"All right. The scotch out there, isn't. Alcohol, tea, three drops of iodine—"

"Wrong. That's *my* mixture, that is. It's all right for people don't drink too much 'n don't know scotch from scheisswasser.

I serve you a bottle of the real, I get the champagne? What a turn-up, eh?"

She rang a bell, and went on looking at her face as if she might have met a stranger.

"Business tonight's a bloater. Most'the girls don't come in. No good wearing their arses out, is it?"

"How many women has Mr. Chamby, here?"

"Had. Ain't here now, dear. All went back. Oh, 'bout'couple 'weeks ago. This business, dear, it's booze and birds. Got any sense, you hold it there. The birds, they get who they can, get 'em drunk, I mean, it's all business. This new lark, they don't booze, but they'll use your place to do what they like. Oh, yes! This man Chamby's lot—"

"But where does he *get* girls, for God's sake!"

She looked at herself, head this side, that side. She hadn't once looked at me except in the mirror. She pulled at the scarf, and dropped it. Her head was a huge ball of fair rolly curls, tight, shiny.

"Going up to seventy four, dear, no holds barred. There it is, look. Three plastics. A fortune, every time. An' what'd they do? Make it a bleedin' sight worse, you ask me. I wish I had me old wrinkles. Least, they was mine. These new 'uns, I don't know how they come there. I told the bloke, I says pull, I says. Pull hard. Pulled hisself, most like, eh?"

The waiter came in with a Cordon Rouge and a Dimple Haig, with goblets, a silver bucket, and a tray of small sandwiches. I hadn't heard her order.

"Ah, nothing like it, is there, dear?" she trolled, to the mirror, nodding at the tray. "Does my heart good, that does. The old days, nothink but champagne. I had more shoes ruined than I ever walked on. Think it's a joke, drinking champagne out of a girl's shoe, do you? More fool, you—"

We toasted, and Curly drank three glasses, one after another, leaned back, belched becomingly, mouthed a charming apology, and took a small brush, this time to darken her eyelids.

"This new lark," I said.

"That's right. You'd never believe they'd have opium pipes out there in that room, would you? Eh?"

She'd stopped dabbing to ask.

"Mr. Chamby?"

"My oath. Couple of nights he turned this place into a real house. Matter of fact, I let it go for a bit just for fun. I was collecting some girls, see? Get a place, look for the girls, make 'em feel at home, I mean, young 'un's. You don't want the klatch in this business. It's the young 'un's make money. I look after my girls—"

"We were discussing something else. What had opium to do with Mr. Chamby?"

She put both fists on the dressing table, and looked at me sideways in the mirror. She had brown eyes that must have been beautiful, and still were not inhuman.

"He started the lark," she said, as if it were a secret. "Come in one night off 'fa yacht, out there. About forty of 'em. Most girls. They filled the pipes. Lit 'em, they did. Everybody was having a puff. It's a little thing, like dirty dough. It burns. I was in here, that first night. I sent for the head waiter. I says, Theo, that's his name, Theo, I says, what is dis horrible stinch, I says. Ah, he says, it's opium. I nigh tore me corset getting out there. Some of my best customers was actually laying down on the floor. Millionaires, I ask you!"

"What was Mr. Chamby doing?"

She patted the curls gently with fattish, glossy hands, short fingers, diamonds dazzling.

"He was dead-soppy," she said, as if it pleased her. "He was give the LSD stuff. Not pounds, shillings, and pence. LSD. It's new. I don't understand nothing about it. Don't want to. Listen, what are you, dear? A nark?"

I laughed.

"No," I said. "I'm nothing to do with the Police. Mr. Chamby's my friend. I'm trying to help him—"

She shook all the curls, but gently.

"He's gone well past it, dear. I only *heard* this, mind. He's taking it twice a week. There's this girl, she's only this high. She dopes him. Oh, she's got him. Funny thing is, he don't look it—"

"Did you hear her name?"

"The girl? Oh, 'course. She used to come in here and wait. She never went out there. Her name was Mo-oy. Well, she answered to that—"

"Where did she stay?"

"The Grand. Had a maid. Her own car. Posh lot. Well, so's he. He was spending a couple of thousand a night—"

"Kroner?"

She looked at me in the mirror, laughing.

"Pounds, dear. Good old pounds. In notes. Paid. 'course, he was a big customer. Sometimes he paid in dollars. Notes. Yes. Oh, he was my right leg, I tell you. But that last one was big. It was three thousand-odd—"

"Professor Tamm paid it?"

"He had to, dear. My girls earned it. My girls wanted it. I got it. I had to. My girls 're my business, dear!"

"How could he possibly run up a three thousand pound account?"

"Easy, dear. That night, he had more than two hundred people in here. This opium and the other stuff costs a lot. Time you've opened a few dozen champagne—"

"But who *were* these people?"

She shook the curls. She didn't look at me.

"Embassies, business, a lot I don't know. Never see before—"

"This particular girl of Mr. Chamby's. Was she Chinese?"

She pulled down her mouth, lifted the glass, looking up at the right-hand corner of the mirror.

"Looked it, but I never asked. Spoke English and French 's if she was born there. The man with her was English, I'm dead sure. Took care of her. Got Chamby out of it when he was well away—"

"Who was this man?"

She leaned back, raised the glass, put it down, and folded her hands.

"Been asking meself the same question, dear. Ask me, he was a funny sort. Youngish, not more 'n thirty five, the outside. Smart, yes. Oxford, I'd say. He had all the girls, everybody like *that*—"

She squeezed finger and thumb.

"What did he do?"

"He just seemed to watch till Mr. Chamby was well away, then him and Mr. Chamby and this girl, they sloped. But he told the girls who to give the stuff to. Mr. Chamby always got took out sleeping—"

"What was this man's name?"

"I never heard it, dear—"

"Was he with this girl?"

"Not sure—"

"Listen, Curly—"

It was time to put her against the wall.

"I'll give you a thousand pounds for the information I want," I said, and let it sink in. "What was this man's name, and where was he staying?"

She was staring at herself, and as I watched, she seemed to shrink.

"Only name I ever heard him called was Pip. About like I said—thirtyish fivish—more or less. The girl in here called him Pip. But he was a bit too much of it, know what I mean? I spit, and you lick it? Don't go down with me. He was staying at the Stradt, just round here. That's where Mr. Chamby got took. Then he slept a couple of days. This Pip always came in to pay me about twelve the next day. The girls got paid by him. I don't pay girls, dear. This is a business, like I said. Birds 'n booze—"

"Where's this man Pip, at the moment?"

"Well, I don't know *his* business, and he don't know *mine*. I get my money, do I?"

She turned to look at me. I've never seen such a pair of coal-burners. Her face was puffy as her hands, but the eyes lived. Under that mass of gold curls they were frightening.

"I could get you took care of, dear," she said.

"If I'm not outside in ten minutes, Captain Lund's coming in to find out why—"

She sat further back to pour the rest of the bottle. She was smiling.

"A nark, I knew you was," she said, and drank and put down the glass. "How 'bout it, Theo? Worth bashin', is he?"

I knew somebody fairly large was standing behind my chair. I sensed presence and size.

There was a move. I did the old pirouette-and-pivot trick, slipping off the jacket, jumping, both feet out, landing, turning face-on. Theo held my coat. He was one of the largest bouncers I've ever seen. He looked sheep-faced at Curly's back. She hadn't moved.

"Well, don't stand there," she said. "Help the policeman on with it, why don't you—?"

I took it from him.

"You'll both stay here till I'm outside," I said, putting it on. "You'll have a number to call in London. Any information you think's valuable will always earn you a check—"

"What, 'n nothink in the bank?"

"That's up to you," I said, writing. "Take that to the proper place—"

She looked at the check.

"Same bank as Chamby's," she said.

"And Pip's?"

"Always paid cash, dear. Not like some—"

"I'm meeting Captain Lund," I said. "Good night!"

I passed Theo—he made way—and went through the dark room. The girl got up to meet me.

"Sorry," I said, and put some notes in a cool, unprotesting hand. "I'm keeping an appointment—"

"An' I been 'n promised meself the tweed?" she said, reprovingly, counting the money. "Couldn't you come back? I'm all right. I mean, anythink y' like, dear—"

"I'll be in London at five—"

"Always find me at the 'Rusty Hinge.' Down Old Compton. Know it?"

A small notion floated from somewhere while the woman helped me on with my overcoat.

"Did you know Mr. Chamby?" I asked her.

"Only by the talk. But the girl who's place I took, she knew him. Knew the lot. Go to the 'Rusty Hinge.' Ask for Benni. Tell her Sid sent you, you're in. Thanks for the present!"

I went back to the hotel to get my bag. The night was cold. There weren't many in the streets. Stockholm went to bed early. A Police car came behind, and Captain Lund asked me in. My bag was on the floor.

"Did you know you had somebody behind you all night?" he said. "Discounting my men—"

"No," I said truthfully. "Who was he?"

"I'll find out," he said, looking through the back window. "You're changing to this car on the corner. The one you ordered from the hotel—"

We pulled up, I got out, my bag went in the limousine, and Captain Lund gave me an envelope.

"That's what we know about Mr. Chamby," he said. "Couple of days more, we'd have put them all inside. A bad lot!"

"Why did you wait so long?"

"He's—what d' you call it?—a psychophagos. That's all. The man was always asleep—"

Paul, a self-eater? That most creative, outgoing, steadfast soul?

"I'm not sure about that. If there's anything I can do for you—"

"I'm paying you back a little. Look out for that fellow, will you?"

I kept a sharp watch back to London, but I didn't "see" anybody. That was a small disappointment.

For some absurd reason I expected to find Consuelo waiting in that freezing wind. The car was warm and I dozed to St. James's Square. Sergeant-Major Tridwell was in shirtsleeves, waxing the lobby floor.

"Late night, Sar'-Major?"

283

"Take turns, sir—"

"We need another man. Ease the pace—"

"Call one in, sir?"

"Leave a note for Miss Furnival—"

"Sir. Lady's upstairs, waiting, sir!"

She was, indeed. In bed. She woke, moved both hands under her hair, and spread it up, over the pillow, stretched arms, legs, in a sort of insidious poetry of constant motion, and suddenly lay there, awake, looking at me.

"They couldn't find your name on any list, and it was *so* cold, I thought I'd wait here," she said sleepily. "I think it's more comfortable, don't you?"

"Much. Are you awake?"

"I'd surprise you how much. Would you care for a cup of *really* good tea?"

"Please. Offhand, can you think of anyone called Pip who might be on the staff, somewhere?"

"Pip? No. Don't think I've ever known one—"

She was out of bed and getting into a thick dressing gown of mine. She looked dream-soaked and cuddly, and I squeezed her, a little overcome by that breath of sleepy femininity. Nothing's more delicate.

"Get me a list of all the people Paul employed, whether they're on the paylist or not—"

"I never heard of anyone? I mean, not getting paid—"

"Is any man, anywhere, known to have been a sort of secretary-companion or something?"

She laughed in my face, a shut-eyed joy.

"*Paul?* Heavens, what a question—!"

"I'm thinking of Master Pip—"

"Not the remotest idea. Of course, there're the Princes—"

"Get on to Marie-France, first thing. Ask her if she knows anything about him, or Stockholm, or about Paul's being there. Get on to Angela. She might know something. Ask Gillian to call me. She knows almost everybody. Didn't she work for Henry Tufton?"

"For most of them. Right at the top—"

A thought almost paralyzed me.

I made the sign of the circle, and a query, to ask if the room had been looked over for a mike.

I saw from the sudden freeze in her face how she felt.

"Tea, darling!" she said, loudly, and took a handful of the dressing gown in imperial sweep. "You know where the brandy is. You might pour *two*. That's because I detest brandy on breath in bed—"

"Whose breath?"

"I never drink after I've cleaned my teeth. You're not so fastidious—"

"Get thee to a nunnery!"

"Love to know what I'd do. Bed 'n brandy's my bag. Dee-ur—!"

34

Heathrow was socked out, and I was asked to stand by.

I had to send Prince Abdullah a telegram. And my friend, Khefi.

Captain Lund's report was a repetition of Curly's brief, more pungent summary, but it had a useful final paragraph.

"It seemed common knowledge that a ship or an airplane would arrive to take everybody, with Mr. Chamby, to Rangoon, via Panama, Japan, Hong Kong. Many of the women came from these places on six months' contract. Their passports and finances were in order. Many had the profession of prostitute, from their conduct. Some, in all, five, were not. These were, two masseuses, one secretary in Russian, Chinese and English, one secretary in French, German, Italian and English, and one without profession. This last woman, Hana Muoy, from her passport, British, issued in Hong Kong, had an English father, Chinese mother from Macao. Thirty-one years, single, no profession, independent, four foot five, blue eyes, black hair, no signs or scars or identifying marks, born in London. She used only Travelers' Checks. We have not yet found the issuing agency. She bought many things to the value of twenty-two thousand pounds sterling, most silver, glass, one picture, one bronze, one sapphire necklace. All sent to Maclas, Capetown, a forwarding agent. Mr. Chamby was always taken to her suite at the Grand Hotel after he had recovered at the Stradt. He was evicted from the hotel for a quarrel in the restaurant. This was because he required service after hours. He tried to go upstairs, and was prevented. Three of the hotel staff were medically treated. Everybody in the party left by air that day, for Paris, London or Madrid. All accounts were paid, including ex-gratia payments for those injured. Mr. Chamby did not appeal to the British Consul. It had not been found where the drugs came from. The other Englishman in the party was suspected. He came to Stockholm three times. His name, as registered, Charles Fribell, Passport No. B55173731 issued in London in January of this year, is found by the British Consulate to be false. His room was searched. There was nothing in possession of this man or Mr. Chamby. Our first warning came with an arrest of a Swedish citizen, found in a car, unconscious from opium and lysergic acid. This was the first of eight arrests. All were respectable people unable to account for their condition. In this way we came to the Round the Corner club, and the enquiry began. It has not terminated."

The Passport Office reported that Hana Muoy's passport had belonged to an amah of an English family, dead for many years, cancelled at the time. All Consulates and Interpol had been warned.

If I knew Miss Muoy, she'd have a dozen others. Her sort never used a false passport for very long.

Especially with a Pip behind her.

I had to find him.

35

I called Superintendent Berry from the I-Unit, and gave him the Maclas agency in Capetown, and the Rusty Hinge address, with the girl's name.

"I'll get an off-duty policewoman to do it, sir," he said, smilingly. "Working without a permit, I suppose. We'll see what she has to say—"

"See if she knows somebody called Pip—"

"Strange, y' know, sir. A supposedly smart man allowing any name to be used anywhere. Still, they all give themselves away somewhere. 'Else we wouldn't have a chance—"

Consuelo came in a flurry to say the airline wanted me at the airport immediately.

We kissed, and she rested against me.

"How long, this time?" she whispered.

"Have a bag packed for Madrid, that's all!"

"Who's going to be in charge here when I leave?"

"Send it all to Miss Toverell in Geneva. Everybody else, stay at home until the accountants have finished. I'm afraid of what they'll find. I'll have to tell Abdullah—"

But it was he who told me.

We were in the sitting room of his suite in the clinic at Gstaad-Brö. He looked better, more rested, without the black patches under his eyes. He wore a heavy white sweater and towelling trousers, despite the steamy heat in the room. Snow lazed down outside.

"We have known for these months, you see," he said, smoking the widest Egyptian cigarette I ever saw, of wonderful aroma. "I told my nephews they must act. But they are very loyal. Except to me. Chamby *did* do a very great deal. Even among our enemies. But we also have agents, you know. We began to hear whispers—"

"What sort, and where from?"

"You are also loyal. Good. Not every man has friends. The whispers came from the bazaars where drugs are bought. LSD is not difficult to find for those whose business it is. Opium is the easiest. Opium and LSD were being taken by women to Bari and on to Rome. Sometimes to Genoa. The men there were selling a great deal to Chamby. So we heard the name. We were surprised, but even more surprised to find Company checks being used. Azil showed one to Chamby. He explained, and it was perfectly acceptable, that shippers, store owners, often exchange checks instead of writing one of their own or paying money. He denied using drugs at any time. But the whispers became open talk. I believe you know Hargel Garagesh?"

"Yes, I do—"

"Well, he personally told me that Chamby had taken a dozen girls on contract. We had to look closer, of course—"

"What on earth would he want them *for*? That's what really stumps me!"

The Prince went over to the window.

"That type of woman is always useful, especially in business," he said. "In difficult negotiations, for example, with a certain type of man, they are indispensable. They take away anger. They provide a certain calmative, no? They earn their money in many ways. They keep their ears and eyes open. *Who* was Chamby entertaining?"

It was more command than question.

"Don't know," I said. "I never heard of that sort of 'entertainment.' At least, in *this* Company!"

"I asked to see you because of two matters," he said, looking out at the snow. "The first, I have reason to believe Chamby has been in close touch with Polish and East German officials about the supply of oil. Not our mineral gas. Oil. From the fields we shall be using?"

"I don't believe it for a moment!"

"My informant is a man of substance, I must tell you. The same Hargel Garagesh. Whether it is true or not, what would Chamby be talking to them about?"

"Possibly our own business—"

"No possibility!"

I knew that.

"Secondly," he went on, still watching the snow, but suddenly he turned. "Now, answer me. Why did you draw two hundred thousand pounds of Company money, and pay it into your private account on Wednesday of last week?"

He caught me quite on the wrong foot.

"You see, smallest nephew, when I take interest in a company, I look into details!" he said, smiling, although it wasn't the sort of smile I liked. "What have you to say?"

"Well," I said, picking myself up, with the pieces. "It's quite untrue, and I'd like to know where you got your information—"

"You have an account at the Zurich Credit Bank?"

"No—"

He stared at me.

"I think you should go to Zurich," he said. "And then let me know where that money went—"

"I shall certainly do so. You may as well know I called our London accountants in. I should have done it when I took charge. I've reason to believe there'll be a large sum unaccounted for—"

He nodded as if it weren't important.

"Where could he use this money?" he asked.

"We'll find out through the bank—"

He widened his mouth, shook his head.

"Common error," he said. "Clever people don't leave signs. I shall expect your call from the bank. This evening I prepare for an operation tomorrow morning. You know, smallest—almost—nephew, I—we—trust you?"

I was touched to the quick. We shook hands. He still had a good grip, a clear smile, nothing behind it.

I went back to the car in a boil of impatience. There was a helicopter service on the flat, but it took interminable time to get there. We went up in snow, but the pilot, I suppose, could have got there with his eyes shut. We weren't up high. All we went over were hills, and snow, frozen rivers, cattle huddled under trees, farmhouses with muddy ruts winding to the barns, and a car stuck in a lane. The pilot waved to the driver, and made a note. We landed outside Basle, and I caught an electric train to Zurich, wondering again at the splendid way the Swiss run everything.

It didn't take the bank manager long to have the papers on the desk. It had never been my bank, and the account in my name, the details, and my signature had nothing to do with me. He called in the chief cashier, and between them they agreed that the man who'd pretended to be me was thirty five or so, dark, and was introduced by Mr. Paul Chamby's secretary, Miss Angela Masters.

"Personally?"

"By letter—"

He passed it across.

"That's not Miss Masters' signature," I said. "You'd better call the Police. I'm going to our office in Geneva. I shall also bring the Police in. Who signed the check that opened the account?"

"It would be at the drawee's bank in Geneva," the manager said, quite pale. "I will have it sent to your bank. It was counter-signed by Carl-Maria Reismann, the accountant in your Geneva office—"

It appeared to me, going back, that Paul would have to stay in the clinic for some time to avoid going to prison. I couldn't see any way out. Checks had been forged, the Company had been defrauded, innocent people had been dragged in. Drugs, alcohol, anything else were no excuse.

I called our law firm on the way in, and Doctor Johannes Buder and an assistant were waiting for me in the foyer. The assistant was sent to call the Police, and in the lift, I went into detail. We didn't have to pass any other office to get to mine, and when we entered, Doctor Buder went to the telephone, told the head porter to close the building till the Police came, and then called our accountants to send the senior partner over immediately.

I called Reismann's desk, and was put on to Miss Toverell, in charge of the office.

"Oh, good day, sir!"

"Send Mr. Reismann here, please, and—"

"But, sir, did you not send for him this morning? He's gone to London—"

"I?"

"I have your telegram, sir. 'Instruct Reismann Report This Office Immediately. Urgent.' Did you not send it, sir?"

I looked at Doctor Buder.

He was smiling a little sadly out at the lake, turned to look at me sideways.

" 'Oh, John, John, the grey goose has gone—' " he sang, in a cracked voice. " 'And the fox is off to his barrow!' My mother used to sing that to me when I was a little boy—"

36

I sent details of the telegram to London, and when I got there, Consuelo told me it was handed in at Pall Mall, near the office, at ten forty, but the clerk couldn't remember much about the sender, possibly a man, she wasn't sure. The form was typed, the sender and the address didn't exist. Reismann hadn't arrived, had no known address in Britain, and Berry had reported that his dossier was a farrago.

"Liaise with Miss Toverell in any matter not covered by immediate instructions," I told her. "Any legal matter refer to Mr. Robarts. Finance, Mr. Simmons. For the rest, you'll just have to play by the seat of your exquisite panties till I get back and marry you—"

"Talking about *that*, I have a favorite little church—"

"Settle a date. I shall be away for five or six days. We shall then meet in Madrid, overnight, and I shall be gone again for another week or so. That's all you're to be told!"

She dropped a small, but touchingly graceful curtsey.

"M'lud 'n monster!—"

"Did you make an appointment with Doctor Tomsett?"

"He'll be waiting at three o'clock. Frederick's gone to Somerton for the registration. His examination starts next Wednesday. Mrs. Tomsett's gone with him—"

"Sorry about that. Did the Company do anything with Onslow Close? Beyond buying it?"

Hands behind her back—in what I'd come to know as her Little Girl mood—always highly dangerous in every way—she looked at me.

"It was restored at a cost of a hundred and sixty eight thousand pounds!"

"A hu—!"

"That was the final accounting. Prince Azil employed the same architect who did the offices. He'd decided to make it his headquarters while he was in London. It's empty, except for the furniture, of course. Why don't you go and see it?"

"Don't think I could bear to!"

"Well. See when you get there. The car's waiting. There's coffee in the flask. It's awfully cold. Don't *dare* come back with one!"

The familiar route, even to the color of the asphalt, brought back all the days-gone-by again. How many times I'd driven Mel—as my fiancée, and as a bride, and then Mel and Frederick as a baby, and Patti—in the same old car that was almost part of the family, noting with regret the tearing down of houses on the way, the building of new, the new roads, new turns, traffic signals, all the minutia of domestic life gone over, compacted in a little room on wheels—yes—how many times!

That road had changed even in the few months I'd been away. I resented the cheapness of most of it, the garish advertisements, bare blocks of "modern" apartments that were merely slums of the future, always the expedient, the cheap, nothing with the dignity of a great people, less with perfume of the royal.

Trothe Common was in front of me before I was ready. The trees were still in leaf. They hadn't grown half my height in my lifetime. They possibly didn't look much different from when my father had seen them as a young man. They'd been planted by my great-great-great-grandfather as saplings in place of oaks cut down for battleships. I remembered Bos'n Jesse Figg, one hundred and three years of age when he came to my seventh birthday party, with everybody else in the village, there, in the middle of the

Common, telling us he'd been given twelve o' the belt by the Beadle for jumping over "they littlish 'uns, ah, 'n takin' they green sprates off 'un—ah!" But that would have been close to one hundred and forty years before this moment—time—my God. And what is there to show?

Doctor Tomsett heard the car and came bareheaded to the Rectory gate.

"I've been told you haven't much time," he called, in his full-hearted way. "Noriss has a pressing appointment, too. Should we walk up and join him? I'm very glad to be able to say that Frederick's not the young man you knew. He's doing a wonderful job. I'm more or less acting as preceptor, but he doesn't require it, really. I'm sure he's going to wear the bay. He's got another two months, rather less, here. Have you decided what he should do?"

"I'd like him to decide—"

"He's taken with the idea of joining your Company. I think the desert has a pull for most of us. I left Bahrein thirty-odd years ago. But I'd go back this moment if I could!"

Doctor Noriss didn't seem to have changed, either. Country life has its glorious advantages, of them all, those hours of uninterrupted sleep. He showed me the clinical cards, the tests, all the documentary. Frederick had, in fact, made a remarkable recovery.

"The only really ugly fly in the ointment is whether he's strong enough to withstand the temptation of another bout," Doctor Noriss said. "A month ago, I gave him the key to my drug cupboard and told him, if he ever felt like it, to help himself. He didn't make a move—"

"Was that wise?"

"It worked. You see, Trothe, there's no 'cure.' It depends entirely upon the will of a man. That's the devil of it. I could be an addict a thousand times over. There it is, rows of it. Anything in the pharmacy's mine. No. Why not? I don't want it. That's not the case with a patient. There's temptation. Memory. Entirely human, of course. I'm greatly attached to the boy. He's a fighter, thank God!"

A telephone call took him away, and Doctor Tomsett and I saw him out to the car.

"Curious man," Doctor Tomsett said, while we strolled. "When the six months was almost up, he gave Frederick another dose of that stuff—"

"*What!*"

"It may or may not have been. But he's the physician. He's ultimately responsible to the magistrates, isn't he? Anyway, Frederick woke, petrified. We had an awful week with him. But from that moment, he changed completely. Where before he was backward, somnolent, merely dormant, he became positive, really very assertive. And he dug into his work in a way that'd charm your heart. Of course, Brenda regards him as her son—"

"All to the good. He missed his mother. I can't possibly tell you how grateful I am to both of you. Words are very poor return—"

We were outside the house before I realised where we'd been going. It was only a step away. But the old lane had been enlarged, a small stone bridge went over the brook, and the wooden gates had been replaced with very handsome seventeenth century filigree iron. The drive had been widened, laid with red brick. The rhododendron had gone, and rose pergolas ran about a semicircle of lawn, with a small marble fountain in the middle, and flower beds. It was open, airy, an enormous improvement.

But the front of the house astounded me. I wasn't prepared for it. Georgian and Victorian "changes" in the front, and the portico, and the blocking of windows—because of window tax—which I'd accepted all my life as historically proper—just as I'd accepted the wen on my Aunt Lucia's cheek—I don't know why I should have thought of that, except that she was a darling, and my favorite—all were gone.

Instead, the house had become its own lovely Elizabethan self.

The brickwork had been lain bare, all the hidden wonders of craftsmanship in that day once again knew the sun. The windows were their original shape, large, wide as an embrace, beaming most excellent welcome. The doorway was twice its size, wide enough to admit husband and wife arm-in-arm, and the portico—which had been lumps of stone overgrown in grass and bushes since I could remember—had been pieced together and restored to its rightful place. I was hit in the throat. The lettering read IN THIS HOUSE LET NO MAN STEP WHOSE STEEL SHALL NOT BREAK THE BARBA-ROUS IRON—a cry back to times when the Tudor bully relied upon his cutthroats. The steps up to the doorway were in white marble, with a dice of red and white tiles on the plinth, and in the middle my ecclesiastical bearing, an Open Book, a Sun Ascendant, a Pair of Hands, Open, a Dove Resting, an Eye above, and the inscription, CEDANT ARMA TOGAE.

God knows where it had been found.

But those were the days of the Faith.

The hall had been cleared of what my father had always called the "Georgian firewood," a box of softly polished rosewood, that nobody—I never had—thought of tearing out. Now it was gone, and the hall was twice its former size, light, airy, with damask panels, each with a pair of suits of armor brought down from the corridor in the servants quarters, where they'd stood, I suppose, since the reign of James, the Bible. The staircase, which had always been hidden since I could remember, was now open, and went up in a balustered arc, with a rare bust of Elizabeth I in a niche, one of the family prizes which I hadn't disturbed when I stored the rest of the items I'd wanted to keep. She was part of the house, and I'd made it an integer of the sale that she and other beauties remain my property, to be taken at will.

My study had been improved by paneling, and library shelves made from the hall's "firewood," and the furniture was all of the period, with a magnificent partners' desk covered in green leather. The library really was a job. Azil had obviously spent heaven knows what on books alone, though the maps and charts were a collection in themselves. The dining room had been walled in pieces of mirror taken from the old bathrooms, and the services of china, silver and goldplate were stored in cupboards that once had been in the corridor of the servants wing, of pale oak, birch, teak and mahogany. I'd never looked at them. They were master-pieces. That corridor was dark. I began to realise I'd always lived in a dark house. Without thinking, I was used to shadows, obscure corners. I'd never thought about it. But the only time Consuelo had spent more than a few moments there, she'd fled, horrified. And I'd never quite understood why, though I'd agreed with her.

I disagreed, now. The kitchen was a delight to any real cook's heart. The garden was three times its old size, replanned with a new, larger greenhouse. I wanted to go in, but I daren't. I'd have wasted hours. The rose garden stretched to the end of the added land, all the trees were replanted, with dozens of newer, the lawn had been replaced, the fountain was Roman, our own Roman trough was at the end, among the replanted rhododendron, azalea, and magnolia, and the banks of hortensia were a marvel of glowing blue, white and slatey-pink.

I didn't want to go upstairs.

I knew I had to buy the house back.

It was mine, it could only be mine. I felt some of the flame of my kinsman, Onslow Trothe. Every tiny piece of it called to me.

I went to the new telephone cubicle, under the stairs, in padded dull blue leather. I pressed the numbered buttons, and almost then, Consuelo answered as though she were beside me.

"Get on to Robarts, I want to buy the house back—"

"I knew you would!"

"You've seen it?"

"When I paid Frederick's account last time—"

"Like it?"

"A perfect joy!"

"Could you live here?"

"Oh, darling!"

"A little different from last time?"

"But it's been most beautifully put back to what it always should have been. I said I'd never live there, because you'd never have let anybody touch it—"

"It's been 'touched' to the tune of more than a hundred and

sixty thousand pounds. Where could I possibly have got that sort of 'touch'?"

"I *know*. But isn't it the most beautiful—have you seen the bedrooms? Bathrooms? The master bedroom has the original bath in marble. A step-downer. It's in the floor. Did they have those ideas so long ago?"

"The Romans had them a couple of thousand years ago—"

"I believe you *are* a Roman!"

"Are you going to be my matron?"

"I wish you were here!"

"Shan't be long. Get on to Robarts. Get my stuff out of store. Ask the architect to see me—"

I felt an entirely different human being. But I knew I'd been most rude to Doctor Tomsett. I found him looking at the roses. He simply smiled.

"We were perfectly sure you'd come back," he said, tranquilly. "There's one small thing. When did a parson never come a-begging?"

"Disgraceful you should have to—"

"No. It's part of our duty to take love, or money. Money's simply the token. Whether of love or conscience, we might debate a little later. You have an old stove and a lot of furniture which came out of the house, and probably won't go back. They'd make a wonderful gift for our school—"

"Take them. Over-all, what do you need in the way of money, or building?"

The wholehearted blue eyes looked down at the rhododendrons.

"What we principally need is a crib for the village babies. Life's become very hard. Women have to go out to work. If we had a place, and a nurse or two—"

"Take the place and find the nurses. What else?"

"This is a very private word. The chapel here was restored. You saw it?"

"No? Which chapel?"

"Well, the Priest's Hole comes off the Minstrel Gallery. It's been bricked-up for so long, you'd never know there *was* a Minstrel Gallery. Off that, down the staircase, there's the chapel. It's a perfect gem. There's a Titian over the altar—"

"I never heard of it!"

"But who did? Everything's exactly as it must have been some night when the estate servants covered it all in. There's a communion set, and a long loaf. My grandmother used to make them the same shape. We don't any more. It hasn't the same taste, either. Aren't those small things extremely precious? Ought they to be disregarded? Forgotten? Oughtn't you to find a priest?"

"Of the Roman Church?"

"But, of course. I'd ask the Archbishop's office at Westminster. Explain the circumstances—"

"You know?"

"Your father informed my predecessor—"

"But in the eyes of the Church—"

"In the eyes of the Roman Church, you were never married!"

"What a funny lot we all are!"

"I so agree. That's why I'm an ecumenist—"

"Would you join Mother Church?"

"But this moment!"

"There aren't many like you—"

"Let us hear the *Venite* in the true voice!"

Constable Parnes held the car door open.

"Where's Mrs. Cloney?" I asked.

"Over shopping in Gridgen's Round, sir. She'n 'im, they proper kick theirselves they warn't yur, zur!"

"Tell them the house is mine, and to act as if I were here. I can't say when I'll be back. I'll simply surprise you—"

"God love y', sir, we'm ben waitin' on y'. Place an't the zame, ah, that it ain't. Be a right welcome yur, ah—!"

I caught a glimpse of Doctor Tomsett's blue eyes, nodded—I couldn't say anything—and the car, thankfully, moved.

But I was back home, and I had no intention of living anywhere else, and I thanked God.

Privately.

37

Joel Cawle bowled me over. He put his hands on his knees and looked down at his wet shoes. It was raining like the devil.

"You know, Edmund, we're all very fond of Paul," he began, carefully. "You don't need to be told much else. When we first got word that he was clanky, we looked into it. Have you any idea how much money he's spent?"

"Yes—"

"Any idea what it's been spent on?"

"No—"

"Armaments—"

"It's not much for armaments. Doesn't quite approach a million—"

"Armaments, a word covering a good deal of ground, can also mean electronics. Communications. Now, it's rather a lot of money. And that's simply a beginning—"

"What sort of communications?"

"Miniature computers, among other things—"

"I don't see where this leads—"

"We wish we did—"

"Are these parts, or whatever they are, made in this country?"

"Some of them. Then there's Sweden, West Germany, Czechoslovakia, and Italy. I don't think I need tell you they go out in your consignments to Tartus. From there by truck to various places, or by air. Generally to Baghdad. Sometimes Tabriz—"

"Russians in this?"

"So far as we're able to judge, no. But we can't put our finger on anyone else. Our contacts 'disappeared'—"

"Seems to be endemic—"

"Any notion?"

"None—"

"Of course, buying that sort of stuff isn't a crime. But whose money is he using? He can't use it here. He'd have to get licenses, bank permits, God knows what. How did he get hold of that cash? Abroad? If it's not Company money being fraudulently diverted, where did it come from?"

"Would that matter so much? Is the Blur really preoccupied?"

Joel shifted. He wasn't comfortable. And I knew he hadn't told me the complete story.

"Well, Paul's an ex-member of the Service. In view of other, recent happenings, it could only redound to the Department's further discredit—"

"In other words, our Intelligence Service apparently's staffed with spies for any other side except our own, or by latent criminals—"

"Not *quite* so—!"

"You might just as well say it. What do you want from me? Paul's well taken care of, and will be for the next six months or so—"

He stood up, tightened his tie, picked up his hat.

"We know you went to Madrid, and sent a parcel to Stockholm by SAS. That parcel contained drugs!"

"I shall want to see proof—"

"You'll have to see the Blur—"

"Then make an appointment. I'm flying to Cairo in two hours' time—"

"May I use the telephone?"

I rang for Consuelo, and she took him to the telex room—which surprised him—and he had his call in private.

While he was in there, I called Simmons.

"I don't want to say too much at the moment, sir," he said, with professional caution. "There's been some really clever jiggery-pokery—there've been fourteen banks involved, so far—"

"Four*teen?*"

"Fourteen, sir. All different. Well, apart from that—it was meant to cover up the manipulation of funds, of course—apart from all that, we don't appear to be a penny out, not, at any rate, in this country. I can't answer for abroad. As a matter of pleasant fact, we've got something like three hundred and seventy-odd thousand pounds in the C account which we can't find any paper for. It's in the bank, snug. But it's not in the books!"

"Could Prince Habib or Azil have—"

"No, sir. We've been right through all that—"

"Who paid it in? How?"

"A check on the Bank of France, sir. Signed in by what looks like G. H. Blair of the Geneva office. But it was paid in, first, to Mr. Chamby's account, and then transferred—"

"Push a cold nose into all of it—"

Joel came to the doorway.

"If twenty minutes from now would be suitable, his lordship would be very glad to see you," he said. "I'll go on and put the file up—"

I had a distinct "feeling" about that sum in Account C. I didn't like the sound of Mr. Blair. I'd never heard of him.

Warrant Officer O'Cerril was on duty when I went down.

"While I'm away, I want all of you to be careful about who goes in," I told him. "At night, you'll be particularly on the alert. You might see the constables on the beat—"

"Most of them's ex-Guardsmen, sir," he said. "There'll be a couple near, you can be quite sure. Everything'll be all right, sir!"

"Don't let anybody leave any parcels!"

It was almost like going home to walk down Whitehall again. The Blur's office looked bleak as ever. He had a new secretary, Miss Purcell, whom I'd known in the old Department.

The Blur opened the door himself, a flourish indeed.

"Welcome!" he said, in his Great Occasions voice. "This *is* a pleasure, Trothe!"

"Brings back memories," I said, and went in, shook hands—exactly like something cool stuffed with cotton—and took off my coat. "I hear you're worried about Paul. No need to be. He's under the care of Roland Ainsworth—"

"It's the repercussions which might ensue—"

"So far as accounts are concerned, I can put your mind at ease. Everything's in order—"

"I'm relieved to hear it—"

He didn't sound relieved. He looked worried.

"—and I didn't knowingly send drugs to Stockholm—"

"I was perfectly sure of it—"

"Is there anything else?"

"Look here, Trothe, this is the position," he said, suddenly, and turned his chair to face me. "Some months ago we became aware of a steady disappearance of our best contacts in a number of countries, mainly in the satellite states, and in the Middle East generally. What we *have* found out, in every proven case, was that though they'd all been paid large sums, and most of them were married men, they'd all gone. But we can't find out where!"

I could only look at him. If the combined efforts of M.I. and Special Service Agents couldn't find an answer, then something was really Up. I remembered Druxi.

"What type of people were these?"

"One kind or another, businessmen, civil servants. I understand you're having the same experience?"

"We've put a few lines out—"

"We might exchange information?"

"Naturally. Who's your contact in my Company? Or should I say men? Or is it women?"

He crossed his knees, and brushed something off his sleeve.

"You don't expect me to answer that sort of question. But I think I may tell you that a good deal of information's been passing from someone in your Company to someone outside. We're not sure where it's going. It's sent by clix each morning and night."

"From?"

"Vaguely, somewhere round London. We haven't been able to locate the transmitter—"

"What sort of information?"

"There are three types of code. One, we haven't been able to break. The other two carry unimportant stuff. To delude, probably. But Chamby's name's been mentioned, so has yours, and Angela Masters!"

"In what connection?"

"Movement, generally. You flew to Stockholm yesterday, broke the flight at Brussels—"

"That was smart!"

"Came through yesterday. We monitor clix. Are you carrying one at the moment?"

"Yes—"

He opened the right-hand bottom drawer, took out the famous black book, turned the pages and looked at the clock.

"Lucky," he said. "In two minutes, switch to two three—"

"Two three? Who's using that?"

"Try it—"

"While we're waiting, what about Errol?"

He pulled his ear, looking out over the treetops and chimney pots.

"He didn't tell anyone where he was going, or what he was doing—"

"But you know where he is?"

"Of course—"

"Have you tried to extradite him?"

He looked round in half-amused surprise.

"Extradite?" he said. "So far as we know, he's living quite happily outside Lille, with his mistress!"

"Mistress? *Errol?*"

"Time you switched on—"

I'd put clix to two three, the extreme end of the band, which, so far as I knew, had never been used.

The signal ripped out. I hoped my face was impassive.

I was taking down the Company's own six letter-group code, the child of Paul and myself that we'd been so certain would take a century to break by any method. That led to four extremely serious conclusions. There were at least two clix in other hands, the Company code was known, there was an operator in or near London, and one elsewhere. Clix easily reached anywhere in Europe, could be picked up in the Americas, or Russia.

The message ended. I had to go back to the office to decipher.

"You can't read it?" the Blur said disappointedly. "I'd hoped you'd have been able to help—"

"It's a shock to find clix in other hands—"

"Why? Chamby's been most careless, don't you think? All the others are accounted for, including three in your keeping—"

"I know precisely where they are—"

"Then these?"

"Weldon would know. There isn't anyone else capable. Two extra sets—or more—are being operated. Who gave permission?"

"I certainly didn't. Let's talk to Weldon!"

He rang Miss Purcell, and told her to ask Mr. Weldon up, with his registers.

"Meantime, Errol," he said, when she'd gone. "We haven't tried to get in touch. We found out where he was, that's all. A farm, Les Trois Fontaines. Perfectly happy, apparently. So our man said. Living a farmer's life. Lovely place, and—so he reported—a very beautiful girl. The slinky sort—"

"How slinky?"

"She's from Calcutta, from her papers—"

I couldn't say a word. Things were adding up.

Miss Purcell brought Weldon in. I'd known him for years, an inventor of real genius.

"Yes, m'lord, I've made extra," he said, and opened the larger book. "I made two last year for VCC. You initialed—"

"Correct—"

"I made two for Mr. Chamby—"

"When?"

"Just before he left Switzerland, sir—"

"I didn't initial that!"

"No, m'lord. You were in Bonn. There's the date—"

"So that Mr. Chamby has his own, and two others. Why wasn't this reported?"

"Always reported, m'lord. It's in my report every month. Here's a copy—"

A little aggrieved, Weldon put the big sheet on the desk, and pointed to the columns.

"Number 19 OB, sir," he said. "We don't call them clix—"

"I see. Now tell me. Why can't you locate one in work?"

Weldon looked at me, as I knew he would, and shook his head.

"Never find it, m'lord. They're special circuits. Mr. Trothe's own patent, matter of fact. But without a lot of trouble, there's another way. You don't *find* them. You send out a zero signal, and destroy them!"

"I'd hoped you weren't going to say that, but it's the fact," I said. "If those sets were stolen—which I suggest—they can be destroyed. But the operator would also be destroyed—"

"How *very* interesting!" the Blur said, almost in a purr. "I think we ought, don't you?"

"It can't be done as simply as all that—"

"I haven't the faintest idea of these things—"

"Then you may leave it to me. Weldon, I'll need an F25—"

"Get it for you, sir—"

He went off, and the Blur turned to me.

"If we *can* destroy them, we'll have done something extremely useful. We'll also have found out who was operating—"

It was on the tip of my tongue to tell him that all clix should be warned to stay off the two three band. But then, I decided that anyone "on" at the time I used the F25 would be grist.

"Who's monitoring clix?"

"Weldon made a special set. Admiralty signals are in charge. Why?"

"That's all right. Weldon knows what he's playing at. Give me Errol's present address, will you?"

He took a red pencil from his pocket, and wrote two lines.

"You're going to see him, Trothe?"

"I am, yes. This isn't Errol's form, you know!"

"I thought it odd. But then, I've known people act in the most outlandish way—"

He was having a jab at me.

Weldon came in with a small nickel box which I put in my pocket, and we shook hands. He knew he wasn't wanted.

I'd put my overcoat on, and I'd picked up my hat, and the Blur'd turned away, facing the desk.

"There's something else!" he said abruptly, quietly, and I thought unwillingly. "I think I should warn you that we suspect we have a renegade in the Service. I believe he's made a special mark of your Company. You don't need to be told that it's not in any sense an 'ordinary' Company. Because of what you're doing, and where you're placed. There's—as I suppose you may well understand—ample scope for action—"

"Employed by us?"

"We're fairly sure of it. We've been receiving—as I told you— these signals for some time. Most of it's nothing to do with your Company, and obviously I cannot give you any details. But if you'd allow me to put a man—"

"Quite out of the question!"

"I'm sorry about that—"

"Have you any reason to suspect—whoever he may be—was recently in Stockholm?"

"Yes—"

"And was he also in Rome?"

"We believe so. Why?"

"Anybody nicknamed Pip?"

Still with his back to me, he walked over to the window, and stood there, hands in pockets looking up at the sky.

"If you know anybody, why not say so?" he asked, as if he feared the answer.

"I don't know, but I assure you I'll do my best to find out!"

"That's what I dread. Fleet Street's got its mouth open. Have you any idea why he should have made a target of your Company?"

"It's obvious he's out to ruin Paul. I wish you'd tell me his name!"

He shook his head a mere half turn, more flinch than denial.

"On suspicion? I couldn't possibly. Chamby got drugs of course, through your couriers. The supplier was working for you in Rome—"

"Thanatis?"

"You *do* know—!"

"Is Thanatis your suspect?"

"Oh, good lord, no! Very minor type. Nothing to do with us. But obviously guided by someone. It's the *some*one we'd like to talk to—"

"Where *is* Thanatis?"

"The Italian Police are looking for him. He had something to do with the death of a man called McGowan in Rome—"

"A friend of mine. Working for me—"

"I'm aware of it. I'm extremely worried, Trothe. So many of our contacts are threatened, d'you see? But there's no hard evidence—"

"If you suspect, you have grounds. If it's anything to do with my Company, why not tell me?"

"Not for the moment."

The perfect Blur.

"Then I shall get after Errol, first—"

"You may rely on any help I can give you. And the very best of luck!"

I was in need of it. A "contact" was so much more important than any sporadic informer. "Contacts," names, places, were in the highest degree secret. If the suspect could threaten "so many" contacts, then he had to be near, or part of, the M.I. hierarchy, close to the Blur. Only the few in top positions had access to those names, and where they worked. That narrowed the field to a handful. I knew them all. I'd worked with most of them. The younger men had been my juniors. Which of them could snake into the Company without my knowledge? Or with Paul's help? I didn't know all the people he'd taken on. But the dossier of whoever-it-was would take some cracking if it had been prepared with help of all M.I. facilities. It could mean months.

Or never.

38

I went to Paris and took a taxi-plane to Lille, a quiet old town I've always had a fondness for, if only for the best fish restaurant in the world. I was there for a late luncheon, and found the bouillabaisse still a matter for verse, the sole with green grapes a dream, and the salad of meddlars and fresh dates in half a dwarf cantaloupe an absolute hymn. I'd already looked at the map. The place wasn't far. There was a train to Paris in just two hours which I intended to be on.

Luck was with me. A couple of tables over, a man wrote in an order book. From the pile of colored pamphlets, he represented Charot, Manet, crop buyers and seedsmen.

I asked the waiter to get me a few, and a contract form. He came back with a handful, among the smiles and seated bows of the representative, pointing to Henri Dumesnil, printed in the right-hand corner.

A ready-made identity.

I took a new Peugeot drive-it-yourself, and told the girl I was going to Arras. Instead, I went a few miles north, and turned off on a side road. A little way down, a sign pointed to Les Trois Fontaines. I bumped over ruts between overgrown hedges, with beet fields on both sides, and came to a white gate. I got out to open it, drove in, got out to close it, and turned into a little dell among trees, downhill to a slate-roofed house in grey stone, two chimneys smoking, and flower beds picking up after rain.

A servant in black, starched apron, laced cap, came out and bobbed a curtsey.

"I'd like to see the proprietor, if you please," I began. "I have reason to believe he wishes to sell his crop—"

"Who is it?" a man's voice called, from a ground-floor window nearby.

"I am Henri Dumesnil of Charot, Manet," I said, in that direction. "I should like the opportunity to present our prices."

A man came out. I almost fell.

Mariotti. No doubt of it. He wore a shirt, neckscarf, waistcoat open, britches, fawn leggings. He looked a typical "gentleman" farmer. He didn't know me. I'd taken some trouble with my appearance.

"What are you offering, the hundred kilos?" he asked.

"I'd like to see the fields, first—"

"If you'll wait a few minutes, I'll take you. I'm waiting for a call—"

A woman came out to lean on his arm.

She didn't surprise me. She'd been the secretary, Nikka Hurryat. She was, indeed, the slinky type, young, very good-looking. I realised that in Rome they'd cultivated a much older appearance. Now they made a handsome couple. I thought of Angela, those eyes in shadow of ashen hair.

I bowed, briefcase between knees, holding out the pamphlets.

"If you'd care to see some specimen contracts—" I began.

"A moment," he said, nodding at the telephone's ring. "Please sit down—"

They went in together. I heard him at the telephone. I'd clipped three of James' explosive stickers to the inside pocket of my jacket. I stuck two of them to the middle panel of the door they'd gone through, and walked outside, stepped over the flower bed, and stuck the third just under the window sill. I pretended to look at a blossom, and paced, looking at others farther away. By that time, I was yards off.

312

I began to count. At thirty, he was still talking.

A pail filled on the other side of the house.

I watched the second hand of my Patek Philippe touch fifty seconds. The stickers should have blown between twenty and thirty.

Three duds.

I thanked God I wasn't in Hauerfurth. I wondered if the rest of the stuff was dud. I'd been fixed. No possible doubt of it.

James had to be told without delay.

But how could the Blur and his department have confused Errol with someone else? Whose word was he taking? I had to do some thinking, not least about the Blur himself. He'd already tried to put me away. Was this a second crack?

The place was quiet. I couldn't hear Mariotti's voice. I could hear myself breathing. It surprised me there wasn't even a dog. I wondered how people could live in such a place without one.

I walked over to take the sticker off the wall, and inside, to lift off the other two.

There wasn't a sound anywhere.

I went back to the car to set clix. Mine was in the thin Patek Philippe wristwatch, with the circuit running round the inner rim. I pulled out the winder, turned the hands to midnight, pulled it out further, turned it forward, and twice back again, and I was ready.

A message was going through. I took down a few groups. It wasn't in Company code, but another, a five-letter-group, sent by someone not too steady in Morse.

I took out the F25, tuned to the sender, pressed the key.

The signal stopped in mid-group.

The house appeared to shudder. I'd expected it.

There was no noise.

I drove that workhorse Peugeot along the tree-lined road back to Lille, wiped wheel, seat, doors with petrol, turned the car in, and caught the Paris train on time. I hadn't long to wait for a London flight, and when I reached Heathrow, I telephoned James, but he wasn't at the office, and hadn't got home. I had a sandwich and read a couple of the evening papers, and tried again, found him in. We decided on a halfway mark from his house, a very good pub outside Greenwich.

All I did was show him the stickers. He dropped them in his coat pocket without a word.

"Would you care for another drink?" he said, and hooked a finger at the waiter. "I hope nobody else knows about this—?"

Clearly he meant the Blur.

"Nobody—"

"I'm glad. My first misfire. Wouldn't you find it intensely annoying?"

"I did, in fact!"

He raised his glass. I didn't like his eyes. They were dry, far away.

"We confide too much, Edmund. There's one bigger fool than an old fool. That's a young fool. They pretend to know. You see, I know where they came from. They're all numbered. These aren't—"

"You couldn't tell me his name? Off-hand?"

He smiled, shook his head.

"You might care to come to the office about noon, tomorrow?"

I got back to St. James's Square at a little after two. Consuelo had gone home with her mother. I got thankfully into bed, with a call for nine o'clock, and it was nine on the dot—I heard the bells—when Groves woke me.

I called Consuelo first, and the maid had to go into the garden to find her.

"Darling! What *are* you doing *there?*"

"Changed the timetable a little. I'm going this morning. Are you coming in?"

"Of course. Don't *dare* go without seeing me?"

"How could I?"

The call to Grass Tree took a little longer.

His lordship, I was told, was at his ablutions. Lovely word.

"The pair weren't whom you'd thought," I said. "I suggest you check the source. And I think you'd better find out what happened—"

"Oh. Did you decipher that message?"

"Didn't have a chance—"

"Could you call me at the office when you have?"

"And Errol?"

"This alters things—"

I took the code book out of the safe, and set to work. I had a distinctly sick feeling to see all that I'd thought secret—figures about growth of construction, the building of the main plant in Beyfoum, mileage of pipe laid, number of pumps installed, rectification of the rhumb from El Khor, the position of the Verschoyle Castle, number of personnel in work—every useful detail —had been transmitted.

Who was the operator? Where? How was the information got? It couldn't all have come from London. Some of it must have been garnered from Geneva, Beirut, and Teheran.

I ran over the possibilities, and then telephoned Weldon.

"Any chance that other 19 OB's could be adapted to mine?" I asked him.

"None!" he said promptly. "The set being 'adapted' would blow. You know that. So would any at the other end. If they were that unlucky!"

"If the F25 was used, how about Admiralty signals?"

"I made the set with that in mind. They're getting a half-echo effect, first, and second, there's no charge—"

I deciphered the text of the partial message I'd got from Les Trois Fontaines. That clix was being used to receive.

"FF GEN POSS RO CAI. C STILL STEM UNC OU."

I picked up the telephone and read it over to the Blur.

"S-t-e-m—St. Emery's? The clinic? A threat to Paul—?"

"All right, Trothe. I'll have him moved this morning. The other—travel indications? Did you, by the way, pick up the clix?"

"No. I left—"

"Very wise. I'll get somebody there. Hadn't you better enquire about those references to travel? Who'd know?"

He was teaching his Granny. I called Miss Peel to the office. I trusted her completely. A big woman, dark hair, fine hands, black eyes behind thick lenses.

"I don't believe anybody could, sir," she said wonderingly. "Everything's under lock and key the whole time. The cashier's the only one—"

I got Berry up from "I," and gave him the problem. I had to be at James' office. I was there just in time for a brew of tea, and the messenger gave me a midday paper, a racing edition.

"Like a look at the horses, sir?" he said. "Won't be long. Sunnik's happen' down the experimental lab—"

I could well imagine it. I found myself among fetlocks and glanders again. The garrulous nonsense of racecourse journalists brought the smell of stables into the room, and suddenly I was thinking of the harness racks at Onslow Close, and I knew I had to be there when the Dorothy Perkins came into bloom, that grafted glory of scarlet with a scent that roamed all that side of the house.

James came in quietly, as usual, and gave me another green-wrapped parcel.

"Won't be any complaints about those," he said. "Send everything in that first parcel back to me. Want anything done, do it yourself!"

"Had some trouble?"

"Don't mention it outside. Won't be released for a little while. Till the relatives have been here. That girl, Alison—"

"That rather nice fat one?"

"Yes. Good brain. We don't know what it was. Don't like to think it was suicide, of course—"

I could only stare.

The parcel didn't feel very heavy. It spoke of other things.

"Well," I said, without quite knowing what to say. "I'm very sorry, indeed—"

"We all are. Very clever girl—"

I went back to the office in less than a festive mood. I was wondering what had happened to the other clix, but I didn't know when to expect the news. It made me a little thoughtful. Consuelo noticed it. She was packing my case.

"Is everything all right, darling?" she asked.

"Class-one order. Why?"

"You're in your cloister mood—"

"I've got to leave you for far too long, that's all. Who's the duty cashier here these days?"

"Mr. Taylor—"

"Ask him to bring me my official allowance of fifty pounds in cash, will you?"

"Aren't you being excessively patriotic?"

"Just in case they search me—"

"Love-ly job!"

Mr. Taylor came in and counted fifty pounds in new five pound notes. I've always admired the way a practiced cashier flips notes. I never could. I noticed his alert air and sharp, dark eyes behind gold rims. He'd come from our firm of accountants, and he'd been with them from boyhood.

"Are you satisfied with the way things are going?" I asked him. "All in order?"

"Well, sir—" he hesitated, pulled down his shirt collar. "Not really. When we first came over from the other office, my wife wasn't too well, and I went home early. I *do* know how I leave my desk. A couple of paper clips, a piece of pencil, a rubber band or two can tell you a lot. It's been gone through systematically. I didn't say anything because there was nothing of importance, and I thought it might be Security. Couple of nights ago, I left carbon paper under my blotter. Next morning, I found handwriting. A copy of my cash report that day. Last night, the same. More writing this morning—"

"Whose?"

"Don't know, sir—"

"Bring those pieces of paper here and give them to Miss Furnival. Say nothing. Has Miss Masters ever introduced anyone to you? For any reason?"

"Yes, sir. Mr. Reismann, he's the accountant from Geneva. I cashed a couple of checks for him—"

"Thank you, Taylor. Not a word outside, please—"

Consuelo put my briefcase on the desk, waited for Taylor to shut the door.

"I'll find out who stays after hours," she said. "There aren't *so* many here. Little nerve-shattering, isn't it?"

"More vermin—"

"Anybody employed by Paul is suspect—"

"I was one, wasn't I?"

Blues flashed.

Consuelo reached across for the On.

"Call from the Leicester General Hospital, sir," Hines said. "Urgent. You're through, sir—"

"Hello? Mr. Edmund Trothe?"

"Speaking—"

"This is Doctor Lennox. Miss Angela Masters is a patient of mine. I'm sending you a certificate that she can't report to you for at least a week. She's here, room one four seven, in the private wing."

"I'm very sorry indeed to hear it. Anything serious?"

"Well, she hasn't been at all herself lately. Then, last night, her older sister died, Ursula—"

The voice was clear. Consuelo turned quickly, back to me, leaned against the desk.

"But such a young woman?" I said, aghast. "What was the cau—"

"That will be the coroner's business. We're all dreadfully unhappy about it. May I speak to the Company's physician, please?"

"Thank you, Doctor Lennox. I'll have you put through—"

Hines took the call, and I looked at my Patek Philippe.

"Time I went," I said, gently as I might. "Coming to the airport?"

39

I made a hurried visit to Geneva. As I'd thought, the other code book wasn't in the office safe. There was no note to show who'd taken it. I called in Lawrence Forbes, the cipher man, old in his ways, steady.

"There's been some sort of mix-up, lately," he said. "Even the Bentley's often been wrong. I haven't had anything in the Company code for nearly three weeks—"

"We're changing it. If any more comes in, try to find out where it's sent from. Priority one. I'm moving you to London to take charge—"

The death of Angela's sister didn't affect me as much as I'd have thought. I was quite sure it had something to do with clix. The F25 had done its job. But it was hard to believe that Ursula could have been the operator all along. I'd met her only once, shorter, darker than her sister, competent, or she wouldn't have been principal secretary to M.I.'s vice-chief. I wondered if Paul could have known. It wasn't a matter to dwell on. But what was nastily bared was a seepage of vital information. I didn't think our diplomatic agreements had been divulged. Neither Consuelo nor Angela had dealt with them. They were in piles of documents in the Geneva strong room, untouched, with all the Governmental correspondence, the master-plan of the Beyfoum complex, the original maps of the pipeline, and all the patent blueprints and connected paper.

I knew the agreements would be the main target. Paul knew. My worry was whether he'd told anyone. The drug horror could have been thought of to force it out of him. Half-drugged, he might be got to say anything, perhaps do anything suggested to him. Except that he—they—whoever "they" were—would need my cooperation.

The diplomatic agreements with eleven countries were what counted. While they remained inviolate, we were safe, as a Company. Any leakage would mean starting again, from the beginning, with the additional handicap of having imperilled the reputations of men-in-office, and the negotiators. Not a pleasant thought.

To enter the bank strong room, the permission of the General Director was required, with the presence of Paul and myself, and his key and my own had to be used. I'd taken Paul's key at Grosvenor Street, that night. It was in my boot pocket, with my own.

The information sent, perhaps, in the past month or so, was a serious loss to us, and a great help to any competitor, and up to a point, it could hurt us. Apart from that, everything at Geneva had been normal, and there was nothing to alarm in the daily reports from the desert or elsewhere, no incidents, no further loss of personnel. I signed a heap, and left.

Rome warmed with a late sun. I was tempted to stay overnight, but I resisted, and had the audacity to feel virtuous. Before I went to the office, I called Arturo and said I'd be in the station buffet on the half-hour. I was gradually changing my appearance. I'd left my heavy overcoat in Geneva, and my grey suit. I wore a frayed linen, and an old raincoat.

I turned in to a barber's shop, and told the man to use the horse clipper back and sides. He did, with elan. I came out with a hat slightly on my ears, sheared almost to the skull, and drafty about the neck.

The station buffet at twenty five minutes past the hour was

crowded with families. It always seemed to be. I ordered a vol-au-vent and a glass of Chianti, and I was reading the paper when Arturo joined me. Nobody would have known it.

"Still nothing on the death of McGowan," he said, at the counter. "Nothing heard of the people who left. A complete mystery. Everything quiet, everywhere. The housekeeper bought flowers this morning. Galvani said they were for your office. London told them you might be in sometime today. The first Miss Masters' lodging in Donna Clementina's house was taken two days ago by a man from your office—"

"What type of man?"

"Thirty—forty. Fair. Small mustache. He uses Mr. Chamby's car. He works late. I've seen the lights—"

"—damn it! London gave the game away—!"

It had.

Paul's office had been turned upside down. Whoever used it hadn't known how to work the electronic switch to Angela's office, and that was a blessing. I called up Galvani and told him to collect all the papers scattered about the floor. There was still cigarette smoke in the air. The ashtray was full. It wasn't a cigarette I knew. I went up to Paul's apartment. Wardrobes were open. The place looked as if it had been given a thorough search.

"How did this man get in?" I asked Galvani.

"He came with a letter from Miss Masters, sir. She asked me to give him every assistance. It was initialed by Mr. Chamby. I have it downstairs—"

"Bring it here—"

It was written on the stationery of Angela's home outside Leicester. A forgery.

"He wouldn't let the cleaner in here, and he wanted to open the office downstairs, sir. But Mazzini wouldn't do it without your permission—"

"When did he leave?"

"A little before midday—"

"Get the car—"

We did a fast trip to Donna Clementina's house. A new doorman let me in. Donna Clementina was surprised in her dignified way, but not by any means effusive.

"You *do* have some curious people, Mr. Trothe!" she said. "The young man Angela sent planked down a month's rent, took his bag, and he's gone. No goodbye, no 'thank you,' nothing!"

"What was his name?"

"His name? Don't you know?"

"No. I *do* know he's an imposter—"

"Oh, Mr. Trothe!"

She was looking up, not at me, but at something over my head. She was frightened.

"No need for alarm, I assure you. What name did he use?"

"Fribell. Charles Fribell. I didn't have a chance of talking to him very long. Very well educated—"

"Did he leave anything? Papers—"

"Let me find out—"

She left me standing in the hall, with the major-domo watching from the staircase. I didn't blame her in the slightest.

She came back, with the big maid carrying a shirt and some handkerchiefs.

"The laundry marks are going to be useful," I said. "And the shirt was made in London. May I have them?"

"Well, *I* don't want them!" she said. "And, Mr. Trothe, may I make it *quite* clear that I shall ignore any other letter of introduction?"

"I think you have every reason—"

"And not a word from Angela! Not one!"

"She's unwell. She's in hospital at Leicester—"

"Oh, heaven above, poor child!"

"May I see that letter?"

"I tore it up and burned it, Mr. Trothe. Now, if you'll excuse me—"

I've never been given a more cutting send-off. And again, I could only sympathise.

I sent the laundry by air to Bernard Lane's office. I thought he'd do more with it. Mr. Fribell must have been in a hurry. It pointed to a mind a little shaky under stress, and liable to forget details. That was a point in our favor. If Mr. Fribell was none other than Mr. Thanatis, he'd begun weaving his rope.

I hadn't heard anyone use those names during my time with the Service. From looking at him, he was at least ten years younger than myself. I didn't think he could face me again in any sort of disguise, and get away with it. I wondered if I ought to think about him in terms of somebody called Pip.

The flight to Cairo was most agreeable, with an excellent dinner of kid in kous-kous, and a strawberry jelly which actually tasted of strawberry. The drive from the airport brought back many a memory. There's something about a palm tree that loads the imagination. Cairo still seemed its old self, though the new buildings added a warning note that the old days were quite gone. But the people in the streets appeared as I'd always remembered, dressed the same, and the coffee houses were filled. Nothing seemed to have changed. But it had. I couldn't see it. I could feel it.

The greatest pleasure was to find Marlq' Ben Ab waiting for me, bath poured, clothes laid out, exactly like old times.

"Chief Commissioner Khefi'l'Amir will be waiting at eleven forty five, sir—"

"Thank you. Telephone that I shall be there. How's everything?"

"Quiet, zar. No mor-r bom-p-z!"

I bathed and lay down to think things over. There wasn't much to be done. I didn't think the Roman Police had any chance of catching Mr. Fribell-Thanatis or whatever other name he'd used. Obviously he had the passports. But who was supplying the money? He could leave Britain with only fifty pounds. If we could find his source of supply, we'd be on to something.

I took the Egyptian passport with me, wondering what had happened to Bilat Khan, and on the way downstairs, looked in at Paul's office from the main door.

A large photograph of Angela looked at me from the desk.

It was rather a shock.

On sudden thought, I tried to get Consuelo, but the operator said there'd be a long delay, and I cancelled. I'd get her on clix as we'd arranged. I looked at myself in the lobby wall. I wore an old, dark tropical, that fitted where it touched, but I was beginning to sweat and I hadn't gone outside. The haircut seemed to have taken off at least five years, possibly ten. I thought I looked fairly fit. I felt fine.

Cairo's older part had always been a haunt of mine, but now the bars and clubs were out of bounds. I was sorry for it. But I couldn't risk it. I loved the music and the dancing girls. But not now. In my position, I couldn't. I was surprised at the amount of construction, all in the "modern" style, though I'd preferred the narrow streets, the smell of age. The Commissariat was partly rebuilt. The place was an assault of new paint. A sergeant told me to watch my clothes on the way up.

Khefi's office was the same, even to the paper balled on the floor. He always missed the basket.

We met as old friends, though he was talking to an Inspector, and apologised, and went on talking in undertones. The Inspector saluted, bowed to me, and went out.

"Now, we have a coffee, and you tell me everything!" he said, in that hoarse and "throaty" accent, which made his perfectly good English sound like a foreign language.

I put the passport on the desk.

"I want to know if I can use that," I said. "I'd like to be an Egyptian for a couple of weeks. A man, up to ten years older. An expert in medical electronics. Machines for the heart, brain, and blood—"

"You make us a great compliment, and this' no good," he said, and put the passport in the drawer. "He was a criminal. Executed some years ago. I will get you one, new. Tomorrow morning at ten o'clock. What are you going to do?"

"I'm going to East Germany. You may guess the rest!"

"If you' found, it will be understood—"

"Don't worry. I'd tell them to call the British Consul—"

He looked at me over the left hand, that always held a cigarette he'd never lit in the years I'd known him. It always pointed to the left, away from his nose. The other hand swung a box of matches between thumb and index. He'd strike a match for somebody else, never for himself. He had the palest grey eyes I ever saw, that in odd light flashed blood-red. They'd seen rather more than most, though he wasn't much older than I was. He was known as the Corkscrew—he signed his letters with a spiral ending in a long point—and he used one for asking questions. It was long, narrow, with a dark bamboo handle. Anywhere, either sex. A probe with a corkscrew can be painful. But it gets the correct answers. I'd seen it done.

"I also have a favor to ask," he said, swinging the matchbox.

"What is it?"

"I require a British passport—"

"I have one in another name—"

"It will do. You mind if that name is used?"

"No. If there's any smoke, it's his bad luck, that's all—"

"No smoke. It's for Israel—"

"An amicable venture, I hope?"

He looked at me over the cigarette. Bright as a spill of pins.

"We speak among ourselves. To others we are always 'amicable'—"

I changed the subject.

"I want to go just beyond El Mir tomorrow. What's the best way?"

"Be at Eilat at a few minutes before one o'clock. You will have a chair on the mail plane. When will you return?"

"In four or five days. Not as myself—"

"You will let me know—you know my number—ask the Police—"

"Thank you. I shall need your help in leaving the country—"

The cigarette dismissed it.

"I get the passport tomorrow in exchange for the other? Good. I'd hoped to take you to a supper. It's cancelled. I must work. You understand?"

"Perfectly. I shall expect your messenger. And I'll call you when I return—"

"It is a pleasure to see you. So healthy!"

I didn't much like that, but on the way downstairs I hoped he might have been groping for a compliment.

On the way back I saw that I was being followed, which didn't disturb me. Khefi was loyal to his friends. Yet I wished I'd had the freedom of the city. Ordinary travelers, without responsibilities, never know how lucky they are. They can go anywhere. But I remembered the bomb attempt, and Khefi must have had it in mind.

When I got back, I went out on the terrace. I'd caught Cairo on a night that was wonderfully clear, with many tones of lights, from oil dips to mercury vapor which almost wrote the country's history, and the palms it was first written on flashed green in a cool breeze. Sometimes, in lulls of traffic, I heard faint music of reeds and drums. I thought of Ursula, and the others who'd died, in truth, for nothing. I wondered why. Nothing I was doing was worth a death. So far as I was concerned, nothing I'd ever done, nothing I'd ever represented was worth a death, or dying for. Memory of the effects of war, the call of patriotism, the mass sacrifice, had long been forgotten in the hideous embarrassment of a peacetime that wasn't.

I knew what I was supposed to do, but I wondered what, in honesty, I was pretending to be.

Other mens' money, hundreds of workmen, the keeping of many a contract, a word of honor, depended solely on what went on in my head. That's what it came down to. I'd never thought much about it before. I didn't seem to give much of a damn now, except that I was sure things were going the way I wanted, if a bug or a bullet didn't stop me.

Marlq' Ben Ab came in with the night tray.

"Why did you speak to me about Miss Masters?" I asked him. "How did you find out?"

"I like Mrs. Chamby, sir," he said. "Miss Masters, she got a friend, take her place sometime. I know the skin—"

"Took her place? In the office? Why didn't you tell me?"

"I am *valet d' chambre*. When this friend tried to come in your apartment, I say no. Then I tell, and I leave!"

"I understand that. Did you know anything about drugs?"

"The doctor had drugs in the Cairo pouch. From Boussaf. Twice a week—"

"How did they get in the pouch?"

"The medical orderly, Kharam, went to the pharmacy. When the doctor left Rome, he also left. Nobody know where—"

"You knew Mr. Chamby was taking drugs?"

"Mr. Chamby always do what we want—"

"In my country, it's a crime—"

"Here, no. I leave, sir, before I kill. In Rome I go to prison. It is safer I am here!"

"How many did you want to kill?"

"Sir, so many, you believe me? Miss Masters, I leave for Mr. Chamby. He must find one day the man—"

"What was his name?"

He pointed downward through the floor.

"Downstairs, sir. He was for three months with the Company. The name is Than-at-is, sir!"

"Thank you. Seven o'clock, please!"

"Orange and lemon juice, China tea, honey, and El Achram, seven o'clock, very well, sir!" he said, chanting in one tone.

"Good night!"

He'd hardly shut the door, when he came in with a cable.

THREE FOUNTS PAIR VOID. ANY REASON QUERY. ORB.

The Blur's call-sign.

Void was code for dead.

I wrote a cable: ORB, IGLOO, LONDON. ASK WELDON. FULL BAG. EOT.

"Urgent," I said.

I was delighted to think it would get the Blur out of bed.

But I quite understood the Prince Abdullah's confusion of mind. I was equally confused, and at last, had to face it.

Angela—or Ursula?—had possibly been in touch with the two at

Lille since they'd left Rome. With Paul's knowledge? I could hardly believe it. At all events, two clix no longer existed.

But one or both had clearly been under control of Mr. Thanatis-Fribell-and-who-else. Who, exactly, was he? Part of M.I.6? Special Service? Some other label? Under control of the Blur? Paid by our side? The Blur hadn't been at all sure of himself. He'd been, in fact, the perfect blur. Not too far one side, not so far the other. Neither yes nor no. Somewhere shadily in between.

The Blur, and well-named. Was he involved in any way? It was a sudden thought, that stuck.

But there was another, far more serious. If Thanatis was the brain, then he was now fairly warned that I was on to him. He'd try to put me away as first business. Then, of course, Consuelo.

I thought of the lonely train ride back to her mother's home, that car trip along quiet country lanes. Her brother had been killed in a lane, and not so many miles from the house.

It wasn't a bit of use trying to dismiss the thought as panicky. The means were available.

I went into our radio room, called London, got information, knew there was a censor listening in, wasn't worried, and I asked for Gillian Roule's telephone number. It was near Market Harborough.

"Gillian? Edmund Trothe—"

"Oh, Mr. Trothe! Yes—"

"Did you hear about Ursula Masters?"

"Isn't it simply *aw*ful? They haven't an idea what it was—"

"Do you know of any close friendship Angela might have had with anybody other than Paul Chamby?"

"Oh, dozens! Lovely girl like that, of course—"

"Could you scribble them for me? Might be a lead. Do you think either Ursula or Angela might have known anything about our barman friend?"

"I'd prefer to think not. But in her job, Ursula might—"

"Examine the possibilities, and call me through the London office tomorrow evening—"

"I hadn't thought of *that* link—"

328

"Somebody's warned. You understand? Take great care, won't you?"

"I'm used to it. I'm beginning to feel our barman friend knew something. So did the same 'someone'—"

"D'you know anybody nicknamed Pip?"

"Can't think of anyone for the moment—"

"Let's talk tomorrow—"

40

Before eight o'clock I'd made certain Consuelo had two good men and a woman always near, and two men on duty at night. Over clix she promised not to move without them, and not to sleep anywhere except in St. James's Square, and asked if I insisted on a chastity belt.

I sent three dots, O.

Gillian called over the radio-telephone at a few minutes before ten.

"There's something in what you say about Paul," she said. "He must have told Angela—"

"What's the evidence?"

"He could be got to tell anything under the effect, couldn't he? Wasn't that the idea?"

"Not impossible. What's the reasoning?"

"How did Angela know my lad had gone before I saw you?"

"How do you know?"

"She called his mother on the twenty eighth. She asked her to a cocktail party and wanted to invite our friend. She was told he was looking at a property in Southern Ireland. But she didn't call me though she knew perfectly well *I'd* know—"

"Why didn't his mother tell you before?"

"We only see each other every ten days or so. Passed out of her mind till I asked her—"

"Not much to go on, is it?"

"But Ursula told someone else he couldn't be found!"

"Ursula?"

"And she either got it from Rome, or there was a mention somewhere—from the way I was told—I believe it was Paul Chamby—"

"I can't believe it!"

"My source *should* know. Can't mention names—"

"All right. No names. When?"

"About a month ago. She'd said he'd absolutely vanished—"

"You were told this when?"

"Last night—"

"She never at any time called you?"

"Never. We'd only met at the Department—"

"Did you know anything of Ursula's friends?"

"Most of them—"

"Was she working for Joel?"

"No. VCC's private secretary—"

"Who's he?"

"Now? Victor Maude. In Bernard Lane's place for the moment. He's in Washington. So's Joel—"

"Were they friendly with our friend?"

"Very. They were both 'in' on what he was doing—"

"I see. I'll call you when I know anything—"

"I'm praying!"

It seemed that the Blur had told me a deliberate lie. If Bernard and Joel *had* known what Errol was doing, then *he* must. But instead, he'd given me the Lille pair. Why? And why should he be "after" Errol? And was Paul really so far gone? Or was he, as the Prince Abdullah and Professor Tamm had said, playing another game? But from long knowledge, playing false didn't equate with his character. He could never be a traitor. Was the link Paul-Angela-Thanatis-Ursula? I couldn't imagine Paul's tolerating Thanatis for one moment as anything more than an office boy. Might he have been aware that Thanatis was an M.I.6 contact? But *was* he? It appeared so. The white rat must have been

331

Ursula. She was in a position to know. With her out of the way, Mr. Thanatis-Whasname's game might be crocked. I had to try to assess where next he might insinuate himself.

At ten thirty, two Inspectors in starched and ironed uniforms presented Khefi's compliments. A photographer with them took my photograph and went away. The older of the two wrote my particulars in a long sheet, signed in the proper places, stamped it, and handed it to me in a bow.

"If there are any enquiries, sir, you will present this," he said. "It covers everything. Where will you be staying?"

"At the house of Mrs. Ulla Brandt Ben Ua, at El Mir—"

"I know it. You will not be disturbed. The lady is in Syria—"

"Is Ouran Khadesh still—"

"He is there, sir. We spoke two days ago when we had your message—"

I was glad of that. Ouran had been a friend of mine since youth. He was dragoman at the Embassy at that time, and we'd gone on many a hunting party. It's one of the best ways of making friends. I'd got him the job with Ulla, and he'd brought up his family there.

"May I rely on it that cables will be delivered?"

"They will be on the wire to Tobruk, and sent by special messenger—"

The photographer came in with the prints, I signed them, and from the briefcase came a new passport, a photograph was stuck in, and the Inspector put it on the desk.

"With the compliments and felicitations of the Chief Commissioner, sir. You are in our charge at all times!"

There wasn't much to say to that, and I knew far better than to offer a gift. When I'd seen them out, I waited for eleven eighteen, and got on clix to Consuelo. NGHREXLNGALWLO—Nothing Here Except Longing. All Well. Out, and I sent SXLGDYSO, Six Long Days, Out, and three dots.

I had an hour with the reports, but all was quiet. At twelve thirty, a Police car, which I hadn't expected, came to take me to the airfield, and I was escorted over the tarmac to a Dart, and given my "chair" by a really beautiful hostess. It doesn't surprise me that air hostesses vary between the extremely goodlooking and really beautiful. They are, after all, the pluck of a nation. And they're always a tonic.

We didn't go into Tobruk. We followed the desert road—so changed from other times!—and went down to the beach. Ulla's house was long, white, wide windows, with a swimming pool that went into the dining patio, cooling the interior with ice water, all bosky in trees and shrubs, and everywhere, for half a mile, surrounded by a garden that sang every color on earth.

My eye went to the rock I'd been dreaming about. It seemed to crawl into green sea in smooth grey folds, lower and lower, till the surf beat in white shock over its forehead. Small platforms in nooks had been tiled where Ulla and her friends could bath nude in privacy.

Ouran met me at the gate with a couple of boys to carry a bag, an umbrella, and a briefcase.

He made a low obeisance. Not a whisker seemed changed. He hadn't moved from the place for almost thirty years. In the gabble that followed, I made sure that the Police driver and sergeant went off happily, and Ouran led the way down, through wonderful flowers and cool streams, to my suite, apart from the house, with a window twenty feet long, facing the sea, a red tiled floor, a bed large enough for at least three couples to disport themselves without faulting, a fine Gauguin at the head that might have been painted for that exact place, and a bathroom with one entire wall of falling, whispering water.

I took my clothes off and stood in the pour till I was frozen, and put a gown on to go outside to dry. Ouran brought coffee, and a jar of clarified goosegrease, nut juice and pomegranate rind stewed together. I smothered it over myself, thick, wrapped a towel, and went through the flowers to the rock, over the hump till I could see the surf, found my place, put the towel down, smothered on more unguent, and lay, arms wide in the sun.

In my opinion, there's only one use of time less wonderful than glorying in the love of a girl, and that's lying nude in the eye

333

of a baking sun, not a sound except for a gull now and then, and the nearby sough of the sea.

I was grossly tempted to send for Consuelo. But I could always bring her later. Now, I knew, Khefi wouldn't understand it. I'd said nothing about it. I knew I could have a troupe of the local girls any time I wanted, without a murmur, even with approval. But not someone from outside. Serious business was exactly that, no less, and Khefi had his own hard rule.

Everything in the world went out of my mind. Once again I saw the electric mauve of the desert sun behind my eyelids. The grease ran, I rolled over, and splashed more on. Before I was aware of it, a pair of hands were massaging my back. I shaded my eyes to see a crone dipping into the pot and kneading the slippery stuff into my skin. Everywhere. Nature had no secrets. When she'd thoroughly thumbed and fingered my head from nape to chine, she went off with the pot. There was an analgesic in the mixture that took the burn out of that first day's exposure. The gong called me back just before the sun lost heart. I stood under that waterfall again. Two women came in with towels, set up the massage table, and one of them patted the mattress. I lay there and let them pound the devil out of me. I didn't think finger ends could go so far into shoulder joints, thighs, knees and ankles. I was helpless when they'd finished. But they didn't ask me to get off. They carried me out to the bed, put me in, covered me over, cleaned up, and left. I slept till seven by my watch. Ouran came in to announce dinner. I put on a linen suit and a scarf and went across the garden to the reception room. It was all tapers, and so was the dining room. My dinner was served at the head of the table. The orange tips of dozens of candles caressed the water, carp rippled among the lilies, and a wide silver platter of green figs in a pyramid took the width of the table midway, with dozens of roses in a copper cauldron at one end and a magnificent cushion of violets nearer me.

Ulla called while I was reading on the long sofa in the library.

"Are you comfortable?"

"I'm in the first of the thousand nights—"

334

"Well, I'm glad. I can't get there for a week—"

"I'll be gone—"

"I've got one crumb of news, though. It's about one of your men. The man who told me is a partner in the law firm that handles my business, so I know it's right. One of your engineers, he didn't know his name, but he'd seen him around, took sick and went to the hospital there. This is about three weeks ago. Well, my man had to fly to Belgrade. Your engineer was on the same plane. When he got off—Belgrade's the end of the line—your man was going south to Tirana. That's Albania, isn't it?"

"It is. And that's a very important item—"

"I'm glad I'm *some* use—"

"I've fallen for the house. I'm going to buy something like it—"

"Look. I'm there for only a couple of weeks in the year. Why buy a place? Go there for the rest of your life—"

But I got Ouran to look at what was available, and in the days that went too quickly in sun that never knew cloud, I walked with him after I'd had a massage in the late afternoon, and looked at small bays, at headlands, with a way down to a beach. Ulla had, of course, the best. But I wanted Consuelo to see the places before I made a decision. I was coming to depend on her. Savagely. I was sleeping ten hours a night, lolling in a fry all day. Eating like an elephant. But I'd lost seven pounds by the bathroom scale on the fifth morning. That night I asked Ouran to send for a car and get a seat on the plane next day.

He looked absolutely stricken.

"Ah, but sir! I had a surprise for you on Saturday—!"

"What?"

"The girls from the caravan coming in from El Ichmir—"

"Not this time!"

He pulled a purely Arab face. The fall of his arms in the white burnous became an aspect of minor disaster.

He got the usual present when I left next morning at five, and I put notes in the hands of the many in line—the cook and four helpers, three water-carriers, five housemaids, two masseuses, two chambermaids, two laundrymaids and four head gardeners—

but I didn't see my gentle crone of the inveigling hands. I hadn't looked at her since that first time. I'd kept my eyes shut because of the sun, and I'd simply call "good morning!" when she arrived, and thanked her when she'd left.

"Where's the old woman who spread the grease?" I asked Ouran.

He pointed to a girl I hadn't noticed at the back. She wore the long blue mantle and white headcloth. But that's all I recognised. She was—I'd say—about twenty, and the prettiest of the lot.

"That's not her," I said.

"Put the cloth over," he told her, and she lifted the muslin over the bridge of her nose. She was shaking with laughter, looking down. I saw what had happened. The thin stuff had been held close to her face by heat and her breath. I'd seen her against the sun. She'd looked wrinkled. I gave her—without looking at her—more than anyone else.

"Must be something the matter with me," I told her.

"She thought there was something wrong with her!" Ouran cackled. "Not a move?"

Everybody doubled, smacking their knees, howling.

Ouran looked at me sideways.

"We have a rude saying, sir," he began, trying not to laugh.

"I've got a better one!" I said, in the car. "See you all soon!"

41

Khefi was at the airport to see me off, though even he had to look twice. I wore a large black felt hat, and a black suit Marlq' Ben Ab had bought for me and altered slightly not to fit. My patent boots were a little too long, and I walked as Ouran did, who'd never worn anything except slippers. Overcoat to underwear, and all in the suitcase, were Egyptian, first quality, excellent but recognisably not quite London or Paris. I was a good blackish-red Bedouin color, with cropped black hair, mustache and beard, and I wore heavy horn-rimmed bi-focals, a diamond on my little finger, and a large gold wristwatch. I left the Patek Philippe, my personal papers and the strong-room keys in the safe. All I carried of my own was my little friend, still in the shoulder holster.

Khefi's attention got me the seat I wanted. We shook hands in a manner befitting two men of import, and I went aboard as the famous electronic surgeon as if I knew what I was talking about. I didn't get off at Rome. People stared at me in the buffet, but when I showed my teeth a fraction, they looked away. I've never known a longer leg than that from Rome to Madrid. I read, dozed, read again and the bump of the undercarriage woke me up. Again, I Ouran'd across the tarmac, through Passports and Customs—Khefi had got visas for everywhere—and out to the thin rain of a Madrileño night. Madrid's another city I have a very warm corner for, and I looked out both sides, more or less blowing kisses at the places I remembered, happy again to see the Plaza, and only sorry I couldn't stay till next day. Thinking of Consuelo, I felt I had a thousand multi-colored balloons in a dance about me.

In schoolboy French I sent a cable to PUSEYINS, BRUSSELS that I would arrive next day, and another to the Metropole for a room and bath. There was a message for me from—of course—Consuelo, and I could have hipped a fandango. *I'm in 317. Where are you? LNG . . . ! C.* I went to the florist and sent up three dozen roses, and a note *I'm in 250. Dot. Dot. Dot.*

Her tap sounded almost as I came out of a towel. I put the horn-rims on, hustled into the jacket, showed my teeth in a rabid grin, and flung the door open.

She almost shrieked.

"Bliz gom een, Senowreeta!" I chittered. "Bliz, you seet, no?"

She came in and sat on the bed, half-laughing, half-frowning. She could barely believe it was me.

"What do you expect to do in that?" she asked, in a small voice.

"Cure a couple of spots, perhaps," I said, in French, and made the "bug" sign. "Dinner?"

We kissed, and there was a knock. She stood.

I opened the door. The valet wanted any laundry or pressing I might have. I asked for a bottle of scotch and a siphon in the room, got my hat and umbrella and escorted Consuelo out. We didn't talk in the lift. We went out to the foyer, but it was really raining. Walking was out. We went to the restaurant instead.

Consuelo was not quite herself, despite her eyes, tender, warm, appealing.

We had a corner table, away from everyone, and I looked at the menu.

"Something very light for me, please," she said, suddenly, and looked away. "I'm in such a rage!"

"Oh, lawks—hold on—that's not awfully Egyptian, is it? Oh, Horus. Do?"

"I've been so looking forward to this, and what happens?"

My balloons stopped bobbing. Obvious.

"You became a girl—"

She nodded, and blew out a breath.

"It really is *the* most exasperating—"

"It's healthy, anyway. Glass of champagne won't hurt you. Chicken broth. Fillet of sole in lemon juice. And look. Mangoes!"

We had a very good dinner, and she told me a lot more about most of them at M.I.5 and 6, and the new department. Victor Maude was son of Sir John, a former Governor-General, still a power behind the scenes, with many friends everywhere, especially in the United States, Canada, the Middle East generally, India, Pakistan, and all through Africa. A word from that type of man can make or break. I had every cause to know. Joel Cawle's father, Sir Poynter, had also been a Governor-General. Joel had gone to my school and Cambridge, took a First, and had one Government job after another, shifting from here to there, and then he'd dropped out for a time, it was said, to manage his father's estates in Canada and Rhodesia.

"That was only an excuse," Consuelo said. "But even the people who pretend to know don't know much. He's known to be a sharp brain. He got into the Russian nuclear plant. Then the French. Then he was in Poland and Czechoslovakia. He began that row in Italy. You remember, between the Army and the politicians? But it seems to have been something to do with Saudi Arabia that put his star well up. Gillian doesn't quite know. We almost didn't get a contract for rockets, or something. The new, controlled type—"

My ears were sticking out a mile. Things were beginning to add again.

"Of course, I could be repeating the most awful nonsense—" she said. "But that's the best we could do. Both Ursula and Angela 've known them all for years—"

"Anybody know what Cawle's doing now?"

"Been in Washington for months. He's always in London for a few days or so. Bernard Lane's there too. It's *the* job next to the Ambassador's—"

339

"Any link between Ursula and Angela and any of the top people? I mean, emotional, apart from social or professional?"

She frowned into a spoonful of mango.

"I've never heard of anything—"

"Did Angela ever say anything about Paul and drugs?"

"Never. I'd never have guessed if I hadn't found that phial—"

"Did you ever see anyone you recognised—I mean, M.I.5 or 6—at any of the Company's offices?"

"Never—"

"Did you know somebody called Thanatis, in Rome?"

"Vaguely. Couldn't stand him!"

"Could he have been, in fact, any one of them?"

She put the spoon and fork together, and looked down the room.

"I've got the dimmest sort of outline. If they were—any of them—they couldn't do it again!"

"I don't think you need coffee. A good night's sleep. Couple of aspirin. I'm going early. I'll have time to call in at Paris—"

"Darling, I can't—I simply *can't* tell you!"

"Mother Eve dictating, that's all. Girl's best friend—"

"Pah!"

We said good night in the foyer, a magnificent bow and a kiss for a limp hand, a sour grimace, and I watched her go into the lift. I went across to the rack and bought a dozen papers to read with a quiet scotch. I couldn't find anything in the English editions about Ursula, and very little about anything else. I called the airline for a seat on the seven A.M. to Paris, and asked the porter for a call at five.

I went to sleep thinking of El Mir, and the sun, and for some reason, of the "crone."

Pouring rain isn't the weather for a flight to Paris. We got there without seeing anything but the clouds down below. I called Azil's apartment from the airport and got the housekeeper. Yes, they were closed to all callers. There was correspondence. Without seeing my credentials, she couldn't read the envelopes. Yes, the Police were on duty in the foyer.

Since I'd never met her, I couldn't do much except get on the flight to Brussels.

Still raining. I went up to my room at the Metropole, took off my clothes, pulled the curtains, and slept, regretting I wasn't in the sun. I called Red when I woke, and he said he'd be round right away.

"I'm in 471. Any good at straight faces?"

"Climb all over 'em. See you!"

When I opened the door, he stared, and fell against the jamb in a sort of hoot. The pageboy took a tip and an order for orange juice. I'd written the plan, and he studied it while I wrote a note to Consuelo.

"Only thing missing's the most important item," he said. "Time—"

"Here're two lists of words. This one, of manufacturing firms, gives you the date. This one's time. Bromide-Actino is ten thirty, Sulpho-Trisodium, eleven forty five. Lilly's the twenty fourth. Got it?"

"Fine. Suppose they won't let you in till the afternoon?"

"That's what I'm hoping. Reverse the list. Bromide-Actino is now?"

"Five thirty—"

"Right you are. I want to arrive at the prison preferably in the late afternoon. Evening's not far off. I'm thinking of pursuit—"

"You didn't get there yet!"

"Don't worry. Here are the cans of 'mixture.' Pill. Mask. Now tell me what you're going to do?"

I had the radio well up, playing one of those hamstrum clatter-yowls, something that's taken the place of what used to be called popular music, a peeve of the impoverished, but it smothered what we were saying.

"I'll have the aircraft at a field I know. Belongs to a friend. It's only four minutes from the border. Then it's five minutes and some seconds from the prison. I'll take off, allowing for time. I'll come in this south-southwest corner, pick my own spot, drop a can just before the halfway, and then at the prison yard. I'll come around and put her down about twenty yards from the gate, turn her, and leave her running. And wait for you—"

"Pill down, mask on. That's it. The moment I've seen the East German lad about the permit to see the other one about the interview, I'll cable. If I cable needing anything—any piece of surgical equipment—that means it's postponed, or not on. I may not get what I want. The prescription I send will be date and time. It'll be relayed from Cairo. Got somebody here to get in touch with you?"

"I told you we have a factory at Brunswick? Send it there, and they'll relay to me at Wildersheim. Minutes away from where I'll be. And we have our own code—"

"Right. They spray again today. For five days. I'll fly tonight for Magdeburg. If you see anything you don't like on the way in, shove off!"

"Pity we can't have a couple of rehearsals. You should have seen my fat gals taking jumps. Your crates are at the airport, and that's the Customs papers—"

He pushed over the folder of documents itemising a cardiograph unit and an encephalog. Both were newest of their kind, and I intended to present them to Magdeburg University. I'd already had correspondence with the Rector. I was to have a session at eleven o'clock with the students on the day of my arrival, and on the next morning with the faculty and their friends. It was on that afternoon or the one following that I hoped to "visit" the prison. I was supposed to be returning that night to dine with the Rector. If it had to be another day, then I'd simply have to play the cards. Once those surgeons got hold of me, it wouldn't take them long to uncover the sham.

It all depended on the permits. But I didn't intend that anyone at the University should have anything to do with getting them.

I had my scotch, Red had his orange juice, we went over it again and we shook hands, and he left.

"I'm not wishing you anything," he called from down the corridor. "You've got it all!"

"Share it!"

There was a flight to Leipzig at ten, and I thought I'd stay the night there and make it a base, rather than Berlin with all the in-and-out nonsense at the East-West barriers.

It was a comfortable aircraft, but the weather wasn't ideal. We seemed to swing all over the sky. We landed at Cologne, and I showed my passport and papers without any word, went aboard, and we touched down—I think—at Kassel, though we weren't disturbed and when we flew on, the steward came round to tell us we were crossing the border. My fellow passengers didn't even look up. They *did* look decidedly prosperous, even glossily so, though, in a curious way, they all appeared to belong to the same family, clothing, neckwear, almost identical, though what most took my eye was an air of restraint about them all. As if they were all thinking something they didn't want to say, even to themselves.

Though it was well after midnight, the airport was crowded. I went out to the Passports desk and presented my papers, one by one. The official looked at them all, stamped them, saluted, and passed me to Public Health. Again I was stamped, and sent into the Customs bay. My bag was gone through slowly and thoroughly, piece by piece, refolded, and put back tidily. But the crates had to be opened, each item verified by the documents, stamped, signed. The officer looked at me for the first time.

"These articles can be collected by the University tomorrow morning with these papers," he said. "You are staying where, Professor?"

"At the Halle Hotel—"

"You will be notified when they are taken. There's no need for you to attend—"

Couldn't ask for anything fairer, and I went out to the taxi, had to borrow a tip off the driver for the porter—I'd forgotten to change any money—and we went through semi-lit streets to the hotel.

The East German concept of comfort doesn't run to elegance, but at least it was harshly "modern"—chrome and plastic—and shiningly clean. I had a hot bath with a sliver of soap that wouldn't lather, and went to bed fairly pleased with myself.

So far, so good.

343

42

Knowing a little of German University hours, I was on the telephone at seven fifteen. A secretary surprised me. She had everything in hand. The items were in process of being collected at Customs, and the Rector, Doctor Voigt, presented his compliments and would consider it an honor to entertain me with coffee at eight thirty, and to luncheon at noon. I accepted, leapt for the bathroom, got into one of my starched shirts, packed a surgeon's overall, and went downstairs. The dining room was full, the coffee was awful, and the same air of restraint—or was it resentment?—still seemed to hang over them all. Outside the streets were grey. It wasn't just the weather. People, clothing, shops, all seemed to lack any life or color. While I waited for a taxi, the shops I looked at flanking the hotel didn't have anything I'd have thought worth buying.

Drab. That's the word.

The faculty building at the University was all I might have expected, Gothic, sombre, hushed in that silence which seems to put a pair of hands round the throat.

Doctor Voigt came out to meet me. The crates were being unpacked in the annex. I showed his students how I wanted the parts put together, and said I'd go across to the lecture hall to check.

"They're very excited—we all are—about your visit," he said.

"We're doing a lot of work with electrical equipment. But not so advanced as this. I'm told you applied to see certain patients in prison?"

That was a jolt.

"Well, yes," I said, fumbling for a moment. "We're experimenting with electronic therapy in diseases of the glands. I've been told they have patients—ah, may one suggest?—under specific treatment?"

"Our students make twice-weekly visits," Voigt said, and folded his arms almost protectively. "They're doing things we wouldn't dare try here—"

"In what way?"

"Oh, well. Operating techniques. Transplants. Some of my professors are consultants. We learn, too!"

"I fear my knowledge of the German language doesn't carry me far in the more technical areas—"

"Permit me to observe that you have most excellent command. May I help in this matter? I could take you on a tour of the hospitals—"

"That would be most gracious. I'm primarily interested in glandular disease. I believe we're about to find out where these aberrations arise. If you're interested, naturally, I'd like to show you what's been done, so far—"

"But I shall be most interested, my dear Professor!"

"I'm seeing the Inspector-General this morning, and the Ministry of Transport—"

"For some special purpose?"

"To enter Hauerfurth—"

His expression barely altered. But he seemed in some extraordinary way to have gone quite cold.

"I think that will be difficult, Professor Afram," he said, after a couple of moments. "Other prisons, no barriers at all. We could walk in. But not Hauerfurth. The—inmates—pay their debt to society by being of use. On many levels. We have graduates there. You could perhaps talk to them? I'd advise it!"

"I shall be glad to—"

"I shall try to arrange a dinner for later this week—"

"I have only until the twenty fourth. I'm going to Warsaw and Leningrad—"

"I'll see what I can do before then. Is there anything in particular—"

"These patients, described here—"

I opened the briefcase to pick out the medical bulletin concocted by Consuelo and Gillian. Paper, print were an exact copy of the real thing.

Doctor Voigt merely glanced, and gave them back.

"I promise nothing," he said. "Completely beyond my small competence. Were it purely medical, I could promise you open doors anywhere. Not in Hauerfurth. There, we enter politics. A domain we all like to keep away from—"

"Unpleasant, I agree. But a patient is entitled—"

"Except in Hauerfurth!"

"I must try. It's the real object of my visit—"

"I regret to say this. I shall do all I can to help you. But I fear you must resign yourself to disappointment. I shall talk to the medical officer there. He's a graduate. But that means nothing. Give me those names again if you please. This conversation is between us? No further discussion? *Anywhere!*"

"Confidential, you please believe me—"

"We don't mention anything—"

"It never took place. We, also, in these days, have to function in a certain way. We're used to it. But we can still get many things done. Well, then, Doctor Voigt, these most interesting experiments with the coelocanth—"

Two of his professors came to be introduced, and we discussed marine life at length, constantly joined by members of his staff until it was time for me to go. Doctor Voigt sent me in his own car to the Inspectorate. I asked for my man, and sent up a card. I'd already written to him from Cairo with my scholastic and professional credentials, and a list of publications. Never mind how carefully his staff went into them, I was fairly certain they were far too well documented—there were articles from the *Lancet* and the A.M.A. *Journal* off their own presses—to give much ground for doubt, and the list of my French and Arabic articles ran to a couple of pages. With the help of Druxi and Gillian, Consuelo had done a real job. Without, of course, knowing what she was doing. But I wasn't *all* that sure. She was just about as smart as the next.

A young officer banged his heels to say good morning, and kindly to accompany him. We went up in an iron cage, along a bare corridor, to an end room. The youngster held up a hand to slow me, footed forward to knock as if in hallowed precincts, and a quiet voice invited us in.

The man I remembered, in a greenish uniform with silver braid, sat behind a large desk. He got up to shake hands—a slither of palms—and nodded to a chair. The youngster left us.

"Now, then, what may I do for you, Doctor Afram?" he said.

"I wish to visit Hauerfurth Prison. I want to inspect two patients. They are mentioned in the prison medical report. You will find their names in that file. Their prison numbers are one one eight seven, and four zero one two. It is work of highest national importance. The test will be sent to the Pathological Institute—"

He held up a finger, as though he were listening elsewhere.

"I've heard about this," he said, frowning.

I pointed to my file in front of him.

"I have no authority to grant a pass for a visit to prisons," he said, leaning back. "All I can do is to sign a travel permit for you to go *to* the prison. To enter, or to talk to prisoners, you would have to go to this officer. And I don't think it would be granted. It is not usual—"

He tore off a half-page, and ringed the heading.

I passed him an envelope addressed to the other man.

"But you have it exactly!" he said, almost gaily. "Wait. I will speak—"

He pressed the button. The youngster opened the side door.

"Get me the Ministry," he said.

"Highest national importance—" I put in.

"That is understood. I know of you. Everything is known. But you see, my authority is limited only to a travel pass—"

I saw how perfectly innocent men could be sentenced to years in prison, or hanged, or shot. There was no hope of appeal to that type of mind. They didn't see the trial, or the shooting, or the hanging. They simply dealt with paper as someone immediately above told them. Other men didn't exist. The man up above did. Because he did, they did. Not the Law, but dictat. Not the vote, but one man's fiat.

The telephone buzzed. He lifted the receiver. He turned the chair, speaking with his back to me. I didn't attempt to listen. I lit one of my Simon Artz cigarettes, and went over to the window. I looked down at a grey quadrangle. All windows. All dark.

"Very good!" he said, swinging round in a creak. "I shall have a pass made out and provide the car. That is, if the Minister agrees. The journey is thirty minutes. Thirty minutes inside. Thirty minutes back, and the driver should report to my adjutant at about ten o'clock?"

I could have carolled.

"It couldn't be in the afternoon?" I said carelessly. "I have lectures on both days, and at ten thirty this morning, I have an appointment with the Rector—"

"It can be tomorrow afternoon," he said. "Or the afternoon of the next day? It depends on whether the Minister gives permission. I have no objection!"

"At your disposal," I said and flicked ash in the tray with a hand steady—I thought—as a surgeon's. "This afternoon, and tomorrow, I'm at the University. The next afternoon? I shall be grateful—"

He thought for a moment, worriedly.

"You're helping work of highest national importance," I said, in the gap.

"Ah, yes," he said, and rang the bell. "I thought I might have forgotten something—"

I blessed Leonart Graeffe.

The youngster came in and put his heels together.

"*If* the Minister agrees, have a travel pass made out for the

Professor for the afternoon of the twenty third at three o'clock," my man said, in a "careful" voice. "Three o'clock, the Hotel Halle. Direct route, B8 to Hauerfurth Prison. Thirty minutes wait. Return direct to the hotel. Driver reports to you at four thirty. No divergence from that order. Accompany the Professor to the Ministry. The Adjutant is waiting. Here. Take this file—"

I put out the cigarette, and we shook hands. He still looked puzzled.

"A privilege to be of service," he said, a little doubtfully. "I didn't know Egypt was so far advanced. I mean, of course, it's—"

"Sir," I said, picking up my hat. "I shall be most happy to welcome you, if ever you should come to Cairo. I shall, I hope, be permitted to show you four thousand and more years of civilised history. It would be my pleasure—"

"Ah, but that's a dream!" he said. "How I would enjoy—"

He half bowed, and I walked out, with the youngster behind me.

He sat in front with the chauffeur, and our tires whistled through grey streets to the greyer Ministry, and although rain makes any city—except perhaps London—because of the red buses?—or Paris?—because of what?—bleak, those streets were the greyest. It seems to be the prevalent tone of dumbocracy.

We went into the hall, to the lift, and up to the mezzanine floor. Another young man, in a blue uniform exchanged a nod with my youngster, and took me down the wide corridor, turning rather impatiently when I stopped to call "Thank you!" and leading on, down to the end door. This one opened automatically.

I was in a room with a window north and east, a large desk, a good carpet—I'd have said Shariz—and a couple of fine oils, one —from the green and apricot—a Raffaele, or a pupil, probably "taken" from a church—and my man came to meet me. He wore a dark suit. Curious, but they never seemed to use a good laundry.

"I am glad to have the pleasure of meeting you, Professor," he said, nodding dismissal to the Adjutant. "I've spoken to the Rector of the University. You have a very full program. Most useful, I understand—"

"I am here for such a short visit, unfortunately. I go on to Warsaw, and to Leningrad—"

"So I was informed. Now, what is it you require at Hauerfurth? I should warn you that facilities are extremely limited—"

I took off my glasses, and looked at him between the eyes. They were indeterminate grey-black. Tired, mentally. I had no time to feel sorry for him. Though I did.

"I want to see two patients," I said, loudly. "I wish to take tests for the Pathological Institute. It is work of highest national importance—"

He turned away, fiddling with a jacket button.

"Yes," he said slowly. "I know. But it's not generally permitted. This is a matter essentially for the Director—"

"It is of highest national importance—" I said, loudly, in my best Arabic-German, when any guttural becomes a cascade. "Ugo Primondi and Levi Dav—"

"What is especially significant about them?" he asked, in a rugose frown.

"They both suffer from a rare disease of the endocrines. It is a disease we have had some success in treating. But not in human beings. If this disease should spread, without the serum which might control it—"

"But how do you know this?" he said, frowning. "How could you know of these men—"

Without hurry, I unlocked my briefcase, and brought out a sheaf of print, all from West or East German medical pamphlets, most of them genuine, except that we'd inserted paragraphs, among them, the one I held out for him to see.

"A report by the Prison Health Authorities, here," I said, pointing. "This engaged our attention. A very rare form. Virulent. It's not yet common outside a few of the lesser-known peoples in Africa. And if it is to spread? And no defence anywhere?"

"Of highest national importance, yes," he said slowly. "Of course—"

"You often meet prison officials? From this prison?"

"Hauerfurth? Yes—"

"No health measures? Protection?"

"Why?"

"These men are in this atmosphere of disease. How do you know they haven't brought it out?"

He stared at me.

"Would this be possible? A disease—"

"The incubatory period—when it doesn't show—is at least two years. You may be suffering unaware at this moment—"

"Ah, but Professor!"

"Have blood tests made today. Lose no time—"

He strode to the telephone, dialed three numbers, and sat back, looking at me.

"I seem to have heard those names," he said, considerably shaken. "Can they—are they—well, will they die?"

"Very painfully, if the serum isn't available," I said, looking out of the window at roofs and chimney pots, and thinking that from my own experience, Civil Servants never seem to look at anything else. "That's the main reason for this visit, you see. We've *got* to find a reasonably safe method of treating people by the tens of thousands—"

"I didn't think it was nearly as—hello? Get me the Director of Hauerfurth—"

We waited. He wasn't looking at me. I offered him a Simon Artz, lit it for him, and went back to light my own. Here, I knew, was the hurdle. He wasn't the type to be jumped over, gone around, or flattened. But he *could* be unnerved. And was.

"Hello? Yes. Look, this matter of the two prisoners. The interview, inspection, whatever it is—"

He listened, turned the cuttings toward him, reached for spectacles.

"I see. Are they in a fit state for a visit?"

Another pause, and the voice of an elf at the other end.

"Yes, I know. Supposing I sent a medical superintendent with him?"

Elf, again.

My man looked at me.

"You wouldn't want to examine them physically, or photograph them?"

"I don't want to touch them. All I want is a full face and profile look at them, their legs and arms, and a blood-slide of both. You understand, we've never seen this in our hospitals—"

"Why these two, and not others?" he asked me.

"Only because they're mentioned. I'd be content with any—"

"Why *two?*"

"The disease manifests in many ways. I'd like to see them all—"

The elf had heard, and spoke again.

"Where did you get the information?" he said.

I pointed to the cuttings.

"It's in a paper, here," I began. "The highly infectious—that one—"

He turned to the receiver.

"You see? The Professor might teach us something. What's the difficulty? A few minutes, it's not much. A look at them—"

The elf again.

"Well now, I'm in absolute agreement there," he said. "Let him see them, and then talk. The Professor's about your height, dark complexion, black beard and mustache, spectacles. Couldn't be mistaken for anybody else. He'll arrive in a Ministry car. He has written permission, fifteen minutes. No more than to see them. The doctor can give the blood tests. Then you can talk to him—"

He nodded.

"I take full responsibility, naturally!" he said, impatient. "We don't want any trouble outside. But I agree. A rigorous enquiry *is* necessary. And you can start there, in your office. That's the place. Right. I want to talk to you later—about the control of—uh —that's right, I'm not satisfied. Ring me in fifteen minutes!"

He clapped the receiver down, pressed a button, and stood.

"The permit to enter the prison will be in charge of the car driver," he said, smiling, at last. "He will be at the Halle Hotel at three o'clock, on the afternoon of the twenty third. Let me advise you to answer the Director in any questions he may ask you. Tell him in detail. Show any printed evidence. A revelation of this sort is a serious matter. But it could turn out to be most fortunate!"

"That is the correct point of view," I said, and picked up the briefcase. "If any further enquiries are necessary, I'm sure my Consul-General will be most happy to be of service. Our Ambassador, also—"

"He knows of your visit," he said, eyebrows up in recognition. "I was on to him this morning—"

Ah, Khefi!

"—and I am deeply indebted for your help—" I said, locking the briefcase. "It is of highest *inter*national importance. If this got loose, you could decimate your population—"

"Yes," he said, and half-frowned. "That's the reason—"

"And take great care of yourself. This is a disease like leprosy. It comes as a thief. Good morning!"

He couldn't speak, didn't offer his hand.

The Adjutant took me downstairs to the car, closed the door, told the driver to take me to the Halle Hotel, and saluted in a half bow as we left.

I didn't want to examine the state of my mind. I found I'd been rigid in every limb for the past few minutes. I was trembling with strain, and although I was warmly clothed, I almost shivered with cold. A curious condition, though I'd imagined I was conducting myself more or less normally.

At the hotel I asked the porter for a cablegram blank.

I wrote "BOUSSAF, CAIRO. In addition prescription Marlq' Ben Ab, add item Beminal-Triclite, Squibb, one daily. Confirm. Regards. Afram."

I hoped it would go direct to the Boussaf Pharmacy. From Boussaf to Marlq' Ben Ab. From him to Pusey. There wasn't much time.

I didn't take a comfortable breath till the porter gave me a receipt and my change.

43

My new units were a tremendous success, and the lecture—which I'd learned by heart from Leonart—was loudly applauded. I could feel the sweat cold under my eyes, and over my eyebrows. Theoretically I know nothing. I'd never been interested in mere theory. It's nearly always wrong. Only practice shows the way. Luckily, I'm an accomplished technician. I'd been messing about with electronics—we've only just begun to call it that—since boyhood. What I lacked in theory, I more than made up in hard knowledge, and what I couldn't explain in math, I could draw schematically on the blackboard. And did. I amazed myself by what I could do when I tried.

We lunched, we discussed Arabic literature, where—again— thank God!—I happen to know a little, and back we went to the lecture hall for an hour and a half on the use of electricity in diseases of the nerves. I'd always been deeply interested, and over the years I'd listened, read, helped my physician friends where I could. My use of the German language isn't halting. But my accent was a joy. I listened to myself. I was delighted. So was my audience. I begged off a dinner with the students that night for a quieter meal with Doctor Voigt, his wife, and some of the professors with their wives, which I insisted on giving at the Halle Hotel. I knew what I was doing. There wasn't time to talk. The journalists and photographers were there, and the Mayor came in with some of his Councillors, and we began a really noisy party, with the Police Chief and his officers, and most of the city's physicians, and a few of the town drunks. I didn't know anybody except Doctor Voigt and the professors by sight—and they seemed uneasy until they'd had a few more—but the manager was a wise man. About the time the Rector began to look for his cloakroom ticket, I felt somebody at my right elbow. I looked up, and found the headwaiter, three chins shaven glossily in a way I've never been able to achieve—truly a baby's bottom-vomping—there's no other way of describing what isn't a smile, isn't a scowl, can only be a vomp—at me.

"Sir, Doctor," he began, in my ear. "The manager begs to say the account is now of considerable size—"

"Bring it to me," I said. "Nobody is to pay. I insist. Everybody is my guest—"

He bowed from the belt, went off, while I saw the Rector to the door with his wife on my arm, and when I turned to go back, the manager was in front of me, inviting me to the desk. The account was indeed, formidable. My letter of credit more than covered it. There was no scotch, and I asked for a bottle of cognac to be sent to my room. The place was still crowded, but I felt I could *imshi,* and did. Nobody seemed to be looking for me, and indeed, most of those I saw couldn't have told me from who. There's nothing wrong with the beer, especially with that chaser.

I was reaching to put the light out, and the telephone buzzed.

"A cablegram, sir, Professor," the porter said. "Should I send it up?"

"Please!"

I waited, trying not to hold my breath.

I opened the door as the steps neared. The night porter held out the envelope, I gave him a note, and shut the door.

I read *Squibb formula Beminal-Triclite added Marlq' Ben Ab daily prescription. Patient gaining ground. Temperature, pulse rate normal. Eating well. Awaiting your return. Regards. Boussaf.*

I drank the health of every Egyptian ever born in a quite good cognac, had another for Boussaf—I could see that bald-head smile with the missing front tooth—and Marlq' Ben Ab—I had to buy him something special for Christmas—another for Consuelo, and a tender thought for Eve, and just that last consecratory gulp for Yorick.

I intended to have him out.

With Help.

44

Both my morning lectures had been even noiser with applause than that of the first day. The craftsmen who'd studied my schematic diagrams had agreed that I might be right, and the circuit drawings I'd invented for heart and lung regeneration were accepted by fourth year students for construction in the experimental University workshop. I found them all "bright" enough. I was sorry for them. As a father, I saw hundreds of Fredericks, with infinitely less opportunity to expand as human beings, unable even to put healthy—but "forbidden"—thought into words. I wondered what was to become of them, but I hadn't the time to think.

I had a cheese sandwich and a glass of tea for lunch. I couldn't risk alcohol because of the pill. The skates I strapped with tape under my waistcoat. I'd had the wheels filed a little flatter so that they "sat" more comfortably, and without any remarkable bulge in my appearance. The oblong "sticker" I put in my hip pocket, which wasn't where most would look for it. Pills I carried in the lower left-hand waistcoat pocket, the smaller explosive stickers in the right, handkerchiefs in the right upper, gas discs in the left, and the masks were in the inner fold of my jacket. At about six minutes to three, I bought a large block of chocolate and two cartons of cigarettes and put them in my briefcase. I'd sprayed all the paper in my room, and the ash had gone down the toilet. I'd left nothing except extra clothing, suitcase, and foot-wear. I hadn't picked up the change from my letter of credit. The balance far more than covered my account.

At a minute to three I was on the steps when the car arrived in the rain.

A sergeant of Police sitting beside the chauffeur got out to open the door. A small extra complication. I got in, and the chauffeur took his cap off to give me a long envelope addressed to the Di-rector of Hauerfurth Prison. The sergeant closed the glass divide, and away we went. I didn't look where we were going. I leaned back and pretended to sleep if only for the sergeant's sake. I saw him looking at me in the small mirror.

I did sleep, and soundly, and I didn't wake till we slowed, and the chauffeur pressed the siren three times at the turn into the prison approach. I yawned, made all the faces of the innocent awakening, ignored the mirror, and looked at my watch.

Three twenty two.

Grey clouds rolled behind the prison on both sides. A guard stopped us at the concrete car shelter on the right. Another hurried with an outsize umbrella. The sergeant and both guards spoke for a few moments, and he got out.

I took the pill.

I didn't think they'd spray in that weather, but from the flapping of the guards' overcoats, there was quite a strong wind. The ser-geant opened the door and invited me under the umbrella. I got out in fine rain, and there was, indeed, a blusty breeze in gusts.

We had about fifty yards to walk. I wasn't paying much at-tention. But the concrete square of the prison was directly in front, with a cube reaching out, and we were walking toward a high white, steel-slatted gate.

The place had altered a little since I'd been there. It looked newer. A paint job. The entrance cube was new. The forest had gone. I couldn't see anything on either side except grey cloud.

At the gate, the sergeant pressed the button, and we waited. The car turned into the concrete shelter. Nothing moved down the long approach.

A speck—a bird?—moved across the sky far over, behind the prison. I didn't look. A window slid in the postern door.

"Visitor with permit!" the sergeant shouted.

The window snapped shut.

A loud rumble began inside. I imagined the grille coming down. At the same time I saw the sergeant breathe hard once or twice, sneeze. I reached into my pocket for a handkerchief, and pretended to blow my nose.

"I'm coming down with a grippe!" he said.

"You chose a remarkable day, Sergeant!"

"Always the same, here. That marsh, out there—"

In blowing my nose I'd turned away from him. The aircraft was over on my right, low down, not yet turning toward the approach.

I breathed deep in thanks, suddenly aware of a curious stoppage at the bridge of my nose.

The postern door opened on the left. A guard looked out and beckoned, and we went down, stepped over the sill, but the sergeant halted at a gesture, and the door slammed. The gate made darkness behind my back, the grille was all the way down a yard away. I gave my envelope to the guard. He went to a speech-box on the far side, held up the envelope to the scanner, and waited, facing the grille. He didn't look very eager. He wiped his forehead under the cap peak with his fingers, and looked at the tips.

The grille rumbled up.

He pointed to the door. I walked on. It was opened before I got there, and I went into a room walled in oiled wood, about thirty feet by forty. James' sketch hadn't been far off, except that he'd had dark green paint. This was cream. There was a smell of linseed oil, floor wax, and an antiseptic. Everything gleamed. Two guards at a counter on the right nodded me over, pointed to the briefcase, hat and coat. The sergeant had kept the umbrella.

The door at the end on the right opened, and a stout Inspector, from his badges, in a blue uniform came toward me. He looked rheumy, cold-ridden. He pointed at the control panel behind the counter, and said something I didn't catch. One of the guards reached up to push a switch. Instantly there was a roar and a rush of cool air. The guard handed him the envelope. He barely looked at it.

I dropped two discs, trod on them.

"Doctor Mahmoud Al Afram?" he said, almost in sorrow. "Over here, please—"

He went across to a plain door.

Apparently I wasn't going to the waiting room, next to the cloakroom. The door was shut.

I heard the jet over the whine of the air-control unit.

The Inspector opened the door.

Two white-gowned figures sat on chairs with a small surgical table between them. I didn't recognise either of them. I hadn't expected to recognise one. But not to recognise the other was simply moments of despair. Others—possibly a half dozen horrifying white shapes—stood in a corner on the right. A medical orderly swabbed under their sleeves. I felt a colossal let-down.

And yet.

Those in the chairs were brownish-purplish human balloons. It was impossible to look at them and imagine a normal human being. Their faces were squeezed behind layers of what I could only think of as grease in creased rolls that hid their eyes in slits, hid their noses except for a reddish blob, hid their mouths in a wide, deep fold. Their hands were swollen pads. Even the nails were hidden in little pits.

An orderly pulled up their gowns. Their legs were the same size from ankle to knee, about as round as my thigh.

The wider, taller of the two seemed to make a convulsive effort.

Only the heels of the feet were on the floor. The toes pivoted. Toward each other.

Once. Twice. Three times.

Three dots?

Yorick.

"How long have they been in this condition?" I asked nobody.

"No questions!" the Inspector said. "No speech!"

"Pardon!"

The Inspector nodded to the orderly and turned to me.

"Now you've seen what you wanted, Professor, the Director would like a few words," he said, in a tone that seemed to say This Is Going to Be Good! "This way!"

He put a hand under my arm in a policeman's grip and turned for the door.

I didn't know how much the current of colder air might have affected the gas. But I was fairly certain the air-intake was working. That curious heaviness at the bridge of my nose was stronger. But then, that might have been the effect of the pill. I wondered if there was a way into the prison through the medical room. But James had been sure that the cage was outside. I had to be careful they weren't taken out while I was with the Director. I went, lamblike, still with my handkerchief up, and managed a couple of good sneezes at the office door.

It was a small room, filing cabinets round two walls, a map and graphs behind the desk.

The Director might have been early forties, cropheaded, blue eyes, the pallid blue that never seems to smile, in a navy-blue jacket, high collar, zipped to the neck. He had the air of a clean, efficient killer.

He pointed to the only other chair. The Inspector put it under me, and choked a sneeze. The Director had my briefcase open on the desk. He was reading the papers I'd brought.

But I felt a blither in the pit of my stomach to find him comparing my cuttings with bound files of the journals they'd been taken from. I recognised the print.

He took his time. He read as if he enjoyed it.

I dropped the third gas disc. Moved my feet.

"I am glad we have had the opportunity of being of service to medical science," he said, still reading. "We like to oblige distinguished guests. I read the newspapers. Wonderful, what you do. How else can we help?"

He was sweating across the forehead, top lip.

"I saw the patients," I began.

"We call them prisoners, here," he said. "They have no identity!" He still pretended to read.

"We like to be correct—"

My ears were alive for any sound in the entrance hall.

I suddenly realised he was looking at me.

Laughing. But as I'd thought, not in the eyes.

"Of course, we must obey instructions, Professor Doctor Afram!"

The gas was beginning to tell. I knew it, because he took out a handkerchief to wipe the run.

"Are you all protected against this disease?" I asked.

He looked up again, laughing wider.

"The medical officer assures me your fear of contamination is groundless, Professor. I told the Minister that, just now. He was surprised!"

I sneezed again.

"There's no need to answer any questions. Here, at any rate. But I would like to know where you found the names and numbers of these two—"

"My information came—" I began, pointing at the papers.

"This is always possible," he said, clipped. "But I shall make sure. You will not return with this car. You must wait here until I have read these articles. When everything is in order, I shall call a car to take you back to the Ministry. There you will be interrogated, if it is necessary. We have no wish to offend you, of course. But you realise that this is a most serious matter—"

"In what way?"

"You have a name wrong, here—Primondi. I want to know where you got it—"

I opened my hands.

"Only from the reports—"

"We've treated you with every courtesy, I think you'll agree? You've seen these two. That is our part finished. Your Government cannot complain, you again agree? Now you will have some time to finish your part. I want to know where you got these names and numbers. You did *not* get them from these publications!"

"But, sir, I do assure you—"

"But, sir, you do not!"

"Where else *could* I get them?"

He smiled through sweat.

"That is exactly what I wish to know. And I intend to know before, Professor, you leave this prison!"

He looked over my head and frowned a nod.

I slipped to the left, stood, chopped the Inspector in the fat of his neck, and he fell forward, hitting his forehead a crack on the chair arm.

A long burst of heavy cannon fire shook the graphs, made the pen roll off the desk.

A siren howled somewhere overhead.

The Director tried to kick back his chair. He was surprised he couldn't. I cut him under the nose with a backhand, and he went over sideways, out.

The door was half open.

There hadn't been much noise. The hall was quiet except for the fans. I went over to the medical room and flung open the door. The two were among a group, all standing, perfectly steady. The medical orderly looked at me, turned, called toward the inner door. The doctor came out, saw me, and gestured over to the cloakroom. He was trying to tell me the slides were there, perhaps.

The orderly plumped down on a metal chair, tried to be sick.

A loud bell rang inside the prison, went on ringing.

The doctor fell to his knees. I went over to Yorick, tallest of all, verified his number on the metal tag hung round his neck, pushed a pill deep into his "mouth," down his throat, spat on a handkerchief and stuck it over the fat rolls covering the nose, pushed a mask over the head. I found Bar-Dav's number, pushed a pill in, plastered a handkerchief, pushed a mask over. I put my own mask on. The orderly had been making attempts to stop me. I shoved him, and he fell and lay there. The other "shapes" made sounds. I wanted to block my ears. The doctor leaned against the wall, looking up at the light.

I ripped at the tape under my waistcoat and pulled out the skates. One I put on Yorick's bare foot, one on the other's.

Neither had made a move. I wheeled Levi on his one foot, and pulled Yorick behind him. I lifted Yorick's arm—God knows what it weighed—but it rested on Levi's right shoulder. I lifted the other arm, and put it on the left, dragged Levi by the gown, and went through the door, across the entrance hall to what I thought was the waiting room. Both guards lay behind the counter. I had to shoot out the lock. It was a store of sorts, floor to ceiling in shelves filled with cans.

I took out James' oblong sticker. By eye, the far wall appeared to be the outer.

I crossed myself, and laid a hand on Levi's shoulder, on Yorick's.

I thrust away a rack of cans, pressed the sticker flat, and wheeled the two a few yards off.

The room filled with smoke and dust. My ears felt as if I'd been clouted on the point. I had my arms round both of them. Cold air came in. The siren *ooo-ow-ooo'd* in screams. Other bells whirred in a tinny clatter.

I saw the rain, felt the bitter wind. Light was going. I lifted Levi over the stones, put him against the wall outside. I went back. I could hear Yorick wheezing with effort. I had to raise an enormous leg, another. I locked my hands into fat round the waist and lifted. I knew only where I was going. I got him out on the gravel outside. Levi had fallen. The wheel had slid from under him. I pulled him on his feet. His legs didn't bend at the knees. I grabbed the rolls of Yorick's belly, held him, pushed the two together, one behind the other, and shoved Yorick forward. It didn't work. I went round to the front, took Yorick's arm over Levi's shoulder, and in a half-step backwards, pulled them.

I heard Red shout. I turned to wave him off, but he was running, mask on, toward us. He took Levi and pushed him, one wheel, at a half run. I followed, slower, with Yorick. The sergeant lay outside the gate.

The road was plowed by a burst of cannon fire from the tower. Fortunately the jet was well under the cube wall. Bells rang far off, and another siren howled.

I went out to turn toward the narrow cleft up in the square tower. I could just see it. I'd never fired my little friend at distance.

I shot three times. The cannon stopped. The loudest bell stopped.

The siren howled on.

Red bundled Levi in the aircraft, just like a sack, and got in to pull him clear of the doorway. I shoved Yorick to the opening.

He was too big. I saw Red's eyes blink over the mask.

He grabbed in fury, I shoved. The gown tore. We folded flesh, we pressed, we squeezed one side, stuffed gross folds on the other. Inch by horrid inch we tugged him in. I bundled the legs, which wouldn't bend at the knee, in, straight as tree trunks, tipped him head-down. I climbed in over him, and had to tip him again to swing the door shut.

Red turned the aircraft.

Two cars were coming down the driveway.

He looked at me.

"Go for it!" I said, but he didn't hear.

The nod was enough.

We went singing down the asphalt. The cars skidded, turned off the fairway. One tipped over. It was full of policemen. Some of them tried to shoot. But the gas was getting them.

We were over, rising, turning.

The two were face down on the floor, almost naked. I was shivering with cold. There was no way to help them. Neither had made a sound. We flew in the darkening evening, in cloud, not more than a couple of hundred feet up. Red was flying by compass and the clock. The map was on his knee. The hills weren't far.

Scarlet tracer bullets streaked past us in spark-spitting paths.

I took my mask off. He took off his. I tried to take Yorick's off, but I couldn't reach. Levi was out of touch, underneath.

Red pointed behind, and winked.

Not far away, a fighter went up, turning for a pass at us. I knew it wouldn't be tracer.

Red poked my shoulder.

On his side, the rest of the flight was in formation just above us.

"Hang on!" he yelled. "We're over the border!"

We dived in a turn. I hadn't seen the hill in front. We went round, over a house, skimming treetops, and down into the dark.

I saw the power pylon too late even to shout.

We went under the wire, down, farther down, and our nose pointed at an avenue of trees. It went for a long way into the darkness.

Behind us there was sudden light.

We ran in between the trunks, and touched down on a long driveway with the leaves flying a mad scurry all round us.

The light was only a little less than sunshine, a pinky-orange, where we'd come from.

"Should have looked where the hell he was going," Red said, and revved, and stopped. "Had my shirt on it he'd hit!"

The trees almost met overhead.

"Ought to be here any minute—"

"Who?" I asked.

"Druxi," he said, in surprise. "Who else d'you think?"

Almost in that moment, a car pulled out of shadow farther down and came toward us without lights.

Red laughed, took out cigarettes.

"She said it, and by God, there she is. Hope she's got blankets, and stuff. Specially in the bottle!"

She had.

45

I woke up in bright lights that almost hurt my eyes. I had a very faint notion how I'd got where I was, but nothing held together. I only knew I felt warm in bed, I was weak in arms and legs, and I didn't want to get up. But I was hungry. I lifted a hand that felt like a zephyr—it seemed to move on its own—and touched a beard. It took me a few moments to remember Doctor Mahmoud Al' Afram.

I pieced it together. We'd had a painful time in lifting the two into Druxi's car. The blankets saved our lives. There was also a small bar, and we gulped straight scotch, one after another. We'd driven to Bemersheim, where Leonart's ambulance met us. I didn't remember much after that except Leonart's scream when they opened the doors.

A nurse came in, elderly, what's often known as an Old Dear, blue linen, white headdress, spectacles, the voice of starch.

"Well, awake at last!" she piped, taking a thermometer out of a case, a sort of reflex.

"And very grateful!" I said, cracking my face. It hurt to smile.

"I should just say so!" she said, and hovered, thermometer poised to dive.

"What's for breakfast?"

I was surprised at the strength of my voice. It seemed to shake the room.

"Breakfast, my goodness, it's four in the after*noon!*"

"Give me breakfast and lunch now!"

"I say, you *are* much better, aren't you? I'll just take your temperature and pulse, and then we'll see what Cook can do for herself down there—"

It was obvious I was somewhere in England, but I couldn't place it, and I didn't want to ask the absurd Where Am I?

"Could I make a telephone call?" I asked.

"Why, certainly, sir. Who did you want to talk to?"

I gave the St. James's number, and she went to the corner table and dialled, looking over, chin up, at the receiver on my left.

"Consolidated Industrial Enterprises S.A. Good afternoon!"

"Miss Consuelo Furnival, please—"

"Who's ca—? Is that Mr. Trothe?"

"Yes—"

"Oh, hullo, sir! You better?"

"Much, thank you, Hines—"

"Miss Furnival, sir—"

Silence.

"Edmund?"

"Consuelo?"

"Oh, *dar*ling mine!"

"Most beautiful—"

"I wasn't there! I've just got back. I've been there every day. I left at one—"

"Where is this, anyway?"

"Sir Roland's nursing home. You missed pneumonia by that much. General Pusey's secretary's telephoned every day, morning and night. He wasn't much better off—"

"*Is* he a General?"

"That's what they call him. Air Force—"

"How're Yorick and his friend?"

"Well, of course, they're both terribly ill. But everything's being done. I've spoken to Doctor Graeffe twice. Sir Roland sends him your bulletin every day. I'll telephone him after this—"

"How are you?"

"I *wish* I hadn't come up here. Something told me not to. You were sleeping so peacefully. May I worry you for a moment? Nothing to do with business. That's going absolutely as it should. Not a single blob anywhere. It's your son-in-law. Mr. Obijijawoy —I don't suppose I'll ever pronounce it—"

"What does he want?"

"He's insistent he must talk to you the moment you're able. He won't say a word—"

"Try to get him—"

"I'll be there in about an hour—"

"I'm waiting to feel your arms round me. I shan't be myself till you do. I love you, my heart. I kiss your beautiful mouth. And the luminous dell of pale blue shadows between your breasts—"

"Sergeant-Major Briggs's here with something to sign, or I'd tell you how—*how* I *adore you*. Wait for me—!"

I seemed to be getting stronger by the moment. The nurse came in with a bowl of beef bouillon and an omelet, and a glass of beer. It didn't take me long. Then I had some pills, an injection in the rump which I didn't enjoy, and the telephone rang.

"Edmund Trothe—"

"Ah, sir! Such a long time, isn't it? Could I possibly see you? This is your damned son-in-law!"

"Don't say that, please. Do come and see me. This afternoon?"

"Ah, if I may!"

"But of course. You know where I am. Come on!"

"Within the hour, sir!"

I called Frederick. What a joy to hear the same operator at Trothe Common! She'd been there for thirty years or more.

"The Dower—" the housekeeper said, and she, a villager, pronounced it in Anglo-Saxon—the Day-urr.

Oh, England, my England!

"Mr. Frederick Trothe, please—"

"Who's ca'n, zur?"

"His father—"

369

"Oh, Mist' Admun'! Ay won'erful to hear 'ee, ah. Mom'n' please, zur. Maz-tur Fred-duy-uh!"

The pause, the tiny voices, footsteps on the tiles, the clatter of the receiver.

"Daddy? Is that—"

"Frederick, how are you?"

"Absolutely in top, sir. That's all. I'm going to get a first. How are *you*?"

"Come here tomorrow. I want to see you. Talk to you—"

"But so do I. Be quite certain everything's in top. I took the liberty of taking a few rose trees from what used to be 'our' garden to the cemetery—"

"Why 'used to be'?"

"Well, you know, one can't go barging in and demanding something that isn't ours—"

"But, Frederick. The house is mine. You may take what you wish, and I wish you would. Take Cloney with you. Do the sort of job she'd have wanted done—"

"It's our house? I mean, could I go there?"

"Certainly go there. Take your room—"

"I mean, could I go there tonight? I'm quite free to—"

"Delighted if you would. Ask Mrs. Cloney if there's any bed-linen or—"

"I'd sleep on the floor!"

"Good. Whatever you want to do, do it. It's our house. Go home!"

I didn't know how to give thanks for that, among so many other gifts. First, that I was alive.

I had a sudden notion.

"Could I get on to Mr. Paul Chamby?" I asked the operator.

"I'll see if Mr. Chamby's available, sir—"

I waited, wondering.

"Hello? Edmund?"

A voice I barely recognised. Yet, I did.

"Paul. What a pleasure."

"Oh, Edmund. All I do is think!"

370

"How are you? How's everything going?"

"I don't know. I don't know—"

"Feel better?"

"Edmund, I'm just lying here, day after bloody day. I want out, that's all—"

"We'll be waiting—"

"Not just that, Edmund. You don't know what happened. I've just begun looking at it. I didn't know I could be taken. At my age. After what I've been through. I tell you, I look at myself as a foreign character—!"

"Good. Anything I can do?"

"You? You pulled things together, boy. I might have taken a lot more notice of you. A long time before. If. But perhaps you're right, at that—"

"If what?"

"If you weren't so bloody old-fashioned!"

"Oh. Old-fashioned?"

I never had such a minus-punch-in-the-nose.

"Well. You know. Everything's got to be just, kind of—oh—the way *you* think. The way *you* want it. Gets sort of irritating when somebody else wants to do it more direct. Cut the red tape. Know what I mean?"

"I'm not sure—"

"Well, it doesn't matter. Fact I'm here, I owe to you. Hadn't been for you, I don't know where I'd be—"

"Talked to Moira?"

Silence. Not the happiest. Even silence can be plus or minus. I hadn't known that before. I hadn't quite felt it.

"No, Edmund. Tell you straight. I couldn't look her in the face—"

"On a telephone, you don't have to. I can give you her number—"

"What, of my own house, can you? My word, Edmund—"

"All the better—"

"Listen. We have to talk. I get periods. These last couple of days, I'm all right. But I go back. It's—it's a tough go, Edmund—"

371

"I'll be up in a day or so—"

"It's this fellow Finlayson. He was second man at Beirut. Know about him?"

"Heard of him, that's all—"

"Better find out—"

"What's the fill? Who put him there?"

"I did. Knew his father. Known him almost since he was born. Often stayed with us. Very quiet sort of boy. Plenty of brains, I always thought. Plenty? He's a razor. I'd told Sir Poynter I was starting the Company. I needed the 'in.' He got most of the people I know for me. Well, when he asked me if I could place his son, of course, I said send him along—"

"While I was with the Company?"

"Before. You see, we agreed he wouldn't use his own name. Obvious reasons. Attracts a lot of attention. I put him in Beirut. He knows a lot of people there. All the politicians. That's important. Let me make this clear. In the Company, he used his mother's maiden name, Finlayson—"

"You're making many things clearer—"

"Well, whether I am or not. Fact is, I went stupid over Angela. Then Ursula died—"

"I'm sorrier than I can tell—"

"So am I. But I was so far down the drain—why can't we see it?—we know it. But admitting it? I just went on dreaming. That's it. Dreaming. Edmund, the dreams I've had. A life so marvelous, you can't stand it when you wake up. It's not just the colors. It's the sense of being much more than you are. You wake up, you're just a tired bundle. A rotten packet. You want to go back. You've got to. That's where you live!"

"How did it start?"

He breathed a long ha-a-a-h!

"I don't want to blame anybody. I'm the one. Angela said she'd like to try LSD. This was in London. More than a year ago. I said anything for a quiet bang, so we had a shot. In this place in Soho. Young Finlayson was at that party. He got the stuff. Anyway, I woke up in bed with Angela. That was the first time. It

372

was a joke. Then it wasn't so funny. I knew it. But it got worse. Angela was marvelous. Edmund, oh, Christ!"

He was weeping.

"That's enough!"—somebody—probably a nurse—said, and the receiver clashed.

I had plenty to think over.

Who was the Sir Poynter he'd spoken about? I knew at least two. And was young Finlayson, who'd got the stuff in Soho, the Pip of Stockholm?

If he was also Mr. Thanatis-Fribell, then he knew a lot more than he should, and he could do a great deal more harm than I'd imagined. His "illness" in Beirut, and absence from the office was explained by his becoming Mr. Thanatis in Rome. In that section, under Mariotti, with the help of Geneva and London, we'd prepared our sales programs, chosen the routes, systems of transport, banking facilities, all the details of distribution in Europe.

Had we known as much about any of our competitors—or as at least one of them evidently knew about us—we'd have been in a very strong position. I had to wait for Consuelo.

Sir Roland came in wearing a grey suit he might have slept in. He looked at me over the tops of the hornrims, and nodded.

"Three or four days more," he said. "Get up for a couple of hours tomorrow. Then go somewhere in the sun. You missed pneumonia by not very much. Effect of gas and the pill. And exposure. You were lucky. Errol and the other are doing fairly well, you'll be glad to know. Can't talk yet—"

"I wish to God there was something we could do for the rest of them inside there—"

"International Red Cross? United Nations? What's the use? No teeth. All they have to do is deny it. And keep on denying it. Can't wage war for a few unfortunates—"

"How's Paul?"

He took the hornrims off, narrowing his eyes to look through the window.

"A very bad business, indeed, Edmund," he said, nodding,

mouth down. "He's what I call a 'conscience' case. Something's worrying him. He can't face it. For one thing, he's sure he was responsible for that girl's death. But there's something else. I believe you might be able to do something. You might try?"

"I can do better than that. Have you a piece of paper?"

I scrawled—I could barely hold the pencil—Moira's number outside Melbourne.

"When that call comes through, perhaps in the early hours, will Paul be awake?"

"I'll see what can be done. Why?"

"His ex-wife. That's a fair percentage of his trouble. When she's had a word with me, first, would you tell the operator to put her through to him? And don't warn him. Let it be a surprise—"

I sat back when he'd gone.

I was thinking of Paul's voice.

And of young Finlayson.

Sir Poynter could only be husband of the Lady Loelia Finlayson. Shipping heiress.

I didn't want to think any more. I was suddenly shrivelled.

I was then and there on the Blur's side. How could the son of those two come under suspicion?

But I saw that the bomb attempts in Rome and Cairo were a misuse of James' "stickers" which he could ask for by the dozen without question. The gas in Angela's office—and in the car en route to the airport—were James', too. The error in the pipeline was simple to explain, since Beirut was supply and distribution center. Theodolites could be tampered with and nobody the wiser.

I had a great deal to say to Mr. Finlayson when we met, certainly the Angela Masters business to discuss, and the "disappearance" of so many men.

The Blur's extra-blurriness was summarily explained.

His next-to-right hand for so many years.

Above suspicion.

E. J. Finlayson. Sometimes—I could hear Paul's voice—we're blind.

Esmond Joel Finlayson.

Joel Cawle.

46

My son-in-law was in the room almost before I was properly out of a particularly gloomy daydream.

I hadn't realised what a big fellow he was. Or how black. A true African. Trust Patti to pick the root and branch. No half measures. But an excellent tailor makes a difference, too.

"Sir, Mr. Trothe—" he began, a tentative, quasi-pathetic approach, which I couldn't resist—"I feel—"

"Look here, we'd better get this right!" I said, not too testily, but enough to bring that stare into his eyes. "What does Patti call you? I mean, when she's in a good humor?"

That big smile broke like a sun.

"Well, sir, sometimes she calls me Nestlés, because it's chocolate, and sweet," he said—and I could hear her saying it—"and sometimes 'you big, ugly tomcat' when she isn't in a good temper —or at other times 'my big huggy teddy-bear'—I'm giving you the secrets of the domicile—and then, when we are reading, or walking, or socially, she calls me Ob—"

"Let's make a pact purely between ourselves. It's ridiculous for you to attempt to call me 'father' or 'dear old dad.' I detest the idea. You call me Edmund. I shall always call you Ob. If that's agreeable to you?"

He took my hand before I could prevent it, wrapped it in both of his.

"Edmund, I have had many wonderful moments," he said, almost as a prayer, eyes up, lips out, with that light in his eyes and a lyric rasp in a bass voice. "When I passed my finals I was drunk. Not with alcohol. When I was admitted to the Bar, I was drunk. When I first wore wig and gown in Court. Ah, no man so proud here on earth!"

I could feel those victories. But in the same moment I extolled the men who'd made them possible.

"But then I met Patti. And she was so different from the others. I mean, the others I'd met. It cannot be explained. I felt I could tell her all the things I wanted to do. The building. Not only roads and houses, and other things. I wanted all the children in my country to have the same as I had. To have the chance. But you see, that chance is taken away—"

"Taken away, how?"

He looked at me. I felt the "African" weight.

"Sir, well, Edmund. I went to a Church school. That's where I started my scholarship. There aren't any more—"

"But why not?"

"Well, because we have our own system of education—"

We looked at each other. He'd had an even better "education" than I'd had. He'd become Queen's Counsel. I hadn't. I was a long way behind.

"But what sort of system?"

"It's a copy. But boys like me won't get the same opportunity—"

"Why not?"

He opened his arms, looking up with those enormous eyes.

"It's the men," he said, and so sadly. "My headmaster. He's dead, now. Nobody to take his place. Nobody to write letters. No help. No pull-up. Nothing for me. Or somebody like me. From a village. You know, it is wonderful to call you Edmund. I was worried about our relationship. So was Patti. But, sir, it is a question of Mr. Paul Chamby—"

"He'll be at least six months in hospital—"

"But I am most sorry to hear it. It is a matter of some urgency. The Police could interfere—"

"What is it, exactly?"

"A question of almost four hundred thousand pounds—"

"Which Mr. Chamby owes? Where does this begin?"

Ob put those big—but delicately bony—hands together, and held a knee.

"I suppose in Conakry, about four years ago. A man called Merzel, a Swiss, wanted to cash a draft on Singapore. As it happened, the same firm were clients of ours for many years. My agent paid in dollars. He cashed a few more in the ensuing weeks. Some were on Tanganyika, Rhodesia, Sierra Leone. But my agent became curious. He wondered what Mr. Merzel was doing with so much money always in a foreign currency, though he only wanted dollars. He found out. We have our own informants. Merzel was paying revolutionary parties in other countries. Of course, he reported to me. I said give any excuse, but no more checks. Am I going to cut my own throat? If it was found that my Company was cashing his checks for such a purpose, how long would I live?"

"You're a conservative, I take it?"

"Politically, I am nothing. I conserve what I have, in every way I can—"

"We share the same view—"

"So does Patti. I thought she was a Communist at first—"

"Not Patti!"

"No. She is highly critical, that's all. But now she is like me. Well, this Merzel was very displeased. We heard no more of him. But suddenly, my agent in Algiers wanted to know if he could cash a Rangoon draft. This man's name was Grancour. Well, the sums got larger. Then he bought machinery through us. It didn't go to Algeria. We found it was going to a port in Thailand—"

"What sort of machinery?"

"For making nylon fabrics. Acrylics. Cotton spinning. Let me see, yes, a lot of electric stuff. A great deal of money. We made a very fair profit, as the buyer. We sold to him. I have many friends in Algeria. Well, a Captain came to see me. He said this man Grancour was a French agent. He showed me a folder of information, and these photographs—"

He showed pink palms.

"No doubt. A little altered. Merzel!"

He laughed as though it were an excellent joke. I didn't laugh. I had a feeling—that extraordinary feeling of "knowing"—that prescience of What-Is-to-Be.

"My agent was furious to be so misused. By this time, I, too, was a little annoyed with him. I started to make enquiries. You know, I have business all over Africa—"

He pronounced it Aah-fric-aah.

"—and I found that he—a dozen of him, in fact—had been working for a long time in the same way. But who was giving 'him' the money? We thought the Russians, or less likely the CIA."

"Why do these men go to you?"

"We are mercantile agents. For every type of business—"

"Why don't they go to a bank?"

"A great deal more formality. Detail. Time. They are, of course, bank drafts, not ordinary checks. Recently, my agent in Marseilles asked if he could cash a draft on the Bank of France, in the name of your Company, by Mr. Reismann, your accountant in Geneva. It was signed by Mr. Chamby. I knew his name only through Patti. Other drafts came in from Rome, Beirut, and Athens. A great deal of money passed. We were then asked to buy gold on Paris. After that, several more. All appreciable sums. Two, I found out, went to Iran—"

"Through the Canal Banking Syndicate?"

He laughed a row of resplendent white tusks.

"Sir Chapman is a friend of mine for many years," he said. "Yes. By now I had a lot of information about Mr. Merzel who was Mr. Grancour who, after being many others, was Mr. Reismann in Geneva, and Mr. Grethe in Paris, and Mr. Thanatis in Rome. But I didn't get him direct until we had—we were doing a large business with your Company at this time—we were buying a lot of machinery in Sweden. Here was the epicenter of disaster for my friend Mr. Merzel and family. Because, foolishly, or luckily, we underwrote the amount of money due to the Swedish company. In all this time, please understand, we hadn't a line of correspondence with this procession of the same men. Everything ordered by your Company was signed either by Mr. Chamby, or by representatives, the accountant—or by you—"

"I never signed anything at any time!"

He lifted his hands, like a flight of blackbirds.

"They were accepted because cash was always deposited with the order, and the balance was on the dot. You see, this man—or men—never did anything wrong. In business, he—they—were quite honest. And really, what does it matter to me how a man does business?"

"Quite sure you're right. Sweden?"

"Ah, yes. Swedish taxes are high. There was some arrangement that the money should be left in an account somewhere outside Sweden. Mr. Chamby signed the letter making himself responsible. Well, my representative there is very dependable. When he found out about it, he was, of course, out of his head. It was a serious crime. He cabled me. You know, I have many companies here. Tea, cocoa, cotton, sisal, property investments, automobiles, agricultural machinery. Well, my Swedish representative showed me all the papers. We couldn't possibly lend ourselves to this nonsense. The machinery had been shipped. I telegraphed to Mr. Chamby. His office said he was in Cairo. I called my agent in Cairo. They couldn't find him. My agent had already told the Swedish company we couldn't look at the arrangement. Very well, they said. Where's the money?"

He leaned back in the chair, hands in pockets, crossing black silk-socked ankles.

"Just a moment," I said. "What makes you believe that Mr. Merzel and all the rest are one and the same man?"

"The photographs, first. The man is different in each. But clearly he is the same man. Besides, he works the same—"

"About the money—"

"We got on to Geneva. Couldn't help us. Only Mr. Chamby could sign the check. But the company in Stockholm was pressing us for payment. It was almost four hundred thousand pounds—"

"Three hundred and seventy-odd thousand pounds?"

He stared blank surprise.

"But how could you know?" he almost whispered.

"Never mind. Let's come to the Swedish matter—"

"Very well. In Stockholm I have friends everywhere. I was told that Mr. Chamby was taking drugs. I was surprised, but I've known many. Brilliant. Quite mad. He often went to Stockholm, I found. Curiously, at this point, my London manager of the property company said he was having a great deal of trouble with a tenant in one of our buildings. When they came to serve the summons, what shocked me was to see your name as the guarantor!"

"Forgery!"

"No doubt. But I had to be careful. We approached your Company here, and a Miss Masters said there must be a mistake, and she would put everything in order. At this point, the Swedish company issued a writ, and I went to Stockholm, explained the circumstances, and paid. When I got back to London, the place had been raided by the Police. You notice I didn't bother you or your Company?"

"Any idea about the sort of people this fellow's working for?"

The nurse came in quietly and stood behind him.

"There's a young lady downstairs, sir. Miss Furnival—"

"Show her up, please!—"

"Only one visitor at a time, sir!"

Not a bit of use arguing with starch, and I didn't want to fall out with her.

Ob gave me his hand. His shadow was over me, a veritable Zeus with a blessing.

"You know I have done business with mercenary armies," he said. "I thought first of all this Merzel-Grancour—and all the rest —were a means of supply to mercenary soldiers. Then the character and quantity changed altogether. If you look at my files, you will perhaps assume, as I do, that it's a country—or perhaps countries—no longer represented in the places where I have agents. Or now, doesn't want to buy openly through its own representatives. I will bring you the main files tomorrow, if I may?"

"You'd be most kind. Which country do you think it is?"

He buttoned his jacket.

"Comparing the list of machinery, the money, the shipping lines, the way it's done, I believe it might be North Vietnam or North Korea, or perhaps Java—"

"Ob, I shall look forward to seeing you tomorrow. If you have copies of those photographs, you might bring them with you. Send Patti a kiss from me—"

"Edmund, it will be a pleasure! We both leave a kiss under your pillow!"

I took off the receiver as he left, and asked the operator for the Blur's number at Grass Tree.

47

The door swung, and I could have imagined I saw a vision.

Consuelo came in and stood looking at me. She seemed in simply magnificent fettle. Just looking at her I felt better. She wore a camel-hair coat about the shade of dark autumn leaves, with a beret of the same color, a paisley scarf, and suede top boots. But the deep blue of her eyes was so tender, her mouth was still that velvet blossom I dreamed of, and when she sat on the bed to put her arms about me, I felt the warm wonder of her, the heart pulsing, weighing joy.

Nothing to touch it for effect.

"Darling, you look a hundred years old!" she whispered. "I love every second of it. I'm only sorry I wasn't there all the time!"

"Bring me my Gillette tomorrow. I'm going to be up for a couple of hours—"

"Ah, but grow a little beard. A little wuzzy? For me?"

"No wuzzies. They'd think I'd gone on the 'art' side. What's been happening?"

She sat up, threw the coat off her shoulders, slipped off her scarf. She wore a silk shirt with a row of small buttons.

"The matron gave me fifteen minutes," she said, and took some envelopes out of her pocket. "A letter from Patti. One from the Dowager Lady Imbritt. For some reason, Gillian wants to talk to you on clix. She's still at the Graeffe Place. And a piece of ridiculous news!—"

"Spill!"

She crossed her knees—the sound of silk I loved!—and opened a sheet of paper.

"Last Wednesday, Bilat Khan's sister—I thought—telephoned and asked where he was. I said he was away on Company business, why? She asked if she could come and see me. I said, by all means. She came yesterday and what do you think? She put his new passport on the desk. The one we got for him!"

We smiled at each other, but only in the eyes.

"She said their mother was very worried, and Bilat Khan wasn't son or brother at all. He'd gone to lodge with them about a couple of years ago, and had been in and out of the house ever since. He left some luggage there. Locked. A new lodger's light-fingered, apparently. He opened the bags, but he couldn't close them. The other sister—the nurse—caught him in the act. She took this passport—using her brain—and called the Police. Well, the original Bilat Khan, they discover, is working in Wolverhampton—"

"Moment. Who's the original Bilat Khan?"

"He's a mechanic. Years older than the passport says. He came here three years ago from Kenya. He chose British citizenship—"

"What does the Passport Office say? We've put them in a very awkward position—"

"Well, Mr. Rodwell put the blame on the issuing authority in Kenya. It's difficult, it seems, to tell one Bilat Khan from another. But it's going to be a very hard job getting a passport for anybody else after this!"

We looked at each other, still with a smile.

"Did Berry turn up anything?" I asked gently.

She opened a couple of sheets of shorthand.

"Several things. First, the Maclas Agency in Capetown's a forwarding depot for freight, mostly Malaya, Java, Hong Kong, and Shanghai. Then the girl in the night club, the Rusty Hinge. She's Swedish, and she said she knew this Pip by sight. He came with Mr. Chamby, and their party had been going there off and on for quite a few months. She was vague about that. He was quite good-looking, this Pip—average height, smartly dressed, fair to brown, didn't talk very much and he was always with this Chinese girl. But she stayed outside until Paul was nodding off. Then she and this Pip took him away. He told the girls who to give the stuff to, and they did exactly as they were told. That is, his girls. The others, the club girls, he paid very well indeed. They all liked him—"

"When did this girl hear him called Pip?"

"Only when she heard Curly say it. But when another girl called him that, he didn't like it and there was a fight with Curly. She didn't hear the details. Curly and he didn't like each other, but she seemed afraid of him. That's about all. Disappointed?"

Pip. Like a tack-hammer on a little bell at the back of my brain, that word kept striking, kept echoing.

"No mention of the other guests?"

"Oh, yes. They all seemed businessmen of one kind or another, all affluent—from the money they spent apart from the 'party'— all sorts of nationalities. They called him by a name she couldn't remember. She thought it was French. Vague about that, too. She was a most unwilling witness."

"I can imagine why—"

"One other little item. This is the sherbet at the end of dinner. The Chinese lady had some wonderful coats. The cloakroom woman at the club's a Finn, and she happens to know a little about furs. She said that a sable coat had the label of Saks Fifth Avenue, in New York. Superintendent Berry got on to them and they identified the customer. She paid with a check drawn on a Washington bank. That account had been opened by an attaché of the Albanian trade delegation. He's not there any longer. That's the crushed ice. Now for the sherbet—"

"I'm slavering—"

She reached to pat my hand, stiff-armed and schoolmarmish, and sat back in a preen.

"On a run-down of the account—of course, FBI and Interpol

were on to it—they found her hotel. One of the doormen's a detective—I imagine—and said she had a lot of flowers sent her, but most by a Mr. Somerton Hales. They got that from the florist. He always paid cash. Well, the more they ran him down, the more he disappeared!"

"Does it surprise you?"

"It must have surprised *them*. Because then they simply *galvanised*, and after a lot of digging, they traced him. Where to?"

"East Wing, the White House?"

"Almost as bad. No. The British Embassy!"

"You've got something maddeningly attractive sticking to your lower lip—"

"Pay attention. Well, they saw the First Secretary. The Ambassador was in London. They simply said they wanted to interview this man. They were told he wasn't on the staff. Nobody knew who he was. Never heard of him. What was their evidence? Well, you know, all cabbies make a note of an address they go to. They'd examined the lists. This particular cabbie said he'd driven this man from the florist's to the Embassy building, and the guard saluted as if the fare was a somebody. Of course, it was only a cabbie, he was obviously mistaken—never mind his fare list—and the interview ended in cordial regrets and shumshaw. But that cabbie was very angry. They put him in a place where he could watch the comings and goings. He picked out—on *sight*—the head of—? Our Intelligence Service!"

That little hammer suddenly became a pile-driver.

Everything gonged.

I knew my Pip.

Consuelo looked at me in surprise, which for some reason made her more beautiful.

"Doesn't it surprise you?" she asked, a little hurt.

"I'm on the floor," I said, with truth. "Tell me about 'our' Bilat Khan—"

"Paul vouched for him. The report from Kabul seems factual. His travels, his arrival here, were all checked. He had a Pakistan passport. But the Pakistan Consul says he's not from Pakistan and isn't registered there!"

"Which passport is 'our' Bilat Khan using?"

"We'd all love to know. Miss Peel got his ticket as far as Belgrade, return. In his name. It was cashed in from Paris. It wasn't used. What's his little bundle?"

"We can all guess. How's El Humir?"

"Everything's going wonderfully. Mr. Bowles has gone there. Wants very much to talk to you. Superintendent Les Vosges's report is in. Prince Abdullah's coming along, he says. Wants to see you as soon as possible. And if you're going to talk to Gillian, you'd better get on clix—"

"Mine's in the safe in Cairo—"

"Mine isn't!"

She took the car keys from her handbag and gave me the miniature tire they were hooked on. I did the turns on the hub, and got 'live' air. I watched the electric bedside clock. Exactly on the minute the Morse came through.

DXIBLV . . . NRPSHB . . . MDMI . . . EVDYKI . . . MPP-LDB . . . IGL . . . ENTWST . . . NSTFUN . . . SURART . . . MWRFRI . . . LTSFRW . . . NS . . . AGCTSA . . . YWABY . . . BMDLYB . . . TRSTLU . . . BLTKLV . . . O.

Consuelo took it down as I read.

"Druxi believes—three dots, emphasis—no report should be made to M.I. Evidence points Yorick's imprisonment was planned by Igloo—three dots, emphasis—entire Washington staff under surveillance. Arrests tomorrow or Friday latest. Further warns against contact with anybody anywhere. Both are moderately better but still unable to talk. Love—three dots, emphasis—Out."

"Doesn't surprise me," Consuelo said, and most certainly surprised me.

I got back on clix.

NBWRDA . . . YT . . . NINT . . . NCTSWY . . . OIOICL . . . V . . . O.

"Nobody warned anytime. Three dots, emphasis. No intention.

Three dots, emphasis. No contacts. Wait your OIOI call. Love. Three dots, emphasis. Out."

"Why doesn't what surprise you?" I asked.

"This, about Washington. I wonder if it's *every*body?"

"Druxi's a hard-fisted puritan with words. Ever noticed? All meat. 'Entire Washington staff' means the lot. The issue—"

"From Bernard Lane, down?"

That, really, was the facer.

"Well—"

"He's there. So's Joel Cawle. 'Entire' she said!"

Again I was reminded of the Blur's extreme blurriness, and again I sympathised. To suspect was one thing, to prove quite another, and there was a nasty chasm in between that wasn't to be bridged by discussion.

The telephone rang. She raised her eyebrows for my nod, and took it.

"Yes. Oh, yes. The Lord Blercgrove? Mr. Edmund Trothe—"

She gave me the receiver.

"Hello? Edmund?"

"Speaking. Are we scrambled?"

"Just a moment. Yes. On this line we generally are except when Cynthia wants to talk to her friends. Edmund, what a marvelous thing you did!"

"Well, we had to do—"

"We're all at your feet—!"

"Question—"

"Yes?"

"Are you still unclear about the identity of X?"

"The creature we spoke about? We *are* scrambled, you know!"

"But do you know who he is, and where he is?"

"I think I may say we have everything we require. But he's gone to ground, somewhere—"

"Vixen, perhaps? Chinese?"

"We've been looking for her. And some others—"

"Any reason for this extraordinary conduct? Where are we going? We're a laughingstock!"

The long sigh seemed to echo in the room.

"Ah, Edmund, if only one knew! How do men of that sort become traitors? One can understand others. The attraction's money. But when they have all the money they can want—"

"—a moment. Did you say 'a' man, or 'men'?"

A pause, while Consuelo ran her hands up a long stocking, as if she didn't know what it did to me.

"We've known each other rather too long, Trothe"—the voice had changed to a brisk patter—"I'll ask *you* a question. What's your reading, based on what you know?"

"I'm inclined to the belief that we've had to deal with two people in M.I. Sorry to have to say it—"

"Go on, please!"

"I believe that Paul's extraordinary conduct was deliberately induced in order, first to penetrate this Company's offices, and then to use us, our staffs and banking facilities for a reason yet to present itself. One of those I suspect is a really superb artist of make-up. I taught him a lot myself—"

"—name, please!"

"Joel Cawle?"

"Unfortunately, yes—"

"I can barely believe it!"

"I can't. But neither can we any longer evade the fact—"

"Then who's the other?"

Pause again. Consuelo sat closer, ran her fingers through my hair.

"I don't think I'm in a position to give you that answer, Trothe—"

"I'm damn sure you *are!*"

"What?"

"Take your mind back. When we last met, I mentioned a nickname. Pip—"

"Pip?"

"Yes. Now consult your Greek. Fifth or sixth form, again. Do you remember the word for 'one who casts lecherous glances at nubile maidens'?"

"Trothe, what *are* you talking about?"

"In our penultimate year at school, the village women made a complaint against some of the senior boys for stealing kisses, pinching, and in other ways bringing a blush to innocent cheeks—"

Consuelo stared at me slightly cross-eyed.

"—the chief culprit was dubbed Pip—a diminutive of the noun —by the school captain who'd said 'it gives me the pip to look at you!' and that's what I've just remembered—"

"But *who*—whom, Trothe?"

"Bernard Lane, of course—"

Silence, that endless churn of soundless time.

Omnipotence, staring at catastrophe.

"Any smallest hope of putting them in the bag?" I asked, to salt the wound.

"Let us grant that your premise was correct. You can imagine they were too well served. They must have had an extraordinary team in this country, alone—"

"In your own office?"

"It hadn't escaped attention. We know most of their connection with your Company. Many others, besides. We're trying to unravel the rest. Lane was something of a financial genius, you know. It's going to be a costly hunt, I fear. They knew our people all over Europe and the Middle East. Most of them have disappeared. You can imagine what the Americans think of us!"

"Are the Russians implicated?"

"They're trying to make it seem so. But we believe otherwise —with reason—"

"I believe a file I have may provide a little extra information—"

"When you're able, do come down for a weekend. Compare notes. Mix tears!"

"Anything more I might do?"

"Take care of yourself. You're a solid mark. You know that, don't you? Assiduous students of James' have to be guarded against. I don't think I need say any more. We're all warned. Get well soon!"

I listened to the strange sound of the scrambler going off the line.

Consuelo hadn't taken her eyes off me.

"I'm afraid," she said. "I really am. I never liked either of them—"

"You keep your mind on getting married. Get the house ready for us. Frederick's there, now. Have the Chapel prepared. Find the priest—"

"He's found—"

"We'll go and lie in the sun for a couple of weeks—"

"Where you got that wonderful tan? I want one just like it. All over—"

"Simply take them all off—"

She stood, pulling on the sleeves of her overcoat.

"What are we going to do about the solid mark?" she asked, nodding at the telephone.

"Ignore it—"

"You can't!"

"Shoot when I have to—"

She clasped her hands, shut her eyes.

"Oh, darling!" she whispered. "What a filthy way to live! I hate it!"

"It's our day, my beautiful. The fact of the time. We're in the era of the brute. I'm having you taken care of—"

"And I've arranged with our Sergeant-Majors for a special escort for you—"

"Aren't we going to be alone sometimes?"

"If you don't see to it, I will!"

Darkness was in the room. She walked a couple of paces, looking about.

Suddenly, she shivered.

In that strange movement of fear in the body I loved, I seemed to see the pieces of jigsaw suddenly shaken to fit together.

The pair of them could do almost as they wished, go where they pleased. Both Angela and Ursula Masters knew both of them very well. They'd worked for them both. Angela had possibly become a little too much of a nuisance to both of them, in one way or another, and putting her in the storeroom was a fair way of getting rid of her. They'd underrated her intelligence, that's all. That fatal lack of attention to detail was a point in our favor. Getting Paul involved must have been fairly simple, once Angela—whether she knew it or not—became the bait. Heroin was a difficult habit to break, once begun, and a man of Paul's temperament wouldn't, perhaps, think of it as harmful, until he realised he was an addict. But then he'd have to find supplies. Bernard or Joel wouldn't have the slightest difficulty, on one pretext or another, of getting as much as they wanted without question, either from the M.I. pharmacy, or from their own resources. It seemed to me that the Swedish adventure both with drugs and women, was planned, first to amuse a circle of businessmen and bankers of use to them in buying materials they couldn't find anywhere else, except in the United States—which they couldn't use because of "enquiries"—and then to involve Paul in a situation which could only lead to his arrest and ruin, first, and the eventual foundering of the Company. They couldn't foresee my joining the staff, or the Prince Azil episode. I didn't doubt they were behind the "disappearance" of our technicians. They'd be useful if only as instructors elsewhere.

For what?

I pushed the entire business out of my mind.

"When you get back, light candles for us," I said. "We need them. We need a clean slate. And help—"

"They burn every day," Consuelo said, putting both palms to my face, warm strong hands, that held. "I've got into Gillian's habit. I find it suits me—"

"Good. Bring down a Company checkbook tomorrow. I want to clear that 'B' account, tell Mr. Simmons. I want the entire file on Pip and his pal. Take it to the Blur, with another from my son-in-law—"

She was looking at me in a strange side-glance. By the light of the small bedlamp, those eyes were a hard, implacable blue, very unlike her.

"Do you really think I ought?" she asked. "I think you'd better talk to Gillian!"

"Why?"

"She knows a great deal. More than she'll tell me. I believe she'd tell you—"

"Find out when she gets back from Germany. Bring her here. And lunch here tomorrow. I want you to travel in broad of day from now on. With escort!"

The nurse stood in the doorway, switching on lights everywhere, click—click—flip!

"That's it for tonight, sir!" she said. "Come along, Miss!"

We kissed like budgerigars, and held hands till she was a yard away. She stood in the doorway for a moment, blew a kiss, I blew three back, and the nurse nodded a smile, and shut the door.

Consuelo's doubt of the Blur hadn't been much of a shock since I'd always, for one reason or another, distrusted him. I had nothing to thank him for. He wasn't by any means forgiven for what had happened some months previously. And Bernard and Joel had been his hatchetmen.

A plan began to work in my mind. While we were on honeymoon, the details could be put into operation. The entire weight of the Company would go behind it without losing a day's work or a pennypiece.

I intended to find Bernard Lane and Joel Cawle, wherever they were.

I saw exactly what could be done, how to bury the traps.

While the thoughts formed, I remembered the tabard I'd worn as a boy, the blue velvet, the escutcheon in gold thread on the breast, the scarlet and white-barred epaulettes, and my father putting his hand on my shoulder. The tabard had been his, his father's and grandfather's, and Frederick had worn it.

In it all, for some reason, I saw the black mask of a fox, bloodied in a kill of chickens. But chickens die quietly, and foxes wreak their will. I didn't intend it should go on. Consuelo could be one. I certainly could. Errol almost had been. There were dozens more, Paul not least of them. We could all, in one way or another, be victims of 'accidents', or of an induced stroke or heart attack, or ruined by scandal or financial jugglery. Or simply shot.

I had to keep well in mind that so far as banking, the stock market, and accountancy went, Bernard Lane was more than capable, and clearly held control of what seemed to be a great deal of capital. But, curiously, in all he did, he was honest, so far as one might judge. That made him even more dangerous.

There, I, too, was competent, and honest, or I hoped so. All three of us had been to the same school, knew more or less the same people. We'd all done more or less the same work. But there was, in solid fact, one big difference.

I'd been very much more fortunate than either of them.

I'd worn the tabard.

I had no fear of the future.

The lights of modest candles reach a long, long way.